Middle Distance

Anthologies published by VUP include

A Game of Two Halves: The Best of Sport 2005–2019
edited by Fergus Barrowman (2021)

Sista, Stanap Strong! A Vanuatu Women's Anthology
edited by Mikaela Nyman & Rebecca Tobo Olul-Hossen (2021)

Monsters in the Garden: An Anthology of Aotearoa New Zealand Science Fiction and Fantasy
edited by Elizabeth Knox & David Larsen (2020)

Short Poems of New Zealand
edited by Jenny Bornholdt (2018)

Twenty Contemporary New Zealand Poets
edited by Andrew Johnston & Robyn Marsack (2009)

The Best of Best New Zealand Poems
edited by Bill Manhire & Damien Wilkins (2008)

Great Sporting Moments: The Best of Sport 1988–2004
edited by Damien Wilkins (2005)

Six by Six: Short Stories by New Zealand's Best Writers
edited by Bill Manhire (1989, 2021)

Some Other Country: New Zealand's Best Short Stories
edited by Marion McLeod & Bill Manhire (1984, 2008)

Middle Distance

Long Stories of Aotearoa New Zealand

Edited by Craig Gamble

Victoria University of Wellington Press

Victoria University of Wellington Press
PO Box 600, Wellington
New Zealand
vup.wgtn.ac.nz

First published in 2021

A catalogue record is available from the
National Library of New Zealand.

ISBN 9781776564323

Printed in Singapore by Markono Print Media Pte Ltd

Contents

CRAIG GAMBLE

Introduction

This collection really was born over the morning coffee table at the VUP office, despite how conveniently picturesque that might sound. It grew out of a discussion of how the literary magazine *Sport* might evolve – if evolution was something we wanted to happen to it.

One of its guiding principles was that, like *Sport*, it should collect previously unseen work. I was keen to read unpublished stories, and I wanted as much as possible to include a diversity of voices and styles. This didn't just come from a place of wanting something new and shiny. I also thought this anthology would be an opportunity for writers to consider the long story form anew. The guidelines we set were brief (new fiction, about 10,000 words, by New Zealand writers) and deliberately so, because I was keen for writers to consider more than length. I wanted them to be free to think about form, about what they could do with that little bit of extra space and time. I imagined that I might receive work which rejected convention, perhaps even broke down the walls between writing and reading in some way I could only vaguely imagine. I was keen to be surprised and challenged, to read the unexpected.

We received many submissions, and immediately obvious was the huge variety of genre, character, setting and subject. Some stories were speculative fiction; others were much more realist. Some focused on a short passage of time; some encompassed a life. There were several ghost stories, two stories about mermaids, and stories that talked about otherness, sexuality, racism, religion – how to be alive in the world.

I was delighted by this variety, and often surprised by the directions many of the stories took. But at the heart of all of the submissions, and exemplified by the fourteen stories published here, was something I perhaps should have expected. Each of them urgently wanted to tell us something. Each made a space in the reader's head and filled it with another life, or world, or feeling, or all of these. These stories kept you reading and gave you knowledge you hadn't previously held. In other words, each story demonstrated how very skilled the writer was – not necessarily at experimentation, though that is there too – at being a storyteller. And yes, both mermaid stories made it in.

In his recent book on stories, *A Swim in a Pond in the Rain*, George Saunders describes a story, wonderfully, as 'a frank, intimate conversation between equals' – the 'equals' being the writer and the reader. This is not peculiar to shorter fiction, but in a short story, obviously, the writer has less time and space to achieve that intimacy and frankness. The writer must exercise a keen focus at every line to keep the reader engaged, to 'respect' the reader, as Saunders has it, and to communicate what is vital in the story. The long story has more space to work with – 10,000 words or more compared with the 3,000 or 4,000 more common in a short story. To my mind, that only makes the task harder. A reader has time to engage with a character more deeply, but their greater attention needs to be satisfied more fully. Setting and world-building can be given more space, but it still needs to be done with an immediacy that keeps the story moving. The writer of a long story walks a difficult middle path between the sharp joy of a shorter work, and the more cumulative pleasures of a novella or novel. They can, if they're successful, make the conversation between themselves and the reader truly memorable. Editing these stories – another sort of conversation, perhaps – has reminded me how much effort this takes, how much care and precision.

These are stories which aren't afraid to play with expectations, to leap for something fantastic while at the same time beautifully detailing the everyday. In Sam Keenan's 'Afterimages', set during the war and seemingly rooted in scientific fact, a young woman begins to feel she is fading away, quite literally. The protagonist of Kathryn van Beek's 'Sea Legend' strives for acceptance among the tight-knit and hard-working crew of a fishing trawler, but comes face to face with the surreal.

Many of these stories feature characters at the edges of things – in liminal spaces or at the edges of society, often pushed there by prejudice or ignorance. But that does not necessarily mean they are made smaller by it. The titular character in Rem Wigmore's 'Basil and the Wild' has been largely ostracised by his village, but living on the edge of the wilderness leads him to the discovery of a more genuine home. In Emma Sidnam's 'Backwaters', a young Chinese immigrant copes with the harshness of his new life and the discrimination of the wider community while simultaneously living another more beautiful and more loving existence. The father and son in Maria Samuela's 'The Promotion' are separated by years and sometimes distance, yet their lives run in parallel as they encounter challenges in a country that is not always welcoming, and in which they might be stronger together.

Events may move more quietly in other stories, but they grow to fill large spaces in our imagination and empathy.

Anthony Lapwood's 'Around the Fire' details the care a single father takes in creating a safe space for his children, no matter the cost to himself. In 'Getaway' by Nicole Phillipson, a woman embarks on a quietly stubborn rescue mission and quickly finds she may have to rescue herself. The young man at the centre of J. Wiremu Kane's 'Ringawera' comes to realise that, through his struggles with his sexual and cultural identity, he might be able to help someone who is struggling even more than himself.

Belief – systems of belief and disbelief, and those who advocate for them – are central too. In Octavia Cade's 'Scales, Tails and Hagfish', a young women stubbornly holds on to her identity in the face of scepticism from all sides. In 'Like and Pray' by Samantha Lane Murphy, a mother beset by grief discovers what the limits of her faith might be, both for herself and for those around her who don't believe.

Three stories are haunted – in places populated by ghosts and spirits – but none of them conform to genre tropes or expectations. In Jack Barrowman's 'The Dead City', the world is ancient and visceral, firmly rooted in its own solidity, and that only makes the monsters more frightening. The group of young women in Joy Holley's 'School Spirit' sneak into abandoned buildings looking for a haunting, but what really frightens them is something much older and more uncaring than a ghost. Vincent O'Sullivan's 'Ko tēnei, ko tēnā' – a story he described in an email as 'a tasteless fantasy' – is a tour de force, a pastiche of a Victorian ghost story with a final twist that will leave you breathless.

The closing story in this volume is David Geary's chaotic, cartwheeling 'The Black Betty Tapes', a story that not only resists classification but openly revolts against it, throwing out revolutionary forms of narrative, dialogue and character as it goes.

What delighted me the most in all of these stories, I think, was the bravery of the authors in attempting something new. Reading them again, I feel none of the writers held anything back. They committed their best ideas to the page from the beginning, and then another, and another, pushing both themselves and their stories to a new level. The places and people contained in these stories are both intimate and world-spanning, and all are able to be absorbed in one sitting. But for that period of time, however short or long, they all have the power to relocate you. To lift you out of the place and time where you live now. I can't promise you'll make it back, and you'll have to find the mermaids for yourself.

Middle Distance

OCTAVIA CADE

Scales, Tails and Hagfish

When Loretta's neighbour failed to turn back into a mermaid, and was instead carried by emergency workers out of her house, her skin having grown into the cheap suede of couch, Loretta was undeniably disappointed.

'Is she gonna die then?' she said, crowding alongside the workers. 'Can I *see*?'

'She's going to be just fine,' said the man closest to her, and Loretta could see the reluctant lie all over his face. She might have been twelve, but she was also a neighbour and could have helped. Twelve-year-olds knew how to use a phone, and the stench coming out of the house, product of months of immobility and incontinence, could not have been missed. 'And no, you can't see! What are you, some kind of ghoul?'

'What's a ghoul?' said Loretta. 'Is it a mermaid? Because I'm a mermaid. So is she.'

'Jesus fucking Christ,' said the man, and turned away. His face was all red, and Loretta thought it was because he was trying hard not to breathe in Mrs Wilberforce. He clearly hadn't had as much practice as she'd had. Loretta practised holding her breath every day, because mermaids dived deep in the ocean like whales did – back when the whales were alive – and she had to learn to hold her breath long enough to dive that way too.

'She's just a kid,' said the man's partner, as they loaded Mrs Wilberforce into the ambulance. 'Leave off, will you? It's not her fault.'

Except it kind of was, because Loretta had sneaked into that house every day for the past four months, drawn by the scent of decaying mermaid and holding her breath longer every time. She'd hidden behind the filth and piles of furniture and the beers cans and empty food cartons left by Mr Wilberforce on his occasional trips home, and she'd watched.

She'd honestly thought the transformation would be quicker. It hardly seemed to have progressed at all. It was mostly stink, and Mrs Wilberforce had been taken into the ambulance still attached to the couch. What was under the silver blanket didn't look like a fish tail at all.

She didn't sound like a mermaid either. Loretta thought mermaids would sound like teeth and wishes, but Mrs Wilberforce just moaned like the possum her brother had run over once and not quite finished off.

It was all very confusing.

There were lots more people in the mermaid's house than were ever there before. Loretta watched them poke and point and shake their heads and she wanted to scream. They had never cared to come and watch the mermaid when all she did was slump on the couch. It had just been Loretta then, all by herself, and when the mermaid had been hard to wake Loretta had pulled away some of the rotten fabric that the mermaid had dressed herself in and tried to see where her skin had broken down enough to come into couch, but she was small and skinny and all the mermaid's weight was against her.

She was always careful, when she finished, to push the mermaid's ankles together as closely as she could, but skin didn't seem to combine with skin as easily as it did with suede, although in some places the skin had broken down into sores and that was hopeful. Perhaps the sores would stick together.

When the mermaid slept and Loretta had finished looking at her legs, she looked at her house instead. It was a boring house, but it was full of hiding places and Loretta searched them all for fish skin. When the mermaid came out of the water to become Mrs Wilberforce, Mr Wilberforce must have taken away her skin and hidden it. That was why she sat on the couch so much – it hurt her feet to walk. Then, when her skin started to grow into the couch, Mrs Wilberforce must have thought it would help her legs to grow back together.

The first time Loretta went looking for the skin, she told herself that it was because she wanted to give it back. Then, when she got frustrated at how well it was hidden, she began to think that Mrs Wilberforce didn't deserve it. Loretta was a mermaid without a fish skin, but if she'd had one she would never let it be taken away.

The skin would be safer with her than with Mrs Wilberforce, but she couldn't find it.

'Can I go see her at the hospital?' she asked her brother.

Her brother said no but she went anyway. He wouldn't be pleased but she liked him better that way. His mouth would fall open and he'd swell up like a puffer fish, which made him angrier and puffier, and when he caught sight of himself in a mirror that was revenge for him never believing she was a mermaid.

Mermaids were good at revenge. They were good at salt water as well, and so when Loretta arrived at the hospital and asked to see the mermaid and was denied, fake tears got her in. 'You're a good girl to care so much,' said the nurse, and Loretta agreed. 'But . . . a mermaid?'

'She's stuck on dry land,' Loretta argued. 'She just wants to go home.'

'I think I like that explanation better,' said the nurse.

Mrs Wilberforce was sleeping, but when Loretta took a bottle of sea water from her backpack and poured it over her face she woke up quick.

'I couldn't find your skin,' she said. 'You need to tell me where it is.'

Underneath Mrs Wilberforce's skin, the mermaid shifted. 'Jesus fucking Christ,' said the mermaid, and Loretta frowned.

'It's not like you're using it,' she said.

It took a long time to convince Mrs Wilberforce that Loretta knew she was a mermaid. Several visits, in fact, but Loretta suffered through it, thinking it must be hard for one mermaid to recognise another when the first mermaid had been pretending to be human for so long. She probably forgot lots of things.

'I looked everywhere,' she said.

'You've been in my house?'

'Heaps of times,' admitted Loretta, without a trace of shame. 'I watched you try and grow a new skin on the couch. It didn't work.'

'Maybe I thought the suede felt like shark skin,' said Mrs Wilberforce. 'Maybe I thought it would protect me better than my own.'

That sounded right, but all the sharks were dead so it wasn't like Loretta could make a comparison. 'Are you lying to me?'

'Yes,' said Mrs Wilberforce. 'Mind your own business.'

'No,' said Loretta.

They stared at each other.

'I've looked everywhere but I can't find your skin,' Loretta hinted, with no more subtlety than she had shame.

'Are you going to steal it?' said Mrs Wilberforce.

'Yes.'

'Then why should I tell you where it is?'

'You've had it stolen before. You'll survive.'

'Not a very sympathetic child, are you?'

'No,' said Loretta. 'I don't feel sorry for you neither,' she added, and the mermaid sighed.

'You just said the same thing twice,' she said. 'Your speech is appalling.'

Loretta scowled. She heard enough of this sort of thing at school, when she bothered to go. Mermaids should be above vocabulary tests.

'Tell you what,' said the mermaid, beached in her hospital bed with bandages holding skin grafts to the back of her thighs. 'You do something for me, and I'll tell you where the skin is.'

The something she asked for wasn't difficult. Loretta had seen the globe before, on one of the bedside tables and far out of reach of the couch. 'He'd never bring it to me,' said Mrs Wilberforce of her husband, and Loretta thought if the mermaid hadn't figured out that she'd hooked herself to someone in love with hoarding, then all the fresh water had run into her ears and then into her brain and rotted it. Perhaps that's what the stink was, and why Mrs Wilberforce found it so hard to remember she came from ocean waves.

The promise of the skin would have made her bring the globe anyway, but if it helped Mrs Wilberforce to remember then maybe it could be useful in another way. The globe was full of water and sand and when Loretta shook it, the sand settled down into a beach scene from an island on the other side of the country.

When Mrs Wilberforce, propped up painfully against pillows, took the globe from her she considered it with salt eyes that looked very far away. 'I was born here,' she said. 'Happier times.'

'In the waters by the beach?' said Loretta, and Mrs Wilberforce looked at her steadily with wet cut glass for eyes.

'Why not,' she said. 'Well, why not.'

There was no fish skin, she said. Mr Wilberforce had burnt it.

Loretta thought that probably sounded like him.

'The truth is,' said the mermaid behind Mrs Wilberforce's face, leaning close, 'you don't need a fish skin to be a mermaid. You can be one your own self.'

The next day Loretta went to school. Not to learn things – mermaids learned all they needed in water – but to steal. The smallest children had classrooms full of the felt-tip pens her brother would never buy her. She took them home and drew scales on her legs. Tiny scales, bright scales, red and blue and yellow, because if the waters were empty she could be safe in them and beautiful, with colours that lit up the waters and made them living again. It was hard to draw scales on the back of her thighs but she balanced in front of the mirror and lifted one leg after the other, colouring in.

She didn't want shark skin that felt like suede, she wanted shark teeth and scales. She wanted quickness and gills. With one of the black felt-tip pens she drew great slits down each side of her throat. They wouldn't open when she tried to breathe through them.

Maybe Mrs Wilberforce could tell her how.

There was still the problem of the legs. She cut up her bed sheets and tied her legs together from hip to ankle, tied them so tight that her feet went red and numb. That was a problem. Too late, Loretta realised that she couldn't walk down to the ocean like that. She'd have to roll, but if that took too long and the gills came in she'd drown on dry land.

She looked in the mirror and sucked in her cheeks like a fish. 'You *are* a mermaid,' she said. 'You *are*.' She had gills and scales and the mind of a mermaid, and that was surely enough.

When her brother came home, he looked at her feet, turned cold and purple, and cut the bed sheets off her. 'You're not a little kid anymore,' he said, looking at her stained and separated legs. 'You're a big girl now. Try to act like it.'

'I'm a *mermaid*,' said Loretta, and when he laughed at her she bit him.

'Jesus fucking *Christ*,' said her brother, nursing his wound. Blood dripped onto the carpet, and Loretta's mouth tasted of iron and salt. 'You goddamn little *ghoul*.'

Whatever, she thought.

'A ghoul,' said Mrs Wilberforce, 'is an undead creature who feasts on human flesh. On that note, close your mouth when you eat. You are not a goldfish.'

Loretta, who had commandeered the lunch tray on her arrival and was guiltlessly stuffing herself with stolen pudding, would have slammed her mouth shut if it wasn't full of squish. The pudding was slimy, with a tendency to squirt. Some spurted onto the hospital sheets, and she rubbed it in with grimy hands. This somehow made the stain more noticeable.

'You look like you're trying to swallow a hagfish.'

'What's a hagfish?' said Loretta. Her words were somewhat indistinct.

'Something gone,' said Mrs Wilberforce, sighing.

Loretta winced. She'd heard all this before and was not in the mood for a repeat. 'Everything's gone,' she said. She tried to sound sad about it but there was a bread roll still on the tray that had been sitting in gravy, and she wanted to see if she could stick her tongue through the sodden bit.

Mrs Wilberforce watched her with escalating disgust as Loretta found that she could, indeed, force her tongue through the roll without benefit of teeth. The roll was so soft she could even fit the whole thing in her mouth at once, though it made her cheeks bulge out so far that her eyes watered.

'And *you* are supposed to be my mermaidenly replacement,' said Mrs Wilberforce. '*You*.'

She didn't want to talk anymore after that, and there was nothing left to eat, so Loretta went home and looked up hagfish. They were full of slime too, like pudding.

She wondered if there was a hagfish walking around, skinned of its skin but oozing anyway, and waiting to see if they could find another hagfish to go back to the sea and be hagfish again.

She thought that no one would want to be a hagfish, probably.

There were diamond cuts in the grafted skin covering the back of Mrs Wilberforce's thighs. They did not look like scales. Apparently the cuts were to let fluid drain from under the graft. Loretta opened a can of tuna to see if the liquid there smelled the same but it didn't.

'I think you've lost all your fish,' she said. The nurse and Mrs Wilberforce exchanged speaking expressions.

'I'm a magical creature,' said Mrs Wilberforce, in tones so dry Loretta knew she hadn't set foot in surf for decades.

'Course you are!' said the nurse, and smiled. Loretta had seen those smiles before. Baby smiles, for babies who had no teeth, and when Loretta showed the nurse her teeth, the nurse stopped smiling and went away. Mrs Wilberforce said it was because she'd finished changing the bandages, but Loretta knew that some people couldn't look at a mermaid smiling without wanting to drown themselves. There was a fish tank in the waiting room but though she sat there for most of the day, watching, the nurse didn't come and stick her head into it, which made the day a waste.

'Life is full of disappointments,' said Mrs Wilberforce, when Loretta slunk back into the ward to say her goodbyes. If anyone knew about disappointments, Loretta thought, remembering the tuna can, it was probably her.

'Why didn't you cut your legs down the middle?' she asked. 'That might have made them stick together, instead of sticking you to the couch.'

It hadn't been a bad idea, the couch – or not exactly. When Mrs Wilberforce had grown attached to it, her legs had been trapped and a little further from separate than they had been. Loretta couldn't quite picture how Mrs Wilberforce could have swum with a couch attached to her backside, but maybe she could have sliced it off with bits of clam or something.

'No more clams,' said Mrs Wilberforce. 'No more nothing.'

If there weren't any clams, along with the there-weren't-any-whales and there-weren't-any-hagfish, Loretta reasoned, there might not be any tuna either. People were always telling you things that weren't true, so maybe the reason Mrs Wilberforce's liquid bits didn't smell like tuna juice was because it wasn't really tuna in the can after all. That cheered her up.

Of course Mrs Wilberforce didn't smell like fake tuna. She was a mermaid, and mermaids would know.

'Maybe I could sew my legs together,' Loretta said. 'Cut them down the middle and sew them together.' She looked at Mrs Wilberforce, critical. 'I'm not saying you didn't try hard enough'

– though she hadn't, but maybe that wasn't her fault, separate from skin as she was – 'but a knife and needle might work.' She'd had to promise not to use any more bed sheets. 'A knife could open up the gills as well.' No matter how often she went over them with felt tip, the lines remained stubbornly closed.

'*No*,' said Mrs Wilberforce, grabbing at her arm. 'No knives! You must promise me that.'

'You said I could be a mermaid with you,' said Loretta, sulky at the prohibition. 'You said we could be mermaids together.'

'That might have been a mistake,' said Mrs Wilberforce. Her face was very pale. 'Maybe you're not meant to be a mermaid after all. Mistakes like this happen sometimes. Wouldn't you rather be something else instead?'

'You were never going to give me your fish skin, were you?' said Loretta. She felt hot all over with betrayal, so hot that even salt water wouldn't cool her down. 'You said that he burnt it but I bet you lied. You just want to be a mermaid by yourself. You think I'm not a mermaid, but I am. I *am*, and you can stay here beached by yourself, because I'm going to take your skin. I'm going to take your skin and wear it, and there's nothing you can do about it!' If there had been pudding she would have thrown it. 'I should never have believed you,' she said.

When she ran out of the hospital room, the mermaid cried behind her, but Loretta ignored her.

She searched the mermaid's house, again and again, but she couldn't find the skin so she burnt the house down instead. If she was going to be stranded on dry land then the mermaid had to be stranded there too. The faded scales on her legs shone in the firelight. 'I'll show you,' she said, hands blistered and ash-covered, except it was too late, because when Loretta went back to the hospital, days later and surfeited on spite, the mermaid was gone.

'I tried to find you,' said the nurse, 'but you never left your contact details. Mrs Wilberforce was transferred yesterday. She's going home.'

'Her home's gone,' said Loretta. 'It burnt down. I saw the fire engines from my window.'

'No, sweetheart,' said the nurse. 'She's gone *home*. Back to her island, the one she told you about. There's a very good hospital there, people who care about her. She'll get the help she needs.'

The mermaid had left Loretta her globe. When she shook it, the sand and the water glimmered in sunlight.

'I don't want it,' said Loretta. It was a baby toy, like felt-tip pens. 'I hate her.'

'I'm sure that's not true,' said the nurse, gently.

Loretta scowled at her, an ugly scowl come out of deep waters. 'I hate you too,' she said, and threw the globe hard against the wall. It didn't break, just made a sad hollow thump and rolled back towards her.

She took it with her when she left, purely so she could have the pleasure of destroying it.

She was the only mermaid left in the world. Mrs Wilberforce might have gone home, but she had left without her skin and she was so little fish without it that it was hardly worth calling her a mermaid anymore. Loretta thought that Mrs Wilberforce would find home less friendly than she remembered. She hoped she went swimming in the empty waters there and they drowned her. Better to be the last living mermaid than share the title with a mermaid who lied.

Loretta stole a hammer off her brother and smashed the globe. Sea water spilled over her, soaking her skin. Sand infiltrated every crevice. Without either, the empty globe was a small cheap thing, but the salt and the sand sank into her and *itched*.

She dreamed that night of oceans, and of Mrs Wilberforce saying *You can be one your own self*, and when Loretta woke the next morning, there were tiny webs between her toes and the beginning of corrugation in her gills.

She went into the sea, hunting for hagfish, and her skin was tight and new around her.

*

Loretta met the hagfish at the doctor's office, where everyone denied she was a mermaid.

The medical profession, Loretta thought, was blind and incompetent, and if they had all been in water she would have scooped out their eyes with clam shell and eaten them.

'You don't have gills, you idiot,' said her brother, scrubbing at her neck with a flannel. 'You're just having an allergic reaction to all that ink.' He had taken away her felt pens and hidden them for the second time. (The first time, Loretta just retrieved them from the rubbish bin but her brother found her out, and with a low cunning she hadn't expected from him had hidden them somewhere else instead. He had probably asked Mr Wilberforce for a good hiding place, and Mr Wilberforce might have said *ashes*, but there was no fire in their house and Loretta would have smelled the burning.)

'You don't have scales, sweetheart,' said the doctor, slathering Loretta all over with a foul cream that smelled nothing like the ocean. 'It's eczema. That's why your skin's so dry and flaky.'

The hagfish was slumped in the corner of the waiting room, leaking. He paid no attention to Loretta, and that was insulting. She wasn't particularly clear about who bossed what in the sea, or if the old scales of bossing were still the same now the ocean was filled with so much emptiness, but Loretta was certain that a mermaid outranked a hagfish.

Perhaps the hagfish was sulking because she had ignored him first. He looked familiar, and eventually Loretta realised that he was in her class at school, which made the lack of recognition acceptable because she hardly ever went. The hagfish was called Jeremy, and she disliked him on principle. Perhaps she should have been more open to friendship with other marine life, but the only real memory Loretta could summon about the hagfish was a general impression of *damp*, and not the good kind that came with rolling in waves. The hagfish just oozed, and maybe he didn't understand he was a hagfish – not everyone could be as sharp and bright as mermaids – but surely the slime should have been a giveaway.

Loretta was forced to concede that hagfish were just not very bright. It was probably the reason that none of them were left. There were a lot of stupid people in the world, after all. It stood to reason that there would have been a lot of stupid people in the ocean too, back when it was full of life instead of old tyres and disappointment. Still, maybe there had been a hagfish magician or something, and they had hidden the last hagfish in plain sight so that one day a mermaid could find it and force it to remember itself and come home.

If Loretta had needed any more proof that she was a mermaid, that was it. She only hoped that the hagfish proved less spineless than Mrs Wilberforce, but then Mrs Wilberforce had been out of the ocean for years longer than Loretta had been alive, and even if the hagfish had lost his skin the very day after he was born, that was still less time without it than Mrs Wilberforce had been without hers. That was moderately hopeful, so Loretta went up to the hagfish to make an attempt at polite conversation.

'You're very slimy,' she said.

'Who the fuck are you?' said the hagfish, and Loretta socked him in the mouth. She had to. The hagfish bled and cried and there was more slime, more of it everywhere. It looked, she thought, an awful lot like snot.

Loretta was dragged out of the doctor's surgery by her ear. 'I had to do it,' she said. 'He was being rude. Also, I thought it might knock something loose.'

'Like a tooth?' said her brother, and Loretta couldn't read his expression very well but it was the same expression he always had when talking to her. She called it his puffy, what-am-I-supposed-to-do-with-you face, because that's what always followed it.

'What the hell am I supposed to do with you?' said her brother. 'You hit. You bite. You're twelve years old. Surely this phase should have been long over by now.'

Loretta shrugged. Mermaids had different life cycles, probably. If she was the only mermaid left in the world – Mrs Wilberforce no longer counted, Loretta had stripped her of her status – then she was normal for her kind.

Her brother drove her home in silence. Loretta wouldn't have listened to him anyway. She was too busy thinking about the hagfish.

'Did you notice how slimy he was?' she said.

'Poor kid's got fucking *allergies*, Loretta. It's spring. There's pollen everywhere. Leave him alone, won't you?'

Allergies, Loretta thought. Not bloody likely.

'Lots of people have allergies,' her brother went on. 'And you'll give yourself one if you don't stop scrawling over yourself.'

That gave her pause. Not the scrawling, because she wasn't going to stop that, but lots of people did have allergies. There was one girl in her class who was allergic to fish. When Loretta found out she had followed her around and grinned her mermaid grin because it was winter and the school pool was empty so there was no way for the girl to drown herself because a mermaid had grinned, and Loretta had wanted to see how a person allergic to fish behaved when confronted with a mermaid. The reaction had been frustratingly invisible but Loretta knew it was there because whenever she went back to class and started following and grinning again, the girl always tried to avoid her, and eventually she developed a stomach ache and went home. She went home every time, so clearly mermaids were fish enough to trigger people who hated fish.

Loretta hoped the stomach aches killed her. People like that were probably why mermaids died out in the first place. They wanted to stop having stomach aches and so they got rid of all the mermaids but Loretta wasn't going to be got rid of. She was the one who got rid of people.

But her brother wasn't talking about fish allergies, and clearly Jeremy the hagfish wasn't allergic to fish, because then he'd be allergic to his own self and then he'd be dead. He was probably allergic to pollen, like her brother said. Loretta couldn't understand why she hadn't seen it before. Did that mean that everyone with hay fever was a hagfish? Had she been ignoring them all along?

No wonder the hagfish was not pleased with her. Perhaps she had hurt their feelings.

But that didn't sound right. Hagfish didn't have feelings. Not important ones, anyway. Loretta thought they were probably what her teacher called a 'lower animal'. Like an earthworm or something, all squiggly and slimy. Loretta didn't think earthworms had feelings either.

It wasn't fair. First there was another mermaid, and she turned out to be a useless selfish mermaid who had spent most of her time trying to forget being a mermaid and her legs didn't stick together very well even when she tried to remember. Now there was a hagfish, and Loretta didn't think the hagfish forgot being a hagfish. He probably never knew he was one in the first place, which meant that maybe none of them knew. That seemed particularly useless even for hagfish, so Loretta suspected there was probably only one of them because surely if there was a whole stinking population *one* of them would figure it out and find her to do homage.

She wasn't quite sure what homage was but thought it sounded like something mermaids should have.

So probably it was just Jeremy, and he *did* seem slimier and leakier than most people. It was just Loretta's bad luck that he was a lower animal, like an earthworm, and didn't know any better, but he was all the hagfish she had.

Later that night, Loretta sat up suddenly in her bed, hooked out of ocean dreams by sharp edges and possibilities.

If you cut an earthworm in half, she heard, you had two earthworms.

It was a plan but not a good one. Jeremy might have been a hagfish but there didn't seem to be much value to him. He already seemed like a lot to put up with. Loretta wasn't sure she wanted more than one. On the other hand, he might be her responsibility. She didn't want the responsibility, exactly, but if he was the only hagfish in the world, he was also going to school with a girl who got stomach aches from fish and who knew what she would do to him?

He was Loretta's hagfish. If anyone was going to get rid of him it would be her. Loretta hadn't decided, yet, if it was worth it to be rid of him but until she did decide no one else could have him. He might end up brained on the head, picked up by the feet and bashed against the side of wharf. He might end up cut up and put in a tin to pretend to be tuna. (She would have to smell him, and see if the scent was the same.) That was unacceptable. The hagfish might be oozy and slimy and wet in all the wrong ways, but if he was the only hagfish in the world then he belonged to the mermaids and Loretta was the only mermaid left, which meant he belonged to her.

There were two possibilities. Either Loretta went to school and grinned her mermaid grin at the girl with the allergies until her stomach ache came back and she went home, or Loretta went to school and followed the hagfish to keep him from harm. Both involved going to school, which did not please her. Loretta thought that hagfish might be more trouble than they were worth. Couldn't she have a shark or a selkie or something? A skin would be more useful than slime, especially as her own skin was withering under treatment. Her brother had hidden the ointment in the same place as he had hidden the felt pens, and wouldn't let her leave the house until she slathered it over her scales. If he thought a mermaid would let her scales be taken he was dead wrong. Loretta stopped at the beach on her way to school and scrubbed the ointment off with sand and salt water. It stung a bit but she didn't care, and there were more felt tips at school. She used them to draw the gills back on her neck, the scales back on her legs.

The hagfish flinched when he saw her.

'Is that a gang marking?' he said.

'Yes,' said Loretta. 'Mine. You want to join?'

The hagfish didn't say no quickly enough, so she held him down and drew gills on him too. She wasn't sure if hagfish had gills but they had to breathe somehow, and the amount of slime he leaked while she was marking him made her think that at least part of the hagfish knew himself for what he was.

'Please don't hit me again,' whined the hagfish, and wasn't that like a hagfish, she thought. They were probably all like that around mermaids. Maybe they were afraid of being eaten.

'I'm not promising that,' said Loretta. 'I won't bite you, though. There's only one of you, I think, and if I eat you up there might not be another one.'

'You want to *eat me*?' cried the hagfish, in rising tones. There was no trace now of the hagfish who had been so rude to her in the doctor's office. She had smacked that right out of him, which was something. She had done well there. Perhaps she could show a little leniency now that the hagfish knew not to snap at mermaids.

'If I have to eat something slimy I'd rather it was pudding,' Loretta admitted. 'And you are *very* slimy.' She wiped her hands on his jumper.

'It's hay fever,' said the hagfish, disconsolate. 'Nothing seems to work. It's itchy eyes and runny nose all the time. I'm sick of it.'

'Have you tried salt water?' said Loretta. 'I could hold your head under for you.' It wouldn't do anything for hagfish slime but maybe the water would help him to know himself. Loretta hadn't needed water for that – she had always known she was a mermaid – but hagfish clearly needed more help. He was a lower animal, she reminded herself. He couldn't help it.

'I don't think I trust you to let me up again,' said the hagfish, and Loretta had to admit that he had a point. She'd be tempted to hold him under until he started swimming, but apparently the hagfish couldn't swim, which, *of course* he couldn't. He was useless, absolutely useless. The only thing he could do was slime.

When the girl with the allergies came round – 'You don't even know her name, do you?' said the hagfish – she flinched at the sight of them together.

'You're going to have a stomach ache soon,' said Loretta, and grinned with all her teeth showing. Then she remembered that it was spring and the school pool was open again and the girl might go drown herself so she clapped her mouth shut out of habit but then remembered that drowning might solve her problem so grinned again, but by that time the girl with the allergies had run away and was looking sickly off in a corner somewhere.

Weak, thought Loretta, scornful. Weak, weak, weak.

'I don't like it when you make that face,' said the hagfish. 'It's scary.'

'I'm only smiling.'

'I know. Stop it!'

'I'm trying save your life, you stupid hagfish,' grumbled Loretta, but he was snorting into a hanky, slime seeping through the material and the whole wet gurgle of it reminded her of Mrs Wilberforce's globe and how the water had leaked out when she smashed it.

Across the classroom, the girl with the allergies cringed. That made sense, Loretta thought. If she was allergic to mermaid she would be allergic to hagfish, and the two of them in one place was probably making her stomach ache even quicker. That was promising.

'Go over there and slime on her,' said Loretta. 'Sneeze or something.'

'What? *Why*?'

'I'm running an experiment,' said Loretta. 'Move it, hagfish. Don't make me tell you twice. I'll sock you again if I have to.'

Ten seconds later the hagfish had sneezed and the girl with the allergies had shrieked and then she was crying and complaining about a stomach ache and wanting to go home, and Loretta heard the teacher comforting her and saying something about stress and that was all right, Loretta knew about stress because her own was gone now.

Perhaps the slime wasn't that useless after all. The hagfish was better off being able to defend himself. Loretta wouldn't always be around to do it for him.

She liked him better when he did what he was told. It might be worth cutting him in two after all, she thought.

'I'm not going to do what you say if you're just going to cut me in two,' said the hagfish, snivelling all over the beach. Loretta had made him leave after she had filled her pockets with more felt-tip pens. It was moments like this when, despite herself, she missed Mrs Wilberforce. She had been a failed mermaid but she hadn't been a whiner. Loretta despised whining. All mermaids did.

'You're going to do what I say whether I cut you in two or not,' she said. It was only the truth. Some people were happier when they were told what to do and Jeremy was one of them.

'And I'm not a hagfish either! You don't have to be mean just because I snot a lot.'

'You're a hagfish, Jeremy,' said Loretta. 'Just accept it. Maybe if you come into the water you'll figure it out quicker. I'll only hold you down for a little bit.' Right now the hagfish thought he was a boy, and mermaids lured boys into water and drowned them, but he wasn't making it easy. She wasn't even sure what luring was, exactly, but she thought it might involve wearing shells over the places where her tits would be one day and that sounded unpleasant. Her brother nearly drooled over girls sometimes, and Jeremy slimed enough that adding drool would not be an improvement. Luring sounded more trouble than it was worth. She'd already drawn the gills on him so if he didn't hurry up she wasn't going to bother with luring, she'd just knock him down and drag him into surf.

'I'm not a hagfish!' screamed the hagfish. 'I don't even know what a hagfish is! And you can't make me one, because you're not a mermaid!'

Loretta went very still and stared at him, eyes flat and dark, and she knew the moment he saw the mermaid rising within her, the scales and the teeth, because he began to blubber. 'I'm sorry! I didn't mean it. You can be a mermaid if you want to. Even if you don't want to. If you're a mermaid it doesn't matter if you want to be or not, I guess. You're a mermaid either way.'

'Yes,' said Loretta. 'I *am* a mermaid.' She would have shown him her scales coming in, the flaky skin spreading over her old human form, but he didn't deserve the proof of it. He'd doubted and looked into her eyes and knew better, but he *had* doubted, and hagfish doubting was different than human doubting. It was worse, because hagfish should know better.

'Perhaps . . .' said the hagfish, humbled, 'perhaps I could help? Not by drowning. I don't want to drown. Or be cut in half. But if you're a mermaid, um . . . shouldn't you have a tail? And, like, scales and stuff.'

'I have scales,' said Loretta. 'And no, I'm not showing you. And I had a skin that would have given me a tail. Least, I nearly had it. It belonged to another mermaid but she let someone else take it and wouldn't share it and I couldn't get to it.'

'Maybe you just need another skin, then,' said the hagfish.

It was a good enough idea to keep from drowning him, Loretta reasoned. She could always do it later if he fell back into his nasty rebellious hagfish ways.

*

The hagfish liked to spend time in libraries because there was generally very little pollen there. Loretta distrusted them for their dryness and for the fact that books didn't do well in water. She would have made Jeremy go in by himself but he might have run away or washed his gills off or done something to make himself difficult. She'd catch him again afterwards – she was a mermaid, of course she would – but if she had to be the only mermaid left in the world, did she really have to be saddled with a hagfish for company?

A shark would have been so much better.

'I can't find anything about mermaid skins,' said the hagfish. 'Closest thing is a selkie: a sort of seal woman who loses her skin sometimes and has to stay ashore like a human woman and get married and have babies.'

Loretta thought some people were just bloody careless. If she had her skin she wouldn't be coming back, and she surely wouldn't be stripping it off for anyone. Seals must be as stupid as hagfish, as stupid as Mrs Wilberforce. It was like she *wanted* to be caught, but Loretta had seen pictures of Mr Wilberforce when he was a young man, Mrs Wilberforce had kept them on her nightstand, and he wasn't that good-looking. Mrs Wilberforce must have been really desperate. Loretta would never be that desperate. If a mermaid wanted a man, the proper way was to snatch someone who'd fallen off their ship and take them down and down and down into dark water, and then after Loretta wasn't quite sure what, let their dead body float back up again. Simple. She didn't understand how Mrs Wilberforce had managed to muck it up. Perhaps the lack of other mermaids had affected her brain, bad enough that even when Loretta presented herself the brain was just too much rotten to recover.

She scratched at her skin, flakes sifting off so she could almost see the scales beneath. The small webbing between her toes was still there – 'Of course it is, stupid,' said her brother, 'you were born with it. A freak from the get-go' – but it wasn't getting any bigger, and her gills stubbornly refused to open. She was stuck between, a mermaid with a human shell that was nearly too small and not sloughing off, and Loretta was afraid that she'd never get her mermaid form without a skin. A seal skin wasn't ideal, but there were no other mermaids left to take skins from, so her choices were limited.

'I know you don't want to hear it,' said the hagfish, 'but maybe you should talk to Mrs Wilberforce again. I know she's a long way away but the internet could track her down I bet.'

'No it can't,' said Loretta. 'She's dead. I know.' A mermaid who gave up her skin, who turned her back on other mermaids, was never going to last long once she got back to the ocean. It would close up her gills and eat up her scale-skin and that would be that. No more mermaid, like no more tuna and no more whales and no more sharks, which all would have been better than a hagfish who didn't believe her. 'I can prove it,' she said.

At the hospital, Loretta asked for the nurse who had looked after Mrs Wilberforce. The nurse's face dropped when she saw her. 'Oh, honey,' she said, and Loretta had to stomp on the hagfish's foot to stop him sniggering at the thought of her being honey to anyone. 'I'm so sorry.' Mrs Wilberforce had died soon after her return home.

'Told you so,' said Loretta, and the nurse looked taken aback.

'Did you know already?'

'Course I did,' said Loretta. 'She didn't want to be a mermaid anymore and the water didn't want her. It was bound to happen.' She hesitated. 'Did she tell you about her skin before she carked it?'

'No, she didn't,' said the nurse, and her tone was colder. She looked past Loretta. 'Do you need to see a doctor, young man?'

'Oh, that's just Jeremy. He's fine,' said Loretta. 'He's a hagfish. He always oozes like that.'

'I have allergies,' the hagfish snuffled.

'Then perhaps you should go have them somewhere else,' said the nurse, and for the first time Loretta almost liked her. 'And wash that ink off your necks!' she said, and Loretta's almost-liking dropped dead as Mrs Wilberforce.

'Well, what now?' she said as they left the hospital. 'You know anyone with a seal skin, hagfish?'

'I wish you'd call me Jeremy,' said the hagfish. 'It is my name.'

'Hagfish is a better name,' said Loretta. 'You're not the only Jeremy in the world. You are the only hagfish – for now, anyway.' She hadn't forgotten the earthworms. 'It makes it harder to mix you up.'

The only seal skins either of them knew about were in the museum or on the seals. There was a colony of fur seals an hour down the coast.

'The colony doesn't have burglar alarms,' said Loretta.

'The colony has *teeth*,' said the hagfish. 'Great sharp shiny teeth! The museum doesn't have teeth.'

'We'll just have to find a dead one then,' said Loretta. The dead seal would still have teeth but she didn't tell the hagfish that. He'd probably use it as an excuse. 'And before you think of backing out, remember that I've got teeth too. And I think they're getting longer.' Her skin was certainly getting itchier, and her gill marks more corrugated. Her brother would have said it was because Loretta was always using the felt tips but that was a lie. It was gills coming through, mermaid gills, and anyone who said different was due a bite.

'Bad luck comes in threes,' said the hagfish, over-cheerful when they couldn't find a dead seal, and Loretta scowled. It was as if he didn't even want to be cut in half, he was so determined to be unhelpful. Worse, he didn't seem to realise that he was the second bad-luck thing. A mermaid that didn't want to be a mermaid (and didn't want Loretta to be one either), a hagfish that didn't want to be a hagfish, and now a bunch of seals that didn't want to be dead.

'I thought the third bad thing was that we'd have to go back to school now,' said the hagfish, and he was a horrible liar because the hagfish loved school. Mostly, Loretta thought, because Loretta wasn't there.

Hagfish were so fucking ungrateful, she thought. Give them gills and a use for slime and a way of going back to the sea and what did they do? Wanted to go to school instead, that's what. 'You're the most gormless hagfish I've ever met,' she snapped.

'And you're the meanest mermaid!'

'If you don't like it, you can bugger off.'

'Fine. That's what I'll do then,' said the hagfish, pettish, and he marched off, but he did it slowly enough that Loretta could have called him back if she wanted to.

'I hope fish-allergy girl cuts you up for tuna!' she called after him, and the hagfish actually stomped his foot.

'Her name's *Frieda*,' the hagfish shrieked. '*FRIEDA*!'

Stupid, horrible name, thought the mermaid.

Stupid, horrible hagfish.

The seals either didn't care or were so stunned by the presence of a mermaid that it just looked like not caring. Loretta was sadly unsurprised. With no mermaids to tell them what to do the seals became fat and lazy and, while they were probably smarter than hagfish, they were doing a good job of pretending that they weren't. That, and their breath stank. All of them stank.

'I suppose I should get used to that,' she said. 'If I'm going to take one of your skins then the stink will sink in.' Maybe it had a bit already, just by her being there. It would explain why the seals were all right with her walking among them. 'I suppose you learned to put up with a lot,' she said. No whales, no mermaids. They probably didn't miss the sharks, but more and more there were no fish and the seal colony was getting smaller because of it. 'That's another thing to thank Mr Wilberforce for,' she said. 'He stole her skin and all right, that was mostly her fault for letting him get near it, but you would have been better off with a mermaid about.' Loretta said it as steadily as she could, because the seals were bigger than her, bigger than hagfish, and she needed one of them dead and they knew it.

'I need a skin,' she said. 'If one of you were dead I'd take that one but you're none of you dead so one needs to be. I don't mind wearing dead skin, but I need to go home.'

Home was not a house with no parents and a brother who wouldn't let her tie her legs together no matter how much she bit him. Loretta took off her shoes. She sat in front of the biggest seal, the one with the biggest teeth and the biggest breath and she held up her feet, toes spread wide apart. 'It's webbing,' she said. 'Look close and you'll see. Like a fish. My legs aren't all together yet but they will be.' She took off her shirt and held up her hair so that the seal could see the gills she had drawn over and over again on her flesh. 'These are my gills,' she said. 'They're not breathing yet but they will be.' She took off her pants and stood naked before the seal. 'Look at my scales,' she said. 'I had to draw some of them in and the others just look like old nasty skin but the scales are there underneath and they're not all the way hard yet but they will be.

'I need your skin, seal,' said the mermaid. 'I need it so bad. And you need a mermaid. All of you do. You had one but she was useless and gave up on herself but I won't do that. I'm a good mermaid. I'm strong. No one will trick me into giving up my skin. And I've already found a hagfish. He's useless, but he's a hagfish so no surprises there. If there are more hagfish out there I'll find them. If there are whales and tuna and all the other dead things walking around like they've forgotten what they are, I'll find them. I'll find them and bring them home and giving up your skin for that will be worth it. I'll make it worth it. I want you to give me your skin, seal. And I'm sorry, but if you won't give it, I'm going to take it. Mermaids get what they want.'

The seal didn't give up its skin. The seal bit her instead, a stinking gape of bite that crunched all the way down to bone, a hard bite, a warning bite and a bloody one. Then it bit her again, and again.

It bit her harder each time.

The mermaid woke in a hospital bed. There was a tray with the same slimy pudding, with the same bread roll sopping in gravy. Mrs Wilberforce's nurse was sitting on the end of the bed.

'That's my pudding,' said the mermaid, automatically.

The nurse just shook her head. 'Do you think you deserve it, really?' she said. 'You've caused a lot of trouble, Loretta.'

'Not Loretta,' said the mermaid. 'Loretta isn't a good name for mermaids. I'm a mermaid.' Her throat ached as she said it, strained from screaming, but she knew herself.

'Don't you think that if you were truly a mermaid a seal wouldn't be able to bite you?'

'Seal can bite all it likes,' said the mermaid. 'I'm still a fucking mermaid.' And the mermaid grinned her big mermaid grin, but the nurse just rolled her eyes.

'Don't try that on me,' she said. 'I'm immune.'

'No one is immune to mermaids,' said the mermaid.

'You're not a mermaid, Loretta.'

'I am,' said the mermaid. 'I will always be a mermaid.'

'You could choose to be something else.'

'No,' said the mermaid. 'I couldn't.'

She clamped her legs together as if they were one piece of flesh and rolled over so that her back was to the nurse.

When the mermaid woke in the early morning before dawn, there was a seal skin draped over the end of the bed. The skin was thick and coarse and damp. The mermaid ran her fingers over it and pulled it onto her lap and the skin was heavy, so heavy, and it stank. The hair pricked her fingers, and the mermaid wept.

When the door to her room opened, the light from the hall spread into the room and made it hard to see, but the mermaid could make out the nurse, standing there and watching her. The nurse's eyes were big and dark and wet. 'I thought you should know,' said the nurse, in tones that Mrs Wilberforce would have described as absolutely non-committal, 'that your brother will be coming to visit this morning. Visiting hours start at eight.'

'What's the time now?' asked the mermaid.

'Nearly six. And goodness me,' said the nurse, 'but it is stuffy in here. I think some fresh air would do you good.' She crossed the room and tugged up the big sash window that opened onto the veranda outside the hospital. The window locks were too high for the mermaid to reach. 'Perhaps you'd like to sit and watch the sunrise,' said the nurse, and placed the visitor's chair by the window. If the mermaid had been able to stand on the chair she might have reached the locks, but barely, and her whole body hurt too much to stretch. Still, the mermaid could recognise excuse and alibi when she saw it, just as well as she could recognise opportunity.

'Are you sure?' said the mermaid, when the nurse went to shut the door behind her.

'Yes.'

'You're not going to ask if I'm sure?'

'I already did that,' said the nurse. 'Make it worth it, will you?'

'Yes,' said the mermaid.

'It's quite a nice world really,' said the nurse. 'I like it here.'

'More fool you,' said the mermaid, which was not exactly polite but she had the seal skin now and if the nurse came to take it back the mermaid would bite her and bite her and then the nurse would know what biting felt like.

When the door shut the mermaid threw off her bedclothes and tried her best to stand on legs that were still sadly separate. They were all bandaged up, as Mrs Wilberforce's had been when she had skin grafted onto the back of flesh that she'd cared too much for and then not enough. There were no diamond shapes from grafting, but the mermaid knew that scales would soon be pushing their way through. More than that, her legs *hurt*, and if the soles of her feet didn't feel as if they had been stabbed with knives the rest of her did. Knives like teeth, and seal breath passing into her body, all bugs and germs and stink.

The mermaid swayed under her own weight. It was harder on dry land, without salt to help with floating. The seal skin was too heavy to lift in her arms so the mermaid wrapped it around her and it was enormous – she was like a kid playing dress-up. The skin dragged along the ground, and she could have wrapped herself in it three times. It was hot and close and staggeringly heavy and the mermaid fell out of the window, trusting to the skin to muffle the thump. Even so she could feel her injuries open up, the wounds starting to seep.

'I don't smell of tuna either, Mrs Wilberforce,' said the mermaid. 'I don't smell anything but seal stink, Mrs Wilberforce,' said the mermaid. 'You were an enormous fucking disappointment, Mrs Wilberforce,' said the mermaid. 'You were a neighbour. You could have helped.'

Forgiveness was a waste of everybody's time. Spite, not soppiness, gave the mermaid motivation to keep going, though her feet tangled in seal skin and scraped themselves raw on tarmac.

'A mermaid, Mrs Wilberforce,' said the mermaid, struggling along the road and doing her best to stay out of streetlights, 'helps her fucking self. Even if she has nothing. Even if she only has a hagfish.'

The mermaid was all wet under the skin. She was sick and sweaty. Her bandages bloomed with blood. That was a good thing. The sickness and the sweat and the blood helped the skin to stick, and the mermaid needed the skin to stick because she couldn't hold it up anymore. Her hands were slick. It was difficult to grip. When the mermaid reached the dunes and fell into them, sand stuck to the seal skin and to the little bits of under-skin and made everything even heavier. The mermaid had to crawl towards the water.

She almost didn't make it, but when the mermaid lifted her head from wet sand, salt crusted over her face, grit on her tongue and in her eyes, she could see the bobbing heads of seals in the surf, watching. The largest seal was missing.

'I hope I poisoned the bitch,' said the mermaid. Gratitude was not high on the list of mermaid traits. It, like forgiveness, was too heavy to carry. The skin was heavy enough for any one creature.

The skin bulked around her, a thick, hot blanket. It trapped her legs, held them together so that the mermaid had to serpentine her way to water, to kick like a fish finding its way to froth. By the time the mermaid made her way into water, she was too tired to swim. The tide carried her out, and the skin, waterlogged, carried her down and down, like a sailor drowning.

The seals watched. They did not help.

The mermaid was used to that.

She helped herself instead. Kicked and kicked like her legs were tied together with bed sheets instead of seal skin, although she didn't have much of a choice because they *were* bound together now, and when the mermaid reached down with long clawed fingers, the scales on her legs were hard and hairy both, the scales of a mermaid who'd become mermaid through seal instead of fish skin, a curved shaggy tail. The mermaid gasped to feel it, and bubbles came out of her gills, open for the first time.

'I knew there were gills,' said the mermaid, smug. 'I fucking knew it!'

The seals circled at a distance, and far off the mermaid could feel the pulse echoes of fish, currents made by small fins and small heartbeats and there were far too few of them. The whales were dead and the sharks were dead and most of the fish were dead – she still didn't know what they put in the tuna cans, but it didn't smell like mermaid – but the mermaids weren't dead, and if she could find a hagfish she could find the rest.

When she sculled her way to surface, the mermaid saw that hagfish, trudging along the road to the hospital, to be there when visiting hours began. She could see the glint of slime trickling down his face, see him raise his handkerchief to swab at it. It touched something in the vicinity of her heart, but the mermaid squashed it down, resolute, because Frieda was with him, fish-allergic fucking *Frieda*, and she was even carrying a little bunch of flowers. The mermaid was certain, suddenly and horrifically certain, that a Get Well Soon card was tucked inside.

'Losers,' she said, and shook her head.

The seals were all around her, and, turning from land, the mermaid went searching for fish.

JOY HOLLEY

School Spirit

It was important that we broke into Erskine College on a full moon. It was in Cancer, which wasn't ideal: we didn't want anyone crying. Also I was on my period. But it was a Saturday night and none of us had work the next morning, which was too rare an occasion to pass up.

Saffron and Frances got to mine at 10pm. I had been waiting since 9:30 – the time we had agreed upon.

'What took you so long?' I asked, opening the back door of the car. 'Oh, hello.'

A girl with very pale skin smiled at me nervously from the other end of the back seat. 'I'm Olivia, I'm a friend of Saffron's.'

'Right. I'm Meg.' I got in and slammed the door. As far as I knew, Saffron didn't have any friends outside of our extended circles. I suspected she'd met Olivia on Tinder.

'Olivia studies fine arts.' Frances turned to pass me an open packet of Oreos.

'Nice.' I took one of the biscuits and split it so I could see its white circle of icing. 'I've been craving sugar all day.'

Frances raised an eyebrow. 'Period? Same with me and Saffron.'

'Witch bitches.' I laughed. 'We're all synced up with the full moon.'

I took another Oreo then offered them to Olivia. She shook her head. I thought about asking if she was on her period too, but decided I better not.

'Can someone feed me an Oreo?' Saffron asked, not taking her eyes off the road. I passed them back to Frances and watched her feed one to Saffron.

'Have you been to Erskine before, Olivia?' Frances asked.

'No, I'm from Christchurch.'

'None of us have been either. But Saffy's done lots of research.'

Frances was the only person who called Saffron Saffy. Occasionally I slipped and called her Saffy too, but it sounded wrong coming out of my mouth.

Olivia shifted the tote bag in her lap. It was one of those black ones with the white square on it. 'Are you all from Wellington?'

'Only Meg,' said Frances. 'Saffron and I are from New Plymouth, we've been friends since high school.'

I met Frances in first year psychology – which we both dropped – then met Saffron at Frances's birthday party. Saffron and I hooked up that night, and at a few parties after that, but over the past year our flirting had mostly steadied into friendship.

'Is the moon out yet?' Saffron asked.

I peered out the window. 'I think the clouds are hiding it.'

'It's in Cancer right? That's no fun.'

'Olivia, what sign are you?' Frances asked.

'Um, Pisces?'

'Uh oh,' Saffron and I said in perfect sync. She spun her head round to grin at me.

Olivia looked scared. 'What's so bad about Pisces?'

'They're our least favourite sign,' I said. 'But maybe you'll be an exception.'

'What's the rest of your chart?' Frances asked.

'I don't know.'

Frances and Saffron glanced at each other. 'Not even your moon? Your rising?'

'I'm not sure what time I was born.'

'Text your mum and find out,' Frances said.

Olivia obediently got out her phone. 'I'll text my dad.'

None of us said anything while she tapped on the screen. I felt somewhat sorry for her, but I was mostly annoyed at Saffron for inviting her along. The three of us had been planning this night for months.

'Here we are.' Saffron pointed up the hill at a cluster of large Gothic buildings.

Frances peered at them. 'So old-fashioned.'

The largest building was four storeys high, with a wide balcony attached to each level. The balconies' white railings stood out in the dark.

'They look so out of place,' I said. 'Like a blip in time.'

'They'll be knocked down soon.' Saffron turned onto a road leading up the hill. 'So we better get a good look tonight.'

Let me tell you what I remember. Steep steps and dark trees dripping. Slipping on the slick and avoiding the cracks, afraid of breaking my mother's back. The smell of pine needles and rain. Magpies squawking. I remember looming buildings, though they loomed less over the years.

A labyrinth of long corridors. Gleaming floors. The smell of polish and beeswax. I remember the ringing of the bells. A chorus of footsteps. Two rows of girls, the Mistress of Discipline close behind. A whisper, then the sharp crack of her wooden clapper: *Silence, ladies!*

I remember brown pinafores in winter and green pinafores in summer. White uniforms on Feast Days. White veils for the Procession of the Lilies. A flower placed before the statue of our Lady, in the Black Forest Grotto. *Mary, I give thee the lily of my heart. Be thou its guardian forever.* I remember curtsying for Reverend Mother – quick curtsy in the corridors, deep curtsy at assembly. Gloved hands fumbling with holy pictures. Needlework classes on Saturday mornings. Standing on the grille to feel the waves of hot air up our skirts – forbidden, but everybody did it. Art books with pages glued together to hide the male nudes. Rumours of a headless nun in the piano cells. Birthday flowers from Best Friend.

I remember pressing glasses against closed doors. Gruff voices on the radio. Ships and submarines. I remember girls arriving from far away. Extra prayers at assembly. A black plane overhead. Girls crying and *what is happening what is happening*. Two girls taken into Sister Caldwell's office to read a letter from their mother.

I remember waiting for Sister Hayes to think we were asleep. Listening to the click-click of her heels as she walked from the dormitory to her room. Pulling back the curtains between our cubicles and climbing into Best Friend's bed. Hushed voices washing in and over each other. I remember voices disappearing.

Saffron parked at the bottom of a tall grassy slope. There was fencing up around it, but other people had broken in before us, leaving a convenient hole in the wire. We eased through it one by one. The slope was rutted and tangled with weeds, which made it easier to climb but took focus to navigate. Frances and I were nearly at the top when we heard a yelp from behind us.

I knew immediately it was Olivia.

'You all right?' Frances yelled.

'Yeah, I think I just twisted my ankle a bit.'

Frances and I looked at Saffron. She sighed and began climbing back down the slope.

'See you up there!' I yelled. Frances and I scurried to the top, her leather satchel bumping repeatedly against her hip until she grabbed it with her hands instead. We ran to the chapel as soon as we were on our feet, and collapsed, laughing, outside the main door.

'Sappho strikes again?'

Saffron had made her Tinder bio *you can call me sappho* back in first year, and this is how we had referred to her Tinder personality ever since. Her nickname in our group chat was 'sappho the serial dater'. Saffron pretended to be embarrassed, but it was obvious she enjoyed it.

'Sappho extreme. She forgot they had a date planned tonight.'

'Typical.'

'Such a dick. She didn't even say sorry, she just texted Olivia back like, "Want to come ghost-hunting?"'

'Did she tell her we were coming too?'

'Well you'd think so, but then we pick this poor girl up and she's obviously completely confused as to what I'm doing in the car.'

'No way.'

'And Saffy barely said a word to her the whole car ride.'

'I can't believe she's a Pisces. She does seem kind of wimpy.'

'For sure, not Saffy's type at all.'

'And how does she not know her birth chart? I thought all gays were into astrology.'

'Same. She did look cute in her Tinder pictures, though.'

The two of them walked towards us, Olivia limping a little.

Her body leaned to the left, weighed down by the tote bag hanging off her shoulder. I wondered why she hadn't left it in the car.

'Let's go round the back,' Saffron said. 'Apparently there are windows you can climb through.'

The chapel itself was intimidatingly tall. The windows were stained glass, with pictures of what I assumed were Jesus and Mary, but it was too dark to see, and they were so high only birds could reach them. Behind the chapel, a smaller building was attached. None of the windows had any glass left in them and most were boarded up, but Saffron soon found a low window where the boards had begun to rot away. She took a jumper out of her backpack and wrapped it around her hand, then pushed hard on what was left of the boards. They fell apart easily. The rest of us helped brush away the splinters, clearing the sill. Saffron swung her leg over and straddled the sill awkwardly while she bent her head and shoulders into the room, then whipped her other leg over and dropped inside. Frances and I did the same, and helped Olivia in after us.

Inside was even darker than I had expected. Saffron brought out a large yellow flashlight and the rest of us turned our phone torches on. At either side of the chapel entrance were two stone basins with leaves and roses carved into them. Saffron dipped her fingers into a basin then quickly pulled them out. She shuddered as she shook off the droplets. 'That is not holy water.' Frances passed her the jumper and she wiped her hands. We stepped into the chapel.

The first thing I saw was all the glass. Light glinted off the floor in a splintered mosaic of shattered bottles and window panes. Most of the glass was clear or dark green, but there were reds and oranges and even some blues. Amid all the glass was a lot of bird poo, some empty spray-paint cans and an abandoned cardigan. Most of the pews were intact. I looked up. The ceilings were so high the light from my phone couldn't reach them: above the stained glass windows, everything dissolved into darkness. Saffron scanned the lower part of the walls with her torch. They were almost completely covered in graffiti, most of it tags or drawings of dicks. Up near the altar were the remnants of a fire and some empty chip packets. I wandered over to a smashed statue and crouched down to pick up a white stone finger only a little smaller than my pinky. I put it in my pocket.

'Hey Frances, it's you.' Saffron was pointing her torch at one of the pictures on the wall. 'Saint Francis.'

Frances and I looked up at the painting. It was about the size of an old TV screen and framed in wood, with three little crosses sticking up at the top. 'Where does it say Francis?' I asked.

'It doesn't. You can tell because he's got a wolf.' Saffron moved her torch along to the next painting. 'And that one's Genevieve because she's holding a candle.'

I pointed my phone light at Saffron. 'I forget you grew up Catholic.'

'So do I.' She smiled, but I could see her chewing the insides of her mouth. 'Block that shit out.'

Frances opened her leather satchel and got out her camera, looping the strap around her neck. She snapped a photo of me before I registered what she was doing.

'Delete that.'

She stuck her tongue out and turned to take a picture of one of the windows. The camera flash was offensively loud in the quiet chapel. Frances stepped into the confessional, then poked her head back out. 'So, is this place actually haunted?'

'People on the internet say it is,' Saffron said. 'One of the nuns died in the study room, back in the thirties. And they used to have funerals in here.'

I sat down in one of the pews. Olivia sat behind me.

I turned around. 'Did your dad reply?'

'Oh, um . . .' She checked her phone. 'I was born around 3pm.'

'You should do your chart now.'

Olivia opened Google. I watched Saffron. She had climbed right up onto the altar and was taking a close look at everything. She picked up a thick white candle from the cluster arranged around a worn-out Virgin Mary. Frances snapped a picture and Saffron's head shot up, grinning.

Olivia coughed. 'I'm a Cancer rising?'

Saffron sniggered. I was surprised she could hear us from up on the altar. 'Pisces sun and a Cancer rising, oh dear.'

'What's wrong with it?'

'Nothing,' Frances said. 'It's just double water, lots of emotions. Your rising is how you come across on the surface, it's not that important. Your moon is the interesting one, it's like your inner self – mood and feelings and all that.'

'It says Virgo.'

I laughed. 'Damn, what a chart.'

'I'm a Virgo moon too,' Frances said. 'Wouldn't recommend.'

'It's the source of all her anxiety,' I added.

'What signs are you guys?' Olivia asked.

Frances sat down next to me, her legs stretched out over my lap. 'Meg's a Capricorn.'

'What does that mean?'

Frances smirked. 'It means she's heartless.'

I punched her shoulder. 'I have a heart! Saffron's the one with an Aquarius moon.'

Saffron hopped off the altar. 'Never felt a feeling in my life.'

'Saffy's a Sagittarius rising, so she seems all chaotic and fun,' explained Frances.

'But don't let it mislead you, I'm actually very serious.'

Olivia was looking at Frances and me. Frances grinned and rolled her eyes.

There was a soft, tearing sound. I looked around for the source. Saffron's mouth had fallen open and her eyes were locked on the altar. I turned towards it. A small flame quivered on one of the candles.

'Did one of you do that?' Olivia's voice was quivering even more than the flame.

'Nope,' said Saffron. 'That's some supernatural shit.'

She rushed back up onto the altar and leaned close to look at it. I couldn't tell if she was faking or not. It was the kind of prank she would play, though I had no idea how she'd have done it. She flicked her pinkie through the flame, back and forth, then pinched it between two fingers. Frances took pictures from multiple angles.

'Can we go somewhere else?' Olivia asked.

I waited for Frances to answer, but she was too focused on the photos. 'In a minute,' I said.

I remember the first half of that year in pinks and blues. I was a senior and had finally been awarded a ribbon: dark blue, draped over the shoulder, tied loose at the waist. Best Friend was the highest blue ribbon – Head Girl. Her hair was long and black, but when it caught the light it glinted almost navy. The best-behaved juniors were given pink bows, then pink ribbons. Pink cakes were served for afternoon tea. Best Friend and I delivered buns to the pink and blue rooms of the infirmary. Little blue lamps lit the chapel altar every evening.

It was mine and Best Friend's honourable charge to be sacristan. We spent an hour each day down on our hands and knees cleaning. The smell of oil and incense lingered on our clothes and in our hair. All the girls were jealous.

While we cleaned, we talked about Altar Boy. My Altar Boy was different from Best Friend's Altar Boy. We didn't know either of their names. We had only ever glimpsed the boys out of dormitory windows, or from a distance at the Procession of Christ the King. We knew there was a girl who had sent letters back and forth with her Altar Boy, but Best Friend and I would never have taken that risk. We would've lost our blue ribbons if we were caught. The girl and her boy got away with it by replacing his name with a girl's name, so when the nuns read over the letters they assumed she was writing to her sister or a friend.

Best Friend had a sister once, but she had died in the earthquake. The earthquake had killed a lot of people in the town Best Friend came from. Here, all we'd felt was a ripple. Best Friend's parents sent her here straight after the funeral. She was seven. Her sister had been eleven. Best Friend never told me her sister's name, but sometimes I saw her flinch when Sophie was called on the roll.

In the week before the Feast of the Sacred Heart, we spent even more time in the chapel than usual. We gathered lily of the valley and filled the pews with their scent, saving a few to press inside the Bible we kept next to our bed. We arranged candles in the shape of a large heart, beginning on the altar and trickling down the steps. The evening before the feast, each girl was given a candle with a thick paper cover for the Procession of the Lanterns. Symbols of the Sacred Heart and Mother Mary were cut out of the paper covers in sharp snips. The chapel was dark. Rows of girls wove in and out of the benches, singing hymns in French, then English.

A message from the Sacred Heart;
What may its message be?
'My child, my child, give Me your heart
My Heart has bled for thee.'

There was no missing the moon when we got back outside. The clouds had cleared just enough for it to take its place in the sky: dramatically bright. Frances and I spun around in circles, throwing our hands up towards it. Saffron howled like a werewolf. Olivia kept her arms folded tight across her chest.

'Now the real magic can happen!' Frances cupped her hands around her mouth and called out towards the college, 'You can come out now, ghosts!'

Olivia looked alarmed, but I wasn't sure if that was because of the way we were acting or the possibility of encountering an actual ghost. She gazed down the hill to where the car was parked.

'Take a photo of me, Frances!' Saffron held her hand up like a crab claw. 'So it looks like I'm holding the moon in my fingers.'

Frances held the camera up. 'It's just a bright circle, you can barely tell it's the moon.'

'Do it anyway.'

Frances took a few steps back then shuffled to the left. 'Your hand needs to be higher.' She gave Saffron more directions, then started laughing. 'This is impossible, I'm just going to take it.' The camera snap, snap, snapped.

I peered over Frances's shoulder while she looked through the photos. The moon was slightly out of Saffron's reach in all of them, but she was grinning as if she'd caught it.

'You look so sweet, Saffy,' I said. Blood rushed to my cheeks as soon as I registered the slip. No one else seemed to notice.

Frances zoomed in on Saffron's face, making the three of us laugh. Olivia made no move to come look at the photos.

We checked multiple doors to the main building before we found one with a broken lock. It looked like someone had smashed it with a hammer. A red sign with the words EARTHQUAKE PRONE BUILDING – DO NOT APPROACH was taped at eye level.

It was easier to see inside this building than it had been in the chapel: none of the windows had curtains, and they let in enough light that we barely needed torches. A cage elevator cast criss-crossed shadows on the floor. Saffron yanked the elevator's gate open and we all flinched at its screeching cry. She stuck her head inside but kept her feet firmly planted in the corridor. 'What a deathtrap.'

I traced my finger along a cross carved into the staircase pillar. It seemed there were crosses carved into every possible surface of this building, both outside and inside. I'd even seen little crosses on the peaks of the roof.

We headed up the stairs and into one of the classrooms. It was long empty of desks or a blackboard, but there was a large pile of wooden planks in the middle of the room.

'It looks like someone was planning a bonfire,' Frances said.

I nudged one of the planks with my foot. 'Or a sacrifice.'

Olivia sat on the windowsill and rubbed her ankle. I wondered why she didn't ask to go and sit in the car. I would have suggested it, but I couldn't think of a polite way to bring it up.

This room had even more graffiti on the walls than in the chapel. Saffron put down her flashlight and picked two spray cans off the ground. She shook them. One still had a bit of paint left in it. She aimed the nozzle at a blank space on the wall and a white blob formed. She kept going until the blob was shaped more like an iceblock.

'It's a ghost!' She dropped the cans and picked up her flashlight again, shining it at the ghost-blob. Frances snapped a picture.

I laughed. 'Would she get into art school, Olivia?'

I turned my torch in Olivia's direction and saw the glisten of held-back tears in her eyes. She forced a smile. 'Ha ha, maybe.'

Everyone laughed except Olivia. She really was acting like a Pisces.

'I'm thinking about Miss Gates, Saffy.' Frances was taking pictures out the window now. The view was all dark suburbia. A wispy cloud was lit up almost gold as it stretched across the moon.

'When are we *not* thinking about Miss Gates.'

'Is this the one that was always going on about school spirit?' I asked.

'Show some school spirit, girls!' Saffron spoke in a posh accent, though it wasn't clear which country it was supposed to be from. 'She wouldn't even let us sit with our friends in class. It wasn't school spirit.'

'She was fully crazy. She had this thing about hair.' Frances put the lens cap back on her camera.

'She made everyone put their hair up in a bun before they came into the classroom,' Saffron explained. 'She couldn't even deal with plaits, it freaked her out.'

'Why?'

'I don't know, nits or something. OCD.'

'And then.' Frances folded her arms. 'Saffy came up with this idea.'

'It wasn't completely my idea. Rosa Martin was the one who said we should leave a lock of hair on her desk.'

'Yeah, but you were the one who convinced the whole class to cut some off.'

I rolled my eyes, but I couldn't keep the grin off my face.

'You haven't changed, Saff.'

Saffron was grinning now too. 'We arranged the hair from lightest to darkest. It looked really cool. You have photos right, Frances?'

'Yeah, on my laptop. But honestly guys, you should have seen Miss Gates' reaction. She fully started crying, in front of the whole class. Her whole body was shaking.'

Saffron giggled. 'And then she had a nervous breakdown and quit her job.'

'No way.'

'Yep.'

I laughed, kicking one of the wooden planks. Olivia was silent. I looked at her, trying to convey with my eyes that she was free to go back to the car, if she wanted to. She forced another smile.

Saffron and I led the way back down the corridor while Frances and Olivia trailed behind. We stuck our heads into every doorway, though most of the rooms looked much like the one we'd just been in. Frances gasped when we came to a room with a little stage in it. The backdrop was painted to look like the countryside, but the painting had clearly been done by teenagers. The hills were lopsided, and the schoolgirls climbing up to the top were smudgy and spaced out at such a distance they barely looked like a group.

'There's four of them.' Frances climbed onto the stage and began taking photos again. 'Like us.'

Olivia sat down on a bench that was pushed against the wall and got out her phone. Her sore foot stayed on the ground but the other one jiggled frantically. Her nervousness was so palpable it almost made me nervous. 'It's nearly midnight,' she said.

'The witching hour.' Frances spun round and took a photo of Saffron and me standing in the doorway.

'I thought the witching hour was 3am,' Saffron said.

'Are you guys planning on staying here that late?' Olivia's foot jiggling intensified. I stared at it, as if staring could force her to stop.

Saffron shrugged. 'If we feel like it.'

Frances hopped off the stage. 'You two come stand up here, be my models.'

We obeyed. For the first round of photos, Frances had us stand back to back in the centre of the stage, facing out into the wings.

'Stop hunching, Saff.'

I felt Saffron's back straighten. Her shoulder blades nudged into mine. I wondered if she registered this too. Unlike Frances and me, Saffron and I almost never touched. It was one of the few unspoken rules that had arisen after we'd stopped hooking up – as if the slightest physical contact could lead to us fucking again. The two of us stood statue-still while the camera snapped and flashed, snapped and flashed.

'All right, now turn round so you're facing.'

When we turned round, our faces were ridiculously close. Saffron jutted her neck out so our noses bumped and we both started giggling.

'Behave yourselves,' Frances ordered and we both stared at the ground, like kids who'd been told off.

'Get closer.' We shuffled forward so the toes of our shoes were almost touching. Both of us were wearing Docs: Saffron's were Oxfords and mine were Mary Janes.

'Heads up,' Frances directed. 'Look at each other.'

We lifted our faces carefully. Our mouths were so close, it was impossible not to think about kissing. I tried to force the thought from my mind, worried that some random impulse would take hold of me and I'd actually do it. I'd felt this impulse at least once with most of my friends, but it was more dangerous with Saffron. It was strange to think how well I'd known her mouth. Her lips were in a funny, pouting position that meant she was trying not to laugh. I racked my brain for something serious. My face settled into a blank. The camera flashed in the corner of my eye and I tried not to wince. Gradually, Saffron's face relaxed to match mine. I had thought her face was the most beautiful face I'd ever seen back when I had a crush on her, but now it seemed mostly ordinary. I could recognise its flaws as flaws rather than endearing imperfections. We stared at each other. Her eyes slowly turned from sources of meaning to circles of colour and black. It scared me how vacant they were: just body parts, blinking mechanically. I had no idea what was going on behind them.

'Done, thanks guys.'

We stepped apart as Frances jumped back onto the stage. Saffron instantly came back to life, her eyes full of spark again. I wandered over to Olivia and took a seat. She quickly exited out of Google Maps.

'Give us a show,' I called out to Saffron and Frances. They rolled their eyes. 'Come on, you were both in school plays weren't you?'

'Only one.' Frances put on a high-pitched warble. 'Double, double, toil and trouble!'

'Fire burn and caldron bubble!'

They both started laughing at such a hysterical volume it sounded like they were still playing witches. Saffron spun in a circle then stopped, swaying.

'I thought you said there were four girls.' She pointed at the stage backdrop, still giggling. 'There's only three.'

Frances looked at the painting again. 'I swear there were four. I must be losing my mind.'

I frowned. 'I thought I saw four too.'

Saffron threw her arms up in delight. 'We're all losing our minds!'

'Check the photos,' I said. I rushed up to Frances so I could see the camera screen. She flicked back through, then zoomed. Our voices were soft and in sync. 'Fuck.'

Saffron hurried over and looked at the screen. She looked at the painting. 'Okay, that's scary.'

A phone started ringing and we all jumped. The ringtone was unfamiliar, but we all checked our phones anyway.

'Hello?' It was Olivia's phone.

The three of us breathed out. Frances turned her camera off.

'Oh no, okay. Hang on.' Olivia put her phone down and looked at Saffron. 'My flatmate's locked out.'

'Oh,' Saffron said. She sounded unimpressed.

'She needs me to let her in.'

'Can she go wait somewhere?'

Olivia spoke into the phone. Her voice was awkward and uncertain. She turned back to us. 'She said she'll wait in McDonald's.'

'All right. We'll try hurry then, I guess.'

Olivia said 'Love you' before she hung up. She stood. 'Okay, we're going?'

'Once we've finished looking, yeah.'

Olivia faltered. 'Huh?'

'There's still heaps of rooms we haven't seen,' Saffron said. 'We'll just do a quick look.'

Tears were brimming in Olivia's eyes again. I resisted the urge to roll mine.

'But . . . I need to let my flatmate in?'

A suggestion hovered on the tip of my tongue. 'Maybe you should call an Uber?'

'It's a $60 fare.'

I raised my eyebrows. Of course she'd already looked.

'I've got all the photos I want,' Frances said. 'But I'm not staying in here. I'm going to wait in that classroom.'

For a moment, I thought Olivia might break down crying. I tensed, ready to respond. She swallowed. 'I'll wait with you,' she said to Frances.

I remember so much silence, and so many sounds. The scritch-scritch of pencils during study in the library. A class down the corridor speaking French in unison. Mother Nottingham's raspy breathing. I remember the static of cicadas, calling us outside on summer afternoons. The sound made us fidget in our seats. A girl tapped her foot until the table shook. Best Friend tensed up. Her eyes darted around until they met mine. I smiled. Her body calmed.

We prepared for our first communion with a three-day retreat. None of us were allowed to speak. It made everything feel like a dream: we were dizzy with silence. Our desks were all turned towards the wall and decorated with holy cards and treasures. A visiting priest read us passages from *The Lives of the Saints*. We couldn't figure out if the stories were true or not.

Talking during meals was allowed on very special occasions. Sometimes Reverend Mother read to us from the pulpit, but most days a bell rang out until the dining hall was silent. Best Friend and I sat at different tables, each responsible for maintaining a group of juniors' dining etiquette. We taught the girls not to ask for things like butter or salt, but to offer them to others in the expectation they'd be offered back. The food was always awful: a grey sludge of porridge for breakfast, a grey sludge of something dead for dinner. We taught the girls not to complain. This rule was cast aside when we were served boiled tripe. Even Reverend Mother apologised. The local fish-and-chip shop received the biggest order they'd ever had.

All day we looked forward to afternoon tea. Sometimes it was bread and jam, sometimes it was sugar buns. One time it was Afghans the size of our outstretched hands.

After the black plane, there were no Afghans and no sugar buns. The jam was spread extra thin. Even the juniors knew not to say anything.

It was much more exciting with just Saffron and I exploring. Every time I remembered the painting, I felt a rush of adrenalin. A good kind of fear pumped through my body.

'The candle in the chapel,' I said. 'Was that you?'

She looked confused. 'What do you mean?'

Another rush of adrenalin. 'I guess not.'

We arrived at a closed door. Words were printed in French on a panel above it.

'Salle d'études,' Saffron pronounced. 'Study room. This is where that nun died.'

She gave the door a push, but it didn't open. I couldn't tell if I felt disappointed or relieved.

We made our way along the corridor until we found the bathrooms. Two long rows of mint-green basins were lined up back to back, the mirrors above them lined up too. The mirrors were covered in grime and the few patches of reflective surface had been written on in marker. *CELESTE & EVE <3 2016. VM & HER HEAVENLY ANGELS, G & A. ADA WAS HERE.* The basins were littered with chocolate wrappers and cigarette butts. Someone had left an old rain jacket on the ground.

Saffron twisted one of the taps, but no water flowed. 'It's good to get away from all . . .' She waved her hand at the doorway. 'That.'

I laughed. 'You invited her.'

She made a face. 'I didn't know she'd be so . . .'

'Watery?'

'Yeah, anxious energy. It's draining.'

'It's her chart, it's not her fault.'

'Mmm. I should have asked what sign she was before I asked her out.'

She dug a Sharpie out of her backpack pocket and started writing in the bottom corner of a mirror. *S – A – P – P – H – O*. 'Aren't Pisces supposed to be into astrology and the occult and everything?' she continued. 'She seems so anti all of it, why would you come ghost-hunting if you're not into ghosts?' She passed me the pen. I drew a star, then wrote *M – E – G*, followed by another star. Saffron perched on the edge of a basin. She sighed. 'I swear every Pisces I've ever met has a victim complex.'

I turned to her and raised my eyebrows. 'Olivia must be having a pretty shit night, to be fair.'

I wasn't sure why I was defending her, but disagreeing with Saffron felt good. I handed the pen back to her and our hands touched. We locked eyes. Something clicked. Disagreeing with Saffron felt good because it felt like flirting.

She rested the pen on the side of the basin, then grimaced. She pushed her fists into her stomach. 'Do you have any painkillers?'

I dug around in my jacket pockets. My hand clasped something cold and hard. I pulled out the stone finger.

'What's that?' She leaned close, touching it with her own finger. I watched her admire it.

'You should have it.' The words left my mouth before I knew

if I wanted to say them, but when she grinned I was sure.

'Actually?'

'Yeah, you brought us here.'

Saffron thanked me and put the finger in her backpack pocket.

I turned back to the mirror and started drawing the Capricorn symbol. 'I used to wish my parents would send me to boarding school.'

'Why?'

'I just liked how it seemed in books, and movies. I probably would have hated it.'

Saffron's reflection shuffled in the mirror as she nodded her head, mottling around the patches of rust and mildew. 'My parents wanted to send me to boarding school.'

'Really?' I faced her again.

'In year eleven. It was a Catholic school, like here. They thought it would . . .' she laughed. Her eyes followed her foot, drawing circles on the ground. 'Straighten me out.'

This surprised me. 'Were you a bad girl, Saffron?'

She laughed again. 'No, they thought it would . . . make me straight.'

'Oh.' I laughed too. 'Teenage girls locked up in isolation from boys, the perfect place to be straightened.'

'Yes. They clicked on that eventually.'

We were both silent. I wanted to ask more, but I didn't want Saffron to feel uncomfortable. She barely ever spoke about this stuff.

She ran her finger along the basin edge. 'Do you believe in ghosts?'

'Isn't that the whole reason we're here?'

She shrugged. 'I don't know if I really believe, though. Sometimes I feel like I'm pretending – to myself, I mean.'

'I get it. Even with the full moon. Sometimes I'm looking

at it and it's like I'm pretending I feel this intense feeling, but really I just think it looks pretty.'

Saffron laughed. 'I hope ghosts are real, though. I want to believe.'

'Me too. If I saw a ghost, my life would be complete.'

Her expression turned sneaky.

I stared at her. 'What?'

She stepped towards me, almost as close as when Frances had been taking photos. She turned her head and looked right into the mirror. 'Bloody mary, bloody mary, bloody –'

I clamped my hand over her mouth. 'Don't you dare, Saffy.' I coughed. 'Saffron.'

She peeled my fingers away to speak. 'You can call me Saffy.' My hand stayed awkwardly close to her face, her fingers clasped loose around mine. Her expression was still sneaky. *Kiss*, said a voice in my head, immediately followed by a *No no no no no no.* I knew in my body that I didn't really want to, but it was like I'd been possessed by some kind of demon, a stirrer-spirit, urging me to make trouble. If Saffron made a move, I doubted I'd be able to resist.

In the silence, I noticed a gentle jingling. I glanced away from Saffron to look at the mirrors, and saw they were moving just enough to bump into each other. Our reflections wobbled like water. She noticed too.

'Is that the wind?'

We looked at the windows. They were all shut. A sick feeling rose into the back of my throat. The mirrors shook like something was threatening to break out of them. My hand gripped Saffron's and hers gripped back. The adrenalin pumping around my body froze into fear: there was no faking any feeling now.

I remember my hair was wet that night. It was winter and the water made my ears cold. We were allowed three baths a week. Other days, we carried basins of water back to our dormitory cubicles and washed behind the curtains we had each pleated when we'd moved in. Wednesday was a bath day.

Before bathing, we polished the dormitory floor with tea leaves and wax, sweeping up with brooms that stood taller than we did. Mother Nottingham watched to make sure we polished right into the corners. The floors became so shiny we could almost see ourselves reflected in the wood. Our arms ached.

We took hot water bottles to bed. Best Friend and I pushed the curtain between our alcoves back just enough to see each other. We made faces until lights out.

I thought about Altar Boy until I fell asleep. I didn't dream of him. I dreamed of black planes and the radio rumbling. Something dropped. I woke up to shouts and pitch dark. My bed sloshed from side to side. Cupboard doors swung open, Bibles crashed to the floor. A water jug smashed into pieces.

'Stay in bed, girls!' It was Mother Nottingham. I had never heard her voice so shrill.

A junior screamed from across the corridor. I could hear Mother Nottingham pulling at the light switch, but the lights did not come on.

'Sing the school song, girls! *As children of the Sacred Heart* . . .'

Some girls joined in with shaky voices for the second line. The room shook around us.

We'll strive till death to do our part
Storms may gather on our way
But we'll be loyal to Island Bay.

The shaking stopped halfway through the chorus. I looked for Best Friend, but the space beyond the alcove curtain was empty. As the hymn finished, I heard girls creep out of their beds. I got up and slipped past the curtain to where Best Friend slept. She wasn't there. Something touched my ankle and I almost cried out, before realising Best Friend was hiding under the bed. She didn't look like Best Friend. Usually I felt younger than her, but now I felt much, much older. I took her hands and helped her out, then we walked towards the girls gathered at the windows. The city was a shadowy blur. The streetlights had gone out and no light shone from any of the houses.

Aftershocks continued to startle us through till morning. Best Friend stayed in my bed, gripping her hand tight around my wrist every time the room quaked. Nobody slept. For months, we were woken around 2am each night by a jolt in the earth. Even after the aftershocks stopped I woke at 2am, certain that something was shaking.

The floor shifted beneath us and we both swore, dropping to the ground. The room swayed with the familiar rhythms of an earthquake. There was nothing to hide under, so I put my head down and covered it with my arms and Saffron did the same. I pressed my forehead to the floor. It shuddered and heaved. I heard things falling and breaking in other rooms.

The quaking continued inside my body even after the room stilled. It took a little while to realise I was the one shaking, not the ground. I kept my arms over my head.

'I think it's over.' Saffron sounded disturbingly calm. 'We need to get out of here. There'll probably be aftershocks. This building is red-stickered.'

She was already standing by the time I looked up. I wanted to stay close to the ground, but embarrassment pulled me to my feet. 'That was big, right?'

'You should know, you're the Wellingtonian.'

'It felt longer than other earthquakes.'

Saffron nodded, but didn't look so sure. We stood an awkward distance apart. The moments before the earthquake felt faraway, imagined.

A mirror that had been propped against the corridor wall had fallen and smashed in silver splinters across the floorboards.

'Seven years' bad luck.' Saffron cleared a path with the toe of her shoe. I stepped after her.

We called Frances's name three times before she stepped out of a room across the corridor. Olivia's tote bag was hanging on her shoulder along with her leather satchel. I'd never seen Frances look so out of it. A large bump was swelling fast on her forehead, and Saffron and I both rushed to her. 'Shit, are you okay?'

She touched her hand to the bump. 'I'm a bit spinny.'

Saffron put her arm around Frances's waist and shifted the tote bag onto her own shoulder. 'You might have concussion.'

'No, that's not it . . .' Frances shook her head, her fingers still hovering over her face.

'We should take you to a doctor,' Saffron said.

I nodded. 'Where's Olivia?' She better not have hurt her other foot. We'd have a hard time carrying both her and Frances down to the car.

Frances looked at me. 'That's what I mean, where's Olivia.'

'Is she hurt?'

Frances went back to shaking her head. 'She's not there, she's gone.'

'What?' Saffron and I looked at each other. She mouthed 'Hospital' and I nodded.

'Let's sit you down, Frances.' Saffron led her over to the wall. She turned to me. 'I should probably stay with her. Can you go find Olivia?'

I nodded and ducked into the room Frances had come out of. Some shelves and a painting had fallen from the wall, but aside from that the room was empty. I checked the nearby rooms and called Olivia's name. My voice echoed. I was starting to feel nauseous.

I went back to the others. They were sitting together on the floor and Frances was shaking her head again. 'She was in there with me, then something hit my head and I covered my face and she wasn't there anymore.'

'That's weird.' Saffron sounded confused but not concerned. This calmed my own panic a little.

'I didn't explain it right,' Frances said. 'I closed my eyes for a second, and then she wasn't there. Like, she disappeared.'

'We better call her.' Saffron got out her phone, and I checked the nearby rooms again. There was a bobby pin on the floor, but it could have been there for years.

'The phone line's down,' Saffron called out.

I stepped back into the corridor. Olivia's tote bag sat slumped against the wall. 'Don't you think it's weird that she'd leave this?'

Saffron looked at the bag too. The white square stared at us.

A ripple passed through the building. 'Aftershock,' she said, before the word could form in my mind. She was already on her feet. 'We need to get out.'

'But we need to find Olivia,' I said.

'Go then.' The harshness in her voice surprised me. I felt a brief flash of hurt. 'Hurry.'

I rushed from room to room again, shouting Olivia's name over and over. The corridors all looked the same. They made me feel light-headed. When I was sure I'd looked everywhere upstairs, I ran downstairs and repeated the process. I moved even faster down here. Even though I knew Frances and Saffron were only a floor above, I was scared to be alone. My hopes of encountering a ghost had transformed into a genuine terror: every time I stepped into a room, I was sure something was going to grab me from behind the door, or slam it behind me. There was more furniture in these rooms, and a lot of cobwebs. One room had a piano in it. I crept further in and peered behind an old couch in case Olivia was hiding. The floor jerked violently under my feet. I yelped and grabbed onto the couch arm, just catching my balance. The room rocked. I looked around, unsure of whether to stay or run. A dark shape moved in the corner. I bolted. My feet flew up the stairs, too fast to feel whether the shaking had stopped. I pulled to a halt when I reached the others. 'I can't find her.'

Frances looked less out of it now. Her face was full of fear. 'Guys, I know I sound crazy but it really was like she disappeared. She was definitely in the room with me.'

Saffron still didn't look scared, but she did look stressed. 'We need to get out. We can't be in this building.'

I took a deep breath and yelled. 'Olivia!'

Frances shook her head. 'She's gone, I swear.'

I stared at Saffron, and Saffron stared at me. This was nothing like it had been in the bathrooms.

'We need to leave.'

'Without Olivia? What if she's hurt?'

'You would have found her.'

'I should check the rooms again, I might have missed one.'

'We have to get out. And we should take Frances to the hospital.'

'Do you really think she's got concussion?'

'I think I'm fine,' Frances cut in.

No one said anything. The building rattled in the wind.

'We're going.' Saffron hooked Frances's satchel over her shoulder and passed me the tote bag. None of us looked at each other.

I remember the weeks following the earthquake. We all had trouble sleeping, but Best Friend barely slept at all. She didn't like to be inside. Because she was Head Girl, she and I were allowed use of Reverend Mother's Garden. We spent our free time doing roly-polys down the sloping lawn, hopping back onto our feet and brushing the grass off our skirts when the juniors came past. Sometimes we crawled all the way up to Spion Kop. On a clear day, you could see across the sea to the South Island. We always slid back down the slope, though Reverend Mother scolded us for the grass stains on our uniforms. We took care to wash them out.

Best Friend was always tired by the afternoon. We lay on hot pine needles, soaking up the sun and sometimes falling asleep. She slept better outside than in bed at night. If the grass was wet, we'd go to the tennis courts or the cricket pitch. If it was raining, we took shelter in the Bunnyhole and watched younger girls practise their roller-skating. If the Armchair was free, we'd sit there, but that was everyone's favourite spot and hardly ever empty. You could talk privately in the Armchair: a flowery snug set into the bank, with a wooden table and seats. No one could eavesdrop unnoticed.

On the warmest days, Reverend Mother sent us down to the beach at Island Bay. We were allowed enough time in the water to swim out to the island and back. Best Friend stayed on the shore. She spent more time in the sun than anyone, but her skin got paler and paler.

Reverend Mother asked us both to decorate the Black Forest Grotto for the procession honouring our Lady of Lourdes. We trailed our hands in the fish pond and arranged flowers around the Virgin Mary's feet. On the night of the procession, we all kneeled at the grotto and prayed for safety during earthquakes. We followed the procession with a bonfire on the hills. Best Friend looked almost translucent in the flames.

The second earthquake was on a Sunday. It shook us from our sleep, but we'd all been dreaming of earthquakes so much it was hard to tell if the shaking was real. Something smacked and shattered. We jolted awake. I jumped out of my bed and rushed through to Best Friend's. It was empty. I dropped to the floor. She wasn't underneath. She wasn't anywhere.

Getting Frances down the hill was more difficult than expected. I hadn't really believed she was concussed until I saw her try to walk. Even with us holding her up, she kept stumbling. The moon had disappeared again, and we didn't have enough hands for a torch, so for much of the walk we couldn't really see where we were going. My arms tired out before we made it halfway.

'Can we take a break?' I asked.

Saffron stopped and looked around. There was nothing nearby that could fall on us. 'Okay.'

We sat down on the grass. My hands were like jelly.

'We should call the police,' I said. 'To report Olivia missing.'

Neither Frances nor Saffron said anything. I could feel the guilt pulsing off all of us.

'We could get arrested,' I added.

Saffron shrugged. 'The phone line's down.'

'It might be better now.'

She slid her phone out of her pocket. 'What do I say?'

'Just say what happened.'

'It's going to sound like we made it up.'

'It doesn't matter.'

'Do you think we'll get in trouble for trespassing?'

'It doesn't matter.'

Saffron hesitated, then dialled 111. A prerecorded message asked her if she wanted the police, the fire department or an ambulance, then she was put on hold.

Olivia's tote bag was in my lap. I wanted to look inside, but didn't want to be the one to suggest it. I stared at the white square. I had always assumed it was some famous painting, since all the art students I knew had one. I wondered now if it was just a label. The white looked like it had been spray-painted around a square-shaped stencil. It was dead black in the middle.

Frances drooped against my shoulder. I nudged her back into a sitting position.

'We should get you to the car,' I said. Saffron hung up and pocketed her phone, clearly relieved. We hoisted Frances up and continued down the hill.

'What are we going to do about Olivia's flatmate?' Frances asked. 'They're going to be stuck at McDonald's all night.'

'There's nothing we can do,' Saffron said, a little too quickly. 'We just need to pretend this whole thing never happened.'

I stared at Saffron, trying to figure out if she really believed herself. Her expression was cold, but her cheek was sucked in, which meant she was chewing the inside of it. We arrived at the car in silence.

'What took you so long?'

We all stopped. Olivia was brushing grass off her pants, like she'd just stood up. She noticed the tote bag and reached out to take it, thanking me. 'I rushed out so fast I didn't realise.' She clutched it close to her. Her eyes were hopeful. 'We're going now?'

We stared at her like she was a ghost. She looked more

alive than she had all night: her hair had been messed up by the wind and her cheeks were red. She was pretty. If she'd looked like this in her Tinder profile, I would have swiped right too. Saffron gave a zombie-nod, then fumbled in her backpack, finding her keys.

The two of us helped Frances into the front seat and did up her seatbelt. Olivia got in the back. The three of us kept glancing at her. I still couldn't believe she was real.

'You're not allowed to fall asleep, okay?' Saffron adjusted Frances's seat so she was sitting up as straight as possible.

'I'm not concussed. It's just shock.'

I got in next to Olivia. It was like I'd just woken up from a bad dream: I felt relieved, but the guilt from before still clung to me. I had to keep reminding myself that we didn't need to drive to the police station. Saffron turned on the radio and clicked until she found a station that wasn't static. I expected a news reporter's voice to fill the car, telling us where the earthquake was centred and what it scored on the Richter scale, but a song was playing instead. It sounded older than my parents: I didn't recognise it. We listened in silence. When we got to McDonald's, Olivia thanked us and got out of the car. We never saw her again.

MARIA SAMUELA

The Promotion

Kura stood on the doorstep barefoot and drunk, a brown paper bag tucked under his arm. He didn't recognise Taki at first, but the shape of his father's eyes looked familiar. Kura's slim build must have come from his mother's side. Taki had a pot belly and Kura's belly was flat and taut, his skin as dark as his outlook. Either the sun in Wellington had been blocked by skyscrapers that drew long shadows on the footpaths and roads, or Taki always dressed in too many layers, his skin shielded from natural light. Also, it was hard to be touched by the sun's rays when you spent your days toiling inside a concrete abattoir. So his father's complexion, which Kura had been told was once as rich in colour as the most fertile soil, had become sallow.

A grey Cortina with tinted windows was idling on the road behind them. Kura turned in time to see the car roll down the street, heard it beep twice. Then his father was coaxing him into the house, clicking the front door, sealing his fate.

'Kia orana, son.'

Kura flinched at the word 'son'. His father's wife, Tu, greeted him and pulled him into her arms, and he felt his body stiffening like the trunk of a coconut tree.

When he was a boy, he used to wrap himself around the tallest tree outside his grandparents' house, the rough edges scraping against the insides of his thighs as he climbed to its peak. At the top, he'd hook his ankles, hugging the trunk, his backside protruding, naked toes erect. He'd look down over the coastal village, searching beyond the horizon.

Tu introduced him to his younger brothers – Abe, Moses and Joseph. They mumbled hello and shook his hand with limp, awkward wrists. His sister Mere lifted baby Teresa to his face and he hesitated before holding her, keeping her wriggling body at arm's length. Her legs dangled uselessly in front of him, but eventually he softened at her gurgling and rested her tiny body against his chest, planted a clumsy kiss on her cheek. He felt her recoil at the whiff of beer on his breath, and he panicked and passed her back.

'Abe,' said Tu, 'go get your brother some socks. Clean socks.' Kura felt the heat rising in his face. He loathed the attention, and also it meant that his father's wife had noticed his bare feet. Possibly she thought he owned no shoes of his own, had no other basic belongings her own children took for granted. He stared down at his feet. They were flat and wide and, though you couldn't tell by looking at them, his toes were turning numb.

Tu spoke to him in Cook Islands Māori, and when he responded he could tell by their raised eyebrows his siblings were impressed. He guessed they knew only English.

He let Tu lead him through the sitting room and into the dining room where the table was set with the family's best crockery. He had noticed the gaps in the cabinet beside the fireplace, where ceramic plates were displayed like works of art. The other children in the family, he noticed, used the plates from the kitchen cupboards.

An extra chair, a stool covered in orange and cream vinyl that clashed with the others, had been slotted in around the dining table. Joseph sat on the stool while the rest of the family sat in what Kura thought must be their usual spots, eyeing up the space at the table that Kura now filled. Abe returned with a clean pair of rugby socks and the whole family watched as Kura slipped them on, his hands starting to tremble. He hadn't realised how cold his feet were until they were swaddled in the knitted wool.

The table was piled high with food – two roasted chickens and a small leg of lamb, two bowls of chop suey, two large mounds of mainese, slabs of taro, and freshly made coconut sauce in an old Jim Beam bottle, the empty bottle gifted to Taki, who prohibited alcohol in his house. Stacks of sliced bread and a brick of butter and two jugs of orange cordial bookended the food. Kura stared at his empty plate as if his thoughts alone could manifest some of that food upon it. When he looked up, his baby sister was gawking at him from her highchair. He envied her lack of knowing and her helplessness. Hers was the kind of helplessness that came from infancy, not from having landed in a foreign country alone.

Taki bowed his head and paused to let his family catch up. Without having to check that they had, he said, 'Let us pray.'

The family said grace as one voice, the words spilling from their mouths in a single long spiel. The siblings recited the words between shared secret glances, peering over at their new brother, who kept his eyes on his plate.

After grace, hands flew across the table. Chicken thighs were torn from chicken breasts and chicken wings, the white meat sucked from wishbones to be pried apart later for empty dreams. The leg of lamb was hacked into thick chunks of meat, the bone stripped clean of its flesh and presented to Taki like a medieval mace. Mounds of mainese and chop suey were heaped beside the meats, and everything was drowned in the salted coconut sauce.

Tu grabbed Kura's plate and covered it with food. 'Eat up, my boy. You're too skinny for round here. You need to put on some weight or the wind will blow you away.'

He picked at a drumstick and mashed some of the taro into the coconut sauce with his fingertips.

'Don't be shy,' said Tu. 'You treat this house like your home.'

Kura's fingers skidded across his plate and drops of sauce spilled onto the tablecloth. Before Kura had a chance to even look up from the spillage, Tu had leapt from her side of the table and sopped up the mess with a tea towel.

'Sorry,' he said.

She told him not to worry and to eat up before his food got cold. Her smile wavered and he wondered how long she'd known about him. If she was the same age as his father, then something made her seem older. Her skin was clear and wrinkle-free, except when her lips turned up at the edges and the lines on the outer sides of her eyes became visible. She wore her hair in a bun, and apart from the few strands of grey at her temples, which you only saw if you were standing right next to her, it was as black as he imagined it was when she was only eighteen. Which is how old his mother was when she died at his birth. It wasn't all those things. Something else about her made her seem older than he thought she might be.

'Mere,' Tu said to her eldest daughter, 'pour your brother a drink. Don't just sit there.'

Mere grabbed the glass beside his plate and poured cordial to the brim. They avoided meeting each other's eyes and she returned to her plate quietly.

'So you can speak English,' Moses said. 'Or is "sorry" the only word you know?'

Tu clicked her tongue at her second-eldest son, who started to sulk.

Apart from the grace, their father hadn't said anything. Kura looked over at him, then back down at the tea towel soaking up the sauce on the tablecloth. He could feel his father's eyes on the side of his face.

'Do you go to church?' Taki asked.

Kura had seen only one photograph of his father. From his parents' wedding day, six months before the day he was born. He'd seen other pictures of his mother – two baby photos, one photo when she was a schoolgirl, and the family photo of the grandparents who brought him up and their thirteen offspring. But that wedding photo his grandmother kept between the pages of her Bible was all he knew of the man his mother married. Until Taki's letter arrived.

'No,' Kura said, shaking his head.

He felt Taki's disappointment. It seemed to float above the table like poison mist. 'Well,' he said, 'as long as you are under my roof, you will go to church with the rest of the family.'

His siblings sniggered. They stopped when their father fixed his gaze on them, giving each one of them the look.

*

Although it was cold, Taki was glad to be back on land. The voyage from Rarotonga to Auckland took twenty-six days and was far from restful. There were eight other islanders on that boat – all men, all young, all seeking a new life and home in a new land. They worked on that trip to help pay their fares, and to save on costs they rationed the taro and bananas they'd brought with them. Fish became their primary diet, so by the time they docked in Auckland's harbour – tired, cold and hungry – they were all desperate for some meat.

'I can't wait to get to my sister's place,' Taki gloated. His English was broken and limited but his optimism was in oversupply. He described the roast mutton and mashed potatoes she would serve him, the fresh peas plucked from her vegetable garden, the thick gravy flavoured with the meat's juices, and the cool, sweet orange cordial served in a glass, maybe with some ice cubes.

'That's what they eat in New Zealand,' he said. 'Then ice cream and fruit salad – then a cup of tea and cake.' At nineteen, he was one of the younger men in the group, but his unquiet manner made him seem older and more knowing.

He caught a taxi to the address in Papatoetoe. His sister's letter, which she'd written in the language of his mother tongue, was deeply creased. He'd memorised the words like a hymn. He twitched uncomfortably in his father's best suit. At least he looked good. He admired his reflection in the window, turning his head to the right, then left, then right again, smoothing back his dark wavy hair with the palms of his hands. He shifted nervously in his seat as the taxi approached the house.

His sister greeted him at the front door. 'Welcome, my brother,' she cried.

They were still hugging long after the taxi had left. For a brief moment Taki was again that skinny thirteen-year-old his sister had known back in 1950, before she'd fled the family home. Communication between her and the family had become sporadic over the years, but when she drew Taki into her home she knew to say nothing about the baby or the dead wife.

Her house was a palace compared to the two-roomed family homestead they'd left behind in Mauke. Family photos of herself, her Papa'a husband and their children decorated the sitting room walls. 'Eis made from polished shells and coloured plastic, cut and shaped into ever-vibrant frangipani blooms, hung like bunting over the Victorian-inspired wallpaper on the walls of the corridor.

The aroma of a home-cooked meal comforted him, distracted him, his mouth watering at the thought of his first roast mutton. His brother-in-law, patient and thoughtful, quieter than Taki had expected, offered him a beer but was unsurprised when Taki refused it. Instead, Taki watched his nieces and nephews play last card on the floor. They snuck a look at their new uncle, which he returned with a wink that made them blush and giggle.

'Aere mai kai manga,' his sister called from the kitchen.

The family seated themselves around the table. His sister said grace – thanking God for her brother's safe journey and asking Him to watch over Taki as he continued his travels south. Taki listened half-heartedly. He was more interested in the safe journey of the roast to the table. He watched his brother-in-law's every move as he delivered it across the room.

'I cooked this meal especially for you,' his sister said, beaming.

Taki stifled his disappointment as the platter of roasted fish and taro was placed on the table in front of him.

'Welcome to New Zealand, brother.'

*

After lunch, Abe showed Kura the bedroom they would share. The first thing Kura noticed was his brown paper bag. The small bundle of clothes that it carried was placed on top of the single set of drawers, his jandals on the floor beside it. Abe must've done that when he'd collected the socks. Or perhaps Tu had snuck out before to help make the bedroom more homely. Then he noticed the guitar resting in a corner. The six nylon strings were taut against its slender neck, the ends clipped neatly at the tuning pegs. He picked it up and ran his fingers over the fretboard, picking at the strings with his thumb.

'You play?'

Abe's voice startled him. 'No,' he lied. He put the guitar back against the wall and stood awkwardly beside it.

'Took me ages to save up for Mary,' said Abe. 'Lucky I could get extra shifts at the college.'

'Mary?'

'The guitar.' Abe picked it up, plucking the strings.

Kura didn't feel the need to press for more details. 'You work?' he asked.

'Part-time, after school, with Mum,' said Abe. 'Hard work, but the money's good.' He grinned. 'Any money's good, eh, when you're skint. That's the best thing about starting at the bottom, brother. Only way is up.'

He handed the guitar back to Kura. It was your average guitar, the basic kind that even children could learn on. But to Kura it was the finest musical instrument he'd ever held. He sat down on one of the single beds and lay the body of the guitar flat across his lap, his hand over the headstock.

'That's my bed.'

Kura moved to the other bed and felt the springs creak beneath him. He sank into the edge of the mattress and worried his backside would leave an imprint. After a moment, he held the instrument up to Abe, like an offering. 'Play something for me,' he said.

'Nah, bro,' said Abe, waving his arms at him. 'You play something for me.'

Kura rested the body of the guitar against his stomach. He strummed a G chord and fiddled with the pegs until he was happy. He played A and then C, and once he was certain all the strings were tuned right, he plucked the notes to a song from home.

'You know this one, brother?' he asked Abe, not missing a beat.

Abe laughed. 'Teach me, bro.'

The song was making Kura homesick. He lost himself in the rhythm, like the gentle sway of his grandfather's fishing boat moored in the reef. He felt lulled back to his grandparents' house, the humble wooden homestead furnished with four queen beds in its front room. He remembered the sparsely concealed long drop and the open-fire cooker where their meals were prepared, both just footsteps from the house. The crowing roosters in the morning, the scent of blossoming gardenias. The warm rain tapping against the tin roof.

He started to sing and his words carried through the room. Abe seemed to be studying his fingers – the way they were crooked at the knuckles, the amount of pressure applied to the strings. Kura angled his body so Abe could see his fingers more clearly. He supposed the lyrics sounded like traffic to his brother, but he persisted. Surely he'd heard sounds like it before – at christenings and weddings and twenty-firsts.

'Dad says you have to shut up.'

They looked up. Moses was in the doorway.

'You have to keep the noise down,' he said to Kura. 'These walls are like paper. We can hear everything.'

Kura stopped playing. He got up and returned the guitar to the corner of the room and the springs in the bed creaked once more when he sat back down. Moses nodded and left. Kura stared at the doorway as the footsteps made their way down the corridor.

'Don't worry 'bout him,' said Abe. 'He just needs a girlfriend.' He grabbed the guitar and handed it back to Kura. 'When did you get here?'

Kura strummed the guitar, careful not to make too much

noise. 'Yesterday.'

'Where did you stay?'

'With my mother's family.'

'Your English is good.'

Kura said nothing.

'Why didn't you come home? We could've picked you up from the airport.'

Kura shrugged.

'In Porirua? Your mother's family, I mean?'

'Yes.' Kura paused, then grinned. 'They had party for me.'

'Don't blame you then.'

More common ground, besides the guitar and their father. 'You like beer?' he asked Abe.

'Yeah, bro. Don't tell the old man.'

Abe showed Kura the empty drawers and the space in the wardrobe where he could hang his clothes. He didn't need much space; the clothes in the paper bag barely filled two hangers.

'That all you got?'

Kura didn't know where to look.

'Don't worry, bro. You borrow whatever you want of mine.' He held open the wardrobe door.

Kura picked a black rugby jersey. His cousins back home had warned him about the weather, but he hadn't believed them and wasn't prepared. He was about to put it on, when Abe said, 'Not that.' Abe took his favourite rugby jersey from him and brushed the palm of his hand down both sides of it to iron out any new wrinkles he imagined were there, and draped it back on its hanger. Then he pulled a sweatshirt from one of the drawers. Kura pulled it over his head and shoulders, the fleece cowl cushioning the back of his neck. He hadn't realised how cold the back of his neck was until then.

It wasn't the sound of crowing roosters that woke Kura the next day. The bathroom door slamming, the gushing toilet bowl, six pairs of feet on the carpet in the corridor – none of these things would have roused him from sleep back home. He'd had a restless night, not helped by Abe's snoring or the cars he heard motoring past his window. The shock of waking up in an unfamiliar room did nothing to ease his nerves, and now he was expected to go to Mass. He followed Abe's lead and dragged himself out of bed. He pulled on the clothes that Tu had laid out for him, a mishmash of items from his brothers and father.

'You walk to church with the boys, okay, son?' Tu tucked Kura's collar down and straightened his tie. The formal clothing itched against his skin; he tugged at the shirt when she left the room.

'Looking flash, brother,' Abe teased. 'Like a Raro Elvis Presley, my bro.'

In the sitting room, Kura checked his reflection in the framed Jesus print, turning his head to the right, then left, then right again, smoothing down the sides of his hair with his palms, his hands now greasy with the Brylcreem his father insisted he use. The slacks and shirt from Abe were two sizes too big, his legs like twigs within the fabric. His feet were close to bursting out of Moses's shoes, and the woollen vest from Joseph would give him a rash. His father's tie was suffocating.

The boys pounded the footpath ahead of him. Kura's feet were beginning to throb. He ignored the pain and eavesdropped on his brothers' conversation about rugby, knowing that even if he had something to say, he would have contributed nothing still. By the time they arrived at the church, the relief of resting his feet overshadowed his dread at facing the throng of strangers outside the building. For a moment.

'Aere mai, son,' said Tu. Again, Kura recoiled at the word

'son', his self-consciousness heightened in front of this crowd. His brothers were quick to disperse, hovering in the vicinity but never close enough for their mother to call on them. Tu held him gently by the elbow and led him to the door of the church, pulling him into the swarm of unknown faces. Of course he didn't recognise any of the parishioners – his mother's family weren't Catholic, and any cousins he'd grown up with who were about his age and who now lived in New Zealand were probably nursing hangovers.

'This is your Aunty Ina, my sister. And these are your cousins. Come, meet them.' Tu gestured to a woman in white, the garland of pink plastic hibiscus in her hat distinguishing her from the other aunties. Aunty Ina grabbed him by the shoulders, stamped his cheek with a kiss and began introducing him to each of her children. They were reluctant to meet his eye, greeting him instead with the crowns of their heads. It pleased him to not have to baby talk with them.

He followed Tu through the heavy wooden doors and joined a smaller group crammed in the narthex. Doors to his left and right led to more seating upstairs. Later, he'd hear the choir in that upper level, delivering harmonies that could lift the roof clean, exposing the faithful to the heavens. The doors that opened onto the nave were set with stained glass windows, the holy family frozen inside mosaic panels. Suspended white halos, humbling robes, piety personified. Kura wasn't so much in awe of it all as intimidated by its sincerity. He stared at the rows of pews in front of him, so different from the ones back home. The pews here were made from oak, ensuring families a seat in this house for generations. The carpet was plush and a deep red, like fresh blood, moving Kura along the floor in waves. It carried him down the aisle, inching him towards the altar of white marble, where the crucified son of God towered despondently.

'Sit with me.' Any other day, the idea of Kura in a church on a Sunday was unthinkable. But today wasn't any other day. Tu turned, urging her children to join them, and when he heard them behind him, it surprised him to feel comforted.

He noticed his father once they were seated. Taki owned the church aisle as if he were God himself. He wore his Sunday best beneath his white catechist robe, and strutted as he walked. Then he ducked in and out of the vestry, placing chalices and offertory bowls on the credence table. When Taki walked past them again, he didn't seem to notice them. They ignored him back, as if it were part of a ritual.

Kura still couldn't see how this man was his father. They shared few similarities that he had noticed, and he doubted that time could heal the disconnection. Nothing had happened in nineteen years, after all; his rapport with Tu felt more important. Meeting his father had been a mistake. For him and his mother.

The parishioners in the pews in front of Kura addressed one another with familiarity, their enthusiasm abundant. Every now and then, they'd turn discreetly in their seats to glance at him. But Tu stared straight ahead at the giant crucifix. Kura wondered whether she'd already started praying.

Then she whispered to him. 'Here, son. Take this. It's yours.'

He looked down at the hymn book she'd handed him. He'd never owned a book before.

*

'This is my cousin . . . Takiora.'

'Tar-key-oh-rah?'

'No. Tah-kee-orr-rah.' Taki's cousin Vinnie enunciated Taki's Christian name so his boss, who could only speak

English, would understand.

'Tarr-keyy-ohh . . . bloody hell.' The boss swore. 'You islanders and your full-on names.'

Taki flinched at 'islander'.

'Do you want a job?' the boss asked him.

Taki didn't trust his English and, besides, this man made him too nervous. He didn't speak.

'Are you a good worker?'

Taki barely managed to push a word past his throat. 'Yes.'

'He's a hard worker, boss,' said Vinnie. 'We worked together in Makatea. That was real hard work, all right. Every day we had to –'

'I know, I know,' the boss said. 'You worked the guano deposits on the island and sent money back home to your parents. I've heard the story, Vinnie. You've told me a million times already.' The boss turned to Taki. 'I could use another good worker. I'll give you one week. Your cousin can show you the ropes. If I'm not happy with you, you're out. Fair?'

Taki nodded, smiling.

'Oh, and about your name . . . how's Tar-key sound?'

Taki was confused until Vinnie nudged him.

'Good,' he said. 'It's good.'

Taki had been in the country for only three days and already he had a job at the freezing works and a room in a boarding house on Marjoribanks Street. Vinnie met him at the train station in Wellington, where the wind was crisp and strong and seemed to carry the crowds against their will. The tall concrete buildings of the city were officious and impersonal, and the roads seemed overrun with cars and trams and buses, the trams snaking their way from the train station towards Lambton Quay and finally down Courtenay Place, where life hurtled by. He had seen no other faces like his on that tram ride to the boarding house and, despite his cousin's company, he felt alone.

But the feeling, like life in the city, was fleeting.

'This is my cousin Takiora. Taki.' The men returned to the freezing works at Ngauranga, and Vinnie introduced him to the rest of the boys. Many of them were new here too. They welcomed him like a brother.

*

On Monday morning the grey Cortina parked up outside the house. They told him they'd pick him up at 8am sharp, but Kura had never known his cousins to be punctual. He waited for them at the front door, expecting delays and untold excuses, so when they arrived promptly, blowing the horn and hollering his name, he felt disconcerted and needed a moment to find his bearings. There was little time to check he had everything: empty wallet, résumé, comb. He looked at his feet and checked for smudges on his father's shoes, which he'd borrowed when Tu saw his blisters after church. His father's feet were oversized, and to aggravate matters the polish was wet still and it smelled.

'Make sure you get the polish into all the folds,' Taki had said. 'See how the leather is cracked? Get the polish right in but keep the polish even.' It felt like the first piece of fatherly advice Kura had received.

He could hear his siblings getting ready for school, lining up for the toilet, fighting over watered-down milk. A scuffle had broken out in the corridor, limbs flying as they karate-chopped the air. It wasn't until they wrestled each other to the carpet in hysterics that Kura realised they were only playing. Their father had left for the freezing works hours ago.

'Good luck, son.' Tu appeared beside him in the doorway and pulled him in for a hug. Kura struggled to relax into her affections, and when he heard his cousins' wolf whistles and caught Abe mocking him behind her back, he withdrew and watched as she threw a quick wave at the grey Cortina. The gesture shocked his cousins into silence, their windows rolling up.

Kura slid into the back seat of the car. 'We go to the pub now, cuz?' his cousin Lucy asked. The car filled with laughter, deep from the belly.

'Is that all you care about?' Kura said. 'Drinking your life away? Don't you know it's a sin to drink?' His cousins hung their heads, the car growing silent, until he couldn't keep a straight face any longer. They started laughing again, raising their voices and wisecracking.

As the car crawled down the street, Kura caught a glimpse of Tu waving out to them. Only when they turned the corner did she go back inside.

'How was church yesterday, cuz?' Tana called out from the driver's seat. 'Did you get saved by the Holy Spirit? Did your father forgive you your sins, my cuz? What happened to you after you showed up on Saturday?'

Kura told them about his siblings, especially Abe. He showed his cousins the résumé Abe had helped him write, and the mocking resumed.

'You don't need that piece of paper, cuz,' said Tana. 'Just flash that beautiful smile at the rich old ladies. They'll look after you. A beautiful, exotic creature like yourself.'

Kura looked out the window in time to see the church disappear down the road. His cousins wolf-whistled at the building and dotted their chests and foreheads.

They drove for several minutes more before the concrete building towering over the hill came into view. Twice in two days Kura had been blown away by architecture.

'Is this it?'

'This is it, cuz,' said Tana. 'Say kia orana to your new home.'

'This is my cousin Kura,' Tana told his boss. The boss grabbed Kura's hand, his hold firm and assured. Kura, panicking, tried to hand over his résumé. He'd neglected to unfold it first and it looked small and crumpled.

'What's this?' The boss sounded bemused as he unfolded the paper. 'Résumé?' A grin spread slowly across his face. 'Fancy pants, eh? You wanna run this place or something?'

Tana jumped in. 'His father made him write that. He said for him to make a good impression.' His laugh was forced and not catching. 'But I can tell you, boss, my cousin – he's a hard worker.'

The boss looked at Kura. 'You do everything your daddy tells you, kid?'

Kura wanted to tell this man he barely knew his father, that he'd only met him two days ago and he didn't think he liked him. He wasn't certain he could obey Taki; his gut told him he wouldn't. His head told him his father didn't want him there, that it had been Tu who had coaxed him into writing that letter. But his heart wasn't sure. His mother had seen something in his father at one time. He had to hold on to that.

'Can you talk?'

'He's just a bit shy, boss,' Tana said.

'You gotta be able to talk to the other workers, boy.'

'He will,' said Tana. 'He can. I'll show him. I'll help him talk to the others, boss. You'll see.'

The boss paused for a long time. 'Things are tight round here. I can't take every Tom, Dick and Harry. I need someone who can hit the ground running.' He looked at Kura again.

'Can you run, boy?'

Kura couldn't see the point in running, especially if he was going to be building cars.

'He's fast, boss,' said Tana. 'You watch. I'll show him.'

Kura didn't know what to say and even if he did, he didn't think he had the words to say it.

'Look at him.' The boss had a sneer in his voice. 'The boy can barely look at me.'

Kura's head weighed on him like rocks; he struggled to lift it.

'Count yourself lucky you don't have to work for him,' Tana was saying.

Kura stared beyond the horizon, into the city at the foot of the hill. The buildings and cars below looked like a backdrop to a movie scene. But this wasn't just a dream now.

'That man's a bastard, cuz. You're better off.'

Kura stopped listening. His mind had skipped ahead to the interrogation at his father's house. Where is your job? When do you start? When can you start paying your way? He hadn't noticed that Tana had stopped talking, until he spoke again.

'You need some money for the bus, cuz? I can give you some money to get home if you want?'

Kura already knew where the spare key was hidden.

'Four pot plants to the left of the back door. Just until we can get your own key cut.' Tu had thought of everything.

But Kura couldn't return to his father's house, not yet. For starters, only Tu would be there, with the baby, and he couldn't impose any more than he already had. Not that she would've minded.

'I'll walk,' he said.

'It's a long way, cuz.'

'I have all day.'

Tana sounded remorseful. 'I thought I could help.'

Kura tried to ease the tension. 'Maybe I go to the pub now, eh?'

'Have one for me, cuz.'

*

After a year, Taki had settled into a routine. The men at the freezing works worked hard for their money, so on Friday nights the young ones like Taki made their way into town. This Friday was no different.

'Taki!'

'Yeah?'

'How 'bout a beer, mate?'

Taki looked down at his lemonade. He didn't drink, and the boys gave him a hard time for it.

'No, thank you, my friend. I got my beer here.' He raised his soft drink at Joe, who'd started at the freezing works after Vinnie had left five months ago. Despite their different backgrounds – Joe was born and bred just south of Rotorua – he and Taki had become good friends.

'C'mon, mate.' Joe's ribbing was constant. 'You're not in church now. God will still let you in Heaven if you have one beer.'

An uproar from the men filled their corner. Taki turned to them. 'Look at him,' he said, gesturing at Joe. 'He thinks he's Eve, leading poor Adam into temptation with a beer. But I didn't know Eve was this ugly.' He didn't mind being the centre of attention, so he liked it when the other men laughed at his jokes. It helped keep his mind off his business back home. His son had turned two, and it was two years since his wife had died.

'Ugly?' Joe said. 'Mate, your dark good looks might turn the ladies' heads, but unless you know how to lead them into temptation – forget it, my friend.'

Actually, it was Taki who led Joe into temptation.

The following Wednesday, Taki invited Joe to a church social in Newtown. It was a weekly event and thrumming with local islanders. When they reached the church hall, the deep bass of the island melodies was already flooding the streets.

Taki glanced over at his fair-skinned friend. His blond curls were slicked back with too much hair oil. His face, though smooth, had a speck of blood on it. His shoes, freshly polished, concealed the creases in the leather, though only just. But it was his suit that made Taki's heart sink. The seat of his pants that rode too high up, the muted shade of grey that drained his complexion. Why did his friend make no effort?

'Be careful, mate,' Taki said to him. 'These island girls aren't like your Kiwi girls.' He watched Joe's tense smile. 'They might like you.' He elbowed Joe in the ribs as they entered the hall, searching the room for a familiar face. When he recognised no one, they huddled in a corner. Toe-tapping. Self-conscious. And then came the women. Taki introduced Joe.

'Kia orana, Joe.' A sultry island woman greeted the nervous newcomer. 'My name is Helena and this is my friend, Kai.' Beside her, Kai lowered her eyes. Joe did the same. Taki resisted the urge to mock him.

Taki and the women danced while Joe bounced from foot to foot. The women swayed their hips and moved their hands suggestively as Taki closed in on Helena, his limbs synchronised with the beats. He danced with the tempo, his movements blending with the music, while Joe continued to bounce out of time. He bounced from one island song into the next, and before they both knew it, it was time to go home.

'I think Kai likes you, mate,' Taki teased. They were walking down Adelaide Road, the cool air like glass.

'Course she does.' Joe combed a hand through his hair.

'I didn't know you could dance like that,' said Taki. 'No wonder she likes you.'

They walked the rest of the way in silence.

*

It was nearly nine when Kura reached the bottom of the hill. He crossed the road to the main shopping area, wishing he'd eaten more than two slices of toast. Tu had offered to cook him some eggs, but he couldn't eat in front of the others. He remembered them fighting over the milk, and how they watered it down to make it last. The taste of it didn't bother him – he was used to powdered milk back home – but it mattered to his siblings, whose taste buds had been trained to want more. He ignored his rumbling stomach as he dawdled along the rows of shops, stopping every now and then to peek through the windows.

'Kura? That you, nephew?' Kura didn't recognise the woman's voice, but she spoke in Cook Islands Māori and the words put him at ease. He turned as Aunty Ina rushed towards him, her grip tight on his arms when she finally reached him. 'What are you doing here?' Her kiss on his cheek was resolute.

He spoke in his own language. 'Work, Aunty. I'm looking for work.'

'Ah, yes,' she said. Kura felt exposed. Had she and Tu discussed this already? He thought again about the watered-down milk. The need to find work weighed heavily on him. He hadn't expected a land of watered-down milk and honey. His father had neglected to warn him in his letter.

It's time, the letter had said. *Come to New Zealand. Here, you will find work, make good money. Send money back home, help your mother's family. Build a life here, you have brothers and sisters ready to meet you.* His mother's sister back home had agreed. 'Some of your cousins can make over a hundred dollars in a week,' she'd said. 'Stay with your father. He's an important man over there. He will help you settle in.'

Kura looked down at his father's shoes; the polish was losing its shine.

'Any luck?'

'Still looking, Aunty.'

'Chin up, boy. Something will show.'

'Yoo-hoo!' Kura turned to watch a woman bounding down the street towards them. She reminded him of a bulldog. He recognised her vaguely, from yesterday's Mass – another woman in the family he had to get used to.

'Hello, Elizabeth.' Aunty Ina drew out her name, emphasising each syllable.

'Kia orana, Kura,' Elizabeth said, ignoring her. Kura's shoulders tensed up when she kissed him. 'How are you, my boy? How's your mum?' she asked. 'Your stepmum, I mean. Your father's wife. How is she today?'

Aunty Ina stared blankly.

Kura used his English words. 'She's good, Aunty.'

She turned to Aunty Ina. 'It must be hard for your sister having another mouth to feed.' She paused dramatically. 'Oh no,' she corrected herself, 'she wanted another baby, didn't she?' She turned back to Kura. 'You're a lifesaver, boy. She's been wanting another kid to look after, even though she already has a baby. Baby machine, that one.'

Aunty Ina said, 'We see you around, Elizabeth,' and pulled Kura down the street. 'She's a troublemaker, boy,' she whispered. 'Stay away from her.'

Kura's stomach rumbled again, and he looked away when he saw she'd noticed. 'Hasn't my sister been feeding you?'

'Yes, Aunty, of course.' He was quick to respond. 'She's very good to me.'

They stopped outside the post office building. 'This is where I work,' she said. The building stood out amongst the other businesses, raised from the ground level, forcing customers to climb its steps. Kura was impressed. He didn't know anyone who worked in an office; he thought she must be the first in the family. 'Come and visit me whenever you like. I work on the front counter, just wave out to me.'

They both knew he wouldn't.

'Don't be shy. We're family now.' Before she left, Aunty Ina pressed a ten-dollar note into the palm of his hand. 'Go buy yourself some food. You're going to need your strength today.'

Kura found a bench and rested his feet. His father's shoes were an improvement on his brother's, but the soles were too rigid. He wrapped his fingers round the ten-dollar note, feeling like a billionaire. There were iced cakes in the window of the bakery in front of him. He caught a whiff of the mince pies and looked at the ten-dollar note in his hand. He hoped it was enough.

'Can I help you?'

Kura knew what he wanted to say but whether he could say it was another story. Through the glass of the pie warmer he eyed up a pie in the front row. The smell of the pastry was mouth-watering, but the only noise he could muster was the rumble from his gut.

'This will fix that,' said the baker. He reached into the back of the warmer and pulled out a pie with a pair of tongs. 'They're very good,' he gloated. 'Best in town.' He waited for Kura to respond, and when he finally did, he slipped the pie into a brown paper bag and handed it over to Kura, who swapped it for the ten-dollar note. The pie was warm in his hand. He was careful to be gentle with it.

Sitting on the bench outside, he bit through the pastry. The meat was tender and drowning in gravy, and the pastry was like nothing he'd tasted back home. He stuffed it too fervently into his mouth and it wasn't long before he was down to the last bite. His stomach had stopped rumbling, but he could easily have wolfed down a second pie.

His energy had returned, enough to make the long trek back to his father's house. It wouldn't be difficult to find – two main streets, a church and some shops. If he took his time, he could arrive at the house just before five.

*

Before long, Taki was the strongest worker at the boning table.

'Taki! How 'bout another challenge, mate?'

He looked over at Joe. 'Aren't you sick of losing yet?'

The men on the floor laughed.

'You scared I'm gonna win this time?' said Joe. 'You know I let you win cos I feel sorry for you.'

Taki shrugged. 'Nah, too busy.' He leaned against the edge of the boning table, folding his arms and crossing his legs. 'See? Busy. Maybe I beat you some other time.' He beamed as the men watching laughed again.

'How 'bout a little wager then?'

Taki couldn't resist a gamble. He knew Joe was well aware of this. But he said, 'I can't do that, my friend. Too easy. Like stealing your money. And I couldn't call myself a good Christian then.' The banter was rife today.

'Not money – *lunch*.'

Taki considered the stakes. Working here guaranteed all the sausages you could eat. The work was hard and made an island fulla hungry. You had to keep your strength up and your mind on the job. But there were only so many sausages he could eat.

'Okay,' said Taki. 'But only so you can save face in front of the boys. Or try to. That's only fair.'

'*Taaa*-ki!'

'*Taaa*-ki!'

The men were gathered round the boning table, watching Taki and Joe strip a carcass each, and cheering on Taki – the reigning champ. Beads of sweat formed on his brow as he hacked away at the lamb's corpse. He was leading; a heap of meat cuts were piled to one side and his knife slid effortlessly through the flesh of the dead animal. It had taken him nine years to master this skill. He glanced at Joe, who looked frantic and beaten, his knife cuts jagged.

Later, Taki licked the salt from his fingers and took a swig from his bottle of lemonade. He raised his drink to Joe across the table. 'Cheers, mate.' He looked down at the battered fish and the few chips left in front of him, then at the sausages on Joe's plate. Be careful what you wish for, he thought, remembering his first meal in New Zealand.

*

By the time Kura reached the TAB at the Cannons Creek shops, it was well after midday. He'd never been a gambling man, never saw the point of it; it felt senseless and wasteful, and also he lacked the funds. He still had several hours before he could show his face at his father's house, and since the TAB looked close to deserted he entered the dark, smoke-filled room and burrowed into one of the corners. The punters, several men and one woman, had their eyes glued to the race lists on the walls. Kura watched them make their way to the counter to bet, then as they listened intently to the commentary from the speakers. They were motionless as the booming voice filled the space. Kura studied them. Their concentration was exemplary, all eyes and ears on the speakers above them. It was a different kind of praying, but just as earnest as the kind he'd witnessed yesterday; they believed in what each race could deliver for them.

But the hope in their eyes was fading. Nearly all of their horses crossed the line in fourth place or worse. Kura imagined too keenly their loss, which was more than monetary. Only one man cheered, sauntering back to the counter to collect his winnings. And Kura knew that later, the others would slink back to their cars, or walk home, broke and broken.

Just after four, his father arrived. Kura quickly turned his back to him. There were just enough other men in the room to keep him hidden. He glanced over as Taki swotted the race lists, comparing each one with the names in his *Best Bets*. Eyes still on his magazine, he made his way to the counter, placed his bet, then turned towards the speakers. He was so engrossed in the commentary that even if Kura had been standing right next to him he doubted his father would notice. Taki's expression became more animated and he raised his arms in victory as the horses turned the final corner. His smile was wide. But then his face dropped. His mouth snapped shut and his arms fell forlornly to his sides. Kura watched his father tear up his tickets.

Kura slipped out of the TAB. On his way home, he went to the dairy and bought two bottles of milk.

'When do you start?' asked Taki.

Kura looked up from his plate.

'Your job. When do you start your job?'

Tu put one of the bottles of milk on the table and smiled over at Kura in gratitude. 'Leave the boy alone,' she said. 'He just got here. He has time. Look at what he bought us?' She held up the bottle. Kura felt ashamed, more so when he saw the guilt on his father's face. 'Anyway,' she said, 'why can't he just sign up for the dole?'

Taki was adamant. 'No son of mine will live on handouts.'

The next day, the grey Cortina arrived promptly. Kura made sure he had his new résumé with him. Abe had helped him tweak it the night before.

'Helped your grandad on the taro plantation? Gardener. Your nana made you climb the fruit trees for cooking? Chef. You cycled by pushbike all over the island? Can use heavy machinery. Don't worry, bro,' Abe had said. 'You'll find something.' Kura felt bolstered by his brother's words.

The cousins dropped him off at the town centre before driving up the hill to Todd's. 'Just go in and ask, cuz,' said Tana. 'Use that island charm of yours.'

Kura could still hear their teasing as they drove off.

He sat on the bench outside the bakery. He didn't want to bump into Aunty Ina again. There were few people in the area, mainly workers, and as soon as the doors to the bakery opened, he went in.

'Good morning, my friend,' said the baker. Kura tried to smile. 'Another pie? Or maybe a cream doughnut?' He pointed at the shelf of cream doughnuts dusted with icing sugar.

Kura was tempted, but he hesitated. Then he reached into his pocket and pulled out his résumé. He unfolded it and smoothed out the creases, then handed it to the baker, studied his face.

'Are you looking for a job?'

Kura nodded. 'Yes,' he said. 'I'm a hard worker.'

The baker paused. 'I'm sure you are, my friend.' His words put Kura at ease. But then he said, 'I can't afford to take on anyone else.' The look of pity on the baker's face hurt more than the rejection.

Kura took back his résumé and stuffed it into his pocket. 'Okay,' he said, and he swept out the door, knowing he wouldn't come back here again.

The fresh air on his face gave him some relief. He just needed to keep moving.

'Still nothing?'

The family ate in silence.

Later, in their bedroom, Abe tried to build him back up. 'Look, bro, you just gotta be confident. Look these suckers in the eye and say, "You need me to work for you. Don't take too long, cos – "'

'I shouldn't have come here.' Kura's voice was a whisper. 'It's too hard for people like me.'

'What's that supposed to mean?' Abe snapped. 'No brother of mine gives up. It's not in our blood to quit.' Then he lowered his voice. 'You want me to come with you, bro?'

Kura could see that his offer was sincere, but he hated it,

knowing his brother felt like his keeper.

'No,' he said. 'I'll be fine.'

*

Every year, the freezing works threw a picnic for its workers. Queen Elizabeth Park in Paekākāriki, twenty minutes north of Porirua, hummed all day with workers' families. Taki admired Abe at the starting blocks; his older son, Kura, was just a couple years older. He wondered whether Kura was athletic like Abe, and whether they shared similar outlooks. 'See my boy?' he said to Joe. 'It's not just his good looks he gets from his dad.'

Joe's arms were folded confidently across his chest. 'Don't be so sure, mate. My girl's in the running, too.' Taki turned to check out Joe's daughter. She was tall and slim, like a greyhound. And from what he'd heard about her from Joe, smart and tenacious. But so was Abe.

The clapper sounded and the race was on. There were twelve children running in this age group, and Abe was second to Joe's daughter. Joe winked at Taki.

'C'mon, boy!' Taki yelled. 'Get in there!'

Taki had never lost a challenge to Joe; he wasn't about to start losing now.

'C'mon, boy! You can do it!'

Halfway through the race, Joe's daughter was still leading, and still gaining ground. But the resolve on Abe's face gave Taki hope. His son pounded the ground with long, unwavering steps. Joe's girl was still ahead, but only by a stride, and as they approached the finish line Taki called out again. His voice was the loudest at that park. Abe's arms and fists punched the air as he bounded towards the finish line. It was as if Taki's words were adding more drive to his pace, pushing him onwards to win.

The winner's ribbon was pinned proudly on the wall in the sitting room. It became a treasured family possession for years – third only to the velvet painting of Jesus, and second to the family portrait.

*

Kura's cousins dropped him off at the town centre the next day. Abe had talked him up so much that when he arrived in town, he was bent on visiting every shop.

By lunchtime, they'd all rejected him. 'It's not in our blood to quit,' Abe had told him, but he wondered if that mattered, that they shared the same blood. He wasn't convinced that quitting was bad, not when the expectations were already low.

By 4:30, his father's shoes were scuffed, their shine gone. He was exhausted and hungry, and the rejections had turned his stomach to rock. He no longer cared what the baker thought of him. He returned to the bakery and bought a pie, and sat outside on the bench to eat it.

It was as fine as the first one, filling and satisfying, warming his stomach.

By the end of the week, Kura was ready to quit. When his cousins dropped him off as usual, he walked back to the Cannons Creek shops, which took him twenty minutes. No point in dawdling or trying to kill time. He made his way to the Top Tavern and waited for it to open. He had a five-dollar note left, plus change.

Taki was waiting for him when he got home that evening.

'Are you drunk? Again?'

Kura didn't answer.

'Is this what you do all day? Is this how you look for work?'

The room was circling, pulling Kura inwards like a draining sinkhole.

'Where did you get the money to drink?' Taki twisted Kura's collar tight around his fingers. Kura could feel his energy depleting.

'What are you doing? This is your son!'

At Tu's words, Taki let Kura go, watched him gasp for air. He turned to his wife, then skulked off to their bedroom. The door slammed behind him.

By Saturday, Kura had been living at his father's house for a week. He managed to avoid Taki in the morning, as the family had already left for Taki's work picnic. As usual, Kura's cousins picked him up, and he introduced them to Abe, who was riding with them because the family car was full. By the time they arrived at Queen Elizabeth Park, the races were starting.

'It's a good thing these races are grouped by age,' JJ, one of the younger workers, was telling Taki, 'or you'll never win yourself an iceblock, mate. Lucky your wife's packed a decent feed for you jokers, or you'd starve.'

Kura's father had never backed down from a challenge. Ten minutes later he was lined up at the starting block, barefoot and stripped down to his singlet. Tu was looking wildly at him but he ignored her. At least he had the sense to save his shirt from ruin.

'C'mon, old man,' JJ goaded him at the starting line. 'Show me how it's done.'

'Ready, set!'

Taki and JJ led the race neck and neck. Taki seemed to

relish the attention he was getting, the cheers of the older men at the picnic.

Kura watched Taki outrun his younger colleague, the crowd rallying behind him as he basked in the limelight. To everyone's surprise, though, another runner was vying for first place. Taki watched Abe run ahead of him, crossing the line to finish first.

Kura was waiting at the car for Abe. When his brother arrived, he was followed by Taki, who towered over him.

'Have you been drinking?' He sniffed the air.

Abe struggled to make words; instead, he laughed.

'Why are you laughing?' His colleagues were watching them, and Abe's laughing was grating. Taki sniffed the air around him again, and lowered his voice. 'Are you drunk? Like your brother?'

Then he spotted Kura. He stormed towards him. 'What have you done with my son?'

Kura was silent; the beer and weed had slowed his reflexes. But the longer Kura refused to speak, the more it irritated his father. 'What's wrong with you? Speak!'

Tu raced over to where the men were standing. 'Taki!' she cried, but Taki ignored her. He was shouting now. 'What have you done with my son?'

Despite the attention they were getting, Taki couldn't stop himself. Before Kura could react, his whole body shook with the impact of his father's knuckles cracking the bone in his cheek.

*

Plenty had happened for Taki in nine years. He'd come a long way since arriving in New Zealand. He was still working at the freezing works and up for a promotion, and, like in those early days, his nerves were rife.

'Well done, Tar-key. We're impressed with your work here. You're a loyal, hard worker, and popular with the lads. And as you know,' the boss continued, 'we're offering the role to you or Joe. The work is more time-consuming and you'll take on more responsibility. Of course, as foreman, you'll be supervising the boys.'

The boss was watching him. Taki didn't flinch. Good.

'And then there's the paperwork – orders to fill and all that. I don't think you'll have a problem, and, just between us, I'd rather give it to you. But tell me what you think.'

Taki breathed deeply, trying to swallow the lump that snagged in his throat. Even after nine years, this man still made him nervous.

'Thank you, boss. But I can't accept it. I'm happy where I am. This is more than I dreamed of. A beautiful wife and family, a good job, my own home – what do I need a promotion for?'

The boss gaped. 'But the extra money? You have a growing family –'

'More money would be nice, but what price do I pay? Time away from my wife and family, time away from my home. Thank you, boss, but I'm happy where I am.'

He could tell the boss didn't understand Taki's logic. But he shook his head: if that's what he wanted. 'Okay, Tar-key. I'll tell Joe.'

*

Tu was watching Taki change the dressing on his hand.

'You remember when you turned down that job?' she said.

Taki remembered. He'd come home and told her, cradled the family Bible to comfort himself. Ran his eyes over the words, which looked like foreign shapes, every now and then finding a word he recognised. But the words he knew were too few and far between to make sense. It frustrated him as much as turning down that job had.

'You remember what you said when you told me you lost that job?' Tu said.

Taki said nothing. He couldn't look at her.

'You said, "We're doing all right the way we are." Do you think I didn't know you lied to me then? Do you think I didn't know the shame you felt?'

When Abe was old enough, he'd taught Taki to read and write. And when he'd written that letter to Kura, it was Tu who'd convinced him to do it. He still didn't know what kind of father he would be to him, or if he could close the gap he'd created.

Kura stood on the doorstep on Monday morning, waiting for his cousins. His eye was still bruised, and he needed to escape. His siblings were at school and Tu was bustling around inside, the baby still asleep. Then his father came out and stood beside him. Kura braced himself.

'For you,' said Taki, and held something out to him.

Kura looked down. A key to the house.

REM WIGMORE

Basil and the Wild

Basil seldom had company aside from the sheep. Mostly he liked it that way. Sheep didn't ask anything of him, and he could lean up against a warm woollen side if he got lonely.

Once a day he walked down the hill to his sister's house, carrying his empty pot from the day before. Today it went the same as always. Maggie had a portion of stew ready for him. He talked briefly with her and her husband, who he both liked. The children were too loud and moved too fast for Basil, a riot of noise echoing off the walls and ceiling, so he seldom stayed long. He took the pot of stew back up and up and up through the fields and into his hilly pastures. He would build a fire to heat it for dinner, and eat it watching the stars.

With his daily visit done, he wouldn't see any people until the next day. But there was a feeling in his head like something was watching from the woods.

He stood and stretched. He whistled idly, and the nearest of his sheep looked at him then went back to chewing at grass. That was fine, and all as it should be. Trying to look like it was a normal day, Basil picked up his staff. The solid length of wood was reassuring in his hand. He tried not to think how useless it would really be against a wolf, or a bear, or a man.

No one else liked being this close to the edge of the forest, where farmers hadn't yet beaten back the trees and tamed the land into pastures and orchards. No one went further than half a mile in for firewood, and even then they didn't like to. Basil tapped his staff against his ankle and tried to think. He roved his eyes over the trees but all he saw were gnarled branches and patches of shadow. He must be indulging in some kind of childish fright. There was nothing there.

It would be better if he had a dog, but dogs were expensive and Basil wasn't worth the cost. He'd have liked the company, but he understood.

He counted. All his sheep were here except the lamb lost two days ago, and he'd checked down in the valley and up the top of the hill already. It could have gone nowhere but the forest.

Twisting brambles moved, branches shifted, and a towering patch of shadow walked out from the forest like the trees themselves could walk.

Basil's breath was coming too fast and quick and his heart felt strange. This wasn't something he'd dealt with before. It was still his job, though. He stepped forward, into the space between his sheep and the forest's edge.

He wasn't much use to his sister or her family, or the village didn't think so. He could mind the sheep though, and he'd done that well for fifteen years, since he was a boy. All was as it should be. He would try to protect the sheep, and whether he succeeded or failed, all would be as it should be, and he was in the right place. Thinking that calmed his breathing down.

It was a giant that walked out of the woods.

He was a man, broad-shouldered and towering, but he looked something like a beast as well. All over he was covered in hair, thick and curling, with leaves tangled in it. For feet he had cloven hooves, and the nails of his hands were ragged and sharp. Basil shifted the staff in his hands and stood looking at him, trying not to let fear make his thoughts race shallow as rapids. This man was half his height again, and Basil was the tallest man in the village.

The wild man bore no weapon, but his arms were massive. He could pop Basil's head off his shoulders with a flick of his thumb. Basil's heart went too fast and his breathing came too quick and he was slipping into what his brother-in-law called *one of his states –*

The fear nearly overwhelmed him, and then he saw what the wild man clutched in his dirt-smeared hands.

The lost lamb bleated and wriggled. Small, from near the end of the season, it was God's own miracle that it survived being born at all.

And Basil was a shepherd, and he knew his job. 'Put it down,' he said. The words were as slow as usual, but he knew what to say.

The wild man took another step, then halted. The lamb looked tiny in his hands.

Basil pointed his staff. 'Put it down,' he said again.

The wild man crouched. He lowered his hands to the ground, then pulled them away with fingers splayed.

The lamb baaed plaintively then tottered forward to Basil's familiar shape. Basil bent to scratch its head. The little creature bore only a few small cuts, more like it had passed through thorns and bramble than been snatched up for food by a giant.

Basil looked up at the wild man. He crouched there, looking at Basil much as Basil looked at the lamb: aware it was a smaller thing, and likely to be scared.

Basil laid his staff down and straightened. He swallowed, searching for the words, hoping the wild man wouldn't leave before he found them.

'Thank you,' he said finally.

Up close the wild man was still fearsome to look at, broad and tall. Aside from his size, he didn't look that unlike a man, though. There were the hooves, but sometimes people were born strangely. He had tangling hair and eyes as black as beetles, and he was naked from his head to his hooves.

He'd done Basil a service. Basil didn't understand most of how people worked, or the complicated webs they stepped through so easily, but he knew that when people did something for him he should do something in return.

The wild man straightened slowly, as though to leave. Basil lifted his hands and managed to say, 'Wait.'

The wild man dropped back down into a squat, hands resting on his knees, and looked at him.

Basil turned and hurried to his hut.

There was little in there, only a bed and his spare shirt and the bucket he used to fetch water. He grabbed the blanket from his bed and rushed back outside. He breathed out in relief to see the wild man still crouching where he'd left him.

As Basil approached, the wild man stood up. The fingers of one of his hands rubbed restlessly together, but he didn't run. Basil stopped just short of him and held out his offering.

The blanket was of fine-spun wool, dyed blue, the most valuable thing he owned. 'Here,' Basil said.

The wild man reached out to touch it with one hand but didn't take it.

'A cloth,' Basil said. '*Here*. They'll be angry at you.'

The wild man stepped back and frowned. The expression was twitching and slow, as though his face wasn't used to unhappiness.

How to explain? Haltingly, Basil said, 'As a boy, I wouldn't wear clothes – they *itched*, they felt wrong.' He squared his shoulders defensively, but the wild man didn't seem judgemental. Basil breathed out. 'And I was beaten and . . . here.' He shook the blanket. 'They'll be angry at you,' he repeated.

The wild man looked at him for a long time, like he was trying to figure him out.

Basil waited. At last, the wild man reached out and took the blanket. He looped it around his hips and Basil nodded. The wild man inclined his head, then turned and strode away. As abruptly as he'd come he was gone again, as if he was part of the woods.

Basil stared after him, then picked up his staff. He had work to do, of course. He picked up the lamb and sought out the mother ewe, still nursing its remaining lamb. He went about his day, washing his face and shaving in the last light of the afternoon. He gathered his wood and lit his fire, and sat and ate his stew.

He tried not to think how nice it would be to have someone else to eat with, like his family did.

A week after meeting the wild man, Basil lingered longer than usual in the house of his sister and brother-in-law.

William was the first to notice. William was clever with people in a way Basil wasn't. He laughed loudly and often, and seemed to have kind eyes. At first, Basil liked him very much. Basil wasn't clever with people, though. It didn't take long after William and Maggie's wedding for William to get fed up with his silences and stumbling speech, and he no longer looked at him with kindness. 'Something wrong, Basil?' he said. Maggie looked up from where she stood by the sink.

Basil didn't look either of them in the eye, for fear his mind would slow. 'It's cold,' he said, like an apology.

'You have the wits to light a fire, don't you?' William said. He glanced out the window to where the children played. 'We can't always be keeping you in blankets and clothes, not with Bill and Joany to look after.'

'Will!' Maggie hissed. She gave Basil a tired smile. 'I know it gets cold up there, and we do appreciate you. I'll find something.'

Basil sat outside the door to wait. Maggie didn't go looking immediately but stood by the sink next to her husband, arguing with him in a whisper, though William didn't bother to speak quietly. 'He's a grown man,' William said, 'he should fend for himself.' Maggie seemed to convince him when she pointed out that Basil helped with the sheep, after all, so they could spare the wool.

The children came ambling closer to stare at him. Basil lifted a hand in greeting. Joany, who was younger, whispered something to her brother. They both laughed.

Basil wrapped his arms around his chest and leaned forward with his head on his knees.

Maggie brought out the blanket, wrapped around the stewpot. 'Here, and don't mind his blustering. I'll look after you.' She patted his shoulder, slowly enough he saw it coming and didn't tense. 'You and me, Basil. We're a team.'

It was like that, once. Maggie used to speak for him when the words wouldn't come, standing calm and defiant between Basil and their parents the few times their father lost his temper, and she always knew what Basil meant to say. He wasn't sure when she stopped knowing.

He didn't know when the lines on her face had got so deeply etched either. 'But don't lose this one, please, Basil.' There was a shout from one of the children and Maggie turned. She squeezed his shoulder in farewell and bustled away.

He was glad to leave the house again, with his pot of stew

and the coarse blanket. The walk didn't feel too long with that warmth hugged to his chest.

Basil always did his work the best he could, but for a week he'd been watching the woods as well. Today something happened, and Basil stood up, brightening, when a tall shape walked out from the trees.

The wild man looked wary, but more like a person than a beast now he had the blanket wrapped around him. Basil nodded to him and said, 'Hello.'

The wild man nodded back. Basil had been thinking about this all week and had a shape in his mind of what he wanted to happen. He sat down on a flat patch of grass and indicated in front of him.

Slowly the wild man came forward and sat down. He was still intimidatingly tall like this, but it was easier to see all of him at once without staring up.

They sat there together. Some sheep wandered close by, and the wild man watched them. He seemed mostly at ease, though his fingers tapped restlessly against his knee.

'It's all right,' Basil said after a while. He put a smile on his face, though he wasn't good at smiling. 'I don't talk much either.'

The other man cocked his head. 'I talk.'

'Oh,' Basil said. He couldn't help being a little disappointed. It might have been nice.

'. . . Slowly,' the wild man finished.

'Ha ha!' Basil grinned and slapped his hand against the ground at the joke. The wild man smiled back. His teeth were crooked and stained, but his smile was no stranger than anyone else's.

Basil put a hand to his chest. 'Basil,' he said.

The wild man nodded and put a hand on his own chest, bare and hairy. 'Makarios.'

Basil wasn't sure what he'd expected, but not that. It wasn't a name he'd heard before. He thought about it. 'That's not an English name.'

Makarios tilted his head in acknowledgement. 'I'm what you'd call Greek, or I was.' He glanced back at the wall of the woods. 'Hard to remember.'

Basil nodded, as though he understood.

One of the sheep wandered up and nosed at him, staying well clear of Makarios. Basil pushed it gently and it wandered away again.

He looked at Makarios. 'Thank you for the lamb. That was . . .' He didn't want to say *kind*. He'd thought William was kind once.

Makarios smiled. 'It was lost. I have been here sometimes, and knew it fitted here.'

'Yes, it fits with me. I'm a shepherd.' Basil tapped the staff beside him. Then he stared down at the ground, embarrassed. He always said such foolish things.

Makarios nodded, though, and said, 'No sheepdog?'

Basil patted his hand on the ground rapidly, building up his courage to tell a joke. 'Stroke of luck for you,' he said.

The other man frowned. 'The village isn't far from here.'

Basil wasn't sure what he meant, but nodded anyway. 'Yes.'

Makarios scratched his chin with a ragged fingernail. 'There are many people there who could surely spare one. You should have a dog. Safer with a dog.'

Basil hesitated. *Kind* did seem to be the word for Makarios, and Basil was as unused to that as he was talking to strangers. He chewed at his lip.

Makarios reached out a massive hand, then lowered it. 'It's all right. I'm sorry.'

'I've been fine so far,' Basil said, then lapsed into silence. He wanted to ask Makarios to share his dinner, but he had little to offer. His stew had been thin the last few weeks. Food was scarce for everyone, not just him. If they stopped wanting to feed him they would stop all at once. There was no reason not to share their food: he was helpful, he knew his work. It wasn't his fault that William had stopped bothering to be kind to Basil once he'd married Basil's sister and didn't need anything from him. And it wasn't Maggie's fault that she had to worry about her children and not him. He knew that.

Basil gave his head a violent shake to get the thoughts out, the memory of William saying *he's a grown man, he should fend for himself.* He thought that was what he'd been doing all these years. At least he was sure of his plan. 'I have stew if you're hungry,' he said. It was nowhere near night yet, so he added, 'For later.'

Makarios smiled, warm. 'Maybe. What kind?'

'Beef, this week.' The neighbours had been generous.

Makarios shifted so he sat more comfortably, cross-legged with his hands laid on his knees. 'Thank you. No. Don't eat meat.'

'Oh,' Basil said, surprised. A second later he was ashamed to have been surprised. Ashamed he'd assumed Makarios was savage, that his first thought when Makarios came out of the woods was that the wild man would rip the lamb apart and eat it raw.

He looked up to apologise. Makarios seemed like he was thinking, though, the way Basil thought hard when he was trying to figure out the right thing to say, the thing that was correct and as it should be.

'I have roots,' Makarios offered. 'In the forest. Berries. We can still eat together.'

'I'd like that. Yes.'

They talked more over the next few weeks. The change was slow, so it didn't bother Basil too much. His days were largely the same, except as well as watching the sheep and making his trek down for stew once a day, sometimes he shared a meal with Makarios. Sometimes he talked to him for a few minutes at the forest's edge, when the wild man didn't want to come out into the open. The new blanket was scratchy, but Basil didn't mind much, not when it meant Makarios had something nice.

A few weeks later, Makarios accompanied him to fetch water from the stream at the bottom of the hill. Basil filled his bucket. Makarios splashed water on his face and cleaned his hands.

Basil watched him. 'I asked to eat something else with the stew today,' he said to his back, which was as hairy as the rest of him. 'But we haven't had bread these last two weeks.' He was sorry. He'd like to give him something better than just a blanket, when Makarios had been so thoughtful, and such good company.

Makarios turned to smile at him over his shoulder. He smiled a lot more these days. Water dripped from his beard. 'That's fine, Basil.'

Basil nodded, and stayed where he was. Makarios turned and lifted more water to his face, and without looking at him said, 'Was there something else?'

Basil nodded again. 'Can I ask why you don't eat meat?' Everyone he knew did, except on Fridays, and was grateful for the chance.

Makarios stopped with water halfway to his face. He let the water splash down and sat back on his heels. He wiped his forearm over his face. He didn't turn round.

Basil couldn't read faces well, but he could read a turned back even less. He took a step back. 'Sorry, sorry, sorry,' he said.

Makarios shook his head. He stood and smiled at Basil again, though there was a different look to his smile. 'Perhaps it helps to talk.' He strode up the bank a little way and sat on a tree stump there, where it was drier.

Basil left his pail where it was and sat down in front of him, cross-legged, looking up.

Makarios scratched his chin then dropped his hand. 'I was a normal man once,' he said, heavily. 'I was not always as you see me.'

Basil nodded to show he was listening.

'But I was not the best of men,' Makarios said. His fingers dug into the rotting wood of the stump. 'Not . . . reliable, might be the best way to put it. My wife grew unhappy with me, with our life together.'

He fell silent. Basil nodded again, struggling with what to say. 'I'm sorry,' he said, which didn't feel right.

'That's fine,' Makarios said. 'It was my fault.' He sighed. 'In any case, she – left.' He hunkered in on himself. 'A few years later, our daughter grew ill, and I could not save her.'

'I'm sorry,' Basil said again, meaning it.

Makarios's eyes were reddened at the edges, and the corners of his mouth pulled down. He spoke quickly now, but more softly. 'After her death, I grew furious at the doctor. I think I beat him bloody in my rage. I cannot remember now. It feels like another life. That's not an excuse,' he added, sharply, lifting his head. 'I'm not excusing myself.'

Basil shunted back, a little intimidated. 'I know.'

Makarios took a breath and let it out slow and long, shoulders slumping down again. 'Sorry,' he said. 'I am . . . ashamed, of the man I was. I don't remember if I left the doctor alive or dead. For my deeds, I was cursed. I ran and lived wild in the woods, mad with grief. Or . . . simply mad.'

Mad was one of the things the people in the village called

Basil sometimes, though they used softer words mostly, as though those wouldn't hurt as much. 'A bit simple, your boy,' the butcher told his parents once, and Basil had stared up with wide eyes, wondering why it was better to be complicated. He leaned forward.

'When I could think again I was as you see me now,' Makarios said. 'Cursed into this strange shape, and appalled by how I had acted.' He shrugged. 'How to explain? If you've never felt such shame, it's hard to know what a weight it is. I swore never to – never to raise a hand in violence again. Nor even eat the flesh of any animal.' He was quiet for a while, hands resting on his knees.

Basil said, 'You are doing well at that.'

Makarios smiled at him, like gratitude, maybe, or like acknowledgement, or like pity. 'I need to avoid people, so mostly I do nothing at all,' he said, with the tilt to his voice that meant he was making a joke. He ran a hand through his tangled hair. 'That's a lie. I look after the woods, these days.' He laughed. 'Are you ready for more marvels?'

Basil nodded.

'You are kind, to indulge me,' Makarios said, and Basil was suddenly unsure where to look. He stared at the ground with his cheeks burning. No one had ever used that double-edged word, 'kind', about him.

Then he swallowed, finding the words. 'Go on.'

'It was pure chance, not anything I truly won,' Makarios said. 'But my refusal to hurt any beasts of the wood won the favour of the King of the Good Folk, Oberon, when his white hind ran through my woods and left again safe and untouched.' Basil gazed up at him, and Makarios looked aside like he was shy. 'He lengthened my life, I think. Altered my form further still, and gave me this forest to live in.'

Basil looked at his cloven feet and then glanced up at him.

Makarios nodded, and Basil leaned forward to rest a hand against one hoof. It felt like any hoof, really. No stranger than feet, when he thought about it.

Makarios waited until he was done, then stood. He glanced over his shoulder to where the hill obscured the trees. 'My woods grow smaller every year.' His voice was heavy. 'Your kind are always hungry.'

Basil twisted his hands together, trying to find words. He wanted to say it wasn't his fault they were always cutting deeper into the forest, but he knew that was partly a lie. His pastures were forest once, and he too lived in a house built from logged trees. He was part of the village's devouring of the woods, even if he wasn't the one who'd held the axe.

Instead he stood up and said nothing about it. 'Do you need more time to wash?' He knew he sounded brusque but he didn't know what to do about it. He touched a hand to his chin, coarse with stubble. 'I need to bring my water up to shave.'

Makarios shook his head. 'Shaving! I remember that.' He stared down at himself. 'It would take me a while now.'

Basil thought there was an odd note to his voice, like sadness. 'It's all right,' he said, lifting his hands with palms out to show he meant no harm. 'I don't mind. I don't –' He shook his head. 'Shaving itches. It's just so they know I'm . . .' He trailed off. 'I don't mind,' he said again. Maybe it was silly to shave every day, when the hair just grew back. Makarios's way was more sensible.

Makarios smiled at him, which Basil hoped meant he hadn't ruined everything by not reacting right to his story.

Then Makarios looked over the top of Basil's head, and his body tensed, shoulders going up. His arms were still thick as clubs, but Basil no longer read any threat in the way he held himself, only fear.

Basil turned. There on the ridge on the other side of the stream stood a boy with a stick in his hand, a rock skidding over the ground in front of him as he played some child's game. It was Bill, and he was staring right at Makarios with his eyes wide and white. Basil's heart thumped.

Makarios shifted his weight, and Basil could hear his breath starting to come faster, deep puffs like a bellows. Basil told him, 'Run.'

Makarios turned on his heel and sprinted up the hill and away. Basil looked at Bill, who dropped his stick and backed away, shaking his head. He had a thin weak hope that it would be all right: Bill was only a boy, still a few years away from the responsibilities and privilege of adulthood, so they might yet take Basil's word over his.

Then William came up the ridge behind his son. Basil turned and watched as the giant, strange, frightening shape of the wild man vanished over the crest of the hill.

He knew, with a dread like sickness in the pit of his belly, that William wouldn't see Basil's friend. William would see a monster, a nightmare come out from the woods.

Right now Maggie and William spoke too loudly too. The children watched them from the table with wide eyes. Bill had his arm around his sister's shoulder and seemed younger than he usually did.

The boy was frightened by that glimpse of Makarios. Basil wished he could explain that Makarios was nothing to fear, less of a threat even than the men from the village, but the words wouldn't come. Everything was too loud, and they demanded things from him then didn't listen to the answers.

'Some monster nearly reaching the house!' William said and shook him by the shoulders. 'You should've told us the second you saw it,' he shouted, but he was looking at Maggie, not Basil, as if she was responsible for him. 'This is your job!'

Basil struggled for words. 'Not a wolf,' he explained. 'Not a bear.'

'Idiot,' William said, and turned away from him.

Basil looked down, curling his hands in his lap and clenching his fingers together like Makarios did when he was worried or afraid.

'Describe it to me again,' Maggie said. Basil looked at her with hope winging in his throat.

William gestured far above his head. 'A monster twice the height of a man,' he said. 'Shaped like a man but savage, with fur all over like a bear and horrible claws that could rip you in two!'

Bill shrank back into Joan's arms.

'He wouldn't,' Basil said. Bill nodded in relief, willing to accept even his slow uncle's comfort right then, but William and Maggie looked at Basil as if maybe he was a monster too.

'Is this the first time this beast has come here?' Maggie said. Her eyes were like pins that fixed him in place.

Basil swallowed, afraid. He stood up. 'I meant,' he said. 'We don't know. We don't know – what this thing is. What it does.'

'I've heard about wild men,' Maggie said, and Basil let out a sigh and sagged back in his chair. Maggie was wise and gentle. She would fix it.

'You have?' William said sceptically. He gave Basil a look that he couldn't interpret. Maybe William wanted him to join in the scepticism.

'Maggie's smart,' Basil told him.

'They're like the old kings in the stories, who got cursed or driven mad and took on the likeness of beasts,' Maggie said. He nodded along, slowing as she continued, 'They're gifted with wisdom sometimes, or prophecy. Even if it's not his fault, maybe we can get some answers out of him.'

Basil stared at her, helpless. It was like he'd never known her at all.

'Even if what's not his fault?' William said, looking at Maggie like now she had something worth saying. 'What's he done?'

'The crops,' Maggie said. 'This blight might not be natural. We need to tell the others.'

They stood, and the children followed. Bill's hands were clenched into fists, like his fear was easier to bear now it had a shape, now he knew it was an enemy. Basil watched them go, sitting for some moments before he could force himself to stand and follow.

Thin rations. He knew that. Weak stew and no bread for weeks. In his mind, he couldn't connect that with Makarios, because what could one man do? Makarios hadn't been running out of the woods and kicking at the crops or salting the earth. They would have seen signs if he had.

If Basil could just find the words; if he could just explain. If they would just listen.

His family were far ahead of him, heading for the one horse they had. Basil broke into a run, shambling after them.

William turned and put a hand on Joan's shoulder, pushing her towards Basil. 'Look after her.' Joan made a face but went to Basil's side.

Maggie looked at William questioningly. 'And the boy?'

William shook his head and put a hand on Bill's shoulder, squeezing it roughly. 'Time for him to be a man.' He nodded to Basil. 'We won't be long.'

He swung Maggie up onto the horse and hauled himself up after her, and they were off at a trot towards the small village. Basil stood next to his niece and stared after them.

They were going too fast for him to follow even if he had the bravery.

'Maggie's a smart girl,' he said. 'She won't let them do anything bad.'

He hadn't been talking to Joan, but she nodded and took his hand. 'It's all right, Uncle Basil,' she said. 'Billy and Da can fight the monster.' She looked up at him, then glanced aside in confusion as he started to cry.

Maggie and William and Bill didn't come back until late that night, late enough that Bill kept yawning and nearly fell from the horse. At least no mob of villagers were following in their wake. There were only twenty people within five miles of here, in any case, so any mob would be small.

'Thank you for looking after her,' Maggie said as she drew Joan into an absentminded hug. She hugged Basil too, then set to cooking dinner before Basil had time to get used to the unexpected closeness. 'You can sleep here tonight,' she added, smiling at him.

He tried to smile back, but he wasn't sure he got it right. He still felt like crying. 'The wild man,' he said. They just looked at him, and he struggled to form the question. 'The wild man.' What were they going to do to him?

All William would say was, 'Don't worry, Basil, we'll take care of it.' And Maggie smiled sympathetically.

Basil curled up on the floor by the fire and left for his hut and fields as soon as light dawned the next morning. He made sure to do all his tasks, work through the day like always, but it didn't help. His skin felt stretched tight and he kept looking back over his shoulder or staring down the hill instead of looking after his sheep. Twenty people would be enough to kill Makarios. Ten would be enough. He was big and strong, but he wouldn't fight back in case he hurt anyone.

There was no sign of him that day, and Basil hoped he had been clever and left for good, gone so far into the forest he'd never be found. As evening fell he crept to the forest's edge to watch for him. Shadows pooled on the ground, and wind rustled the leaves so they seemed to whisper to him.

And then Makarios was there, walking silently out from under the trees like the day they met.

Basil wanted him to be far from here, and safe. Still, he sighed in relief.

He reached up to lay a hand on Makarios's arm and said, 'I don't think you should be here.' He looked Makarios in the eye, so he'd know it was important, but he could see little of the other man's face in the shadows. 'Not safe.'

Makarios clasped his hand in his own larger one, squeezing it in comfort. These little tricks that people had came easier to Makarios than they did to Basil. 'I keep wolves away from here,' Makarios said, his voice low. 'Do you still feel unsafe? I wish they would give you a dog.'

Basil pulled his hand away. Normally Makarios understood him more easily than this. 'No. Not safe for you,' he said. 'They're angry. I don't know what they're doing.'

Makarios looked at him for a while, after he said that. Basil was almost glad he couldn't see his face so he didn't have to try to understand what he felt.

'I'm fast,' Makarios said at last, and he gave Basil's hand another squeeze. 'Hardly the first time I've been run off from near towns and cities.'

Basil shook his head, wishing he could explain. 'I don't think I can stop them.' Horribly, the tears were welling up in his eyes again. Bad enough to cry in front of a young girl. Surely it was far worse to cry in front of another man. 'I'm not – able to stop them. No one listens, I'm too slow, I'm stupid.'

'Stupid?' Makarios said sharply, and caught his arm. 'No. Your mind turns differently. Is that wrong?' He tugged him into the shade of the trees and sat down, and reluctantly Basil sat beside him. He wished he could find the words to make him *run*. He wished he wanted him to.

'People say it is,' he said. That wasn't being fair, and when his parents were alive they'd often talked of the importance of being fair. 'They don't say it to me. But they say it.'

Makarios leaned forward. 'They can be wrong, same as anyone.'

'Thank you,' Basil said, eyes prickling. He hated pity. He stood up.

'I –' Makarios said, and swallowed his words, and said, 'My mind turns differently too.'

Basil stood looking down at him. He still wanted Makarios to run, but he was curious.

'My mood, it changes too fast,' Makarios said, like he wanted the words over with fast. 'I swing from grief to rage. From impossible laziness where all is dark into a, a hot and dangerous state.' He breathed in, out, and continued more slowly. 'When I'm in the throes of emotion, I cannot remember the world being any different.' He shrugged. 'I wait until I am fully myself once more. And then it is only a matter of time until the coin flips, through some mechanism wholly outside of my control, and I am transformed again. And how can I say what is truly myself, when I go through such changes? How can I know for sure what is real?'

Basil was listening, but it hurt. He thought when they'd first met that Makarios was like him, but Makarios wasn't like him. He'd just been alone too long. Now they'd been speaking to one another for longer, Makarios spoke cleverly, with a depth of understanding of himself and the world. Sometimes he even understood Basil better than Basil did.

If anything, he was twice the man Basil was, not just in size. Makarios seemed to feel so much and be so aware of those feelings, always ready to brace himself for the next change. Every mistake he made, he atoned for. 'Your village is not wrong if they call me a monster,' he said now, and Basil knelt in front of him and laid his hands on his shoulders. His hair was warm and thick like fur.

'They are,' Basil said. He shook him. 'They are.'

Makarios let him, looking at him with his mouth curved up at the sides. 'Careful, there, don't hurt me.'

Basil stumbled back, realising it was a joke only when Makarios laughed softly and said, 'Sorry, Basil. You treat me very kindly, you know. In your company, I feel merely a man. So I don't mind too much if they think I'm a monster. There's still you, and you don't.'

Basil sat down again. The grass was wet. He plucked one blade of grass then another and another and braided them together, until the words came. 'They can be wrong same as anyone, too.'

Makarios smiled again. 'Thank you, Basil.'

'You are welcome, Makarios.' Something in him felt gleeful. Of course they knew each other, but it felt good that they knew each other. He knew this man's name and this man knew his name, and they had sought each other out. Makarios had sought him out.

Basil knew it wasn't safe for him here, knew he should convince him to run, but he couldn't find the words and couldn't make himself want to.

William and Maggie stopped talking each time he visited for his day's stew now. They would wait until he left before resuming their conversation in hushed voices. Maggie still smiled at him, but even the children fell silent when Basil came too close, Bill puffing up with importance, and they didn't play outside anymore. He came down one day and saw a heavy club leaning against the door, a clumsy thing carved of wood. William didn't bother to make up a lie about what it was for. He didn't say anything about the club, but Basil knew it was for Makarios. Makarios, who could never bear to hurt anyone again, and would be killed.

And still Basil sneaked out to talk to him, not in the middle of his pastures where Makarios could be easily seen but at the very edge of the woods, between the trees and the grass, before the dark grew deeper.

He stopped shaving his beard, too, and let it grow out. He started to think about what it would be like to live in the woods. He'd never needed many people around, and Makarios was good company. Maybe he could bring some of the sheep. He didn't want to abandon the flock, but sheep were useful; someone would take care of them. Bill was nearly old enough. He hoped they wouldn't be lonely.

He needed to get Makarios to leave this place. And he wanted to leave with him, if he could only find the words to ask.

One afternoon, when Basil went to get his stew, a dozen people were outside the house. They carried rough-hewn clubs like William's, and Basil knew his time had run out.

He knew most of these men, though he hadn't talked to them much. Old Robert, Geoffrey, Thomas the farrier. Young Bill was there too. Basil went to the group and stood in front of them and said, 'Please don't. Please stop.'

'You don't have to worry,' William said, shifting his grip on his club. 'No one asked you to come. It won't hurt you.'

'But he won't hurt anyone.' He lifted his hands up with his palms out, wishing he could find the right words to stop this and save Makarios. 'He hasn't hurt anyone.'

William snorted and said to the others, 'Basil's too scared, but the real men will take care of it.' He thumped Bill on the shoulder.

Bill was thirteen if Basil remembered right, a few years younger than Basil had been when he became a shepherd. Too young to kill a man.

'Please,' he said, but even his nephew shook his head, and he and the others walked past him. Some knocked into him with their shoulders as they went by. They were on their way up to his pasture.

With fear shaking through him, he went into the house. Maggie was sitting at the table, for once not in motion. He gestured until he caught her attention, then pointed to where the men had gone.

'You don't have to worry, Basil,' she said. 'And we'll have more wood once the forest is safer. We could even build you a room here in the house, if you like. That'll be nice, won't it?'

He shook his head in silent despair and ran outside.

The way back to his hut and the forest edge was familiar, but he took a longer route than usual because he didn't want to run into the others on the way. He ran, tripping a few times over rocks.

He still got there before the mob, and stood by his hut to think. They would be here soon. What could he do? If he yelled out '*Run!*' then the people from the village would know he'd been talking to Makarios. They would kill him, too. Anything he did to try to stop them, they would kill him too.

He wrapped his arms tight around his chest until the worst of the shivering had stopped, and went into his hut.

He was the only man in the village who didn't carry a knife.

No one trusted him with one. His staff was for protecting the sheep and he couldn't imagine hurting someone with it.

Then he remembered: he had his razor. He grabbed it, but his hands were shaking so much he dropped it. Outside the hut, he could hear the shouting of the men as they approached. He picked up the razor once more and ran back outside. Twelve men. As well as clubs they held a thick net between them, weighted at each corner with chunks of scrap iron.

Basil ran in front of them again. He couldn't think what else to do. 'Stop, please stop,' he said. Then one of the men, Henry, raised his club.

Basil froze. He had been hit and sometimes beaten, but never with a club. It could crack his bones like eggshells. It could pulp him into mince.

His brother-in-law sighed and shook his head. 'Put it down,' he said to Henry. Basil was relieved, but then William turned to face him and shoved him back hard.

Basil fell, and cried out in pain. Lying on the ground, he unclenched his hand. He'd been holding the razor and it had sliced into his skin. The cut was shallow but dripped with blood.

'There,' someone said, and Basil looked up, closing his hand on his injury.

They were all looking at the woods, hungry as dogs. Basil looked and saw a dark shape striding out of the trees, a tangled patch of wilderness, a towering giant. Makarios.

No no no, he tried to say. *No no no*. The words didn't come out.

Makarios's head was turned towards Basil, intent on him. His strides were quick even though there was a group of armed strangers here. Basil pushed himself to his feet and pushed the word out. 'Run!' he cried, but it was too late now.

The net fell over Makarios, the crowd of men tugging

and pulling it over him. As he clawed at the knotted ropes, the weight of it pulled him down. He struggled, but the net entangled his limbs and trapped him.

Even then, even as the villagers approached with their clubs, Makarios was looking back at Basil. But then he looked away and pulled at the net to try and free himself. The movement was deliberate, as though there was still a chance he might stop their anger from falling on Basil for knowing him. Basil's chest hurt and his hand ached in quick pulses of heartbeat.

Geoffrey lifted his club and brought it down in a vicious swing, and Makarios cried out at the hit. All the others went still, suddenly, at the cry of pain from the giant.

When he did nothing else, Geoffrey lifted his club again and brought it down, shatteringly hard. So did another man, and another. Makarios twisted and howled and took the blows, and didn't raise a hand to any of them.

If Basil could just find the words to stop them. If he could just make them see.

All his sheep had scattered. He could smell blood. He shifted his grip on the razor.

Makarios went still. Basil crept closer, behind the ranks of his attackers, to stare at him. He couldn't be dead, he couldn't be dead yet –

Makarios was still alive, chest heaving with breath, though his hair was stained dark with blood on his legs and chest and arms. His eyes weren't on the villagers or Basil anymore. His gaze was fixed on the trees, and his body trembled with effort.

Basil looked, too. Creatures were creeping out from the forest. Some looked like deer, some like wolves, and a few were hopping creatures like birds, but they weren't living animals. They looked like they were made of branches, bound together by vines with shadows beneath, like an effigy of an animal powered by night.

Makarios was the protector of the woods, a friend of Oberon. Perhaps these strange creatures guarded him as he guarded the woods, and had been summoned by the spilling of his blood.

The villagers kept swinging their clubs, oblivious to the danger. Deer's antlers gleamed with thorns, and the wolves panted out a thick black slime that sizzled and bit at the ground as it fell. More creatures came from the woods, halting at the edge. There were more than enough of them to tear the whole mob apart.

In that moment, Basil wanted them to. He looked at Makarios urgently.

Makarios's mouth moved, though it was hard to hear him. 'Stop,' he said. 'Stop.'

The villagers jeered, but Basil knew it wasn't them he was speaking to. He looked up in despair. The shadow-wood creatures came no closer, though the deer tossed their heads and the wolves snapped their thorny teeth together. Basil's brother-in-law and nephew, and all the men from the village, kept beating the bound man bloody, jeering at him, none of them looking up to see the threat that hovered so close and was held at bay.

Even faced with death, Makarios wanted no harm to come to them.

Basil stepped forward. He had to shove to get past them all. He pushed old Robert aside, flinching back from the disgusted look the man gave him. He forced his way through until he was in front of Makarios, who lay motionless and bleeding in the net, and threw himself between Makarios and the armed villagers. He pressed his back to the wild man's side, feeling the knots of the net bite at him.

He tapped one hand against Makarios's side and dropped the razor, hoping desperately that Makarios could reach. No time to look, when looking would draw attention. Then he spread his arms out wide like a shield and stared up at the men from his village. In a way, it was a relief. He couldn't find the words, but for once he didn't need to. This was the right place to be, by Makarios's side, honouring his choice of peace by being peaceful in turn. This was as it should be.

He looked right at William, who stared back. 'Basil, you idiot,' he said. 'Get out of the way.'

Basil let his arms fall, and gripped the net. 'He hasn't hurt anyone.'

William hissed a curse through his teeth and the others watched him, waiting, holding their clubs. Geoffrey laughed.

Makarios shifted a little. 'Basil,' he said in a low rumble. 'They'll hurt you.'

Basil shrugged, keeping his tight grip.

William glanced around at the others. He lifted his club, and the muscles in his shoulders tensed, ready to swing.

'Da,' said Bill, in the voice of a much younger boy. Basil looked at his nephew – Bill who looked so much like Maggie, who looked so much like Basil. He saw William looking too.

William brought the club down hard on the ground, sending a clod of grass flying. Then he lifted the club again. 'You should listen to your *friend*,' he said to Basil, derision dripping from the word. 'Don't get in the way of this.'

Makarios shifted in the net but Basil didn't dare look at him again. He swallowed, his mouth dry. 'He hasn't hurt anyone.' They were the same words as before, but they were the right ones. It wasn't his fault people didn't listen.

There was a flurry of motion behind him. Basil fell backwards as Makarios stood, and stood, unfolding to his full height. The others paled at the sight of him, and Basil looked up at him and smiled. He'd bought enough time for Makarios to slice through the ropes.

Makarios looked down at him, then at the villagers. Then he stooped, picked Basil up in his arms, and was off.

The wild man ran in great long lopes, eating through distance. They were out of range of the clubs in a heartbeat, and then they were in among the trees, passing thick trunks and gnarled branches.

Makarios ran for half a minute before Basil started battering against him with his arms. He said, hearing the shrillness in his voice, 'Put me down, put me down, put me down,' until Makarios all but dropped him.

Basil crumpled onto the forest floor, more root and moss than soil. Makarios stooped over him. 'I wanted to get us to safety.' He didn't apologise, but he looked wretched.

It had just been fast, and unexpected. 'Ask me first next time.' Basil stood, brushing the dirt from his clothes.

'Yes.' Then Makarios straightened, looking over Basil's shoulder, back through the woods. It was dense and dark in here. They had covered a great distance quickly, but not far enough. 'Can I take your hand?' he asked.

'Yes.'

Makarios took his left hand, the uninjured one. His grip was firm but careful, his nails curled away so they didn't cut. He ran, and Basil stumbled beside him. They rushed through the woods together, faster than anything. No vines entangled Makarios and no roots tripped him. He moved through the trees like a bird through the air.

They ran until Basil's legs ached, but with his hand in Makarios's giant one, he was able to keep up. Makarios didn't outpace him, or leave him behind.

Eventually, Makarios stopped in a little meadow where a great fallen tree had left room for grass to grow, and wildflowers. Big mossy rocks were scattered here and there. Basil sat on a rock and Makarios sat in front of him, so they were eye to eye.

Makarios took his right hand as well. In a low voice he said, 'They hurt you.'

Basil tried to laugh, but it was a choked noise. 'Not like they hurt you.'

'I am well,' Makarios said.

Basil saw there was blood on his mouth. There was blood all over him, matting his hair in dark red clumps. He squeezed his hands tightly. 'Please don't lie. I don't like it.'

Makarios squeezed his hands back. 'I'll tell you this, then,' he said, deep and grave. 'I've had worse before, and recovered.' Basil considered this then nodded.

Makarios smiled at him, the dried blood cracking on his lip. Then he let go of Basil's hands and stood.

'If you wish I can find another town for you to live in, though I can't promise they would be kinder.' Makarios half turned, so he wasn't facing him. 'This forest borders more places than you might think.'

Basil looked down at his hands, flexing them as he tried to think. He should wrap cloth around his cut, or clean moss. Makarios's wounds needed tending, too.

While they had been running, he hadn't even thought of the fact that Makarios was only saving him from the others, not bringing him to live with him here. Now that he had to ask, he was shy. He clasped his hands together.

But Makarios stood, waiting. He gave Basil as much time to think as he needed.

'I don't think you're unreliable,' Basil said.

Makarios turned to him, frowning a little.

Basil twisted his hands. 'I wouldn't leave,' he said. 'I wouldn't leave like she did. If you spun too fast from shadow to light, I wouldn't mind.'

Makarios looked at him. Basil hoped he heard all the

things he wasn't saying.

'Basil,' Makarios said, deep and low in his chest. He knelt in front of him.

Basil gathered his bravery. He'd faced down half his village, after all. He could do this.

As if in a dream he reached out his hand and touched it to Makarios's chin. He moved slowly, ready for him to pull away.

Makarios leaned into his palm, dark eyes fixed on him. Basil looked down. He was still no good at looking a person in the eyes. But he pressed his hand to the side of Makarios's face. He brushed a thumb against his bloodstained mouth.

Makarios kissed his hand, then pulled back. 'I have a house,' he said, then coughed. 'Something like a house, anyway. There's room for you.' He looked at him intently, searching Basil for something. 'I'd like you to stay. If that's what you're asking. I can make room for you.'

'I can make room for you,' Basil repeated, and it felt profound and good. He added, 'If any of the lambs wander into the woods, we can keep them, I think, only two or three, because they were mine. Then I can have wool for clothes.'

Makarios nodded. 'I would force no one into my wildness,' he said, with a note to his voice Basil didn't like.

Now Basil cupped Makarios's face in both hands. 'I like your wildness.' Makarios smiled, and he could feel it against his skin. 'I'm growing a beard,' Basil added, and he didn't have to know why Makarios laughed to like the sound of it.

NICOLE PHILLIPSON

Getaway

Jean had understood that Shawn, her new nephew-in-law, was picking her up from O'Hare soon after her arrival. But half an hour after she landed, her niece Lila had texted saying this would now be impossible. Jean must instead wait alone in Chicago, silvered city of strangers, until the afternoon, catch a bus alone, and then walk a full mile, over the crusted snow, to Shawn's workplace, so that Shawn could drive her home after he clocked off.

Lila hadn't responded to Jean's many subsequent questions – But hadn't they agreed? Wasn't it right that Elgin was only an hour's drive away? So what was the matter? – nor picked up any of her phone calls.

So Jean had spent the day wandering the city streets, careening between resentment and determination. She had come, after all, seeking the truth, and here was the first ill omen.

Chicago, she thought, had deteriorated appallingly over the last fifteen years. When she had last visited – soon after her thirty-sixth birthday – the city had felt bright and new. Light striking wet streets and car hubs, bright triangles of skyscraper in the lake's waves. During her absence it had devolved, somehow, to this world of screaming grates and lonely, swathed people. And the sky was so soupy today that the sun was lost.

Her bus was due to leave in less than half an hour, so she turned in the direction of the nearest CTA station. She passed by a homeless couple giggling under a dirty rainbow blanket, and one of them cried out to her – something she couldn't understand, his breath twisting up in chaotic plumes. Jean walked quickly away. Once she was out of their sight, she removed her right glove and checked Lila's text again.

Rosemont Station 603 to Elgin transport center walk to Shawns auto repair shop Bay no 2. Be careful aunty Jean its icy.

Lila still sounded just the same: in text, on the phone. This was one point of reassurance. Another was the bias of Jean's own mind. Long before she'd found Roland, Jean's best girlfriend, Bethie, had called her Man Hater (intended, of course, to vex her, but she'd half-loved that title), and although even Bethie agreed that Jean had softened considerably since her pre-Roland era, she had still laughed and dismissed Jean's dark suspicions of her nephew-in-law when she voiced them.

The first suspect detail was that Shawn was twelve years Lila's senior, and he had met Lila when she was just twenty. Not two years ago, he had come to the Maryland town where Lila and her family lived to replace the local auto mechanic – a stroke had left the man mute, crying uncontrollably out of one eye. This former mechanic retired to Montana, and Shawn filled that empty space: hulking, ruddy, fervently evangelical.

The second was the period between encounter and marriage. Six months of courting, just six months, and then her niece had been white-veiled.

At the wedding, however, everything had been doused in gold light, and Jean's sister Kay and her daughters had swarmed contentedly around Shawn. He'd danced with all of them. Jean had shaken Shawn's vast hand at the reception and he had clasped her wrist with the other, said he had heard an awful lot about her. Kay had even gotten drunk enough to amble over to her estranged elder sister; she had burbled triumphantly (scathingly) to Jean about how wonderful it was, having three daughters in love and happy. But Jean didn't trust Kay's judgement like she used to.

The wedding was over a year ago now.

Every month, Lila sent Jean pictures and videos from Elgin, Illinois, where Shawn had grown up and where he now owned a small tract of land, which Lila sometimes called 'the farm'. Chickens swarming around her dirty feet, a chubby loaf on the windowsill, and the corn fields, always looming. Shawn wedged into various rusted tractors and diggers, baring his neat little teeth.

'Hello, Shawn,' Jean called into the darkness of Bay 2. 'It's so nice to see you again.'

Shawn lumbered into the frosted parking lot and squinted at Jean. He was even larger than she remembered: his gloved hands seemed three times wider and thicker than Roland's. She pressed her knees together to stop them shaking from the deep cold.

Neither of them advanced towards the other.

'Get in the car,' Shawn said, jerking his thumb behind him to where a four-wheel drive hummed in the garage.

The muscles around Jean's mouth tightened. 'Excuse me?'

'Get in the car,' he said again. 'Driver's seat.'

Then he disappeared back into the garage, into the concrete

cavern beneath the four-wheel drive where he must stand all day, arms craned up, tinkering with car innards.

Jean crossed her arms and did not move. In her head she screeched – to Bethie, to Kay – *do you see? I was right. I was right.* She would not acknowledge such rudeness. She was a guest – family – not to mention that Shawn *knew* she taught biology at Rivermont Collegiate.

Shawn called up to her from his cavern, but his voice reverberated in nonsense layers. She couldn't make head nor tail of it. For a moment she considered just ignoring him entirely – walking over to the door of the reception and waiting silently for him to take her to Lila. But if she did that, she would have to leave the scant protection of the garage, and already the cold was scraping at the exposed skin of her neck and wrists.

So finally, scowling, Jean lifted her suitcase into the back of the car – where crushed tomato juice cans were littered, extruding red dribbles over the fabric – and climbed into the driver's seat. She untangled a grease-stained pair of jeans from the emergency break.

Jean became aware that Shawn was again shouting at her.

'What?' Jean hollered back, and craned her head over to look down at him. But, in the dark hollow beneath the car, the man was wholly invisible.

'Press the four-wheel-drive button.' Shawn was roaring now, and over-enunciating every syllable. '*Press* it, hold it for three seconds, and then release it again.'

There it was: tiny, grey button marked *FW.* She pressed it twice.

'Wait – three – darn – *seconds*,' said Shawn.

Jean's voice had always been strong. Michael, her ex-husband, used to grip her upper arm when they were in public sometimes, shushing her, glancing around apologetically – and he'd wince if she ever accidentally let loose her real laugh, a raucous cackle. So she'd grown steadily quieter for the years they were together.

I could get loud now, Jean thought, and how would you like *that*, sir? But the truth was, she knew, instinctively, the rhythms of altercation. Raising your voice back wouldn't help you. It would feel good in the moment and then you would be somehow punished, and you wouldn't be able to go back to how things were before. And anyway, she wasn't here for herself. She was here for Lila.

Jean straightened her jacket collar and pressed the button.

'Put her in park and turn the engine off,' Shawn called.

From beneath her came a rhythmic *shink* of metal on metal, and all around her the car trembled with Shawn's blows. 'Is the red light off?'

'Still on,' she said, and Shawn grunted. He resurfaced, waved her out of the driver's seat, got in the car, pressed a sequence of buttons, then got out again.

'I've got to finish closing up in here. Drive her to the entrance for me.' He held out the keys. Without thinking Jean extended her hand. Just before he dropped the keys, though, she snatched her hand back.

'No,' she said, and Shawn looked up at her. His pupils in the snow-light gleamed pale.

'I'm sorry,' Jean said, faltering, almost dropping his gaze, 'but my licence expired – seven years ago. You wouldn't want me to crash your car, would you?'

For a moment something seemed to rumble deep within him and then Shawn sighed, lumbered into the four-wheel drive, and started the engine himself.

Since way back, before Jean and Kay had stopped speaking, Lila had been Jean's favourite niece. As a little one, white-blonde and docile. Bending to embrace any animal that came her way. Mouth moving, always, expelling a sweet tangle of thoughts to anybody who would listen: about animals and books and all the things she was learning in school.

In her teens, her conversation had narrowed to a few topics. Lamenting how many pounds she had gained this week and setting out the new method that was sure to melt them off. Entering into inevitable raptures about the latest nondescript boyfriend. And confessing secrets – that her mother had been on the bottle again and shouted at her, calling her stupid and lazy, and so she'd gone out in the pitch dark and put her bare hands in the snow until they hurt so bad she nearly fainted; that she'd yet again spent all her babysitting earnings at the second-hand book store, another stack of romance paperbacks, and Mamma would be mad, but the cover was just so pretty, and just look how lovely his eyes are, Aunty Jean.

None of the boyfriends had stuck around for long, back then. But nonetheless, Jean had slowly transferred her own dreams onto her young niece, who was growing prettier and prettier by the day. Maybe, she had thought, Lila would find it: that soft swathe of romance Jean had imagined as a child. Even if she was a little clumsy with her words. Silly sometimes, even. After all, Lila possessed the essential tools that Jean didn't: a naturally adoring gaze, a propensity to worship. Jean knew it could all go wrong. Lila trusted almost everyone immediately. It was the most dangerous quality a girl could have. But Jean had chosen to hope: someone would come along, one day, who knew how to treasure Lila's large and honest heart.

Shawn drove them down the highway towards Elgin. At first, on both sides of the road, there was just spinning white emptiness. Then a long line of garish American flags fought the gloom, and then they plunged into deep, black forest. Jean peered out at the trees, at the tiny worms of snow on the gossamer branches. A faint path snaked through the woods, and Jean imagined disappearing down it: into the wet damp smells of earth, the creaks of the branches, the desperate calls of the birds.

She thought then of Roland (somehow, he had hardly entered her mind today) and of Fort Lauderdale, where they were scheduled to take their yearly holiday in a week's time. When, a month ago, Jean impulsively booked these flights to Chicago for early January, Roland had been surprised. He said it was not at all like Jean to make such whimsical plans, and added that it would make Jean stressed (meaning it would make Roland stressed) to land back in D.C. on January fourteenth and then to have to depart for Fort Lauderdale the next day. Besides, it was such a waste of money. She really should have planned to visit her niece later in the year, when flights weren't so expensive.

She knew that Roland was right on all counts. He had been very thoughtful in scheduling the trip, partly because Jean hadn't quite been herself recently. She wished he'd asked first, though, whether she actually wanted to go to Fort Lauderdale. He had been asking her other questions over the past few months: eyes watery with anxiety, he had wanted to know if she was becoming depressed, as she didn't seem her chatty self, was growing withdrawn and sometimes, more and more often, he thought she was angry with him, but didn't know why.

Jean had tried to put her feelings on the table for Roland. She told him she didn't know what the matter was with her, only that she needed space just now, and that she was only sad when she thought of her sweet young students, who were so gentle and who had such a difficult world to inherit. And Roland had stared at her feelings sitting there on the table, bewildered and uncomprehending, before retreating. He'd eventually settled on Fort Lauderdale as a watertight solution for Jean's malaise. And perhaps it would be. Warm seas, Roland kept saying. Impossibly warm. We'll swim all day, in the middle of winter. And after all it was very kind of him.

Shawn turned the radio down and mumbled something.

'Pardon?'

''M sorry,' he said. 'For – I was in a bad mood. You know, I'm working flat out lately, we're so darn understaffed. And I guess I felt pretty sorry that I couldn't pick you up and you had to come all that way over the snow.'

'It's no problem at all,' Jean said stiffly.

'You know, I was feeling excited to get to know you better this week.'

'Oh?'

''Cause Lila, she really looks up to you a whole lot. She was, you know, jumping for joy that you were flying out. She sewed new pillowcases for the guest room – specially for you.' He laughed. 'Been waiting a couple weeks for her to patch a hole in some jeans of mine, but this took precedence, I guess.' But he said the last fondly, without a trace of resentment. Jean tried to find it in his eyes and she couldn't.

'Well.' Jean couldn't think what else to say. It was as though she had met one Shawn at the auto mechanic's, and now, here in the car, another one entirely.

All her life she had hurried to make sense of things and package them up. Classis, ordo, familia, genus. Perhaps Kay and Bethie were right, and she was wrong, and Lila had found her happy ending after all. It was a cool, relieving thought.

They drove in silence for a while, but Shawn kept the radio turned down so it was just a staticky murmur. After a short time, he announced they had arrived at the village. It could hardly be called a village; it looked temporary, a smattering of flimsy houses around the highway. At their centre a single, flaky diner with a snow-crowned egg atop. A boy wandered the roadside in yellow shorts, his legs pink-spotted with cold.

Shawn turned on his indicator, then let out a sudden noise, like an aborted groan.

'Ahh. Did Lila say about my firearms?'

'I'm sorry?'

A sigh. 'She said she was gonna. I have firearms in my house.' When he looked at her, his expression was almost nervous, like a schoolboy about to be scolded. Could he be intimidated by her? 'As I like to be in control of my own safety. Lila was worried that'd shake you up or something.'

Jean and Kay hadn't grown up with money, but they'd been well brought up regardless: their nails were always cut neatly to the quick, and their parents had thin, high voices that folded away unseemly emotions. Guns had been shut out from Jean's world in D.C., although she had gradually become aware of how they lay around her, invisible, like fragments of glass suspended in the sea.

Jean imagined a pistol clanging into a black safe, safely locked under the bed.

'Of course it doesn't upset me,' she said, warmly.

Shawn's answering expression was hard to read, but he almost seemed to smile. He turned the car down a side road, and pointed – 'Home,' he said – and there it was: shabby little box, hanging off the curve of the road like it was about to fall right through those miles of whispering corn fields. There was a strange, rusted farm vehicle in the drive, like a tractor with a large metal arm. The car wheels crunched on the grass, and, oh, there was Lila at the front door, in too-big jeans, glancing at them then turning her eyes to the ground. Many new heavinesses slackening her face and body. Oh, honey.

Shawn lumbered up to the house and quickly kissed his wife – not on the mouth or the cheek, but right on the crown of her head, like a child. Then he was gone. Jean was left to tug her own suitcase across the icy grass and up the steps, but she didn't mind too much. She didn't like being babied. The sky was darkening. Jean felt a little unsteady with hunger.

Lila submitted to her aunt's tight hug. Once released, she didn't offer to take Jean's coat, or even show her to her bedroom. She just drifted aimlessly into the kitchen. Jean swallowed a tut, hung her coat over a chair and followed, stepping over three large pots of dirt-crusted potatoes. The kitchen countertops needed a good scrub. Outside, a group of chickens roamed among dying, black eggplants, pecking food scraps out of the snow.

Lila hunched over a bowl of wet potatoes and began hacking at them with a knife. She tumbled into speech as though they were already mid-conversation, telling Jean about the troubles they were having with the washer this week. Something was wrong with the drum. It banged about like it was fit to break, and all the clothes came out sodden, smelling like old damp. Shawn had tried to fix it himself, and it had worked okay for a while but now it banged and rattled even worse than before, and she had to wring all the clothes out by hand if she wanted them to dry at all. She couldn't bear to call in a mechanic because she knew he'd charge so much. Shawn said the problem was that everything was built to fail these days; they did it just to get money out of you.

Jean's throat clicked dryly. 'May I have a glass of water?'

'Oh!' her niece said. 'Yes. Help yourself, Aunty Jean.'

She pointed at a jam jar on the table, spotted with oily fingerprints. Jean cleaned it and filled it at the faucet. Lila was still hacking at potatoes, scattering peel all over the floor, and not even noticing. And, yes, Jean had forgotten this quality in the girl, but maybe it had always been there: some blur that separated Lila from the rest of the world.

'Did you grow these yourself?' Jean said, picking up a potato. Close up, the skin was badly pockmarked.

'Yeah.'

'Well! I'm impressed.'

'Oh, you see those nibbles, though. The critters keep getting 'em,' said her niece. 'Mice, or voles, maybe. And Japanese beetles got my basil and my raspberries the last two years. Cabbage worms got our broccoli last winter, and I heard mustard was the thing for cabbage worms, so I went down to the store and bought a whole bunch of mustard plants, and they were so darn *expensive*, too, and then I came out one morning and the mustard was all crawling with worms, so.' She sagged. 'I don't know what I did wrong.'

'That's all right, honey. You're still learning, is all.'

Jean found a second knife and began to cut potatoes. Lila said they were having biscuits and gravy and mashed potatoes for dinner, but she was also going to cut up a whole pot of potatoes to freeze for later.

They worked together on the potatoes for a long time, with Lila chattering on in a low moan about the decaying framework of the house, about their failed attempts to exterminate the floods of mice, about being frozen in an indifferent winter. Then she broke off, dropped the knife in the sink, and kneaded wildly at her neck.

'What's wrong?'

'Nothing, oh, just – just this back pain. I've had it months.' Lila's other hand was fluttering and fumbling over the dirty counter. 'It goes all the way down here,' she said, pointing to her tailbone.

'That's no good, honey. Have you been to a doctor about it?'

'Also, I've got this tingling pain in my toes that stops me walking much. And this cough.' She coughed to demonstrate, and something within her rattled.

'Lila. *Sweetheart.* Have you been to a doctor about it?'

'A month ago I did. The doctor couldn't find anything.' Again she drooped. 'Doctors don't know anything, Shawn says.'

'And have you told your mother about any of this? Doesn't she worry about you, all the way out here?'

Kay would surely interest herself in her youngest daughter's physical health. She had often bullied Lila and spoken about her poor grades with evident shame, but Jean believed she did at least want the best for her.

'Oh.' Lila put the knife down. 'Well, Aunty Jean, I don't talk so much to Mamma anymore. I guess, because you're – well – I guess no one would have told you anything about it. But we had a fight, about my moving so far away with Shawn, and then my sisters took her side, so – so – I don't speak to them much, anymore. But I'm doing really good. I'm just so lucky to have Shawn here, on my side.'

'Who do you talk to, then?' Jean demanded. She felt she should have called her niece more often, asked her more probing questions. Drawn these truths out of her. The fluttering doubt that had appeared in the car receded, and that low, bitter roar was back: *I knew it, I knew it, I knew it.* 'You got friends out here?'

Lila blinked her grey-blonde lashes. For a second Jean could see the kid she had known – half wild, half the most vulnerable thing in the world.

When Lila was a toddler she'd trotted around with a towel on her head, being a model, batting her eyelashes to make them laugh. She'd scuttle under the table and bark like a dog, begging for treats. When she'd talked to you, sometimes, she was so palpably needy, so full of yearning, that it felt like her small fingernails were scratching at your chest, trying to get your ribcage open.

'The thing is,' Lila said. 'In this neighbourhood, they seem nice at first, like, they're real nice to me at church and all, but then, you know, you ask them over for coffee and they say yes, but they don't ever show, or they all go on a trip down to the city together and forget to ask me, and I see their pictures on Instagram and I ask them to ask me along next time, and they always say they will, and then they always forget.'

Lila got out her phone to find her neighbour's Instagram pictures, but it took such a long time that Jean sighed and took out her own phone. Roland would almost certainly have emailed already, to check she'd made it okay – he always did. There was just one bar of reception, but after a minute or so the email showed up. Dozens of photographs from Roland's morning walk grew over her screen in stuttering lines. Icicles pouring down from neighbours' roofs; a tricycle buried up to its neck in white.

Below the pictures was a long block of text. Roland had a bad day at work yesterday, and he felt his aspirations – to be useful, as meaningful a particle of society as he could be, to live a life of enjoyable variety – were not being fully achieved. He felt, increasingly, that he might have made a mistake in choosing to focus on piping design. Maybe he ought to move firms, after all, so he could work more with liquid engineering, which he was starting to feel was his true passion. Could they talk tonight about all of these thoughts he was having? He missed her already. Jean closed the email. The chickens had dispersed. Her suitcase was still discarded on the floor, beaded with fresh-melted drops.

'I can't get the biscuits right,' said Lila to Shawn over the dinner table. 'They didn't rise, *again*. I'm so sorry, baby.' Jean took a bite of a biscuit, which fell apart and crumbled down her chin.

'We say grace first,' Shawn said abruptly to Jean, who hesitated for a moment then set the biscuit back down. Then: '*Lila*.'

Lila startled and folded her head over her hands, for all the world like she'd done it her whole life, though Jean and Kay had been raised without God, and she knew Kay would never have been so humble as to seek Him out. Shawn must have trained her in this.

'Th – thank you, thank you, Lord,' Lila said, 'for, uh, for the food we're eating today, and thank you for watching over us, and protecting us from all the people who might want to hurt us, and please – please help me to find some better work, more nannying if you can, and please help me to resist temptation whenever I want to eat something bad, because I get – so tempted, you know, and, I know I need to lose some weight and get healthy again, so please help me stay strong and healthy, and yes, please protect my loved ones, thank you, Lord, amen.'

Then Lila lunged for the skillet, heaping great ladlefuls of gravy over her biscuits. She spooned and spooned until it was half emptied, not seeming to notice Shawn's stare, then set it back on the table. Before Jean could reach out herself, Shawn seized the skillet and began scraping at it vehemently.

'Oh, now,' Lila squawked, staring at Shawn, eyes popping in horror, 'now, I've taken too much, look at that. Oh dear, I'm sorry, baby. Shawn, you'd better have some of mine.'

'*No*,' said Shawn, still scraping hard at the skillet.

Lila was cringing in her seat, twisting. 'Oh, please, baby, I'm sorry, you'd better –'

'It's *fine*,' he said, and set the skillet down with a huge bang. Jean retrieved it and scraped out what little was left onto her own plate.

'Oh, well, thank you for understanding, sweetie,' Lila said

to Shawn, then turned to Jean. 'Look at us, each trying so hard to be the nicest.' She said it with complete sincerity.

Over dinner, Lila burbled away to both of them. Shawn was dead-faced. Jean nodded and made hmms and smiled at Lila, until Lila began to look at her more than she looked at her husband. Beneath Lila's chatter – about these new special gluten-free oats she'd found and how good they were for her acidy stomach, how spelt really tasted almost like wheat flour, just healthier – it felt like Lila was rolling on her back like a lost puppy, wanting a scratch, and Jean was reaching out to tenderly rub her belly.

The talk turned back to the land: the crops that kept dying; the unnatural, see-sawing temperatures that had descended upon them, screaming Elgin from too hot to death cold. The homeless, Shawn said, were freezing dead in the Chicago streets this week. Jean thought of the giggly, rainbow-covered couple. Lila sighed, looked out the window, then, seeing something, perked up. She told Jean about the heated water bowl Shawn had rigged up for the chickens.

'He didn't even want to *get* the chickens in the first place! Oh, he moaned and he said he hated them. But after two weeks –'

'*One* week,' said Shawn, smiling, tight-mouthed at his plate.

'One week, he'd fallen in love. Given them all names. Every one of them! And he marches in one day and says, all sad like a little boy, he says, Lila, we can't kill the chickens. They're my *babies*.'

'They *are* my babies,' Shawn said, ducking his chin into his collar.

Jean looked at him, at his lowered eyes, and that flutter of hopeful doubt returned. She *had* to work it out for sure – before the end of the week, she had to get to the bottom of him. Had to know to what extent he was capable of fulfilling those vows he had made: of cherishing, cherishing till death.

After dinner, Jean gathered up all the dishes. The weight of the skillet and plates was more than she had expected, and her arm trembled beneath them. She turned for the kitchen.

'Oh, I wish you'd've been able to come to Christmas or Thanksgiving, Aunty Jean,' Lila burst out, and Jean turned back to her. 'You could've met Shawn's family! The spread they make is amazing, just amazing. The crispiest potatoes – and *three* different kinds of meat. Shawn's mother makes *six* whole pies for Thanksgiving every year!'

'Six!' said Jean, stacked dishes wobbling. 'That poor woman.'

Shawn beat his hand on the table. 'Not six. Seven pies. Seven.' He fixed Jean with his gaze, began counting on his fingers. Apple. Pumpkin. Key lime. Pecan. Strawberry and . . . and rhubarb. And – and –'

'Blueberry? Now, Shawn, wasn't it blueberry?'

'Don't interrupt me,' he said, waving a hand at Lila. He was still twisted to face Jean. Her wrists were aching. She wanted to retreat. Lila shifted silently back and forth on her thighs, looking fervently at her husband.

'Cherry,' Shawn yelled finally. 'Cherry. And – and blackberry.'

Jean nodded at him and smiled. 'Sorry' – why sorry? – 'but I'd just better go now, and get these soaking before the sauce dries up.'

'I'll help,' said Lila, and together they scuttled into the kitchen. Jean shut the door firmly behind them and felt a little better.

After they had finished cleaning, Jean asked Lila if she would show her where she was staying. Lila led her upstairs to their spare room. Two of the walls Lila had painted herself, she explained: they were badly done, turquoise bleeding into the white. But there was a pretty wooden desk, and a green velveteen chair, and on the bed a crocheted, peaches-and-cream blanket.

The next morning Jean again spent with Lila in the kitchen. Shawn slept late – Lila said he always slept late on weekends. It was kind of a shame, Lila said, as she really wished he'd help her more around the house and in the garden while it was still light out, but after all he worked so hard and needed his sleep. Together they peeled endless potatoes, sliced them up and lay them on trays to freeze. Outside, snow fell in hesitant spirals, the flakes making no difference to the hard, dark earth.

Three hours into their work, Lila was still talking. It seemed that she was able to exert even less control over her words now than when she was younger. She was recounting, blow-by-blow, an argument she'd had with her eldest sister a year ago. She then listed every single one of the trinkets she was trying to sell, cataloguing the expenses that kept draining away at their funds, explaining about the baby-sitting work she was advertising for all over town – yet no one had responded to the ads, save the next-door neighbour with eight mad children who hardly paid Lila anything at all.

'You really ought to see a doctor, honey,' Jean broke in, almost without meaning to. Lila looked at her askance. 'I mean like a *therapist*, Lila. This is all far too much to be dealing with on your own.'

Lila said she didn't want to see another doctor, she hadn't liked the last one at all, and anyway it was expensive. Jean almost offered to pay. But she saw how Lila's fists were clenched oddly in her pockets, and she was reminded of Kay. Kay would never accept charity, would never allow her daughters to, either. And yet she could still offer – couldn't she? Now Lila sighed, sucked in her lips and checked her phone. Jean lost courage and copied her.

Roland had again thoroughly documented his morning walk for her: some tangled branches, a dog writhing in the snow, a grimy coffee cup. And he had attached another multi-page diary of his day.

Lila lowed, and rubbed her back, then went upstairs for a nap. A few minutes later, down through the ceiling, there came the mourning high keen of her niece's voice and the rumbling low response of Shawn's. Jean kept on at the potatoes for a few minutes, then she opened Roland's email again, pressed *Reply*.

'Sick of potatoes?' Shawn said. She had not even heard him come down the stairs. To her own surprise, she smiled at him.

'A little,' she answered. He crushed his feet into his shoes without undoing the laces and beckoned, once, for her to follow him outside.

She buttoned her coat and tied her boots, slowly and neatly, before following him. In the yard, new sunlight was uncovering greens and browns in the earth. Shawn showed her round the two sheds, the garage, the winterised blackberries, the chicken run with its electric bowl. He stopped to run his fingertips over the metallic brute in the drive – a 'tractor-digger' he called it – then hauled himself up into it and made the great rusted neck sway up and plummet down. Grinning down at her, showing off.

'Now, when the wife asks me to dig up a new vegetable patch, I don't have to break a sweat, do I?' He bounced proudly in his seat.

'I think you're quite good at finding the efficient way to do things,' Jean called up to him. A soft wind had picked up, bringing scents of wet earth and manure. From here she could see a few of the chickens ambling about with renewed energy. One fluttered her wings; another had laid herself down in the sun.

'You're saying I'm lazy!'

'No,' she said, quickly, but it was all right: his eyes in the fresh light were mellow.

'Come up here, now,' Shawn said, patting the seat beside him. 'Have a go.'

Jean backed away. 'Thank you, but I wouldn't want to smash down a wall of your house.'

He laughed down at her, and she laughed back. She noticed, behind him, the propped-open kitchen window. For some reason, she felt a little embarrassed at the thought Lila might be able to hear her.

'You cold?' he said, dismounting. 'Can you stand it out here a bit longer?'

'Certainly I can,' she said stiffly.

He strode off once more without reply, and after a pause she followed him into the garage. She nearly tripped over an orange cable: cables and power tools were strewn all over the floor. He turned round and held out a tiny belt of golden bullets.

'For you.' In his other hand was a delicate silver pistol.

She shook her head rapidly. 'Oh, no, thank you.'

Shawn sighed, grabbed her hand, and pressed the pistol into it. She opened her mouth to protest, but his hand was still around hers, gripping her wrist tight. It was so large – the largest hand she'd ever seen. Firearms, he'd said in the car. But how many?

'Is it loaded?'

'Of course not. *Don't* put your finger on the trigger,' he said, and she removed her index finger, curled it against her palm. 'Go out and wait by the shed' – he pointed across the yard towards the corn – 'and I'll show you how to load it and shoot. You'll love it, you'll see.'

Jean walked alone with the pistol to the back of the property. Here, beneath the immense, tap-water-blue sky, was a hole-ridden target; up in a tree perched two dull-winged goldfinches. She heard a shout, and turned back. Shawn was stalking across the frozen ground towards her. He was cradling two hunting rifles and a long, gracile machine gun. The automatic reminded her of the pictures she'd seen in the newspaper a week or so ago: those blurred phone photographs of the fifteen-year-old Iowan boy who had gunned down fourteen of his classmates.

Shawn bent down and set all the guns on the ground by Jean's feet.

He picked up the bigger of the two rifles and slung it over his chest. Jean stared down at the automatic until Shawn reached out and took her hands again, curled them gently around the silver pistol. He manipulated her fingers to push a bullet into a chamber.

'See, once you click the cylinder over, you can't turn it back.'

She tried, and she couldn't.

He told her to hold out her hand. She did, and he tipped ice-cold bullets into her palm. They glimmered; they were bright and lovely. The first bullet stuck in the chamber so she had to tip it out again. Her hands were trembling now. He noticed; he laughed at her for it.

'There'll be a real loud bang and a kick-back. Don't be scared,' he said, and to her surprise his voice was soft. He showed her how to hold her wrist taut.

She imagined her eardrums bursting over the earth. 'But – I'll need ear plugs!'

'You'll be *fine*, jeez. Now, listen to me. This is important information. In the case of an attack, you *must always* remember to turn sideways. For a big fella like me' – he demonstrated, turning – 'it don't reduce the target too much.' He looked her up and down, very slow. 'But for a lady like you with such a slender figure, it'll offer some protection.'

She found she was shaken up and not able to moderate herself nearly as well as usual.

'You talk like you're in a war,' she said. 'There are no enemies around here, Shawn.'

'In fact,' he said, 'we're in one of the most dangerous areas in the whole country. I'll bet you didn't know *that*, did you, Miss Teacher? There were three armed invasions this month, right in this neighbourhood. In the case of an aggravated assault, I *will* protect my home.'

And for a moment she could see the intruders moving through the corn, their smoky figures and flashing eyes.

She was still feeling reckless. 'Isn't it a sin to kill?'

'A sin to murder,' he said. 'There's a difference. Protect yourself from evil, and the Lord will forgive. Now, hold the pistol up. And hold your wrist out like I showed you. No, *no*, like *this*.' He positioned her like a doll. 'Now, go on, switch the safety. And shoot.'

She lifted the gun, but her hand was unsteady, and again he could see the shaking and again was laughing at her, so she turned her back on him. Re-aimed. A noise ripped out of the gun, but nothing at all showed on the target. Perhaps the bullet had gone on and hit a tree, or a small bird, far in the distance.

'My goodness,' she said, dropping the gun, rubbing her knuckles. 'My goodness!'

'Pick it up and try again.'

This time, she just clipped the edge of the target. 'That's enough, now,' she said, laughing in her harshest, ugliest way, but Shawn ignored her. He stepped closer to her and, without warning, buried a hand down his pants. Jean flushed, tried to jerk away – but now his hand was free again, and he was only clutching a small handgun.

'I keep this one on me everywhere I go,' he said. 'Sleep with it under my pillow.'

He was standing oddly close. She thought, he's just trying to reassure me.

'There's no safety. You just have to push the front and the back.' He handed it to her.

'No,' she said, 'thank you,' but again he pushed it into her hands. Again she fired; again, only just hit the target. They had scared away the goldfinches and all the chickens. She pictured Lila sucking in her lips, and those endless potatoes. Why had she ever come out, alone, to this awful place? She thought of Roland and his sedative voice. She needed to get back to him.

'Stay here and watch me,' Shawn commanded, taking the handgun and pushing her out of the way.

He can't hurt me while God is watching, she thought. Also, I'm family. Also, she thought, he's happy. The days Michael had been happy, his dark days had seemed to her like half-forgotten dreams.

'Watch,' Shawn said again. He fired the handgun at the target, hit it right in the centre. Then again and again, the same place each time. Then he shoved the handgun back into his underwear, strode over and hoisted up that vast, slender automatic onto his shoulder. There was a seizure of gunfire, and white smoke misted out the muzzle. He tossed the automatic aside and went for the second rifle. He was in a dazed and joyful frenzy; he'd forgotten she was there.

'I think I'll go back inside now,' she said.

He nodded. He wasn't looking at her. 'Take that one back in for me,' he said. He jerked his head at the automatic on the frosted earth, and she didn't move.

'Safety's *on*, d'you hear? Go and put it on the kitchen table.'

The machine gun was as light as a plastic toy in her arms. In the yellow-lit kitchen, Lila was upturning a ceramic bread tin onto a wire rack. The quiet smell of bread floated all around.

'Hello, darling,' Jean said, working to make her voice normal. 'I'm to put this down here.' She rested the machine gun on the table and quickly went up to her room.

That night, beneath the heavy blankets, across the hall from where Shawn and Lila slept, Jean lay very still. She could not stop thinking of Shawn's huge hands on that automatic. But he had still done nothing to overtly suggest he would harm either her or Lila.

The problem, perhaps, was that Michael had misaligned Jean's warning sensors. She was rendered permanently oversensitive – though, really, when you thought about it, Michael had done very little – just some slammed doors and punched walls and, sometimes, threats hissed through teeth, teeth that seemed only just to hold back an unfathomable rage. But nothing like what you heard about.

When she was thirteen, Jean had been walking with her mother in the forest, three miles from their house, and she had tripped over a root and sprained her ankle. Her mother piggybacked her all the way home. In the kitchen, her mother knelt at Jean's feet, unrolled her sock to expose the engorged violet flesh. She swooped tape around the ankle in a figure-eight: criss-cross, loop, up-swing. And Jean's thirteen-year-old trust was absolute – these hands would make her better.

That trust, she saw now, had radiated outwards to encompass her street, her neighbourhood, the whole world perhaps. She had limped around on crutches for four weeks, and she had trusted that the bus driver would wait for her when he saw her hobbling to the bus stop, and he had; she had trusted that other students would hold classroom doors open for her, and they had; and when she dropped her crutch on a busy staircase, stood wobbling and unsteady amid a flood of students, she had trusted that someone would pick it up and return it to her. And they had.

If only she could delineate every incident that had chipped away at that trust – graph the pattern of erosion – but it was impossible to trace a clean line through the murk of her life. All she knew was that she was left like this: fifty-one and hard and afraid.

She remembered how Shawn had looked at her after she fired the gun for the first time. Something wrong in the way his eyes fixed on her, something she could not understand. She thought too of that black handgun, under a pillow, beside Lila's sleepy blonde curls.

She turned on the light and texted Roland, telling him about the guns. It was the first time she had contacted him in the two days since she had left, but she trusted he would answer quickly, because he always did. And almost instantly after her message had sent, he began typing. He had perhaps been sitting up, waiting for her. Needing her. Even from here, she could feel Roland's immense, sucking need.

He's probably got them under the floorboards, Roland answered, and then he was asking her about Fort Lauderdale, telling her about the weather forecast, but she couldn't gather up any excitement at all, and fell asleep thinking of white, drifting smoke.

At breakfast, although she wanted to avert her eyes from Shawn, she instead smiled at him as brightly as she could manage, and at the same time willed him to leave so she could speak to Lila. He had noticed the change in her, maybe, because he kept twisting to talk to her, fixing her with a strange stare. But even as he ignored his wife, Lila looked at him puppy-eyed all through breakfast. Jean ate her dry biscuits as quickly as she could, powered through the dishes alone, then went up to her room and leaned heavily against the door. She told herself that she wouldn't go downstairs again until Shawn had left for work.

Maybe, once he was gone, she and Lila could go for a walk – she could take Lila out to that diner, for a coffee with cream and sugar. She waited a long time but did not hear the front door close. Restless, she decided to shower.

The bathroom door had no lock. The shower walls were dotted with black grease stains, which must be from Shawn. Even with hot water running over her body, Jean shivered at the noises the house made around her: the gutter rattles, the groan of the decaying framework. Lila, downstairs, was now laughing with Shawn. Jean stepped out of the shower, went to her room and sat on the bed. There were still crusts of snow on the ground, over which those fat chickens anxiously moved, their tiny, squished heads bobbing. She sat in her towel until she heard the front door swing shut, and then she pulled on her clothes and went downstairs.

Lila was sitting at the kitchen table, scrawling in a leather diary. She looked up to see Jean, and almost smiled.

'My sinuses are giving me terrible pain today,' she said, and sniffed violently.

All that pain, Jean thought, it's not caused by the body. It's the brain, surely, crying out.

'Have you considered,' she said, 'my darling, that some of this pain might be psychosomatic?'

Lila frowned. 'That's – that's *exactly* what the doctor said. *Psychosomatic*. That's what he said, to me, but he' – Lila glanced out the window at the empty drive – 'he said it was – because of Shawn. He told me to get *rid* of him! I mean – just because I told him Shawn was being a bit – but anyway, it doesn't matter. Shawn's gotten better since then.'

'But has he *really*?' Jean coiled her advice, ready to dispense.

'Oh, yes, *so* much better. We've really – really worked on things. I just think that the doctor shouldn't have given me that advice. He was just supposed to help me with my back, and he didn't help at all. I just don't *know* what the point is, in saying, oh, it's *psychosomatic*, I just don't know how that's going to – to *help* me.' She was getting worked up now, her face bunching. 'Because I'm *never* going to leave Shawn. *Never.*' She looked down, clicked and unclicked her ballpoint. 'Sorry for talking so loud.'

'You don't need to be sorry, honey. You're just telling me how you feel.'

'Yeah,' said Lila uncertainly, staring right at her as if for the first time. She added, 'And how are things with – um, with your partner?'

'Oh, Roland's fine,' said Jean. 'He sent me these pictures, look.'

How nice, to have some physical evidence of one's happiness. See these pictures of snow-blobbed pines? It is proof that I am loved.

'He seems *so*, *so* lovely,' Lila burst out. 'He seems to *really* care for you, Aunty Jean. I'm so, so happy for you.' And one could not miss, now, the faint tone of condescension. 'Do you, you know, think you might *marry* Roland? I don't mean, like, *now*, of course. Just one day.' Nervous, tiptoeing laugh.

'No,' she said. 'I don't think I will.' And for the first time, she understood that this was true.

'But – oh, Aunty Jean, why *not*? You really should think about it, at least. You'd look so *pretty* in a white dress, you're really so, *so* pretty for your age –'

'I don't want to talk about this anymore, thank you.'

Lila dropped her eyes. 'Sorry, Aunty Jean.'

'Anyway, Lila, I've been waiting till we were alone, to talk to you about Shawn.'

'Shawn?' Again they both looked out at the drive. Empty.

'Darling,' she said in a hushed voice, 'I have to ask you. Shawn, he seems – I've noticed sometimes he seems to treat you with' – here she had planned to be tactful, but the words came out of their own accord – 'I mean, *appalling* disrespect. I know it's prying of me, but I have to ask, just for my own peace of mind. When he gets very angry like that, does he ever –'

'Shawn's a good man,' Lila interrupted, a chill in her voice. 'It's *your sister*, actually, who treated me bad, Aunty Jean. Shawn *rescued* me from my old life. You're just making all these judgements, as usual.'

'No, darling.'

'Mamma said you always thought you were – *better* than us. When *you're – you're* the one who couldn't find a man for *years*.'

'I didn't mean to insult you, Lila,' Jean said coldly.

'You always are, though,' said Lila. 'You always act so superior.'

'I'm very sorry I tried to help you, then.' Jean stood up. 'I'll know better than to do so in the future.'

Her niece looked down and did not answer. From this angle she reminded Jean of her sister Kay. The cut of those lashes against the full cheekbones, just the same. Only, Kay had grown thin and brittle after she'd married Dylan. Jean had begged her, just once, to leave him, but Kay had only curled her lip.

It didn't hurt Jean anymore, this severance between herself and her sister. Amputating a whole person ought to leave you bleeding, but instead, each time she had done it – first Kay, and then Michael – it had felt just like she'd papered over a corner of herself that had once been vivid and aching, and turned it into smooth space.

Jean thought suddenly, Roland was right – I should never have come. I have to get out of here today. Somehow get myself back to Chicago, book a hotel for a few nights, and damn the money.

'It's just,' Lila said, and now her voice was softer, younger. 'I don't think I can be like you. I just don't think I'll ever be able to – I'm not strong like you. I wish I – but I'm *not*.'

'All right, darling,' Jean said, patting Lila's hand and squeezing it briefly. 'All right, then. Never mind what I said. I'm a busybody, you know that. Sticking my nose in. Can't shut my trap to save myself.'

And Lila leaned into Jean and threw her arms around her.

Several days later, Jean woke to a silent house. It was her last day in Elgin. She had slept late. Shawn was already at work, and Lila was looking after the neighbour's kids for the morning. Shawn had promised – very kindly – to return during his lunch break, so he could drive Jean to the bus station. Roland had once more messaged Jean photos and another long string of words, which she hardly read. She walked around the house, peering at the photographs of Lila and Shawn on their wedding day, standing in Kay's pin-neat garden.

She remembered her bravado on the flight over: how determined she had been to swoop in, square up with Shawn, see what kind of a man he was. She'd had fantasies, even – if her suspicions proved correct – of rescuing her niece somehow, gathering her up into her arms, saying, come back and stay with me for a while. And of Lila's abject gratitude. And here she was, at the end of her visit: bewildered, small, with no clear answers, afraid but with no concrete basis for her fear. And somehow further away from Lila than ever. She had failed in every way, and worse still, her previous ambitions had vanished and been replaced with the simple desire to escape Elgin and never come back.

She put the pictures down, inspected some bullet casings and an antique cake knife and a rusty old alarm clock, all of which Lila had been painstakingly sanding and polishing to sell online. Under a side table, she found a crate of yellowed books – she recalled how much Lila had loved to read as a child, and indeed some of these were novels Jean had given her years ago: Forsters, Austens.

She went around the house and tidied. She wiped the benches, stacked the dishes, polished the rusted clock until it was shining. The house seemed to press close, walls going slightly convex, ceiling sinking down almost to touch her. And now a harsh, groaning metal sound from outdoors made her look up. Ah – it was only that damned digger, its arm creaking in the wind. Still two hours until Shawn returned. She would go for a walk, then, and soothe these silly nerves of hers.

She opened the back door. She didn't have a key, but she was safe to leave it unlocked – she would be back in a few minutes. She pulled on her boots and knotted them tight. The air burned her nose and throat, but after a time she stopped noticing the feeling. She made for the razed-down fields, dodging pools of melting snow. The further she got from the house, the bigger and warmer her lungs seemed to become. She came upon a grassed-over path that lazed beneath the power lines. No one was here – it was clear both ways, far as you could see. She heaved in a breath, let it out and out till she was empty.

Oh, how would Lila stand it here, day after day?

Jean recalled how, just last month, some young, beautiful girl had been murdered, out walking beneath the power lines in her own neighbourhood. She bent, picked up a stick, and threw it as hard as she could at the frozen river. But it just bounced and skittered away.

She thought of the novels that she, and then Lila, had read when they were young. In their heads they'd both become the girls in fields of violets, those girls with twisted ankles, rescued and carried home in the rain. And, somehow, still, in her fifties, Jean was waiting to turn the page and find violets.

She could not go to Fort Lauderdale with Roland. It was breathtakingly clear, now. She must – when they went out to dinner – this *evening*, it was far too soon – she must explain everything. She checked her phone, looked over his email, wrote a few hesitant sentences. *I've been feeling so lonely. I just think I might need a little space.* She deleted those, tried something less honest. As she wrote she ambled through the snow, on and on, until finally she looked up and around at the unfamiliar surrounds, and then at her wristwatch. It was ten minutes till Shawn was due back. She had gone too far.

She thought, I'll text Shawn to tell him where I am, but when she tried to open the messages application her phone, which had always disliked the cold, shivered and shut down. She tried to warm it against her neck, her stomach, but it was comatose. The only thing left was to go back. But it would take – twenty minutes, to walk back? Thirty? She began to breathe hard. She was going to miss Shawn when he came back. She was going to miss her flight home.

She did not know how much later she reached the house. Shawn's car was not in the driveway, and she stood for a few seconds, staring at that empty space, gormless. Then she heard the sound of wheels on gravel, and turned to see the four-wheel drive. Perhaps he had been hunting her down, speeding about the narrow roads. She waved. He looked away from her, parked the car, and shoved past her into the house.

'I'm so sorry,' she said, following him in. 'I went out for a walk, and I hurt my leg, and –'

'You left the door to my house unlocked.' He did not turn round.

'Oh, dear. I'm sorry. I didn't think about – I'm so sorry for putting your home at risk.'

'Lila called me,' he said. His back still to her.

Then she realised. Lila, of course, was loyal to her husband.

'You come into my house,' he said, turning finally, 'and eat my food, and use up half my internet and take up all this *damn* space, boss my poor wife around. You're smiling at us the whole time. And inside, you hate us.'

'No.'

'You do – I can see it. You've hated me since the moment you arrived here. I know what you're trying to do with my wife. Trying to pull her away from the Lord.'

She was frightened of how little she had managed to conceal from him, how her innermost thoughts had, perhaps, the whole time, been plastered across her face. He slammed the front door, walked up very close to her. She thought of the gun nestled by his balls.

'Please,' she said. 'I'm sorry, I didn't – oh, God. I only want the best for her. I love her. I'll leave, I'll go, I won't bother you again.'

He laughed, seeing where she was looking.

'I scared you, didn't I, the other night?' He patted his crotch, burrowed his fingers down into the fabric there and pulled out his weapon. Casually flicked it around in his hand.

'Put that away.'

Slowly, with a curious, childlike expression, Shawn raised the gun and aimed it at Jean's throat.

She screamed, a gargling confused animal sorrow, and sank to her knees. The muzzle followed her down. On Shawn's face was a blank and pure delight. She looked at her dear hands and thought, *He won't, won't –*

– a noise cracked and all the atoms of existence spun away.

He was laughing. He had pointed the muzzle away from her at the last minute, and instead – she turned – hit the crate of books. Dark puncture in the side. She watched him slide the gun, with ease, back beside his cock. Her crotch was slightly warm. She had wet herself.

And then he was looking down at her, no longer laughing. Suddenly she could see how she looked to him, saw herself just as he saw her. And she hated herself more than she ever had.

'Just a little joke,' he said, and winked down at her. 'Don't get yourself in a tizzy, now. Get up.'

She couldn't get up. 'I'll give you money. To pay for the internet. And the food.' Wiping her mouth. 'Let me get my wallet from my bag and I'll give you some money. To say sorry.'

He nodded.

She gave him sixty, all she had in cash. He pocketed it. 'Go and get your things,' he said.

She went up to her room. Perhaps she had missed the train; she didn't know the time anymore. She would get on any moving thing that would take her away. She gathered her belongings, confused and slow. She wondered if he would turn the crate of books to hide the hole from Lila, or if he wouldn't bother.

Probably Lila hated her now, too. She thought of calling Roland when she got to the station, but she didn't want him. She wanted her mother's soft hands forty years ago.

Jean got in the car beside Shawn. The handgun was still right there in his pants. The only barrier between him and her, between him and Lila, was that cruel, smoky God of his, plunging all who failed Him into hellfire. Oh, Lila. Let him be frightened enough.

'I'll send you a present. Not wine, of course. Chocolate, maybe.' It was words like snow, words to smother and erase.

'Lila needs to lose weight.' He was resting just his fingertips on the steering wheel. 'No chocolate.'

'Oh, of *course* not.' They were driving into the bus station now. 'I'll think of something else, something very healthy, and send that to you both,' she babbled, and when he parked she tumbled out of the car, fetched her suitcase herself. Shawn said nothing when she bade him goodbye. Right as she slammed the door, the car began to lurch away. She sat hunched over herself, made herself watch until it was gone.

Slowly, she began to feel the blissful shock of wind against her jaw. She breathed in and out, but her mind jittered and vibrated. To calm it, she shook out an old, stale dream: Roland drawing a glittering wedding ring from his sleeve, the ringing chorus of glasses around them. How everyone would look and see that she was loved. That she was capable of being loved.

She walked restlessly up and down alongside the road. *Baby*, Lila had called him. *Baby*.

Jean stood on a metal-grate platform at Rosemont CTA, waiting for her train to the airport. Beneath the grate, a twenty-foot drop. The cold blowing from all directions, up through the holes and down from the sky, chilling her blood. Beneath all the stamping feet, the grate shuddered desperately. Jean's scarf, however she arranged it, was yanked again and again away from her chest, and the cold slapped the triangle of exposed skin on her collarbone. The skin there felt thinned-out, fragile.

And now there was an old, familiar whiteness in her head, a whiteness that she was endlessly spinning out into, alone. And without Roland, she saw, she would just slide into that whiteness, on and on. His long emails, his droning, self-absorbed stories: they were all necessary. They tied her down.

She realised she had completely forgotten to check the time. Desperately she pulled out her phone and tried to switch it on. Over the journey it had warmed in her pocket, and it shook back into life. She still had twenty minutes left before she had to be at the airport.

She deleted the email she had composed to Roland, explaining all the things that were wrong. She texted, instead, *I'm really looking forward to seeing you.* The whiteness receded, but stayed close by, waiting. She looked away from it and opened Solitaire.

Her underwear was still damp. She needed to change it, or certainly other people on the plane would notice the smell. The train would be here in two minutes, but she could always catch the next one. She went downstairs and approached a coffee cart with a cashier who wouldn't meet her eye.

'Where are the bathrooms?'

'There aren't any,' the cashier said with a sigh. Jean checked her phone again. Well, she had time. There must be a bathroom somewhere in this area. She just had to make sure to be at the airport within twenty minutes. She wandered out of the station and down a narrow, snow-swept sidewalk by the droning highway.

She eventually saw two figures far ahead of her, and hurried to catch them up, tiptoeing over the iced concrete. It was a dark-haired woman with a young boy grasping her arm, tilting her slightly towards him.

'Please,' Jean said. 'I'm sorry, but do you know where I can find a bathroom?'

'Oh,' said the woman, and smiled at her. '*Yes*, actually! We just came from the conference centre, my husband's in there. There are bathrooms in there! Just walk on that way and go in, no one will mind.'

She pointed, and Jean nodded at her and stumbled on.

She entered the conference centre and was enveloped in a rumble of men. Men in suits and denim jackets, in ties and short-sleeved shirts, old and young. She waded through them to the women's bathroom.

There was no one else in here. She was finally alone.

She splashed water on her face, stared at her red-cracked eyes in the stained mirror. Wanted to stay, to catch her breath. But she had to get back to the station.

She walked out into the conference centre and was buffeted by streams of bodies. She crawled for the wall and huddled against it, looked around. She couldn't see the place where she had come in. She checked her phone, checked it again. Impossible. More than thirty minutes had passed since she had left the station. It couldn't be true. If it were true, she would be lost. She would miss the flight back home; she'd be stuck here, and how would she get to Fort Lauderdale then? She wandered back into the throng, walked in dazed circles, looking for the exit.

EMMA SIDNAM

Backwaters

1878

They stand in the garden. His hands easily remove the stalk from one thick stem of corn. He's hungry, smells it, wishes he could inhale it. Instead, he lets it drop into a woven sack. Over the sack, he catches her eye and smiles. She glows in the afternoon sunlight, her skin almost translucent.

His name is Ken. Hers is Kate. Two names still fresh as a plucked apple. They chose them for being easy to pronounce and remember but still sometimes forget to respond when called by them.

'Ken.' The name tastes exciting, the flavour of new.

'Kate.' The name feels like a toy that he's bought; it makes her yet more attractive to him. It has been eight and a half months, and to him her hands feel roughened, her once delicate skin now seems to blink in and out with the light. They don't grumble, though. His hands, too, are mountains and valleys where once there had been plain field. It hurts them to intertwine their fingers, to kiss with chapped lips, but the pain seems to capture their shared months. The sting when they kiss makes them feel that maybe they're working towards belonging to this land.

They are eternal strangers in the streets, and for that reason the streets feel endless. If they're hurrying down the streets they can feel hard eyes following them. It's like they're famous, only they're not adored. In fact, the opposite is true – sometimes, children follow them, hissing and spitting like cats. They can't always understand the words, but they understand the meaning perfectly.

English is a hazy new skin, one in which the veins are barely in focus. She's the one pushing both of them to learn.

'Practise with me,' she says. 'Repeat after me.'

He never wants to. He doesn't like English. Speaking it makes him feel like he's stupid, which he isn't.

He's heard things about language, about how pronunciation can taste like new life, and he knows it's achievable, but a large part of him doesn't want to try. He's already a master in his mother tongue. But he made the decision to take a new life, and here he is, and he doesn't regret it.

He's more than grateful that she's by his side. The thought of the gravel of her voice is enough to make him breathless somewhere in his upper body. Her eyes are a deep earth brown, but reflective like moons. You can see his face reflected in her irises, that's how often he looks at her.

The garden is where they spend their whole lives. They have become part of the landscape. You could let your eyes wander over rows of corn, cabbages, white turnips, potatoes, cauliflowers, peas – and blink and miss them entirely. In their plain brown clothes and hats, they truly are one with the earth.

Normally the women aren't allowed to come. It stands

against all reason in a world where a married woman's role is to be a good daughter-in-law, a good mother.

He couldn't go without her.

'It's not possible,' he'd said. 'It's impossible.'

But then heaven intervened.

He looks at her and thanks the moon, stars and skies for her presence. She's the only thing that keeps him rooted in himself.

As a child, he was always quiet.

He was the fifth of six brothers. There was already too much noise in the small house, too many opinions in the muddy air. Kai-Ming, the sixth brother, was famously loud, making it easy to forget Ken, although he was known as Kaineng then.

'Stop staring,' Kai-Ge, fourth brother, said one afternoon. 'You're distracting me.'

Kai-Ge was playing some kind of marble game with the other older brothers in the courtyard. Kaineng had been watching, sitting on the dirt under the solitary tree. The space was small, but he still felt far away, watching four of his brothers roll marbles at each other, the glass sending speckles of dirt through the air.

'Why don't you go hang out with your friends?' said Kai-shek, third brother.

'Does he have any?' asked Kaiyang, second brother, laughing.

'Don't think so,' said Kai-Shek.

'Must be difficult,' said Kai-Ge, 'being that quiet.'

'Must be difficult,' said Kaiyang, 'being that stupid.'

'Leave him be,' said Kai-xi, the eldest, but he didn't repeat himself when the others kept talking.

Eventually Kaineng ran away, the house a ripple behind him.

Thanks to his brothers, Kaineng learned how to be by himself.

Although he longed for closeness with his mother, she had little time for individual affections. She was overburdened as it was. With six children, it was assumed that the older would care for the younger, while she, the mother, routinely rubbed her wrists raw at an iron washboard, prepared hot meals three times a day, kept the house and her sons respectable, and helped out at the fields when necessary.

Kaineng would wander the edges of the fields, drawing in the dirt with a stick. In the mornings, the dew combined with the mud and manure created a throat-clogging stench. To Kaineng, it was the smell of home.

He felt comfortable outside in the starry sheen of morning mist. Much more so than in his house, which was small and old, with walls of mudbrick and a ribbed grey roof. For all its smallness, he never felt warm in that three-roomed house where he shared a room with two of his brothers.

There was no bathroom, only a tiny shelter and stinking hole in the courtyard. He was terrified of darkness and held on throughout the night if he needed to go. He would never have asked a brother to accompany him outside.

All the village doors faced south, but Kaineng didn't feel he had good fortune with the family he'd been given, even though his family was better off than most because their father owned a small but fertile piece of land. There was always food on the table – rice noodles, turnip cakes, yam – though never enough for leftovers. Perhaps once every two weeks they even enjoyed the luxury of meat, perhaps a piece of char siu pork or spare ribs with preserved plum.

They were still poor, and they couldn't afford luxuries like toys, holidays or daily baths. But when his mother cooked meat, the little rooms filled with fragrant smoke and all of them would breathe deep, inhaling the scent of wealth.

School should have been Kaineng's refuge, but he never made friends. If someone asked him a question he would answer politely, but quickly, ending the conversation with a ducked head and a side glance.

At dinner, his parents didn't talk much. His father, a large and quiet man, was usually exhausted from a day in the fields. He would smile as he listened to his sons, five of them squabbling loudly to be heard over the others, and he would laugh and nod in the right places, not noticing that one boy remained speechless.

His mother, also exhausted, usually felt that her work was done by the time dinner was on the table. She tuned out most of what her sons said, while inwardly longing for the escape of sleep.

He told himself he didn't mind. He had two imaginary friends, Dog and Sky, and they were all he needed. Dog was the bigger personality of the two, the one who always teased Kaineng about not having any real friends.

'I don't want any,' he'd tell Dog. Dog was a bit like his older brothers, except, thank heavens, on his side. Sometimes, Dog would cross the line and then Kaineng would wish that he'd never invented him.

'Go away,' he'd tell Dog, but Dog always stayed.

Sky was the supportive one, but he too wanted Kaineng to root himself in reality.

'You can do this,' he'd say, placing an invisible hand on Kaineng's shoulder. 'Give it a go.'

Whenever the other kids were playing a game, or even just sitting together and talking, Sky would encourage Kaineng to join in. As if it were that easy.

'Go up and say hi.'

'Go and ask if you can play too.'

'You should make some real friends. We might not be around forever.'

Deep down, perhaps Kaineng felt lonely. But if he did, he wasn't aware of it. His imaginary friends may not have been flesh and blood, but they sprang up around him whenever he needed them, felt as real as the pain of tripping over in the street. Dog and Sky had their own distinct personalities, and as Kaineng grew up, so did they.

By the age of eight, he was spending most of his plentiful free time making up stories which he'd recite to Dog and Sky. Apart from his house chores, helping out in his father's field, and school – in which he learned only rudimentary reading, writing and mathematics – his time was his own. Sometimes he would wander the streets, talking to Dog and Sky, or watching the movements of the clouds.

He set himself the task of learning how to write at a high level, and stole some of the limited paper from school and carefully wrote his feelings and stories across it. He borrowed every book that the school possessed (which wasn't many) and read them over and over again, until he knew the Four Books and the Five Classics by heart.

Every student could recite ancient lyric poetry, but most of the students didn't think much of the actual verses. Kaineng absorbed them. 'Thoughts in the Silent Night' by Li Bai was his favourite. He felt the words, the reflections of moonlight, the frost on the ground.

At the age of eleven he started writing poems on the stolen paper. He wrote about the village, the smell of the earth in the mornings, the whisper of mist as it fell. He wrote about feeling small and alone, about how he wanted to see a bigger world.

Deep down, he knew it was unlikely. He knew little about the wider world and couldn't find out more because none of his teachers had ever left the village and none of the schoolbooks talked about other countries. Although a few men had scraped together enough money to leave, sailing to foreign lands to make their fortunes elsewhere, none had yet returned. For all anyone knew, those men were dead in the ocean.

Around his early teens, Kaineng sometimes felt cold, like when the rain soaked through his thin clothing. Especially when his older brothers were laughing together, he felt cold.

The truth, and he acknowledged it, was that nobody would miss him if he disappeared. They would wonder about him, perhaps look for him for a day or two, but their lives would not be changed. And that's what he wanted, on a very basic level. To matter to someone.

She, on the other hand, had a soul full of laughter, a palm full of light. Her mother had prayed for another child, prayed to some unknown god, never truly believing in anything but praying to everything.

And when Kate – or Qiu, as she was then known – was born, it was summer rain after drought. The year before Qiu, her mother had lost an unborn child.

Qiu was loved by everybody – her parents and three older sisters, her grandparents, neighbours, friends, and even a boy in her village with whom she'd never spoken. She was bright and vivacious, talked easily and with everyone. If she had been born in a different place and time, her life might have opened to her like a budding flower. As it was, and especially without education, Qiu's life lay ahead of her straight as the dusty path next to the town's river. Her prewritten destiny was an inside life, a life where dreams never moved beyond a closed eyelid or were perhaps never formed at all. She was to be a good woman, selfless in her regard for her parents, husband, in-laws. She was to be gentle, humble, softly spoken.

And Qiu didn't resent any of this. If she had tasted and then lost the opportunity to take wing, perhaps she would have led her whole life crippled by bitterness. But she hadn't, and in fact had never known anyone to deviate from the path. She couldn't regret what she hadn't known, and her reality was no landslide. It was the way it was.

She was also luckier than most. She was a peasant girl in a family without sons. Her parents needed their daughters to help out in the fields, so her feet remained free.

She was wanted with the kind of love that can rise in a mother like a tsunami. Qiu had carefully prepared food, a hand through her hair, meticulous attention when she was sick. She was disciplined to become her parents' approximation of a good person, taught to give light where it was needed.

Often, she would sit beside her mother while she cooked, the food warming the air and diffusing clouds of oyster sauce and spring onions. Whatever her mother made, she would let Qiu try a spoonful before it reached the table.

Qiu loved her mother, loved her home.

But she was also tired of shining. Tired of being the lampstand on the tabletop. She sometimes felt like a shadow but there was no space in the house for darkness.

She did sometimes dream, and her dreams were small but still impossible. She wanted a life where there was room to change colour. A glimmer of independence. She secretly hoped that one day she could own and run a small shop which sold daily, mundane things: vegetables, rice, soy sauce. A shop which would be her own tiny kingdom, and would mean she would never need to rely on a husband or anybody else. Of course, she could never have that in her village, so she imagined leaving. Leaving to somewhere. Packing up her life in a shoulder bag and walking away, letting the village shrink to ash in her wake. She imagined walking into a blood sky, her legs streaks of tireless air, and never once looking back.

They finally spoke to each other on a Wednesday afternoon, seventeen years after being born in near-identical houses three streets apart. They had both finished their respective chores and daily activities and they were down by the river. She was with a group of girls dangling their legs in the water, their bony feet swaying like minnows in the freshwater. He was alone, as always. He was aware that she was there. He was always aware of her. Whenever she shared a space with him, she was like a moth flitting around his mind. He took great care not to look at her too much, desperately hoped she'd never look at him directly.

Inside his head, she was an eidolon. He didn't want his vision of her to shatter.

He remembered the first time she entered his mind, his life. They were four, maybe five, and he was wandering the streets under the pretence that he was playing. Dog and Sky were with him, and the three of them were in amiable silence. It was a blustery day, the wind whipping past in angry blows. His arms were cold.

'Maybe we should go inside,' said Sky.

'I don't want to,' Kaineng replied, and Sky didn't say anything else after that.

The gusts grew each minute, rolling along the grey paving stones with force. The street was nearly empty and the gates to the ramshackle houses were all shut.

With the next gust of wind came a mother and daughter. They were hand in hand, running in the same direction as the weather which seemed to carry them, that's how fast they were moving. Kaineng barely noticed the mother, but he saw her and even in that tiny pocket of time he recognised a glow in her. He couldn't say what made her different from all the other children in the village, just that there was some quality about her, and even at the age of four or five he recognised it. His chest sang.

'You like her, don't you?' said Dog.

He could only nod.

'You'll never have the guts to talk to her.'

He nodded again.

Later, he told her all of this.

'I'd never even noticed you,' she'd said. 'That day at the river was the first time I laid eyes on you and we'd lived in the same village our whole lives. How strange is that.'

He hadn't been surprised. He'd have known if she had ever noticed him. The first time her gaze met his, that day at the river, he'd been transfixed.

'Hi,' she'd said, 'what's your name?'

It took all his strength to stammer out a coherent reply.

The community is small but nuclear. In this particular town there are only twelve men, and that means the twelve are intimately and vitally connected, held together by invisible strands weaving a blood tapestry of Saturday night gatherings. Daily silenced by strange words and shame, they are always eager to talk. Words flow thick as rivers after rain; they talk and talk and talk. They talk about loved ones back home, the younger siblings, nephews and nieces they won't see grow up. They talk about the gardens changing with the seasons, the vibrancy of growing pumpkins, the tallness of tomato stems. They don't talk about their homesickness or loneliness. Instead, they fill those spaces with observations about the strength of the wind, the threat of storm.

Ken didn't want to go to the gatherings at first, but Kate pressured him.

'You need this. You have to go.'

And then one day a group of four of them appeared at his door, almost aggressively pulling him into the road, so the choice was made.

The others peppered him with questions, and bit by bit they began to get an idea of him. They realised that despite his quietness, there's a depth to him – and a darkness too. He's a lake, they've realised, and nobody quite knows what he contains.

The men live a little outside the main town area, in huts surrounding the gardens. The huts are built of kerosene tins, packing cases – anything they can find. The roofs are mostly thrown together from rice or flour sacks, and because they're built quickly, they often leak. With water dripping off the frayed edges of the sacks, the roofs seem to be crying.

The mudbrick houses back in China seem luxurious by comparison. At least there the rooms were filled with years of living, the tiny things that make a house a home. At least there the men had women.

It's not like they didn't choose to come. Nobody forced them bodily onto the ships, set them adrift, sent them thousands of days away. But they're not here to stay, and most of them don't want to.

Four of the twelve men grow fruit and vegetables; the other eight work in the mines each day with hopeful golden axes. Working in the mines means dust. It means straining legs and knotty necks, stubby fingernails, faces screwed up in concentration.

Peter, like Ken, is a gardener. He's got a crooked smile and a perfectly round head, like an onion. And he's likeable. He's always making everyone laugh, has the sort of energy that seems to revive both the plants and the people around him. When everyone else is dragging their iron toes, he's dancing like a mountain bear.

Daniel works in the gold fields. A short man with a thinning crown, he isn't handsome but for his eyes. His eyes are a strange, hazy amber.

'It's from dreaming of gold,' he joked when he first met Ken.

Ken half believed him. The eyes, on first impression, seemed slightly inhuman.

Daniel is somewhere in between Peter and Ken in terms of how much he talks. He's not as quiet as Ken, but he's no showman either.

Every Saturday they each bring a dish to Peter's shack, and every Saturday the shoddy kitchen is a vibrant cacophony of spices and scents, steam and the crackle of oil. Cooking gives many of them a feeling of closeness to their mothers. They remember watching food being prepared with all the precision of eternity. Ken, who didn't cook at all before leaving China, finds an enormous satisfaction in transforming raw earth into delicate broths, strings of noodles. He sprinkles chives into round bowls of rice, and it feels like the echo behind a waterfall, like an idea of the past he didn't have. He can't fully recreate the flavours of his mother's food. And although he looks for them, he can't find the same herbs, the same wines, the same salty preserved plums.

But it's still something. It's more than edible. And now, when he eats foreign-grown food made by his own hands, with people who want him around, it's a childhood of sorts.

While he cooks, he watches Kate pace the room. She hovers in the shadows, sometimes meets his gaze while his fingers press dumplings into shells, strip the leaves from thin green stems.

Sometimes they play traditional music or mah-jong, but mostly they let their full belly laughter waft above it all. And they drink. Some of them long for the sweet haze of spirits, but they deny themselves such a pleasure, fearing that the white locals will see them as debauchers.

For now, they focus on their families and the possibilities painted with gold and green. Seven days a week, from dawn until midnight, colours border their shrunken worlds.

When the gardeners are at work, they look like moving scarecrows. Clad in baggy brown, the cloth hanging loose at their wrists and necks, they seem to stump their way down the rows of carrots, the lines of runner beans.

They grow everything, and the quality of their produce is good. That, at least, is appreciated. But the men themselves, trundling their wheelbarrows into town, they're a spectacle. Particularly when it rains, because half of them put sacking on their heads and on their feet. They don't buy rain jackets, because they don't want to take a single dollar away from their families back home.

It's difficult to talk about how it feels to be an alien, far from family, friends, and the known. And they don't try. There's no point, and these are men who have long accepted that life is hard. Men who are simply trying for better in the ways that have opened to them.

But there's a rare hour, when the night has dried up, the plates are empty, and the room is quiet. It's an hour when they all fall silent, each one alone in his thoughts, thoughts almost certainly of loved ones. The men look upwards, as if stargazing.

Sometimes, they cry. And if Ken is feeling open enough – perhaps once every lunar month – he'll read a poem. Then they all cry, definitely.

It's a Saturday night, and Peter and Daniel and Ken are sitting on the front porch of Peter's shack. Everyone else has left. Ken still doesn't consider himself close to the two men, but they've asked him to join them, have a smoke with them, so he does. He's beginning to open up a little bit, one cell at a time, and the others embrace every piece of himself that he shares.

On this night, the sky is clear like the glint of a knife.

'It feels like we've been here forever.' Peter leans forward, his elbows on his knees, and his eyes gleam. There's something in his tone that the others haven't heard before.

'Are you complaining?' asks Daniel. 'That doesn't seem like you.'

'I'm not complaining,' Peter says, 'It's just . . .'

'What?'

His shoulders slacken slightly. 'Nothing.' His sigh sounds lost.

'No, what did you want to say?' Ken speaks quietly, but inside he's a spiderweb.

'It's nothing.' His voice is stronger now, so Ken doesn't persist. But he knows what Peter means.

Some of them share shacks, but Ken built his own. He wanted privacy for him and Kate. Their small sanctuary is the only place where he can exhale.

Kate always deflects when he asks her whether she's happy with their new life, always smiles a resolute smile and rests her palms on his shoulders.

'It doesn't even matter,' she says. 'Life isn't about being happy, anyway.'

'It matters to me,' he says. His hands flutter to her waist.

'Well, we're here to work hard. That's what's important right now.'

The room is a galaxy, and they are the only moving parts.

'I can think of a few other things.'

She's still standing, hands on his shoulders, and something runs through his body, gluing his feet to the swept dirt.

'As can I,' she says, and she meets his gaze.

And then he doesn't have to think about how he feels, he can just look at her.

'I love you.' He traces the edges of her ear with the back of a fingernail.

She blurs in and out of his line of sight as he tries not to falls asleep, his eyelids heavy, his head in her lap. She's reading to him and her voice is a waltz.

In the early days, back in China, he would eye every boy who looked her way and would tighten his grip on her hand.

'That's too hard,' she said once, prying his fingers from hers. There were little dents on her skin.

He was aghast, apologetic. He looked at his hands, disgusted by the fact that he could hurt her. Although he'd always wanted her from afar, he'd never felt that he deserved her – and here was proof.

Back then, they would walk around the Guangzhou village, where they traced the edges of the houses and the working fields. The village streets had always seemed grey and drab to Kaineng. Streets lined with grey paving stones, small brown brick houses, open drain rivers with little stone bridges for people to walk over. Yet when Qiu walked them, these streets became beautiful. Kaineng would watch her approach and time would slow.

At nights, they went to the grassy copse on the side of the hill and sat for hours beneath the pale moon, trading stories and wishes and feelings. His: new and explosive and burning.

Hers: swooping and bright as blood.

His poems changed in tone, because she filled up his frame of vision. He wrote short poems, love poems. She wanted him to read them out loud to her, but he felt shy. Instead he would press the paper into her hands before the two of them parted.

She touched him first.

He had spent weeks locked in himself, locked in nightmares about lips, butterflies, water – he had no idea what to do. Eventually, one afternoon, she asked him.

'Don't you want to kiss me?'

He hadn't known how to respond, but then she leaned over and kissed him, and it was done. From there it was easy. Even in the cool of autumn they were never cold. They seemed to fit together perfectly.

She loved his hands in her hair, the way he gently raked his fingers through it as if she were leaves.

He loved her touch but craved her voice.

Kaineng hadn't realised how starved he'd been before. He'd never really talked to anyone like this. Their conversations seemed to both stop and accelerate seconds and hours – these were his first times truly expressing himself out loud.

'What do you think about this?' she would say, in relation to some idea she had had.

'I don't know,' was his automatic response.

'Then think about it,' she'd reply.

She always pushed him to think something concrete, and it made him reflect on who he was. Did he prefer this animal or that one? Sweet foods or salty? Night or day?

He was used to expressing his feelings in writing. He was safe behind a shroud of metaphor. But he wasn't used to confidently stating his opinions or preferences, or even deciding what he liked and didn't like. Nobody had ever cared to know.

As he found himself answering each of Qiu's questions, he found that he had a lot to say.

She told him her fantasy of leaving.

He, too, used to have that dream, although only before he met her. To sail, sail, burning the backwater into blood – to never, ever think of coming back. He used to imagine faraway lands, exotic trees with branches spiralling in every direction, strangers smiling and extending their hands. But now, he didn't want any of that. He hated imagining any future that didn't include her.

'I would never want to leave,' he said. 'I'm perfectly happy right here.'

'Don't tell me you haven't thought about leaving,' she said. 'You have to have imagined some alternative life somewhere.'

'Not really,' he said. 'I've never even thought about it. The stories I make up are never about me, they're always about other people.'

'Have you ever made up a story about me?'

He was grateful she'd changed the subject.

'Do you want me to?'

'You didn't answer the question.'

'Millions. Before you talked to me, I had this story where I went up to you and talked to you.'

'How did that story end?'

'How do you think?'

Dinners with her family were slightly tense. He was desperate for them to approve of him, yet he was painfully unused to speaking in the presence of anyone but her. Considering that most marriages were arranged, Qiu's parents were particularly wary of him. If they didn't deem him suitable, he would be out the door and a replacement found at lightning speed.

Her sisters, at least, tried to make him feel comfortable.

They asked him questions about himself which he attempted to answer, but he would stare haplessly at his hands.

'Which of your brothers do you think you're the closest to?' they once asked.

'Well, I'm not really close to any of them,' he said, before trailing off.

'His older brothers aren't that nice,' Qiu interjected. He looked at her gratefully. 'And his youngest brother is always with his friends, so Kaineng doesn't see him much either.'

In the end, Qiu's sisters didn't dislike Kaineng, but they didn't love him either. They found it strange that their sister would be with someone like him. She was like a spring bubbling out of the earth, but he seemed like the earth itself.

Kaineng's own family didn't seem to notice or care that his life had so drastically changed. He was out all day and half the nights, but that didn't make a difference to the noise levels of the house. Kaineng realised that he'd never once felt at home in his house. Sometimes when he was with Qiu, he imagined his family as a pair of eyes bearing down on him, judging him.

But he also remembered the time he had a conversation with his second brother, Kaiyang, by the river. Kaiyang was with a group of friends. They were jostling each other and laughing, and then he spotted Kaineng and Qiu. Quite accidentally, Kaineng caught his eye and the next moment Kaiyang was with them.

'Kaineng,' he said. 'When did you get a girlfriend?'

'A while back,' was all that Kaineng could say.

'Hello,' Qiu said. Her voice was a delicate balance between polite and wary.

'Lovely to meet you,' Kaiyang said, and to Kaineng's surprise, he bowed to Qiu in the proper way. 'Be good to my brother, okay?'

And then, before turning and returning to his friends, he

gave Kaineng a friendly smack on the shoulder. 'See you later.'

Afterwards, they dissected that brief conversation together.

'He seemed nice,' said Qiu. She was surprised because Kaineng had painted such a black vision of his family. She'd believed him, but she was also aware that his interactions with most people weren't quite normal.

'He's not the worst one,' said Kaineng. 'Kai-Ge is the one who gets the most pleasure out of making fun of me.'

'You would think he'd have grown out of it.'

'You would think so.'

Privately, Qiu wondered if perhaps Kaineng's loneliness as a child was like a dark film over his family. She feared that even if his brothers changed, he would never allow them into his life.

'When was the last time Kaiyang made fun of you?'

He was surprised that he had to think about it. He cast his mind over the previous weeks – and all he could think about was Qiu. She'd become the centre of his days. The mundane chores and physical labour faded from his memory the moment they happened. He realised that he hadn't had any incidents with any of his brothers for weeks, maybe even months.

The thought of his brothers still brought him an almost physical discomfort, but none of it was new.

'It's been a while.'

'Don't you think you should try to talk to them?'

'*I* was never the cruel one. All I ever wanted was to be left alone but they always pursued me.'

But he was beginning to doubt it. His memories had congealed into a thick marrow and he could no longer separate emotions from fact. Did his shyness come from the way he had been treated, or was he treated that way because of his shyness?

The next time he saw Kaiyang, he offered up a half smile – and it was something he had to flay his heart to reach.

'You always were overdramatic,' said Qiu, when he told her this. 'And what did he do?'

'Well, he smiled back.'

It was the beginning of something.

From then on, Kaineng and Kaiyang smiled at each other, and soon that progressed to short conversations, and then Kaiyang began attempting to talk to his brother for longer.

He wanted to talk about their versions of childhood, their different experiences under the same roof. But he soon found that it was difficult, because while Kaiyang had good memories, Kaineng remembered his early years as a run-on sentence of trauma. Then he became reluctant, again, to talk. How much light does it take to cut through mud?

Qiu kept encouraging him to open up. 'I know it's hard, but a family is always worth fighting for,' she said. 'They're the only ones who can never leave you.'

She found Kaineng's family situation depressing. Although she'd never lacked friends, she believed that family was the most important thing in the world.

'They were never *with* me,' he said. 'My family isn't like yours. My family was never family. I've never had anybody to rely on except myself. And now you.'

'But don't you want a real family?'

'Maybe one day. With you. But now? Isn't it too late? We're all grown up.'

'It's only too late if you say it is. It's not too late for you and Kaiyang, if you only speak to him.'

One evening, when the light hit the ground in streaks of peach, Kaineng was walking with Kaiyang. They were talking about how Kaiyang had left home two years ago, at the age of nineteen, to live with their mother's sister and her family. 'Going away made me realise a few things,' he said.

Their cousins lived only a few streets over. But it was the

furthest that anyone from the family had gone before – the periphery of what was possible. Kaiyang had gone after a fight with Kai-xi had turned explosive and then violent, both of them with blood blooming from their palms.

Their parents had packed him up and sent him to the cousins' house. He ended up staying with them a few months, and in that time the family hardly saw him. During the days, he worked in their uncle's field instead of their father's field, and when he had free time, he spent it with their cousins instead of with them.

'I didn't think it would be any different,' he said to Kaineng. 'They're still family, after all. But I was surprised. Aunty and Uncle were different from Mother and Father, and the way they spoke to our cousins . . . the energy was different. And it made me think about my own family. I thought a lot about our parents, each of our brothers . . .'

He paused, and he looked pained. He was twenty-one now, an adult, but to Kaineng he looked very young.

'You were the one I thought the most about, because you're the one I know the least. And I realised that it was largely my own fault that I don't know you. And the realisation wasn't an easy one, but I realised that I don't want to be that kind of brother to you anymore. So, I suppose I wanted to apologise to you. For all the times I laughed at you with the others, or purposefully left you out.'

Kaineng didn't know what to say.

'You don't have to say anything,' Kaiyang said quickly, 'or even forgive me. But I want you to know that I really am sorry.'

'He really is sorry,' Kaineng said. 'I think that's true.'

'You should forgive him,' said Qiu. It was an easy answer for her.

'Why should I forgive him?' Once Kaineng had found his words, they wouldn't stop gushing out. 'A childhood of torment, and one apology? Why should I forgive him?'

But even as the words escaped him like steam, he was calming down. Qiu sensed it as well; she let his anger spend itself, and even as he continued to talk his words meant less and less to him. Finally, he was done.

'Well?'

'I suppose I could forgive Kaiyang. But only him.'

'We're only talking about Kaiyang.'

'But we're still never going to be close. He'll never even get close to what I feel for you.'

'I know.'

She never told him, but she felt the pressure of his words – and she carried it.

A few months into the relationship, when the rose-tinted period – at least for her – was beginning to fade, she began to realise what she represented in his life.

It terrified her. The things he said were so grand – she was his sun and moon and heavens, flowers and mountain and sky. At first, she had been floored by his romantic nature, by the way that he talked. She mirrored him, said everything back – was excited to experiment with new ways to express her feelings for him, which were indeed expansive.

She thought of him as a dark well which nobody had ever thought to climb down but that had come to contain god-breathed gold, ghost-kissed moonlight. She liked that she had to press him to get an answer to anything, and she felt a certain pride in being the only one who really knew him.

She began to feel out of her depth. She couldn't float anymore, and the waves came faster.

One day, they were in their copse on the side of the hill and she shivered.

He drew her closer into him, rubbed her arms to warm her, but it wasn't enough.

'I think I need to go back,' she said.

'Do you want my jacket? I don't need it.'

His skin was ice and she knew he was lying, that he didn't want her to go.

'I should get back to my family,' she said, and she could feel his sigh.

'I wish I didn't have to share you with anyone,' he said.

'That's not how the world is.' She extricated herself from him. And then she left, although she kissed him goodbye.

'We need to do something fun.'

Peter stands and announces this on a sweaty Tuesday afternoon when the New Zealand sun is baking through the pathetic scatter of clouds and the men are squatting and smoking, taking a ten-minute break from the endless cabbages.

'What do you mean?' Josh, the tallest in the group, squints up at Peter, using a dirty hand to shade his eyes.

'What do I mean by *fun*?' Peter throws his hands up. 'My point exactly! All we do is work, morning until evening. Every. Single. Day. Seven days a week.'

The men all stare at Peter as if his head is an onion that has started peeling itself.

'Well, that's why we're here,' says one of the men, and the others nod like clockwork.

But Peter persists, and Ken recognises an iron will in him.

'Come on, there has to be more to life than work. The pumpkins will survive, the gold will stay in the ground. We can't work every day, or we'll die. We've come hundreds and thousands of miles away from our homes to a beautiful country that we haven't even seen because we're so busy working. Why did we even come here?'

In the end, five of them agree to take a single day off.

The day they choose is Saturday. That way they can go back to Peter's shack for their regular dinner. They agree to cook in advance, and bring the food to the shack early Saturday morning. After that they'll go for a hike to explore the mountains and beaches. It won't be warm, but they all swear to swim if the others do, get their blood running for the fun of it.

Ken arrives early on Saturday morning, carrying a bowl of noodles. Peter lets him in with a grin.

'Looking forward to the day?'

Ken nods and ducks into the shack. Peter thumps him affectionately on the back as he passes.

Inside, it's quiet and still dark. The shadows hang from the ceiling like curtains, and Ken thinks how strange it is to be at Peter's place so early in the day, with the warmth and glow of the night dinners melted away with the morning. He sits awkwardly on a chair as Peter prances about the room, singing traditional Chinese songs and slapping his hands on every flat surface.

Ken wonders where Peter found his enthusiasm for life, his smiles which he throws around cheerfully as he fills and stows sacks of tomatoes. He thinks about his own childhood, wondering if the answer lies there. He thinks about his brothers and parents, about how they're surely living as if he never existed. The same way they always lived, really. He thinks about Kaiyang and all that could have been.

How he feels – it's a colour, a greyish purple that travels irregularly through his body, passing molecules in and out of his lungs as he breathes.

But Peter breaks him from his reverie. He grabs Ken's hands and pulls him to his feet to dance. Despite himself, Ken smiles.

It's a good day. The air's neither too warm nor cold, and the light breeze keeps their spirits high. They climb up to a cliff and Ken feels a stirring within, a feeling like evaporation. He can't remember the last time he did something just for pleasure.

The five men walk noisily – laughing, singing, racing each other up particularly rocky sections. At one point, Ken and Peter race onwards and Ken trips over, sprawling over rock.

'Are you okay?' Peter runs to him.

'I'm fine.' Miraculously, he's unhurt. He laughs, loudly. He picks himself up and looks behind them, only then realising how far they've come.

'Look at that!' He feels his voice go wild with delight. They all look, all marvel at the sight of blue. The lake is spread beneath them, smooth and incredible. They take a moment to drink in the sight. The sun is high in the sky. They throw their shoulders back and charge upwards.

Later that night, they sit on the steps. Somehow the conversation turns to the future, to family. Ken looks at his hands.

Some of the men discuss visiting China in six years or so, to find a wife, start a family. They will then leave her there, sending her a letter and New Zealand dollars every few months, providing for her in the best way possible.

Those who already have wives talk about visiting home every eight years or so, before going back to retire. Nobody wants to die here.

'What would it do to our souls, to be stranded here?'

'Forget our souls, what about our bones?'

Ken sends money home to his family, but he has no intention of ever visiting, sees no reason to awaken old ghosts.

Even when he's apart from her, he imagines her.

'What are you thinking about?' Peter asks him as they sit there on the steps.

'Nothing,' he replies, and Peter doesn't push, for which Ken is grateful.

Now, he sees her sitting on the edge of the bed, feet flat on the floor. Whenever he imagines her, she's not moving. She's still as a closed window, glowing against a slightly hazy image of home. Sometimes she sings, with a new voice like a perfectly played viola, and the sound reverberates in his chest like tears. She looks directly at him.

'I love you,' she says. Her lips are the only part of her body that moves.

'I love you more,' he says, or tries to say, because his own apparition cannot speak. But he feels it with all his heart.

She is his beginning and end, his first and last.

Qiu began to think about leaving him, but the thought of his reaction scared her.

She wasn't afraid he'd hurt her, more that he would hurt himself. He wouldn't threaten her, or beg, but he would break. Perhaps irreparably. And she didn't want to see that happen. She did love him. But she was also growing up, and he was too. She wanted new experiences, new people to fall in love with, more than life in her village could offer her. She would never leave the middle of her nowhere village – she knew that with a depressing certainty – but she could leave him.

Once, when they were walking and the night was closing in with frost, she tried to tell him how she felt.

She couldn't.

Then, when she was still feeling that it was impossible, whispers began to gather in the town.

For a few years, families had been scraping together funds to send men overseas. Overpopulation meant that village officials were encouraging people to leave, and men had sailed off across the globe in search of fortune or simply to escape poverty. And, although it took a while for the news to reach them, there was a new gold hill now. An island next to the old gold hill, Australia. Another place, another opportunity. New Zealand.

Apart from the rare exception, women would not have the opportunity for another fifty years. But here was an opening for men to earn more, to support their families more comfortably.

Here was a chance for change.

Usually, men would rely on relatives who'd gone before to vouch for them, to help their acceptance into foreign lands. Leaving was affordable, just barely.

'The family could probably raise the money for you to go,' Kaiyang said. He ran a hand through his hair, a habit that Kaineng now recognised.

'You think they would do that for me?'

'A son overseas is good for the whole family,' he said. 'And anyway, as the eldest, Kai-xi has to take over the fields here. My bad knee means I can't go abroad. And Kai-Ge has no interest in going away.'

His brother didn't mention Kai-shek, because he had fallen ill and passed away the previous year. His shadow hung over the brothers even now.

'You're also the dreamer in the family. You're the one who's always wanted to leave.'

'I never said that.'

'You didn't have to.'

*

'Wouldn't you be afraid to go somewhere you'd never heard of before?' Kaineng asked Kaiyang a few weeks later.

He felt guilty, wanting to forget about the possibility of leaving but unable to forget it.

Kaineng didn't mention any of his thoughts to Qiu. He knew she would encourage him to follow his heart as far as possible. But she was his heart. He couldn't leave her.

'I mean, I suppose so,' said Kaiyang. 'But it's also a once-in-a-lifetime opportunity. What do you have here? A life of working the fields, maybe marrying someone, and then working until you die.'

He gestured around them, and Kaineng followed his gaze to the same streets, the same river, the same rundown houses they'd walked past their entire lives. Their village was isolated and tiny. It was several days away from the harbour where the ships set sail.

'Work in New Zealand would probably be even harder.'

'But it would be an *adventure*. No one in our family has ever left this village. Most of us will die without ever having left it. Could you really pass up on the opportunity for a completely different life? For a girl?'

'Not just any girl,' Kaineng said, but his insides were roiling. It was hard to see past Qiu, to imagine that he wasn't with her, that he was a completely free man, but when he let himself, even for a second, did he want to go to New Zealand?

The answer whispered to him like a sin.

The day everything changed, it was cloudy and freezing with a screaming gale. The air was thick with wary hopes and dreams, the indignance of those who had no hope at all.

Kaineng dressed slowly that day – thinking about maybe leaving, mourning his certainty that he never would.

Because there was no choice really. Every time he imagined some beautiful New Zealand, he imagined Qiu, alone, in the same village she'd always been in – and his fantasies all evaporated on the spot.

A life without her was no life at all, no matter where it was.

On that day, Qiu woke up feeling like she had been punched.

She felt like a million moths were engaged in a kind of war dance inside her. But as she dressed, she felt a certain stillness as well – and she carried that stillness with her as she left her house to meet him.

She walked with her head in the clouds, and she wasn't looking in front of her, although her hands hugged her arms in an attempt to warm them.

There are a few differing versions of what happened next, each one a river torrent, a burst of agony like hope every time he imagined it.

She is walking, her head in the sky, when the rush of blood in her veins meets some invisible wall, and pressure builds, like the wind that gathers before a storm. It's true she's young, but bodies are mazes and sometimes people get lost in them. Qiu loses herself here. Her vision goes dark, her feet slip out from under her, her head rolls forwards.

And then the tree falls.

She is walking, beautiful and chosen. It is at this moment that they decide to take her, reaching invisibly through the atmosphere, hands shaped as great buffets of air, pushing with devastating force. The hands caress her soul as it tilts upwards into the universe, lit up with gold from within, higher, higher, higher.

Her body is below her, in a bark grave.

She is walking when the ground opens before her as her life might have done and she sinks into a different reality. She finds herself on a mountain, stretching in peaks and crags in all directions with ice and flowers, and her futureless village seems suddenly far away. There are stairs in front of her, and she knows they lead somewhere wonderful.

'Do you want to climb the stairs?'

The voice is both powerful and soothing, and she nods. It's the easiest yes she's ever given. She tries to move her feet, but they are rooted in the dirt.

'To stay, you have to leave your body in the other world. Do you wish to do that? Say yes or no.'

'Yes.'

She's walking upwards and upwards, mountains curling around her like prayers while her body is left behind, beneath a tree.

She is walking. She doesn't see the falling tree; the tree doesn't see her.

Kaineng was down by the river the next day when Kaiyang ran up to him. He was gasping, his hands on his knees.

'Everyone's been looking for you,' he said.

'Where else would I be?'

'You have to come with me.'

Kaineng let himself be led, saw no point in resisting, no point in anything. Once he got to his own backyard, he stopped, uncertain what was happening.

His father was there. He touched Kaineng's shoulders, for the first time in what felt like forever.

'We heard what happened and we're terribly sorry for your loss,' he said. He paused. 'But there is some consolation. The extended family have discussed it, and, if you want it, will lend you your passage to New Zealand. We know you were wanting to go.'

There was a moment when the ground seemed to dance, as if it were trying to get away. Then the shockwaves subsided just as suddenly.

'You can go to New Zealand,' Kaiyang was saying. 'If you want it, it's all arranged.'

Kaineng could hardly speak but Kaiyang kept talking.

'Listen. You have to go. This is your one shot. You're fading here. And what's left for you here anyway? A family you hardly speak to?' His voice wasn't bitter, but it cut through Kaineng and he felt like he was bleeding.

The waves hit once again, but this time when they subsided, he was left stranded. Kaiyang was right. There was nothing left for him in the village, no one left that he loved. He'd never really had a family, and the friendliness from Kaiyang was nothing more than that – they were friends at most. The one person he'd ever loved represented his entire world, and without her, the streets and houses here meant nothing.

'Let this be the one thing your family does for you,' said Kaiyang. And then he said, 'She would have wanted it.'

Kaineng's face shone like a private sun. It changed colour, and so did his vision – black, red, white, green. Gold.

The pathway ahead was clear. He started the ascent.

'What's your name?'

He gave his new name, the one he'd chosen from a list a few days before.

'Ken,' he said. 'What's yours?'

He received an answer but promptly forgot it. He didn't care. He had no idea what he was doing, where he was going. Instead of talking to the other men, he stared at the waves and imagined himself sinking to the bottom of the sea.

Once, he had imagined walking across the sea, his feet

burning with the sunset, disappearing into a new life where nobody knew him.

Now he imagined his body drifting listless and cold along the ocean floor. He imagined a million tiny fish nibbling his toes, working their way up until he was no more.

He imagined the cold like frissons of fire, burning him up, numbing his heart until it beat a slow, slow dance, and then silence.

I could throw myself off, he thought.

I could throw myself off.

The days passed like the waves. He spent all his time at the helm of the boat, his eyes filled with sea.

The days passed and nothing seemed to change except the shades of sky. The same worried faces appeared to ask him how he was doing. Always the same answer.

'Please, leave me alone,' he said, and they did. They didn't really exist – not in his heart – so it didn't matter if he offended them. Maybe later he would end up living with some of them, befriending them even, but that didn't matter now.

Day after day after day.

That's how it is with long voyages. The boat is a mother, sweetly singing towards sleep.

God, he wished he could sleep. Nights were worse than days.

One morning rose with a metallic sheen. The sun was a single bright note, and when it shone on the water it swelled into a chorus. It was beautiful, and he didn't care at all. Against the soft light, he felt like a stone.

I could throw myself off, he thought. Perhaps he said it aloud.

'But why?' A voice cut through the silence.

'Look at me.' A voice like a viola.

He looked up, and shock like life pulsed through him.

A hand gripped his wrist.

Gold, rivers, sun. Heaven, trees, flowers.

'Why do you look so sad? I'm here.'

When New Zealand came into view, they'd been sailing forever. At least a month. The winds had risen and fallen on them, storms had whipped their blood, and everybody was sore, salty and wrung out. Dry land had become a dream, and New Zealand a mirage.

Arrival day carried a light breeze, patchy white, a pale blue sky like the number eight. They arrived early in the morning. In fact, he was still asleep when he heard the shout.

'Land!'

The rising voices, excitement like swells of tide. He sat up and almost instantly arrived at the helm of the ship, staring out at the mounds of distant green, strips of golden white. He looked forward. This was it.

His first step felt surreal. He double-tapped his foot on the plank, and that made everything more solid. He reached his hand back for Kate, who took it, then stepped out after him.

JACK BARROWMAN

The Dead City

> In this world there are three types of people. Those who follow the Great Pattern, those who stay Still, and those who walk a Pattern of their own. The last kind think themselves free, but even a self-made routine is, in the end, a cage.
> —*Notes on the Long Walk* by Weaver Crow of the Central Parish

'See how the colour drains?' Kanta Yoru tilted the bowl, and there was a rustle as the nurses craned to watch the thick greenish sludge turn incrementally greyer under Yoru's stir.

'You want it here, a faded green like dying coriander.' She lifted the pot from the flame and placed it on the straw mat beside the invalid's white bed. She took a spoonful of the liquid, and poured a line around his mouth.

'Not too much, and wait, see?' The sludge began to ripple, as if the man's skin was bringing it to boil. Yoru drew her long pipe, and lit it with a length of straw. She hunkered down and blew smoke over the man's face. As the coils caught the rippling slime they revealed little silhouettes. Tiny, near-invisible creatures, plump and many-limbed like gently wriggling shell-less slaters. They swarmed from the man's mouth and nose and fell upon Yoru's concoction, and the nurses cooed and gasped.

'These are minor spirits, parasites really, that get into rivers now and again.' As Yoru spoke one of the feasting wisps shuddered, and burst. The slime was both a grand feast and a deadly poison.

'Keep applying this until there are none left. Then apply again. They multiply quick so you can't be sure they're gone until you're sure you're sure, if that makes sense.' Yoru looked past the nurses, down the long and full tent. Over fifty afflicted, the caravan hamstrung; not something that could be afforded when every hour idled along the Pattern could spell doom. 'Be careful where you get your water from. Avoid streams with no moss.'

'We've drawn from the river many times in the past. This has never happened.'

'Spirits follow Patterns too, ma'am. Perhaps next time you come through they'll have moved on. In a way you were lucky. There are hungrier things out here.'

'Indeed.' The Head stood. 'Thank you, weaver. I hope you too are careful, on your own journey.'

Yoru smiled. 'I'm not a weaver.'

The Head led Yoru out of the stuffy quarantine tent and into the tepid day. She waved a hand north, along the many columns of tents that clung to the mossy and root-bitten mud of the lumpy hillside, a spare clearing in the dense rainforest, at the top of which sat an ancient longhouse under tall wet trees. This was a typical clan of the Great Pattern, of perhaps two thousand people, going about their day with unease – dropped shoulders, subdued greetings. They had plenty of time to nurse their ill back to health, but Yoru couldn't fault them for their anxiety.

She bid the nurses farewell, and headed up the freshly trodden track to the longhouse where the clan's Lord had the luxury of staying. Down by the stream, workers were gathering the reeds she'd identified. The Lord had been resistant, wondering how a cure could come from the same stream that had poisoned them, until Yoru explained that the vast majority of curses could be lifted by something in the area in which the curse occurred, since the spirits were usually just mistaking people – or something within them – for food. For now her old ways were reliable, but they wouldn't last. The Pattern spread.

Further down the stream a group of old women were washing clothes. Yoru watched as tendrils of bubbly oil trailed into the shadowy forest. By the longhouse was a tilled field where men were planting new potatoes to replace the ones they'd just harvested, an offering to the next caravan after receiving their own from the one before. They were pulling weeds as they went, and piling them by the rim of the forest. Yoru could see the undergrowth there changed, thinned by tall and prolific coastal grass. The trees were hunched by foreign vines. A boar made of shadowy smoke watched her from a hollow. Mountainous bush rose above, dense, green, wet from recent rain and from itself, its own dampness that oozed from every leaf and trunk. Thinner trees on the wind side, and the Lord waiting for Yoru on the longhouse porch, his clothes simple, the air around him a little warmer, brighter. A Lord who understood the burdens of his position and had lived accordingly, so his Touch was only a gentle one.

Haru was on his lap, and she looked up brightly as Yoru came near. Haru the plump brown chicken, with a fluffy white head.

'Nice bird, this,' said the Lord. 'I never thought chickens could be pets. Not in the cuddly way.'

'Anything can be, if you treat it right.'

The Lord smiled towards the medicine tent. 'All sorted?'

Yoru nodded. 'She knows what to do. Your folk can be on the road again tomorrow.' Haru clucked again, and the Lord let the chicken down. She shimmied over to Yoru, who bent to ruffle her feathers.

'Tomorrow, eh?'

Yoru heard the pause in his tone. 'Another problem?'

The Lord nodded towards the mossy longhouse. 'Traveller from ahead. A bit of an odd one. He says there's trouble afoot.'

The longhouse was dim, lit by small windows and a few lanterns that rested on the big stump that took up most of the floor: the remains of an ancient tree, its flesh scoured with a map of the Great Pattern, edited over the years by many different clans. The elders sat around it, arguing as elders often did. Kids were playing in the warmth near the hearth.

An old man whose neck wobbled worse than Haru's seemed particularly upset. 'We've never gotten along with the Blue Goat! Stinky mouthbreathers.'

'The Blue Goat is better than the Black Guard,' responded a woman with leathery skin. 'Or worse yet, Stillness.'

'We may have to accept a few weeks of Stillness in order to survive,' the Lord announced as he entered with Yoru in tow. In his presence, the others calmed. 'Survival comes first.'

The traveller wasn't taking part in the discussions, nor did he react to the Lord's aura. He stood out to Yoru immediately. His outline was blurred, catching the light wrongly, as if he'd been sucked from another moment in time and spat into this one. The others in the longhouse seemed relatively indifferent to the traveller. They could not see his aura.

Yoru saw the boar again. It ran over the wall like a shadow

cast by a swinging lantern, and the traveller followed it with his eyes.

Nobody else in the room knew it was there.

'Stillness isn't so bad,' the Lord continued. 'There's no Walk due for a month. We could wait out the war.'

'War?' said Yoru. The word jolted her back to reality and she slipped into a seat opposite the traveller. She couldn't see his eyes beneath his wide-brimmed black hat, but he had a long bushy beard and reddish skin.

'Blue Goat and some coastal upstarts,' the chicken man sneered. 'Stirring for months, rumour is the time's come.'

'That's annoying.'

'You're more than welcome to stay with us,' said the Lord.

'No, thank you. I have to keep moving.'

The traveller finally looked up. He had a tendinous neck that sprouted from a rough grey wool tunic, and small, dark eyes. There were a sword and an arquebus resting on the wall behind him, both with light brown handles engraved with figures of a jaguar. They were out of his reach, so he was trusting, or confident, or stupid. 'The Duke's Spring Citadel is near, so the first battles won't be starting too far from now. It'll be impossible to travel north, and south you'll hit the Walk before you reach any longhouse.' His eyes again tracked the boar, and then he grinned at Yoru. 'You might be stuck here.'

'We could always turn around, go south.' The leathery woman spoke with a thoughtful frown. 'Divert early, join the Blue Goat's tail. They'd let us pass off-season if we explained the situation. It means going off the path –'

'The forest is too deep,' said the Lord, darkly.

Yoru avoided the traveller's stare and studied the map carved into the ancient stump. She didn't care about the intricacies of Pattern society, so the wattled elder's retort faded into the background. The map was large, the country unfolded like a tanning hide, the ringed Pattern a faded scar. Fishable lakes, drinkable rivers, good hunting spots, the widening Walks, notations on wildlife and titles for the domains of the Still; mountains were an afterthought, and there were no recorded spirits or secrets. There were only roads on this map. A world that demanded you look only in the direction that you travelled.

'What about here?' Yoru pointed at a branched trail a little further into the forest. A later editor had scratched much of it out, and the name, but further through the woods the road emerged again, exactly in the direction Yoru had planned to head.

A quiet fell, and the elders looked at each other.

'Not an option,' said the Lord.

'Why not?'

The silence was thick, until the Lord said, 'These valleys were once the Kingdom of Kaowai. Down that road stood the city itself.'

'And now?'

'Dead. Fallen to a Walk.'

Yoru nodded. *Superstitious migrants avoid them, but they're safe enough if you're careful.* She stood. 'Thank you for your hospitality.'

The elders stared at her in disbelief. The traveller's eyebrows were raised.

'You don't mean to go that way?'

'I have to keep moving,' she said.

The forest towered over the stream and the road. Moss-choked branches, ferns and vine-laden canopy, all the same sodden, deep green. The birds were green too, or off-brown. The air was wet, but cold, and the bush was so dense that only the path was traversable. Turning off was as likely to cause death from exposure as the snowiest mountain.

Kanta Yoru walked along the grassy edge of a wide road. She wore red, and carried a straw cabinet on her back. The toad sat on top, inside its locked polished bowl, peering at the world with black eyes as it was jostled in fresh, parasite-free water. In Yoru's left hand was her red umbrella, and under her right arm was Haru. They'd left camp with haste. Yoru wanted to reach the dead city before nightfall so she could find a ruin intact enough to sleep in. Thankfully, the traveller had stayed behind. Men who could see her boar were always a bother, always trying to save her.

The forest was staggeringly full of life. Living trees had no visible bark beneath jackets of moss and creepers. Dead trees were misshapen fungal habitats for smaller plants and coursing colonies of insects. She passed a waterfall, and the rocks below were so green they could have been plants themselves. Spirits were everywhere, geometric lights floating in the few spaces between the leaves, bouncing off the surface of the crystal water, emerging from rotten trunks in great bright plumes, hovering over ferns like sunlit dust. Pencil-thin white eels swam in patterns in the stream amongst the pale wriggling slaters that had infested the migrants. Yoru saw great birds in the trees, their shadows on the leaves moving independent of their physical bodies. Birdsong was at once loud and not there at all, and made her sleepy and calm. She saw no mammals, not even the broken brush or scoured trunks to suggest that any lived there. This was an oasis in the rainforest, free of boars and bears and monkeys, belonging to the moss and the birds alone. A deep forest, the Lord had said. He'd been right.

The shadow boar walked the surface of the stream, a proud jagged blackness against the indomitable green. With each step the water spirits gathered beneath its hooves, like eels swarming to a scrap of meat. Sudden water lilies of white light that glowed upwards through the boar and revealed the thinness of its smoke. But as the minor spirits touched the boar they were consumed, and with each Yoru felt a sparkle in herself, a rush of energy, as if she too was eating. She thought of the Walk, of the hordes of ghosts that followed the same Pattern they followed in life, each nomadic clan of the continent trailed by its own hungry ancestors.

She remembered seeing the Pattern fail, ghosts swarming living bodies, their silent feasting.

Soon she saw another shadow, following her. It slipped behind a bush, but it was too late.

'Are you going to be polite and say hello?' Yoru called.

A figure emerged. The traveller, his sword sheathed and his arquebus on his back, but his shoulders a little tense. 'Hello.'

'You know only creeps follow women through the woods. You're not giving a great impression.'

'We're both creeps here.' The traveller grinned, gap teeth in cracked lips. 'Kanta Yoru.'

'You're a fan?'

'How could I not be? You are the Lady Night, ageless and undefeatable, a legend of the Pattern.'

'I am? I mean, night is fine, I suppose, but I don't really have a preference.'

'You joke. But the signs are all there! You must be her, Kanta Yoru, a medicine woman accompanied by a black toad, a chicken and a formless shadow. Although' – the traveller squinted at the boar on the water – 'it looks a lot like a person.'

'Does it?'

'I am known as Guada the Jaguar. I am from far away, and just like you I have never been defeated in combat. A hundred duels, a hundred victories, always hoping one day to meet my match, the Lady Night, the greatest of them all. And now the

Pattern has brought me to her feet.'

'I'm not going to fight you.'

Guada's smile drooped at the corners. 'But you are the Lady Night.'

Yoru knew what kind of person this was. Most ended up as food for the Parish. She had encountered plenty; they were all the same. She turned to go.

Guada said nothing, but after a few minutes Yoru looked back and saw that he was still following her.

'Seriously?'

'I have been dreaming of this day, waiting, hoping, honing my skills.' Guada had a very serious frown as he said all this. Yoru felt a little sorry for him. 'Why don't you fight me? Just try it. Give it a go. One little fight.'

'I don't want to.'

'Ah. And there is no honour in a non-consensual duel.' He nodded gravely, apparently coming to terms with her decision.

'Why not go north? There's good fighting there. A war, wasn't it? I bet you'd like that.'

'Battles lack the particular tactical nuance of duels. One cannot express oneself in quite the same way when one is amidst the flailing and the screaming. Besides, I didn't mention this to the migrants, but I saw a band of weavers up the way. Six including a mature one, poking around, asking for directions. If I'm right then they have designs on this Dead City of ours.'

Weavers? Damn. 'It's not "ours". We're not a team.'

'Well, the place that I'm following you to.' Guada jogged up alongside her, grinning again. 'And you wouldn't want to go alone against six weavers. I know I wouldn't. There would be inordinate flailing.'

'I'd prefer to avoid them entirely.'

'Suits me.'

'Go away,' Yoru sped up.

Guada's gear clanked as he did the same. 'Cute chicken, by the way.'

The Kaowai road was wide and overgrown. The trees had long ago been carved with curly folk wards, now vague shapes in the moss.

The afternoon was deep when the forest thinned.

'It's not far,' Guada said.

'You've been there before?'

'I have a good sense of direction.'

And he did – or he was lying about having been there – because within minutes they rounded a bend and found the walls. Tall, old granite, big enough to block any view of the city bar a glimpse at a tall and distant keep. The stone was entirely bare, despite the wetness of the encroaching forest. Bare and dry.

'It's quiet,' said Guada. Indeed, the only sounds Yoru could hear came from the forest behind them, while the city was a towering silence, as if she was deaf to the world in front of her. She noticed the barred gate was covered in tags of warning and spiritual suppression. *Beware. No entry. The city is dead. The city is quiet.* A few feet in front of the walls there was a ring of protection. Animal bones, hair, wooden figures carved in the same style as the trail markers. The moss and grass ended abruptly at the barrier, and the earth beyond was bare and cracked as if suffering a vile drought. It was the same all along the walls, the city the forest were two different worlds. The barrier must have surrounded the entire place.

The air on Yoru's face felt cold and dry, as if she'd opened a long-shut cellar.

'Dead,' said Guada.

'The ring's still whole. Has nobody come by? Is it just

the isolation that's preserved this place? Or are people more superstitious than I like to think?' Yoru watched the boar step past her, check the barrier for breaks and find none. 'We're not getting in here.'

Guada turned east. 'Let's look this way.'

Yoru went west.

Guada chuckled. 'Thought so.'

'Thought what?'

'Nothing.'

They moved west around the walls. The ground past the road was overgrown and hard-going, but they agreed that breaking the barrier wasn't a good idea until they'd found a way into the city. As Yoru was bashing through a particularly dense patch of ferns, Haru squawking from her perch on the toad's bowl, she felt a shudder in the membrane of the world, and looked to Guada to find him frowning like he'd felt the same. They nodded at each other, then crossed the now inert circle, onto the hard dirt. 'Can you tell where?'

'Up ahead,' Guada said. 'Not far.'

'Those weavers you mentioned?'

'Must be.'

They hurried, the way easier on the hard ground. Haru ceased her complaints.

'There.'

A smaller gate hung on its hinges, the dirt scattered with shattered wood. The circle had been kicked open; on the forest side Yoru could see the rotted skeletons of stables and barns in the shadowy ferns. The city side showed the last gasp of a thin road. There were footprints there, one set. A group of weavers, moving single-file to conceal their numbers.

Yoru bent down, and slipped her rice jug from its spot.

'What are you doing?'

'The barrier must be here for a reason. It's unwise to leave it broken.' She began filling the gaps with rice.

'Rice?' Guada was frowning.

'Any staple works.' Yoru kept filling, until she felt pins and needles in her arms. Then she slipped her knife free and cut off a length of her hair, scattering hair over the rice to ensure the new section was similar to the original.

'Could've asked for my hair,' said Guada. 'Shame to waste such pretty curls.'

'Shut up.'

There was a tunnel past the gate, dark and dry like a deep cave, and at the end there was the light of day, and the dead city.

The silence ached. There were no trees, no grass, not even weeds. No birds, no bugs, no people, no rats.

No Walk.

'Shouldn't this place be full of ghosts?' asked Guada, quietly.

Yoru's neck tingled. She walked slow, scanning the street. With no plant or animal life the buildings hadn't decayed like they should, and there were few collapses. It was well-preserved, enough that it could easily be repopulated with only minor renovations. The paint was faded, stained by rain, but dry. Every dirt road, clay or stone or marble wall, terracotta roof – all dry as the outer walls. Yoru already felt it affecting her; her lips were prickling, and she had to keep pushing down her frizzing hair. The architecture was typical of the region: curved eaves, flicked arches, lightly rounded clay and dirt roads with the gutters along the rim. Screen doors. Bamboo. But the distant keep was solid granite, and Yoru could see other stone roofs deeper in the streets, which suggested Kaowai had once been a cosmopolitan city. *Makes sense. Surely it was quicker to pass the forest this way than the way I came.*

Kaowai was once grand, once full, an oasis of civilisation deep in the rainforest. Now it was a desiccated husk, a cicada's shell left to shrivel in the sun.

'They're not far,' said Guada.

'The weavers? How do you know?'

'Ah . . . the prints are fresher. They're heading for the keep.'

Yoru peered at the prints. They didn't look any different to her. She stopped, and laid a hand on the buckle of her umbrella's head. 'Is this a trap?'

Guada looked at her with bemusement. 'Would it matter if it was? You'd probably kill us all with little to no effort, right?'

'Probably.'

'I thought so.' Guada tilted his head. 'I promise it's not a trap.' Then he smiled. 'At least . . . not for you.'

'Explain.'

'These weavers . . . remember I said there was a mature one among them? Gannet. She's *very* mature. Spent half her life chasing Walks, eating ghosts, and she's probably not far off hatching.' He tilted his head, considering, then added, 'She's been sent for me.'

Yoru looked at the man, then past him, down the long street to where the keep loomed in the tan dust. 'I don't appreciate being tricked. I already said I don't want to fight. How did you know they'd come here?'

'I overheard them. There's a cathedral below the keep. They're investigating it.'

'Overheard? You seem to be awfully good at having information just . . . fall into your lap.'

Guada shrugged. 'You never asked about my spirit.'

'Because that would be rude.'

'Would it?' He laughed, and continued down the street. 'Well, I don't want to offend the Lady Night.'

Yoru watched him go.

He stopped. 'Are you coming?'

'I don't have to go with you.' She turned away and took a path down a separate street, away from Guada.

He laughed, but didn't follow, instead calling out, 'See you in four minutes!'

Four minutes later Yoru turned a plaster corner to find Guada walking towards her.

She sighed. She had specifically tried to keep from running into him, while moving towards the keep, so she could sneak into the cathedral while the weavers went about their feast. 'Are you following me?'

'No.' Guada pointed at the ground, and sure enough the street she'd come to had cleft in its dusty dirt the weaver's prints, and for a moment she felt incredibly stupid. 'Weird place huh? It's like it's only a few days away from just, poof! Blowing away on the wind.'

They were nearing the keep. The sun was low, the sky a harsh orange.

Guada yawned. 'So what's the chicken for anyway? Dinner?'

'You disgust me,' said Yoru.

As they reached the central square a dry gust greeted them, tossing Yoru's hair into her eyes and making her squint. Through tears she saw a tiled expanse lined with dusty marble buildings, once decadent, now bleached skulls with eye-holes picked clean. At the square's far end loomed the blank granite of the cathedral and its keep, a gigantic lump of stark stone with low doors and few windows. Yoru hadn't been in a Parish town for a long time, and the sight made her skin crawl.

At the heart of the square was a wide circle of loose dirt surrounded by shattered tiles, as if a fountain had been torn away. The weavers were gathered around it, six of them, all but one in typically anonymous clothes, tunics and straw hats like migrants or farmers. But the weaver in the middle, who

Guada had called Gannet, was anything but anonymous. She wore bright white – a long jacket, trousers, and wide hat with a thin screen that partially obscured her white-masked face. Her gloves and boots and scarf were black, as was the sheath of her well-fed sword, and she was inhumanly tall and long-limbed, standing straight and uncannily still. In that dead square she was like a lone conical white flower sprouted from a bare desert valley, and Yoru noticed the boar cower into the shadows of a half-collapsed door.

Guada didn't break stride. Yoru sighed and followed. Their footsteps were loud, and they were quickly noticed, the weavers turning to face them, including Gannet, whose mask had thin eye-holes and another gap that showed snow-white lips. The wind had died now. There was nothing to hear but boots and the clank of Yoru's umbrella on the dry stone.

Gannet stepped forward. 'Guada the Jaguar.' Her voice sounded wet and sore.

Guada and Yoru stopped. Yoru stood a little behind him, trying to avoid meeting any eyes. This was not how she'd wanted her day to go.

'Gannet.' Guada fingered the hilt of his sword. 'How long has it been? And to think when we last spoke you could still show your face. Shouldn't weavers as far gone as you be confined to the Central? Or does your rage burn too bright for even the vicars to bear?'

Gannet raised a hand, making a gesture Yoru recognised as a blessing. The lifting of her arm revealed the skin between glove and sleeve. White too. 'I could not leave this unfinished.'

'But you will.'

The younger weavers anxiously watched their leader, who turned her mask to Yoru. 'And you've managed to seduce an accomplice.'

Yoru snorted. 'Seduce? Him? Please. I'm only here to study

the city. I'm a travelling ecologist. The only thing I'm seduced by is natural history!'

Nobody laughed.

'That's not how you smell. You smell like ghosts.' At Gannet's words her whelps sniffed the air and looked puzzled, having smelled nothing.

Yoru had no illusions about the quality of Gannet's senses. She met the weaver's gaze, insectile in the shadows of her white mask, and held it. 'I'm not going to fight you.'

'The Mother damns all who walk with ghosts.' Gannet drew her sword. At that odd, old sound, wet ceramic on wet metal, not a normal sword's sighing hiss but an anguished squeak, the others followed suit in a mad rush. Seven white blades shone bright in the sunset, curved like ribs, wet with mucus that dripped in thick off-white blobs onto the dry tiles.

Yoru stepped back, slowly undid the straps of her cabinet, kept her eyes on the weavers. 'Like I said, I'm only here for study.' She saw Guada hadn't moved. 'Hey, want to lend a hand?'

'We have to run,' he said, quietly, his brow furrowed and his eyes on the city.

'Run?' Gannet let out a choked laugh like the hiccups of an old dying bear. 'You've finally seen a future where I beat you? I am honoured that –'

'No. We *all* need to run.'

To Yoru's surprise, Gannet stiffened and followed his gaze. There was a cloud of dust in the streets beyond the cathedral. Something big, moving closer. The young weavers kept their swords high, the ichor dripped on their scruffy clothes and hung in beads like pale sap that began to tremble like jelly, and soon Yoru felt a rumble through her boots. She eased the cabinet to the ground. Haru was conspicuously quiet, bristled like a cat. Yoru lifted the cloth to check on the toad and found the creep looking, as ever, blank. 'Nothing fazes you, huh?' she muttered.

'You, Finch,' Guada suddenly said. 'You die first.'

'Huh?' One of the youngest weavers looked around with confusion. He had so many pimples she doubted he was even an adult. 'How do you know my name?'

'Do not fall for his tricks.' Gannet kept her pose. Behind her the dust was coming closer; the thing must have been bigger than a score of carriages to make such a cloud. The ground rumbled. 'Draw your sword, Jaguar. I am here. You will fight me.'

But Guada wasn't looking to fight. Guada had found his opening – Finch. 'If you push her in the back and run for the cathedral, then all of us will live.'

Yoru took the chance to unlatch the toad's bowl and slip it under one arm.

'Don't believe him,' said a weaver.

'Keep the faith,' said another.

The rumbling was loud now, constant but staggered, like the thumping of a thousand running feet.

Finch glanced between his companions, who were looking at him nervously. 'All of us?'

Guada grinned. 'Me, you, and Kanta Yoru.'

Finch frowned at him.

'You want to live, Finch. Canary is waiting for you.'

Yoru began to edge around the group, towards the cathedral.

Finch frowned. 'I –'

'Ah,' Guada sighed. 'Too late.' He nodded then to Gannet. 'You're going to have to fight it now.' He took a step back; Gannet took a step forward. He grinned. 'Ah, you know I can't dance, Gannet. That night was all for you.'

Yoru had made it past the weavers. Half of them were

distracted by Guada and Gannet, the other half, the smarter half, were watching the rooftops for the coming dust.

'Draw,' Gannet said again. Yoru wondered why she was letting Guada have a chance. Weavers weren't usually concerned with such things; most were more likely to stab a back than a chest. Perhaps Gannet and Guada's relationship really was as complicated as his jibes suggested.

Then Gannet raised her head like a dog tasting the air, and with apparently total trust she turned her back on Guada to focus her gaze on the corner street. 'The Lord.'

The weavers looked at each other, then at Guada, then again at each other.

'Our Path has diverged,' said Gannet.

Beyond her, Guada grinned, grabbed Yoru's cabinet, and jogged after her. He caught up as she was entering the cool shadow of the cathedral. 'Won't last out here. Weavers or knick-knacks. Not with *that*.'

That came around the corner.

It was gigantic, as big as any of the square's marble mansions, smaller only than the towering cathedral. It was solid flesh, and it was moving, but to Yoru's trained senses it felt as dead as the city it ruled. A mess of human arms, with blushed pink skin like a white man after a scrub. Each length had a hand, and it used them as feet, or perhaps wheels, as it rolled itself like tumbleweed into the square, kicking up dust as the tiles cracked under its weight. That mess of arms, pink and writhing with buoyant purpose, it was like a sea anemone, Yoru thought. A sea anemone with human hands instead of tentacles. A Lord, a greater spirit formed by a collective unconsciousness, in this case the Walk that should have greeted them as they entered the city. Yoru had seen a thousand different Lords – one even dwelt within her – but she had never seen one like this, so physical, so large, so alone in its dead, dry city.

Then it froze, totally still, like a startled cat. Its feet-hands tensed, its air-hands waved like grass in wind. Yoru's boots clattered on the tiles. The young weavers watched their leader, waited. Their toxic sap dripped onto the stone and evaporated in milky steam.

Yoru's shoulder thumped into the cathedral door.

Gannet let out a scream like a cornered rat, and charged. Her weavers flocked behind her. The Lord of Hands bent its lower arms and launched its impossible weight into the air, a graceful but heavy pounce that made the ground shudder. Guada slammed the latch and Yoru stumbled into the cold cathedral hall. The crash of the Lord's landing threw her off her feet. She twisted, hoping to land on her back and lessen the –

Guada caught her, tipped her upright. He'd stowed her umbrella and cabinet beside the door. He didn't wait for thanks, just took off up a tiny tunnelled stairwell cut into the wall. Yoru followed. It was dark. Haru squawked and wriggled under her arm. The steps were uneven but Guada moved with ease, and he was already waiting halfway down a long corridor by the time Yoru reached the top. Thin windows let in the square's grey light. The tiled floor was furry with dust.

Yoru hurried to him. 'What do –'

He held up a hand to halt her. 'Wait.'

'But –'

He pushed her against the wall.

'Excuse me –'

A crash, bright light, stone burst and wind flung her hair, a Lord's strike. Dust and flecks of brick splattered her cheek and stung in her eye and she saw one of the Lord's many arms rip down the corridor, weaver in hand, tearing a wound in the cathedral, only to toss the weaver at the last second to collide with a sickening crack against the far wall.

The weaver fell to the floor, silent. The arm retracted; the shouts and thuds of the battle outside continued. Rubble and dust thudded down the corridor.

Guada let Yoru go and stepped away. 'Let's go.'

Yoru followed. She saw the smoky boar roll out of the stairwell. *Some help you are.*

Through the new hole she could see the square. Only two weavers were left, one of whom was Gannet. The others were dead. One had been driven into the ground near the square's centre, and only their twisted arm was visible around shattered, bloody stone. Another was stuck halfway down a far mansion wall, squashed like a bug, slid on a glistening trail down from point of impact but still suspended by their own juices. One was in the hall with them, one was missing. One was running support to Gannet, following her as she attacked with wild speed and power, chipping away at the anemone Lord's arms wherever they could. The Lord itself fought in ordered rage. The limbs acted in pairs; the movements of one always corresponded to the reverse side. It seemed to be panicked, half its arms arguing with half the others, so in the sunset as it writhed and flailed it looked to Yoru like long lashes of flame blown by a swirling wind.

Then another cold stairwell closed over her head, and she was rising, then running out into cold light, different light, warm and sleepy through the massive, clouded windows of the cathedral's main hall. They were up on a gallery and she could see down into the dusty scattered pews and up into the shuffled stones of the vaulted ceiling. There were no decorations on the walls, only cold bricks curving to the altar, a lump of plains rock dragged here centuries ago. Upon it was balanced the only symbol of the Parish, a giant clamshell, the Great Pattern drawn with charcoal onto the brown-speckled and ridged white.

'Here!' Guada skidded to a halt by a door that looked just like any of the others that ran along the gallery's outer wall.

'Here?' Yoru paused beside him, then frowned. Footsteps were coming up the stairs. Finch emerged, sweat-drenched and out of breath, waving his hand to show he wasn't a threat. The boar loomed next to him, but he was unaware of it.

'Ah!' Guada wore a proud grin. 'You chose life!'

Finch waved the hand again, clearly too puffed to speak.

Guada then took a step back and with a massive boot caved in the door, revealing a big, handsome office. One wall was all books, behind a desk covered in dusty stacks of dry, brittle paper. The Vicar's office, neat, austere, with a miraculously untouched liquor cabinet beside a dusty window that showed the square below.

The young weavers were dead. The one that had hit the far wall had slid all the way to the ground now, and the streak of blood was black in the new moonlight. Another weaver was a lumpy patch in the square, crushed like an overripe feijoa and left to ferment. The next was in many pieces in a long line, crushed too but dragged, like mud wiped on a mat. Fragile, soft things, that had tried to fight in a world they weren't built for.

Gannet was missing.

'Eaten?' offered Guada.

When the sun had gone, the Lord had come to a rest in the middle of the dirt scar of the lost fountain. The night was bright and dry and deathly still. Guada and Yoru were out on the vicar's balcony, the square below. The Lord looked to be crouching. Most of its hands were on the ground.

Its upper arms twitched, and began to rise.

'It's doing something,' said Guada. 'May –'

'Shut up please,' said Yoru, politely.

Slow and steady as a deep sigh, the Lord's arms opened.

Fingers grasped at the clouds, while others ground deeper like gardeners plunging into soil for the roots of weeds. As the outer arms spread like the petals of a blooming flower they revealed smaller hands hidden within, some the size of a man's, some a child's, all crowded together in dense rings like the maw of a limpet. With a great wave of motion the hands folded back on their wrists like they were bracing against the sky, a pit of hands within a tulip of arms, down deep into the Lord, beyond where they could see. It pulsed, swung its layers like reeds buffeted by a current, and then a light began to build, a sickly glow down in the hidden heart. The smaller inner hands clawed at each other, as if they hid bodies fighting to clamber free.

Then the first ghost appeared. A puff of pale brown yellow, transparent clothed body, a blurred face. A ghost of a human, just like any other of the Walks, being helped from the hidden depths of the Lord by the wall of hands, spectral cloth trailing on non-existent wind.

'So we know where the Walk went,' muttered Guada.

More ghosts followed, age and gender indistinct – the blurred afterimages of people swarming from within the flower of hands until the square was bright with their strange, pale light, a light that was brightest in the corner of the eye, but near imperceptible if looked at directly. Yoru didn't need to count to know that the whole population of Kaowai was there.

'I guess we're stuck here until morning.' Guada walked the edge of the balcony, looking straight down at the ghosts spreading down the alleys, filling the town. 'Aye, that's bad luck. We're gonna have to move when the Lord's awake. And that's bad luck too, huh? I've never been fond of getting squished, except in certain circumstances.'

Yoru watched the ghosts enter homes through shut doors,

saw them through windows, sitting at tables, climbing onto sunken beds. They were following the routines they followed in life, as most Walks would. Still, a few remained in the square, circling the resting Lord. The square was bright now, the light of ghosts stronger than that of the moon. The Lord appeared smaller in the surrounding light – perhaps it was smaller, after having shed so much . . . *so much what?* Yoru thought, shaking her head. *They shouldn't be able to reform like that.*

'I'm tired,' she said, and she was – her head felt full of hot wax. She waved off their questions, and left the sight of the resurrecting Walk behind, retreating to the tiny room at the rear of the Vicar's chambers. The files.

By candlelight she learned of the Kaowai Walk, how the Pattern had been broken by the density of the forest and the building of other roads. The city had brought in more weavers to try to stem the sudden flood of ghosts. They'd Touched the walls, widened the outer roads, even offered the Patterners free lodging if they passed Kaowai rather than take the forest way. Nothing worked. The city had once been prosperous, but as the Pattern shifted it had withered away in poverty and destitution and then, one day twenty years before Yoru arrived, the vicar's journal ended. There was no mention of the invading Walk, or the developing Lord of Hands, or what happened to the weavers. No mention of the barrier around the city, or the exodus of its citizens. *If they got out at all.* Yoru looked out the window, down on the mingling ghosts and the glimmering dust and the flesh rose of the Lord. The moon had gone and the city beyond the square was invisible. The only light was that of magic. She could taste rain on the air and sure enough the tiles soon darkened, the window was flecked, and a hiss rose, echoed loud and long through the empty cathedral. The Lord began to pulse, as if it was drinking the rain. Haru was asleep; the toad sat in silence. Yoru got her blanket, folded it, placed it on the tiles, and sat. From her cabinet she drew her jug of rice, and she poured an even circle around herself, and closed her eyes.

'So it's true.'

Yoru opened her eyes. The rain had stopped, the window was long dry, her circle of rice unbroken, bright in the returned moonlight. 'What's true?' She blinked away the sleep. It had been hours, passed in a moment.

Guada stood in the doorway, his face hidden in shadow. Yoru could see another looming behind him – the boar, hungry. She ignored it. 'You sleep inside a barrier,' Guada said.

Yoru said nothing. She stood, kicking that barrier open and going over to her canteen for a drink.

'You're not protecting yourself, are you?' Guada looked over his shoulder, down to the boar. 'You're locking this thing away.'

'Did you want something?'

'No, I'm just curious. See, my spirit is –'

'They're different. We're different. That's life.' Yoru sat back in her circle, her headache already returning and the water not helping. 'Now go away, and don't wake me up again.'

Guada snorted. 'All right then, Night Lady.'

After another instant, dissatisfying sleep, Yoru went back through the cathedral. She spotted Guada and Finch out on the balcony, watching the ghosts mill about the square and drinking the vicar's forgotten whisky. She hung back in the doorway.

'Central's gotten quiet,' Finch was saying. 'My ma insists that when she was a girl the old songs rarely stopped, that she could walk from Karan Motte down all the way to Lombard

Street without even hearing her own footsteps. Now there is no Lombard Street. It's all walls and keeps and chapels and graveyards. Quiet. Quiet rain, quiet wind. Quiet people walking with their heads down. Weavers watching. The Parish hulking over it, quietest of it all, that fuck-off stone mountain. No work to speak of, no markets or anything, just the rationing. Not that you'd ever know there was no work – nobody survives long enough on the street to make a scene of it.' Finch fixed Guada with a sparkling eye. 'You wonder why I'm a weaver, Jaguar, if I don't trust the Parish. It's simple. I didn't have any other choice.'

'What of Central Bay? Surely the Parish hasn't consumed the whole city.'

'I've never even seen the Bay. That way's all walls. City's spread and spread, chewing up the plains and absorbing the inner rings. The old Pattern. All those ancient clans with their legendary Lords, one-time stakeholders of the great heart of the country, now nothing but meat for the Mother. The Plains crowd, caravans run into each other, barely a spare blade of grass between the clans and their Walks. Like spilling wine on a white sheet, and how the patches spread as the wine soaks in. Soon they'll have nowhere to go but together, and I can't see any colour coming out bolder there than the Parish's. Give it another ten years and there'll be nothing but ghosts and quiet fucking masonry. And outside? So many clans stuck following the same loops they've followed for generations, all with Walks near as big as themselves. Miles and miles of grass that should be barren, but everywhere you go you see roads and boot-prints, and the moment you reach the slightest incline you can look in any direction and see a clan, and another beyond that. Any direction, every.' Finch shook his head. 'When I left . . . when we came here . . . from the mountains I looked back and saw it for the first time, the Pattern as a pattern. Walk, clan, walk, clan, in rhythm with perfect timing, in the night just lights and shadows stretching for a thousand miles below you, so densely crowded you could see the Pattern in torch orange and ghost white.'

'Morbid.'

'Like seeing an old friend for the first time in years, expecting the same person from your memories but instead finding someone tired.'

'I wonder if the Walks expand too far – if the Parish might cull the living too.'

'You think they don't?'

Guada laughed grimly. 'So you joined? Even knowing that most weavers die young? Even knowing the Pattern is doomed?'

'I'll either die young and abroad, or live long enough to feed the Mother. There's a lot of comfort in knowing your life can only go one of two ways.'

'You could always end up like Gannet, dying in some dead city despite having finished your holy mission.'

'True. Her hatred for you trumps her piety,' said Finch. 'Frankly, I'm jealous.'

'Of me? But what of our other companion? She should be the target of your jealousy. As she is mine. Some say that the daylight is just a cloth pulled over the night, and the Lady treads the rim like a needle. Each stitch she goes deeper, but the Lady pulls no thread, and the seam flails at her back.'

Yoru frowned. She'd heard pretentious descriptions of herself before, but this one was special. *So . . . bold*, she thought. *I wish I was that impressive.*

'You speak as if she is a weaver.'

'No. I see it now. She is a stitch-ripper, slowly picking apart –'

Yoru decided to step into view.

'And here she is.' Guada grinned as she approached. 'Isn't it dangerous if you don't sleep?'

'The opposite. Anyway, I'm stepping out. I need to see inside a house, see if anyone left anything behind.'

'Want company?'

'No,' Yoru replied, turning away.

'This could have been a nice place to live.'

'Mhm.'

Guada made an ooh-ing sound as he followed Yoru under an iron gate, into the skeleton of a garden. The rain had seemed strong but the ground had already dried. The two were wreathed in smoke cast by censers they'd dug out from the Vicar's storage, that were burning lampflies and crushed rice and warding off the Walk. The ghosts had followed them all the way from the cathedral, and now flickered silently just beyond the smoke, waiting for the fire to die. 'This would've been pretty. A garden like this probably had carnelias. Do you know carnelias? They . . .'

Yoru tuned him out. She crouched in the doorway to check the sill. Bronze, well worn, covered in the same soft dust that coated everything in that dry city. She entered, walked the width of the main room, dusty furniture, upholstery like corn husks, dishes forgotten on the cracked table; no corpses, no sign of struggle, all the drawers and cupboards full. *Hypnosis? Poison?* She looked back the way they'd come, to the hulking shadow of the cathedral. It didn't look too different from the silhouette of a boar. 'What do you think happened here?'

'The Parish wanted to let a big Walk gestate in total isolation. An experiment, I guess. This was the unlucky place they picked.'

Yoru nodded.

'But it has been years. You'd think the Parish would have culled the Lord by now.'

Yoru looked away, over the roofs, to where the glow of the hidden Walk faded a bulb of stars. 'They probably forgot about it.'

'Ha. That would be typical. But, eh, what can you do? We can't kill that thing. And we certainly can't stop the Parish the next time they decide to breed one. Changing the Parish? Ha. Like trying to make water run upwards.'

'I won't answer for the Parish's crimes.'

Finch sat defiant before his two interrogators, his eyes sparkling in the waning moonlight. The doors to the Vicar's chambers stood open, and the Walk had followed them up the stairs. The corridor was a brownish blur of pale ghosts lingering at the edge of the barrier.

'Is a weaver not their hand?'

'The Parish has as many hands as that fucker out there. I'm nothing, a nobody, barely qualified to carry a sword let alone hear about some theoretical experiment. Do you think something like that is common knowledge? I doubt even Gannet knew.'

Gannet. Her body still hadn't turned up. Yoru had a bad feeling.

Guada continued to loom over Finch. 'Are you going to report this city to Central?'

'Of course! You think I'd return alone and not mention why? "Oh, my companions just decided to retire young." Come on Jaguar. I'm not that stupid.'

Yoru watched the flickering ghosts arriving from deeper in the city, flowing back to the Lord, clambering up its sides, helped by welcoming hands that emerged from the pillowy folds of its many giant arms. A reverse of the evening's strange ritual.

'It's not like it's bothering anybody,' she said.

The two stopped their bickering, and looked at her with confusion.

She frowned at them. 'Nobody comes here, nobody is likely to come here. So long as we remake the barriers, there's no chance of the Lord getting out. It seems to live entirely on rain, and this strange recycling of ghosts.' She fished out a bundle of seeds for Haru, who had been patiently hovering around her ankles. The seeds crackled on the tiles and Haru's head bobbed gratefully, the seeds clicking in her beak. 'I don't see any reason why we can't just leave the thing be.'

Finch laughed. 'Leave it be? You're mad! The –'

'It's nothing to laugh at,' Guada interjected. 'We can't kill it ourselves, and if you tell the Parish about it I expect they'd botch the hunt in some way. Our initial goal should be getting out of the city. Our only goal, I suppose, since no doubt the Lady will slip away at the first opportunity, never to be seen again.'

Yoru nodded.

Finch looked for a moment as if he would continue to argue, but instead he closed his eyes, and sighed. 'You said I'd live if I came with you, but now it just feels like you've dragged out my death.'

Dawn came, and the Lord swallowed its ghosts.

The three accidental prisoners slept through the morning. It was decided that the only time they could escape was when the Lord was active but away from the cathedral. This meant a day of heat and deprivation – there was little food between them, and only a scrap of water. The cathedral provided cool and cover from the aggressive sun, and Yoru spent the day following the shade, watching the Lord where she could. It was a strange thing, gentle with its home. She watched its slow movements down the streets, the way its hands coursed tenderly over walls and windows, like an old woman straightening out a quilt. She watched it roll back and forth, climb the taller buildings, leap like it was playing, like it was a cat that just whittled away its days.

'You call this a Lord?' Finch asked. They were watching it try to fit between two buildings, squishing tight. 'But the Lords of Walks aren't like this, they're usually ghosts too, tall pale trees, pillars of light, rivers in the dark. At least the ones I've seen.'

'These things never evolve the same,' said Yoru. 'The caravan leaders are Lords, because their presence in the minds of their people gives them power. The ghosts walk the same patterns as they did in life, as long as they can. But everything has a ghost, and sometimes they have nowhere to go but deeper.'

Yoru found a moment of privacy when Guada fell asleep, his large black hat over his face, puffing dust as he snored. She explored the cathedral's keep, and discovered an alcove with old water in dusty barrels, saved from the Lord's drought by the cathedral's barrier. She cracked the lid of one, and discovered the water was infested. She purified it with rice and the bright purple skin of a particular eel. The little parasites formed an odorless pink scum on the surface, and the boar returned, sliding past Yoru's shoulder in a great black cloud, and stepping across the barrel, turning the scum to steam.

'You know I don't like it when you do that,' said Yoru.

The boar slipped away.

She glared at the spot on the wall where the smoke and steam had been. 'I find you very rude sometimes.'

At noon the Lord was on the far edge of the city, doing

something that involved tossing great plumes of sparkling sand into the blue sky. The three were packing up to leave when Yoru found Finch about to touch the toad's bowl.

'Don't do that.'

Finch frowned, his hand outstretched. 'Why not?'

'You'll die quite horribly.'

'It's true.' Guada passed, his pack clanking with the vicar's silver. 'It'd even kill me, and that's notoriously difficult.'

Yoru rolled her eyes.

Soon they were hurrying to the gate through which they'd entered, their hearts thumping. The hills beyond the walls looked impossibly green. The wind was picking up, howling through the hollow buildings, making dry shutters crack like distant whips. The maze of streets was heady with uniformity, and in the heat Yoru found her head spinning, like she was half-awake, half-drunk, and the whole while straining to hear a thud, a crash, a sound that meant the Lord was coming. That they would soon be smears to be washed away by rain, and then pale blurs that would crawl in and out of the Lord's thousand-handed throat every day until there were no days left.

They entered the cool of a long stone tunnel, and an awful stink hit Yoru's nose. She pulled her collar over her nose, then her foot hit something soft.

Gannet's wide white hat.

'There.' Guada pointed upwards.

Above their heads, nestled against the bricks of the great arch, there pulsed a gigantic cocoon that was as clear as glass. Transparent mucus trembled in long dangling trails. The tiles were warped and blurred through layers of glassy silk. There was a human shape at the bulbous heart, fetal, nearly impossible to spot in the shade because it was transparent now too, the only colour left a slight clouding of the skin, and the pink of drained veins near the twitching milky heart. Gannet, curled into a ball, shoulders arched long, already sprouting wings. Her mask was in the cocoon with her, shattered and smeared over a lengthening snout. The tiles she had latched to were already visible through the frosty folds of her soon-to-be totally transparent skull. As Yoru watched, the lumpy brain twitched, and the wide black eye at the end of the salmon-pink stalk swivelled, and focused on her.

Finch retched, and another smell filled the tunnel.

'First time?' Guada grinned, although he looked a little pale himself.

'This is bad,' Yoru muttered, dragging her eyes away from Gannet's and sliding off her cabinet. The toad stared down at her with its typical creepy blankness as she started rifling through her drawers, and she put a hand over its face. 'I can't deal with you right now.'

Meanwhile Guada had sidled back the way they'd come, and soon she heard a crackle of breaking wood.

Finch recovered a little, wiped his mouth. 'What are you doing? We can't afford to stop.'

'We can't let her mature. If she hatches mature she could kill the Lord, and I don't want to know what kind of moult would come after.'

'You can't just kill her!'

'I'm not going to. Here.' Yoru found what she was looking for – a fat paper parcel that contained over a kilogram of delicious dried chillis. 'Super-hot fire.'

'Super – what?' Finch shook his head. 'Look, Lady . . . Yoru. I can't let you kill her. I might have abandoned her before but this isn't right. She's defenceless.'

'The Lady Night already said that we're not killing her.' Guada appeared with a large stack of brittle timber, having once again known what Yoru was going to ask for before she managed to do so.

'Then what, a spell? Reverse the change?'

Yoru laughed. 'Reverse it? If only I could. No. There'll be no magic here.'

Finch frowned, but backed away, leaving them space.

Yoru began to build a bonfire, Guada going back and forth for more wood, the strange eye in the cocoon following him the whole way, straining to keep focus. Yoru reluctantly filled the bonfire with the chillis. They were worth a lot. This whole journey had become a financial nightmare. What did these people think she lived on? Sarcasm alone?

'Is that it?' Guada stepped back and admired their cone of scavenged wood and wasted condiments. 'It'll be enough?'

She nodded, and drew a golden feather from her cabinet. She circled the fire, lighting it with the feather's glowing tip. Soon the dry timber caught, and with a bark of displaced air the flames sprang to life. She lifted Haru and nodded for the exit. 'Quick.'

But they weren't quick enough. The tunnel's end was still an apple of light when the chilli hit their eyes, and by the time they stumbled back into the sun they were a snotty, coughing, weeping mess – other than Haru, who was looking down from her perch on top of the toad's bowl with some superiority.

'Why do that?' Finch managed between sneezes. 'Surely the smoke will kill her.'

'Not directly. She'll panic and hatch herself before she's ready. Premature birth, premature end. No glass butterfly to pester the Lord. And a safer forest too.'

Finch narrowed his eyes. 'So you did kill her.'

Yoru said nothing. She looked past him, to where Guada stood at the tunnel's end, looking back, his lips moving as if he was speaking to Gannet, far off in her cooking cocoon.

'How did you know her?' Yoru asked as they passed through

a metal gate into what had once been a park, and was now a bland flat of packed dirt.

'Ah, times gone,' Guada said, and then he lifted his sword and eased it out, just a peek.

Ceramic.

'I knew it,' breathed Finch, coming to a stop, his eyes hidden in shadow. 'No way would Gannet care so much about some vagrant. You were one of us.'

'Aye, a long time ago.' Guada stopped too, offering Finch something approaching a smile. 'Me and Gannet . . . ah, young and intrepid, chasing ghosts through the rainforest. It was a good time.'

'You're a traitor.'

'I am, but I didn't choose to be.' Guada stepped closer to Finch, who stiffened, guarded. Guada leant in, until his face was only inches from Finch's, and then Finch's eyes widened.

'Can't you walk and talk?' Yoru said, watching the smoke and dust deeper in the city. Haru wriggled in her arms and let out a thoughtful cluck. 'We don't have time for this.'

'His name was Alax May,' Guada went on, leaving the stunned Finch behind. 'And they said he was the greatest swordsman in the land.' Guada stepped closer to Yoru. 'We'd been ordered after him, another pair in a long list of weavers sent to die at May's hand. We left Central in spring, and didn't find him until the next. A long ride through endless rainforest, mist, Walks, forgetting the day, the season. We were young, stuck together, and so we took comfort in each other. You know how it is. Then we found May. He was better than us, stronger, shining with his legend. An infested man halfway to Lordship. But he didn't have eyes in the back of his head. He didn't see my thrust until it was too late.' Guada was near Yoru now. He leant close, so she could see his eyes. She looked between them, and her neck prickled; the left sparkled with sunlight, rumbled with motion, the reflection of the dry empty road, no Yoru, only the distant hills of the rainforest. 'And I didn't know the spirit would infect me.'

'It's reflecting the past,' she said, staring into his strange eye, seeing for a moment the back of her head, as her past self stepped in that Guada's vision.

'You should have turned yourself in.' Finch had remembered how to speak. 'The Parish is always merciful to unlucky weavers. And that . . . that's too much. I've heard of your eye before, and May.' He shook his head with disbelief.

Guada made his way around Yoru and headed for the city walls. Yoru and Finch looked at each other, and followed.

'I didn't have much in life,' Guada said as they walked. 'Born poor, and it was just me and Mum for years. I became a weaver for money, same as you, kid, but I didn't hate it nearly as much as I'd expected. The work was strange I'll admit, but the people . . . ah. Of course the spirit changed all that. I knew I'd be killed if I returned to Central, but I didn't want to die, no matter how merciful said killing would be. So one night when Gannet fell asleep I packed my things and ran home. The Parish never knew where I was from, so I knew I could hide out, have some time and space to figure out what to do. Mum was glad to see me. But then I learned the limits of this power.'

Guada nodded to indicate a turnoff, and they left the park and entered a skinny alleyway.

'On my long walk I'd missed the letters, and so I didn't know she was sick. By the time I made it home she only had a few weeks left. I did what I could. Tidied the garden, sold off the chickens. Made her lots of soup, too much soup. She grew tireder, quieter. Then the day came. I was sitting at her bedside, the room was warm but stuffy, the blinds drawn. I can still remember the smell of it, that particular scent of a failing body. I can still remember that dog that barked just a few seconds before . . . ah. But of course I remember it. I lived it a hundred times. See.' Guada tapped the temple beside his strange, stuck-in-the-past eye. 'I can go back in time, but only seven minutes. When she died the first time I went back, I tried to save her. But I couldn't. It was like . . . a great heave washed through her, she took in a sharp breath, and then she was gone. She was still talking before it happened, but only a little. I can't remember what she said the first time. And then . . . I tried to save her a few times, until I realised I couldn't. So then I just . . . I kept going back, and going back, trying to find the right words, how to say goodbye, how to say goodbye without letting her know she was going, even though she knew it, she knew it the whole time.'

Guada shook his head. The alley turned onto another dry park, the walls were near, a block of brown slicing the blue sky.

'I remembered everything. Every time I ever hurt her, or upset her. I apologised again and again. I told her stories, told her it would be okay. But it never felt right. No matter what I said it was never the right thing, never a goodbye that felt . . . I saw her die over and over. That gasp, that long croak, the stillness, that barking fucking dog. The ancient curtains, the cobwebs in the corner that she'd been too frail to get at, that she'd insisted I leave. "No pet, they're not doing anything wrong," she'd say, and she'd smile. So up by the ceiling were these great lumps of grey webbing covered in brown beads. A thousand unlucky flies. Ah . . . I never knew what to say. I kept going back, going back, so futile – I know now that it isn't something that can be done. There is no right way to say goodbye. To say . . . ha.' Guada grinned, his teeth white in the sun. The shadows were long now, the evening imminent.

'But I took it too far. I didn't realise the strain on me. I grew tireder and tireder and finally I couldn't cope, my body gave in, I passed out right there in the chair by her bed. When I woke up the sun was gone, the moon was bright, and I could see this long shape, half fallen. I lit a candle, and saw her. Mum had seen me pass out and despite everything, her weakness, the distance, she'd tried to climb out of bed to help me. But she hadn't made it. She'd come halfway then fallen, died all twisted in the sheets. Her arm was reaching for me. She was already cold.'

Yoru said nothing. Guada didn't look at her. He didn't seem to expect a response.

'So there are limitations.' Finch said.

'Aye, there are,' said Guada. 'I couldn't go back anymore, the time had passed. I had to leave it like that. In the end I never got to say goodbye. I never got to say anything at all. She died . . . ah. I think she died afraid for me.'

He was looking at the ground now, watching the soft dust fold around his boots.

'You have to actively choose to go back?' Finch asked. 'You have to be aware of it?'

'Aye.' Guada smiled at Yoru. 'And boy does the Lady Night make that difficult. Do you know how many times I've tried to fight you? I can't even land a blow. I've decided it must be impossible.'

'It is,' she said.

They reached the wall an hour later. The Lord's dust trail was far away. There was smoke above Gannet's tunnel. They found their tunnel, the one they'd entered through. Guada chattered away as they trudged towards the heavy smell of the rainforest and the chorus of evening birds. 'Leaving that thing feels wrong. It's a crime isn't it? Parish just playing with people.'

'We don't have a choice,' said Yoru.

'Ah, you think? I've always –'

A crack cut him off. A thud of hard on hard, and then he was on the ground, and Finch was upon him, slamming again, slamming the rock into the back of Guada's head.

Yoru gasped and dropped Haru. 'Hey!' She pulled Finch away, but it was too late. Guada's skull was caved in, his leg twitching, blood pulsing to the dusty tiles.

Yoru pushed Finch against the wall. 'Why!'

Finch grinned with defiance, his eyes wide and mad and his face flecked with blood. 'When did I ever say I'd given up, huh? You think I'd let you kill Gannet like that? Damned infested vermin.'

'You're the vermin.' Yoru let him go, stepped back, stepped over Guada's corpse. 'You weavers are all the same. You find a thing, a mystery, a person, a place, and you crack it open and suck out all the juice.'

'Damn the Parish! I'm pragmatic, I want *more*. Are you so taken by the Pattern? It does not answer for me, and I've heard all the Parish's musings. Belief is poison, icons only reinforce our doom. Our waning hope, see the Pattern, walk the Pattern! Watch how we cling to this world with great Control. They're awfully naive, aren't they? But surely a famous touched traveller such as yourself knows that.'

'I think you're both naive.'

Finch laughed again. It was well-practised, habitual, annoying. Yoru wondered if he'd ever been honest about anything before this moment. 'Is that so? You, who made a demon your own. You, the Night Lady. The Parish shuns the magic of the world, but *we* embrace it. Because magic is a part of us, isn't it?'

'Magic only wants to eat and reproduce, Finch.' She frowned, a thought coming to her. 'No, magic is like water.

Water only wants one thing – to go down. Sure, you can bottle it, but what happens if the bottle breaks?'

'Exactly! The Parish knows just as well as us that the Pattern is a failure. They'd been seeking the secret to Guada's magic for years, and he just gave it away! He was the stupid one. Stupid, dead, and – a . . .' He tripped over his words, his jaw hung open. His entire figure flickered, like it was a reflection in a rain-tossed pond. His left eye sparkled with a different light to his right.

Yoru stepped back, lifted her umbrella.

Finch stepped forward, grinned.

And then his face fell. Yoru watched as the colour deepened under his eyes, and little flecks of red appeared at their corners. He stumbled, paling, and looked at her with disbelief. 'It . . . it really is impossible.'

He passed out.

Yoru let him fall with a thud, then she looked for Haru, who was calmly pecking at the ground a few feet away. 'Should we leave him?'

Haru clucked.

'You always were the nice one.'

She walked from the dead city, crossed the barrier, and reformed it behind her. The boar greeted her at the edge of the ferns. Finch snored down the tunnel, by the seeping carcass that was once Guada, and Yoru went east. As she stepped into the trees a gust came from behind, bringing the sound of a wail, inhuman but somehow deeply sad. Gannet had hatched, and was mourning herself. Yoru shivered. She thought of the many versions of her own self that Guada had fought, and Finch after him. Many Yorus that Yoru had never known. *What a strange magic*, she thought, *and what a strange sensation. As if they experienced a part of my life that I didn't.*

Along the road she spied a falcon, young and brown,

wheeling in the sky as it readied to stoop. It noticed something, its head turned, its body in a somersault, and it buckled its wings, and for a moment hung still as if an invisible membrane of air was straining to resist it. And then the membrane tore, and the falcon fell, its jagged folded wings fluttering like kite flaps in the current, and with a crackle and hiss of breaking leaves it vanished into the forest.

A few moments later the falcon rose from the trees, beak and talons empty, hunt failed. It took off on a laboured flight west into the ailing blue. Yoru watched until it was gone. Smaller birds sang in the trees, the sun fell, and the ridgeline folded away into blackness. The forest quieted but for a few hidden owls. Yoru followed the road on.

VINCENT O'SULLIVAN

Ko tēnei, ko tēnā

i

Quercus Park is not the most favoured part of its county, if you have progressive agriculture in mind, nor the most social, should hunts and gentry house parties come into your definition. But a reasonably fine prospect is commanded from the amusing turret erected no more than thirty years ago in a stand of ancient oaks. The Tower, as the family consider it, is out of keeping with the handsome stone of the two-century-old house. Those with nothing more than quick curiosity might glimpse the recent folly as they pass the high stone wall of the estate's western boundary. They may puzzle at what rises above the oaks, the legacy of the present baronet's eccentric father. For 'Mad Sir Jack' had exhausted his failing ingenuity on its forty-foot-high brickwork, its four raised corners shaped to replicate the stems of sugarcane, mingled with the overreaching foliage of palm trees, all worked from now discoloured limestone. For this, the Tower declared, was the seat of a man who had done well in the plantations of the West Indies, where his slaves, he boasted, were treated as if part of his family, while sweetening the lives of his fellow Englishmen at home. A sad irony, that Sir Jack died of natural causes, within months of the Act of Parliament that punished such men of enterprise, and washed England's hands of tolerating slavery.

And so Sir Jack's clever and reclusive son, taking up such privileges as his father had bequeathed him, committed himself to the sciences at which he had so excelled in Cambridge. Now in his middle years, he contentedly lived in what he called 'our little menagerie'. By which he meant the gathering of five who most evenings dined together, with so little formality, in a panelled room with its dull portraits of forbears the younger generation seldom raised its eyes to acknowledge.

Oliver's social notions, quite apart from his intellectual remoteness, would have placed him at odds with his equals for fifty miles. There was a cook, and a local man who filled other roles, from serving at table to grooming for the small stable kept on the estate. Oliver and his friend, the urbane Dr Osmond, referred to Godwin and Wollstonecraft and Thomas Paine, heroes of their student days, as familiarly as they did to Fothergill Cooke or Wheatstone. During the years when his thinking was given mainly to electricity, Oliver corresponded with and indeed met the great Faraday. They had spent an afternoon discussing the induction principle, and the closed-core electric transformer. But the humanities also held his interest. He admired enormously the younger Wordsworth, as much as he detested the curmudgeonly Tory who alas still lived. But above all he was a man of science. In recent years Quercus Park had been webbed with copper wires. 'Speaking threads', he called them, anticipating what he hoped would be his achievement, his belief that electrical impulses and the human voice might be brought together. He safely spoke of his ambition with Osmond. Other acquaintances might, kindly enough, think him deranged. Although apart from his greyish discoloured teeth – the result of sensual indiscretion which Osmond treated with mercury – Oliver was not a man easily disturbed. At times it bothered him, but not intensely, that his younger brother was not quite a gentleman, and without capacities one could point to. Possibly a wastrel, but Sir Jack's plantations, which neither brother had any inclination to manage, kept Quercus Park afloat. Their managers, of course, were Englishmen, while its workers were now men as free, you might say, as a Scot.

At twenty, it seemed not to bother Mason that he had nothing of Oliver's gifts, and no consuming interest beyond himself. They sat together in the study, which was as much a workshop as a library. Various metal objects, large and small, were set seemingly at random, and a bench held flasks, tubes, and a brass wheel that once started continued to turn under its own impetus, driving a series of smaller cogs. Other moving parts connected to a device whose glass tube could glow with agitated gas. Oliver happily explained why this was so, but failed to hold Mason's attention for more than a few minutes. Even perpetual motion proved too tiresome for the younger brother to comprehend. A dead frog, ticking with what seemed signs of restored vitalism when a wire was held against it, bored him too much to ask about. For a moment Oliver was tempted to gift Mason the sensation of an applied current, and then regretted the thought. Instead, he sat cleaning beneath his nails with the point of a Mercator compass as he quizzed his sibling. Each found the conversation tiresome, although for different reasons. They spoke a little about finances, inheritance, the need for even those whom the French so rightly designate *les gens fortunes* to find something worthy of their time, their duty even. Mason admitted that, to be direct about it, there was no profession he was drawn to, nothing, actually, that he could see holding his interest for a year or two, let alone a lifetime.

Oliver found it difficult to hold his patience. 'Elizabeth is younger than you, Mason, and without the schooling that so favoured you. Yet in some areas of learning she knows almost as much as I. She works with me on my projects not as an assistant but as an equal. Her gift for calculation already surpasses mine.'

Mason laughed, as though he were the one indulging Oliver. 'Then how fortunate she arrived here when she did. As it was becoming apparent that she might be useful to you as I should never be.'

Oliver threw the compass he toyed with on the papers in front of him.

'Marcus Aurelius,' Mason began. He was about to offer a quotation on calm and equanimity.

'For Christ's sake, boy!' Oliver's face reddened as it seldom did. 'I could buy you a commission with the simplest note to a friend in Whitehall! Service would *thrash* you into something.'

'Nothing I care to consider,' Mason said. He enjoyed the quick returns on truculence.

His brother altered tack. Oliver prided himself on a rational mind. His anger abated as if it were no more than a matter of turning down the flame on a burner. 'There must surely be something, Mason, that is all I am saying, something that interests you for longer than a fortnight? Something in yourself to elevate?'

And Mason, with as much sincerity as he could muster, held his brother's eye. 'What I want, Oliver, is adventure.'

'Adventure?' A word, he could tell, that startled his gifted brother.

'Discovery, then. You of all people should know the magnetism of that.'

A long pause, as Oliver considered that perhaps, after all,

he did not do his brother justice. He folded his hands and asked, as a cleric, say, might enquire in an Austen novel, 'Of what, exactly?'

'Myself,' Mason said. 'To know the boundaries of myself. Of what I might be capable of, for good or bad. That is what each of us should be saying, Oliver. There is nothing in life we might know as we do ourselves. To know exactly what we are. The limit of life is the limit of ourselves. To know what our boundaries are.' And another pause, before he said, 'You must understand me now?'

Oliver looked again to his hands. He accepted there was nothing he might say to such a statement. He thought, we are no more brothers than are elks and dolphins. But what he said was simply, 'Shall we leave it there?'

Yet the gatherings for dinner were always congenial. The two women and the three men who ate together each evening gave every sign of being at ease with each other, their conversations variously domestic, learned, amusing, informed by the London papers Dr Osmond received every second day, and so politics and even social gossip were part of their evening fare. The occasional dinner guests – usually scientific persons of some eminence – would leave, gratified and surprised by the confidence with which the women spoke, the good humour that defined the table, the quite natural intermingling of simple family accord, and a level of discourse that was unlikely to be rivalled within an afternoon's ride in any direction. Apart from the fact that the monarch's health was never drunk, nothing was likely to strike a guest as untoward. Although on reflection, slivers of memory might well come together, and a number of questions raise themselves.

Of the marvellously impressive Elizabeth – Lizzie as the family call her – foremost, naturally. The rumours were rife enough of the tall, dark-complexioned young woman. As she entered the room she seemed, as one guest thought it, like the sudden striking of a gong. No one was unaware of her for a moment, however long the evening might be, or the pauses between her remarks. What the blunt might have called the sexual exchange between English males in the Indies and female slaves on the plantations was too delicate a matter to be spoken of openly when ladies were present. Yet it was not uncommon, God knows, for even the finest families to host 'wards', sent back home from those parts of the globe in whose climate, as Byron's verse reminds us, the very word 'sultry' finds its darkly obvious rhyme. But where nothing is said, all things seem possible. The baronet and his brother treated Lizzie with the easy courtesy they might a relative, shall we say. She and Oliver's wife Isabella seemed as close as confiding girls, as well as mature women. As one of the younger Huxleys – once a contemporary of Oliver's on a staircase overlooking the Cam, and as given to new knowledge as the rest of his distinguished family – wryly enough remarked, 'Whoever else might be guests at Quercus Park, Mad Sir Jack still haunts the table.'

As with any group of humans, the studious calm of Oliver's estate flowed above deeper currents. Oliver himself, with that signalling of symptoms at each partly concealed smile, had now of course settled to a more placid married life. Placid, although the word demands qualifying. Bella was the frankest, the least sanctimonious of women. With the assumed hopes for children so patently ruled out by her husband's condition, the couple admirably refused to take that as *final*, so to speak. On such matters they were unconfined by church teaching, or the commonly assumed English sense of decorum. As a tribute it might seem to Thomas Rowlandson, the great and amusingly shameless artist of moral and sensual excess, Bella and Oliver had refined a marital game named after him. Not that Oliver in the least was a man of excess. But occasionally he might ask, as if enquiring of something of no more importance than a mislaid hat, would his wife mind should Mr Rowlandson call that evening? And so the lurid depictions of art, the fantasies of an infamously proscribed novel from the previous century, Bella good-naturedly acted out. As Oliver, in his own curious selection of clothes, or lack of them, found the kind of satisfactions that might seem trivial or perverse to persons not sharing his own preferences.

Of the others who gathered to dine together each evening, less might be said. Whatever emotional promptings Lizzie harboured none might guess at. With her startling and marvellously springing halo of tightly curled hair, which ran with threads and tints of bronze when lit by candlelight, she seemed as removed from mere sensuality as did an Italian devotional image. While added to that her formidable gifts, her intellectual grasp of the work she shared with Oliver, and it was apparent enough that most men who came her way were in awe of her. Yet in conversation she was so amiable, so reserved. As Dr Osmond thought, but without admitting as much, she was one of the few persons he had met who was, at the last, impenetrable to him. Which could mean, could it not, that what so puzzled them was her simplicity beneath all else. Do we not always assume that if a woman is beautiful, and then clever as well, there is a greater mystery than may be the case?

Dr Osmond made such observations in a notebook he carried always with him, as those men are likely to do who believe each passing *aperçu* too valuable to risk its loss. As he had written for example the word 'volcanic', after examining young Mason several years back, when the fourteen-year-old boy was recovering from a fever. It was a minor enough event, but one that at the time startled him, and proved itself a harbinger, might one say, of the years between then and now.

Minor, but enough for him to mention it to Oliver, who had seemed to take a more tolerant, less moral slant. The boy stood in his nightshirt in front of Dr Osmond, his head level with the doctor's shoulders. He had grown surprisingly in those last few months, 'outgrowing his strength', as was sometimes said of youths who suffered from mild symptoms.

'Raise what you are wearing,' Dr Osmond had asked. His tone conveyed that, familiar as they might be to each other, this was a professional exchange. This was doctor and patient. Mason bunched his nightshirt beneath his chin so that it seemed curiously like the rufflings one sees at the throat of cathedral choir boys. But Osmond then struck by the paradox that forced itself upon him. He himself felt the prickling of embarrassment, which the boy quite obviously did not. His shock – for it was no less than that – as he took in the boy's 'moral disposition' as no other had yet done. Mason held his gaze with a sense of command, defying him to look elsewhere. For his naked body ticked with a raw insistent excitement. He had moved the ground from medical distance to a covert, indecent display. His upper lip raised slightly, showing the edge of his teeth, their resting on the scarlet tip of his tongue. His now a blatant challenge that Dr Osmond lower his eyes.

'The boy will take careful surveillance,' the doctor had said that evening. The two friends taking as usual their after dinner brandy in the scientist's study.

'It may be a stage he is passing through,' Oliver said.

'A stage that may last a lifetime.'

'I expect it was mischief rather than indecency. You know how intractable he can be.'

'A word one uses of horses,' Dr Osmond said. 'It does not do for men.'

As Oliver dredged up the old Latin tag of nothing human being beyond our sympathy, his friend sharply noted that the way educated men hid behind the barricades of Latin at times disgusted him. It was out-and-out evasion. 'It is the way a peasant crouches behind shrubbery to relieve himself.'

'Well, here's to shrubbery,' Oliver said, both men laughing, raising to each other the dull glow of their glasses.

They had agreed, up to a point, that Cambridge might do wonders for Mason, as it had for each of them. The rough-hewn timber the great university took in, that left as polished Chippendale. Oliver laughed again at his friend's extravagant comparison.

'We may be the last generation to claim such luxuries,' he said. 'God knows where our radicalism will one day lead the likes of us, Osmond. Privilege trimmed back. The vote extended. Women offered the same freedoms as ourselves. Fine as it may be in so much, the future will have less need for the great Dr Arnolds than we might think.'

'First God, then Rugby School!' Dr Osmond said. 'So what have we left?'

'Science,' Oliver said. 'That, not Empire, is what those like ourselves will offer.'

The two men had sat in silence for several minutes. Oliver touched a small controlling lever at the side of his chair. There was a click, then the soft metallic running of a chain. On the other side of the room, a bucket tilted above the red coals of the fire, and fresh clumps replenished it. Such gadgetry amused him. He considered, but quickly put the thought aside, how much it would mean to have a son about the house, to entertain and instruct in such simple demonstrations of motion, gravity, transference of energy. The thought brought him back to his marvellous good fortune of having Lizzie's precise assistance wherever his experimenting led him. Yet if such a gift in her, why so little of it in his brother? It troubled him, the thought that what paternity might pass on so meagrely to one appeared so fulsomely in another. From where then, might her intellect come?

So a story moves on several years, as simply as beginning a new line. Mason's academic terms in the rising mists of the famous fens, in the springtime of youth exposed to those more clever than himself, to the constant presence of young men who thought deeply of what existence might mean, what social duty entails. How knowledge is the privilege, as one of Mason's great teachers put it, of passing on Promethean fire, a thought in fact that made as little impression on him as if such things were discussed in another room, and he heard them dimly.

The brothers walked the estate together and chatted on Oliver's recent successes, the pinnacle being his election to the Royal Society, with Faraday himself proposing him. He conveyed the news as if it meant rather less to him than it did, but was hurt when Mason accepted it as if it were admirable enough but scarcely the crowning honour that it was. The boy is unchanged, his brother thought. His surface has been burnished, but little else has altered. They spoke of Mason's future. The young man said airily, 'Oh, the future, Oliver, it will come whatever we do about it.'

Oliver recalled, so long ago as it now seemed, that day they had sat at his desk and the teenager said to him, with such scouring frankness, that what he wanted from life was to press the borders of what his temperament demanded. He rejected, as if Oliver joked, the suggestion that he might travel to the West Indies, to the island the family still owned. The plantations had become all but a burden with their mismanagement. What an opportunity to prove himself, Oliver said. The opportunity, too, to show perhaps a gift for commerce? What Sir Jack had left them might enrich the family yet again.

'And do the work that slaves once did for us?' Mason said.

He said as much again at dinner that evening, with the awkwardness you might think of doing so with Lizzie facing him. But he smiled at her as he spoke, knowing she would feel the sting of it. Her loveliness provoked him, as much almost as the shame, which Oliver so absurdly seemed never to feel, of how close they might be in blood. When Bella too asked what he might do with his life, now that he was so equipped to face it, he surprised them all – the women who watched him with a certain feline alertness, the two men who presumed to think of themselves as exemplars. He said, 'I have decided on the furthest bounds of where Englishness counts for something.'

Almost a sneer, was it, in the words he spoke? Bella could not be sure. She tried her best for Oliver's sake to interpret them more kindly. Mason's attempt, she thought, to impress us all. Detestable as he might be. She felt for Lizzie's hand beneath the table, its lovely smoothness. Its barely perceptible pressure against the entwining of her fingers. She supposed it must still be in his mind at times, as she half intended it to be. The morning on one of his vacations between terms, when he had come into her room without knocking. It was a lapse of attention, an accident, which he knew at once his sister-in-law could only take as deliberate.

It had been a perfect August morning. She sat naked on the side of her bed, in the pouring of sunlight through the high window facing east. He stood with his hand on the broad doorknob, about to mutter an apology and withdraw. In thinking of it afterwards, Bella herself was uncertain why, instead of turning from him with a curt command, she not only stood but faced him. Mason's pulse raced with the brute fact of her provocation. It was as though she stood edged in flame against the shock of light behind her. The dark aureoles of her breasts as large as pennies. The taste of metal flooded his saliva. He stepped quickly back and left the room, clicking the door behind him. He rested his forehead against its cold hard panelling. Had she tested him? Made mock of him? He felt a deep rage against her. One day. One day there would be a reckoning, she might be assured of that.

And now he was on the eve of leaving them all. Dr Osmond spoke smoothly and proposed a toast. To whatever good fortune might come his way. Mason held Lizzie's eye across the rim of his raised glass. His returned words were cordial. He said he well knew what advantages life at Quercus Park had given him. The utter importance to him of each of those who so kindly shared this moment with him now.

'Then you must bring us something special,' Lizzie said, 'on your return.' Smiling broadly at him as she seldom did.

'Oh, I shall,' Mason said. 'I shall.'

ii

From his first stepping to the wharf at the end of a street that rose to the crest of a low hill, Mason felt the attraction of his country's furthest possession. It was the main street he would quickly become familiar with, as he would with the lanes and side streets that ran from it. After the purity of the Gulf he had just sailed through, the views of forested ridges from the deck as he came closer to land, the distant beaches, the clotting of huts of what he supposed were the natives, he felt the exhilaration as the ship he had lived on for two tedious months swung into what the captain announced, with a kind of pride, as the Inner Harbour.

Imagine, the captain invited, what all this might become, with the energy and expansiveness the colony already so displays? But what came to attract the new arrival far more was what he did not speak of. It was the rawness and uncertainty of the new town that so excited him, the more so as he became acquainted with its canvas and timber huddle, the parodic business structures, the stage-set churches, the drive and naked self-interest of those he spoke with. His own mind curiously elated by its abrasiveness, the town's pretence already to be so much more than it was. Its edgy impression of peace, with the military casually present morning and night.

Mason watched the natives as closely as he did his fellow Britons. He accepted there was a wall between them that he naturally could not scale. Yet their distance, their frankness on one level and what he took to be curt indifference on another, drew him in ways he could not define. So that in his letters home he would speak blandly enough of their enterprise as part of the town's economy, the ferocity of their art and even personal appearance, that concealed so much more than it offered to view. He did not report how it was his sense of encroaching chaos, the loss of his own identity, that he felt at times, especially in the grog shops, in the illicit bordellos, in the swirling fumes and stink of places he found himself in, that so appalled, delighted. There was no way to write of such things, even had he wished. To please the two women who would be interested in his observations rather more than Oliver or Osmond, he wrote of the working-class females who still spoke as if at home yet already had taken on an independence that so readily crossed into presumption. But they – Lizzie and Bella – would be diverted, as indeed he was himself, by the fine English dresses, the close-buttoned bodices, the finely needled skirts they might expect women of some refinement to wear, the manners so carefully kept up in the salons (!) of the officer and business classes, the attention paid to fashion, 'even at this distance, and, as you would expect, not quite in season'.

And the social pinnacle – where else, but at the governor's charming enough residence, where the replica of such events at home was well done yet slightly comic too. 'It takes so little in society to lapse, for the fault quickly to seem irreparable,' he wrote. 'Still, the pantomime keeps up with spirit enough.' Mason knew the women at Quercus Park would read past his irony to their shared contempt for 'standards'. His telling them as much. 'There is a good deal here that I believe you might enjoy.'

Yet so much more he did not convey. The depravity, for example, that was not to be spoken of openly. An officer, well taken with the wine so generously laid on as Government House celebrated the anniversary of the young Queen's coronation, asked frankly, had he observed the way a native's eyes rolled back *in flagrante*, the merest strip of mother-of-pearl between fluttering lids? He spoke of the shadowed lives in the huts and grog shops along the downtown lanes, the scrim palaces of forgetfulness and delight, once the darkness came down. The respectable capital went about its lawful business a matter of minutes away. The lights of the deserving shone distantly from what, within years, would be the finer reaches of the city, along the ridges that ran like the rim of a bowl above the seafront.

Late at night, Mason liked to lie smoking a thin and expensive cigar in the rooms he rented on one of the town's eastern slopes. His own forays into business went well for him almost instantly, his partner a serious Methodist, a member of perhaps the only religious sect one could entirely trust. Almost nonchalantly, he invested handsome capital in an enterprise his partner would manage in all its details – the bringing across of farming equipment from Sydney, the kind of thing that new settlers had such need for. Once the governor had settled the problem of natives who for the moment wrangled about the purchase of land, 'the fruit was there for the picking', as he enjoyed informing Oliver. Some evenings he spent an hour or two in the Gentlemen's Reading Room, which a London agency provided for a small subscription. But he preferred to talk with persons of all stations, discovering a gift for penetrating character that surprised him. He felt that almost weekly, he became aware of aspects of himself that may never have surfaced had he remained at home. He quickly assessed how language serves to conceal more than it reveals; that clever men may also carry a lifetime of naivete, the way an illiterate, beneath what may seem a repellent shell, is capable of subtlety and intuition. He wished Lizzie were here to speak of such things. He missed the sharpness of her mind, even as his troubling lust for her blazed at times so that he loathed her for the game she played with him. Yet appearance too, like language, he thought. How it wraps, conceals, the core of what we are. How many layers must one be willing to divest, before one's essence is arrived at?

After six months in this still new and yet familiar place, Mason seemed at home in whatever company he kept. He had a good head for drink, and with means enough to be acceptable wherever a few flung coins might earn a man an instant loyalty, or half an hour's quick obliging. The governor himself was taken with his charm, his education, his connections in a county where distant relatives of his own resided. The two men talked horses, and the bookish administrator liked his quickness in picking up his literary tabs. Thanks to his half attending to his brother, he bluffed convincingly enough in his offhand talk of the sciences, and could say, quite truthfully, that yes, he had dined with Lyell. He was the kind of young adventurer a new colony so needs.

An American friend, 'stranded', as he put it, between changing berths, and hoping soon to travel north to sign on for a whaler travelling back to New Bedford, taught him simple card tricks, but not so simple they were known in the capital. The profit Mason drew from them was not the point, so much as the delight to be taken from the sleek fleecing of the naive. How far would he go, he thought, with a quickening that itself was a pleasure. How far might a man dare to reach his own boundaries? The elation of escaping the snares that convention throws at one? He knew one boundary at least was touched, when he heard how a nervous middle-aged man he had played with the previous evening had shattered dawn at Freeman's Bay with a gunshot that woke the street.

Another friend, a German who traded liquor and ran various semi-legal businesses, was the man he felt closest to, the one who to any eye but Mason's was the furthest imaginable from his own cultivated demeanour. Gruber's left ear was no more than a bulb of flesh. His chest was scored as though a bear had swept its claws across it. Yet he spoke quietly, even in the late-night clamour of his grog shop. He looked at whomever he talked to with what most men might consider candour, but Mason knew instinctively was something so much colder, calculating. It was the German who told him the details of the practice. Who picked up at once on the thrill that coursed through his English friend as he spoke of it.

It was a rare spell without customers as they stood at the counter beneath the dim inverted V of the roof. The rain that pelted in one of its quick passing squalls compelled them to speak more loudly than either customarily did. Not that it was an occasion for extended speech. Gruber unfolded three pieces of paper on the bar's long slab of kauri. Each displayed similar yet distinctly different patterns, the kinds of curves and swirls familiar to him from the faces he noted each day in the street, that seemed to him of all he saw in the colony, the deepest intricacy of what he failed to comprehend. His explaining how one must be patient, patient and careful, as the administration was severe in such matters. But their very rareness sharpened with some men the desire to risk the law. Gruber understood how Mason was already snared with the very thought of it, that the Englishman's will had frayed, as if an addict.

It was two days' sailing, in a scow of the kind built for what could be challenging seas, yet pliable in the shallow inlets as it travelled north, the tidal creeks with their mudflats and mangrove swamps. A young native called Matthew, handsome and polite and the product of some zealous mission school, adroitly managed the craft while its heavy built captain, with his peaked cap and his boasting of naval service, sat in the small cabin with his single passenger. He spoke kindly of his deckhand, who kept the craft's brass polished to a mirror, kept its tackle trim. The boy scanned the sky and horizon as if there were not a minute without a call for vigilance. Mason feigned a passing illness to escape the captain's torrent of reminiscence, his commentary on the coast they sailed off yet always kept in sight.

Several figures were waiting on the frail wharf after Matthew steered the craft up a narrowing creek. The wet banks glistened mud. The young man joked with those who had come from missions and remote solitary farms. Some came on board to help with unloading the sacks, the bales, the dozen sheep, the lengths of dressed timber, the heavy metal blades for a flour mill. A tall man with a broad-brimmed hat waited to greet Mason as he stepped to the wharf, although 'greeted' is too fulsome a word for the curt nod he gave him, without offering his hand. The man referred to by Gruber, as well as the captain, as 'the trader'.

The visitor was led to horses beyond the wharf. A native, already in the saddle of his own mount, stayed at some distance, a rifle slung across his back. The trader said, 'You can be back here in two hours. Once you've made your choice.'

Mason attempted frank good-fellowship. 'Supposing I buy,' he laughed.

'You'll buy,' the trader said. There was nothing more to say.

In twenty minutes the track opened to roughly knocked-together stockyards, enclosing half a dozen cattle. Much of the land on the slope beyond had been cleared of bush, the grass as lush as the meadows on the estate's tenanted farms at home. From a wooden house with a veranda running its length, two women – one English, he supposed, one native – watched the men arrive. His mind was thrown back again to the two women at Quercus Park. They dominated his thinking, even here, in this weirdly pressing landscape, the pulse of strangeness he felt following the trader through what he had been here long enough to think of as 'bush'. Its dark pull towards whatever it was it might conceal, so distant from the earth's other side, with its landscape so timidly packaged, so exposed to certainty.

The men halted in the stink of the cattle yard, yet the odour still there, fragrant and foreign, from the tunnel of trees they had just emerged from. Perhaps because of the slim, silent women twenty yards off, the vivid image came back at him of an evening shortly before he had left. A small gathering in the drawing room after dinner, a scientist whom his brother so respected reading aloud from Shelley's verse. Mason had thought, What elevated rot. But the small group hushed with reverence.

It was the instant he knew, beyond doubt, that he and Lizzie were not only of the one flesh but capable of a deeper bond as well. From opposite sides of the room they had held each other's gaze, while Dr Osmond pressed one knuckle again a leaking eye. While even Oliver, pragmatist that he was, sat with his chin supported on his joined hands, attending to the poet's 'ethereal beings'. Mason felt the glow of so desiring her, the tall, graceful woman with her tightly curled hair, the richness of her colouring. The *hauteur* which none who met her failed to remark upon. The slight swell of her breast beneath her bodice. A boy's body, almost, which so drew his will towards her.

But memory, with its random startling threads, was hauled back sharply to the moment as the trader too dismounted, tossing his reins to a youth who grinned up at the stranger. He led Mason to a stone shed without windows, not much larger than a prison cell. The trader lit a lamp, worked the wick so it flared higher, steadied, so that the small space was brightly lit. A long table was stacked with boxes and packages, piled papers, folded fabrics, and beside it the squat heaviness of a small printing machine. The trader cleared a space and said, 'I will give you time to make your choice.' Mason raised the first of the muslin-wrapped parcels the trader brought from a curtained alcove in a corner of the room.

It seemed no time had passed before the men were riding back into the green, diminished light of the bush. There was the echoing shot of a rifle to let him know the captain was intending to depart in thirty minutes. The tide had lowered the scow several feet. The sleek mud banks were more exposed, the scabbed spindled stems of the mangroves inches above the dark slurp of the broad creek. But in his riding back an elation rose in Mason unlike anything he had known, the kind of thing, as he later thought, that he had once seen among the crazed farm workers and itinerants after Wesley himself had preached not a dozen miles from Quercus Park. It was a feeling of attainment, of touching some chord in himself that was now fulfilled. But from so unexpected a thing, from the tapping against his knee of the large flax kit tied to the front of his saddle, and inside that, wrapped in finer softened flax, the whole point of his being here – a human head.

iii

His brother Oliver was absent when Mason arrived back. A note explained that he and Osmond were in London, which he was obliged to visit more frequently since his election to the Royal Society. He was there to attend a meeting where the guest speaker was a great geologist. But hoped to return within a day or so. He longed to see his brother, to observe the changes which must be inevitable, as he heavily joked, after 'more than a year among savages. Or was it all far more cosmopolitan than that?'

The women welcomed him with both the frankness and casual distance that had always marked their dealings together. Yet Lizzie and Bella suspecting, too, from the minute he was back in the large familiar house, its furnishings and pictures still carrying as ever the mark of Mad Sir Jack's freakish taste, that he was quickened, even more so as he again took in his sister-in-law's fullness, the younger woman's slender *hauteur*. After such absence, they struck him afresh with a brute sexual force he was unprepared for. That image from years before of Bella's turning to him in her nakedness, her seeming indifference as to whether he looked at her or turned to leave . . . Or the evening when Oliver's friend read the poet's verses, the air so charged with Lizzie's protracted boldness. Her staring back at him, while the poetry's beat seemed that of his own blood, its words lost completely in this other raging silence. Until he had been the first to lower his eyes. But all that was then, he assured himself. This was now.

This first evening back, without Oliver's good-natured but solemn heaviness, or Dr Osmond's tendency to share his education with all, there was a rare levity when the three met at dinner. Mason's was a more generous hand with burgundy than his brother's, and the women pressed him for details of the new colony. He told them he was rather unobservant on flora, fauna, the things he knew the menfolk would so quiz him on, and Bella smiled across at him, telling him thank heavens for that! He amused them with his sardonic chatter of social life, at least of its upper reaches, its playing at social gradation, its discretion on mankind's usual follies. He lowered his voice, and the women leaned slightly towards him. 'Even the governor,' he said. The handsome young Māori woman who was part of the vice-regal menage, and Mr Grey's evident pleasure in 'refining' her. Mrs Grey's starchiness so making it clear that it was a tutelage she herself played little part in. He told them too of the lighter side of military life, the resentment some officers, and their wives especially, held that they must travel to the empire's furthest flagpole to forge a career. There were those, of course, even among the womenfolk, who took to the new country, who found ways to ascend, succeed, as would never have come their way had they remained on the lower rungs in their motherland. 'An unfortunate taste of freedom,' as one cleric had said of them, 'that one day may lead to political *fracas*, God forbid.'

Then what had never taken place at Quercus Park before. After the one servant, who had served at table and helped the cook and housekeeper in the kitchen, had left with the elderly woman for the short walk back to the village, Lizzie said simply, with the calmness of knowing how profoundly she violated the customs of the house, 'Time I think, don't you, for our mad father's rum?' Oliver had long refused to touch the bottles which had come from 'Sir Richard's island', that lay beneath decades of gathered dust in a corner of the cellar. 'I will fetch it,' she said.

Bella looked as though a physical shock had struck her. Even Mason, part of whose *sang froid* was to place himself beyond surprise, held back his impulse to call out, No, Lizzie, not now. But the girl was gone. They heard the slamming of a door caught in the high wind that was rising across the park, then sat without speaking until she was back with them, holding a bottle at her side. A grey smear from a veil of cobwebs in the cellar lay across her shoulders like a shawl. As if one breaking of the house's customs had dispensed with others, and with a directness that took Mason back to one of the Fort Street drinking houses, Lizzie said, 'The glasses we have will do,' not bothering to cross to the cabinet where the small glasses called rummers had lain untouched for years.

Her defiance, her bravado, seemed to let so much convention off its leash. The three brimmed glasses tapped against one another. There was laughter and even a raucousness the dining room, with its sombre panels, its few stiff-figured paintings, had not previously known. The harsh dark liquor was a novelty for each of them; 'Our family blood,' as Lizzie said. As if she had waited since girlhood to mock them all. And a loosening too from whatever Oliver, and his friend Osmond, might consider good behaviour. The two women sang a moving Robert Burns song together, and then a more sentimental piece by Thomas Moore; the delight the music afforded them of wallowing in unearned tears.

'Now you!' they demanded, and Mason, in his fine enough tenor, remembered the decent variants of things the sailors had sung on the voyage out, and again back home. Things that were rollicking and jolly. The women tapped their glasses in time on the dining table. They leaned towards each other, and Bella's hand moved so naturally across to stroke Lizzie's bodice, tampering with its laces to reveal the almost childish breast. Yet rather than hinting at depravity, there was now an air of extraordinary naturalness in the room. Mason touched his sister-in-law's cascading hair as he stood and said, 'The present I promised Lizzie, before I left. You remember that?'

'I remember everything,' she said.

'Give me long enough to fetch it.'

He was back in the trader's windowless stone storeroom, his hand shaking slightly as it rested on the long bench of thick-cut timber while the three shrouded heads were exposed for him. He recognised the patterns from the papers Gruber had unfolded for him. There was no sense of revulsion at what he looked down to, but a heavy curdling excitement. So *this* is what we have arrived at, the buying and selling of dead slaves! He had come to the boundary of what human experience permits. The heads were placed on folded sacking, each tilted slightly back so that when the trader raised the lamp he held, they seemed to be confronting him, the teeth of two of them exposed beneath the upper lips, the discoloured gums oddly prominent. The eyes of two were closed, but with one, slivers of some pale polished shell had been inserted, so a narrow sleeve of greyish-white showed through narrowed lids. He looked closely at the swirl and close incisions of the green scorings of the tattoos, covering the cheeks and foreheads of what the trader offered. Mason's forefinger touched the hardened cheeks. The hair, black and shining as if lacquered, was drawn back tightly and knotted at the crown. Its effect of dignity, for all that it may have been subjected to, struck him as perversely handsome. It was as if something thrummed in Mason's being, this standing beyond the bounds of what most men would consider decency. The head dragged at him with a magnetism he feared and welcomed.

He now carried it through from his bedroom to the dining room, surprised as he always was as he first lifted its compact weight. The candles on the polished table seemed to slur against the darkness. But the women had refilled the glasses with the tar-black alcohol. They stood arm in arm smiling at him, impatient. Bella had let down the glinting fineness of her hair. As he passed her he leaned to put his lips briefly against the warmth of her shoulder.

Mason placed the muslin-hooded gift at the centre of the table. 'I'm afraid you must share him,' he joked. He drew back the cloth so his gift was tilted towards them, the slightly wavering candlelight brushing a drift of mobile shadows across it. He watched intently how the women might receive it. Bella's breath caught in a gasp, one hand raised so the fingers were against her mouth. Her other hand became a clenched fist that she pressed against the table. But nothing, in the many times he had imagined Lizzie in the long voyage home, had come near to this. She smiled slightly as she leaned towards it, and then again stood erect. 'A fourth person,' she said, 'has come into the room.'

'We must drink to it,' Mason said. Her words had shaken him. 'Drink with respect.' The women raised their glasses, but only he emptied his in one prolonged gulping, as God knows he had seen often enough in the Auckland grog shops with the stink of their habitués. He felt that first reeling of the room as he placed his glass back down, the bleeding together of the candles as they slipped across his vision. He felt for the first time the wiry springiness of Lizzie's hair as she leaned in front of him, tilting the bottle she offered him. For something less than a fraction, he was thinking – and yet that too can carry the significance of hours – their heads touched. It was difficult for his mind to hold reality in place. Yet a pulsing aura, was it, that press of such seeming clarity as he watched the dark glitter of the bottle set down, and Lizzie's hand come forward? The bodice Bella had tampered with now fallen to Lizzie's waist. Her forefinger traced lightly above the engraved lines on the face in front of her. She touched the raised upper lip, but again so lightly. And her voice so distant to Mason, now that he needed to grip the back of a chair, as the clarity of a few minutes before crumbled into flaking darkness. His final memory of the night, Lizzie turning towards him in her part nakedness, unperturbed that he might see her, and saying in a quiet voice, the voice of a child almost with its hint of wonder, 'His gums are purple. See?'

The race, then.

Since Elizabeth's first arrival at Quercus Park, she and the then teenaged Mason had loved to race what was called 'the course', the long rising stretch close to the walled boundary of the estate, the turn at the very upper limit of the park, to the ten-yard-wide descent through the forest, with its various by-paths where for the most part walkers must go singly. From angles and breaks in the trees, Sir Richard's folly rose up, then disappeared. It was there, before Oliver and Dr Osmond returned, that the women, without telling Mason, placed his gift in a small higher room, in a chest that carried still the fragrance of camphor. No one had used the room for years. More respectful than Mason, they had swathed the gift in folds of white silk.

The drunken night of his return was not referred to the next day, nor the one after that. Only a note that was slipped beneath his bedroom door, before he woke with his head beating as if inside a gong. His sister-in-law's fine copperplate handwriting, signed with Lizzie's name as well: 'Last evening, dear Mason, was so much more than we expected.' Both women, by lunchtime, had returned to the warm but slightly distant manner that so defined them. Mason walked in the bronze air of the autumn oaks, wrote business letters to what he casually thought of as 'our colony', went over and over in his mind the stark details that persisted through the confused memory of his homecoming. No words came to him that held it accurately, its sexual weirdness, its *farouche* excess. He was glad when Lizzie put to him, on his third evening back, the proposal that they ride the next morning.

'The race?'

'Of course. This weather. Before the ground softens with the rains a tenant this morning told me are bound to be here next week.'

'I remember I beat you last time,' Mason smiled.

'The mare was almost lame.' They laughed together, as old friends. As family almost, Mason sardonically thought. Yet that barrier always, tissue thin, between them, remember as he might such times as the evening before he left. Shelley's flighty vagueness skimming the drawing room from where he sat to Lizzie on the other side, her returning his own scepticism with her steady gaze. As if they flipped flat stones towards each other across a river, a child's game, yet heavy as jewels with their erotic charge.

'This time,' Lizzie said, drawing him back to the race she proposed, 'a new challenge for you. We ride upright as we gallop.'

He laughed again. 'Isn't that slightly irregular?'

'You mean you think you'd lose?'

'I never fear what isn't likely.'

'We finish where the two pines narrow the track to ten yards apart.'

'Elaborate planning,' Mason teased her.

'It needs to be a race worth winning,' she said.

The early sky next morning promised a perfect day. The lawns and branches drenched still with glinting webs and runnels of dew. The sun was not yet above the level of the trees. There was chill enough for the riders to be wearing scarves. Lizzie as always in leather jodhpurs, a tight black riding jacket, a matching beret slanted and held firm with marcasite pins across the spring of her hair. She handed down the thin riding crop she carried to Bella, who stood in her deep green travelling coat, telling her, 'Skill won't need this to bring us home.'

Bella would act as starter and judge. She walked twenty yards ahead of the two nervy and circling horses. When she dropped a white handkerchief the race would begin. It was a touch almost of levity, like the starting of children at a village picnic. Mason grinned at the women. So much fun, he thought, so much seriousness threading it as well. The best sort of game. And the thin edge of anger, the feeling that for all his knowledge of them, the women toyed with him. But with his extensive riding in the colony, he was so much finer a horseman than when he and Lizzie last took the course their mounts now leaped to. He let her quickly gain several lengths on him. He would give her confidence, and then draw it back. The hooves of her mare flung up clods towards him. The pounding of the horses pulsed as if his own. He saw the veins begin to stand on the dark gleaming neck his reins crossed on either side.

Yet when Mason made what he intended to be an advantage on her lead, Lizzie remained those few lengths in front of him. The distance between them had barely changed. He felt the awkwardness of continuing to ride upright, resisting the natural urge to lean forward as they picked up speed. Lizzie's perfectly poised back provoking him. It seemed no more than seconds to the swing of the course at the far end of the estate. His heels drummed at the flanks of his mare. He saw how the tall woman ahead of him gave no more indication of urging her horse, than of restraining it. That sense of exquisite unity when a rider attunes to the force that so finely carries her. His irritation now rising to the blur of anger, as it came to him he was not likely to gain on her, any more than she would be reeled in. They crossed the upper boundary of the park, past the last acres of the season's dying oaks, before the turn to the long sloping descent at whose end Bella, not more than the size of a nursery cut-out, stood to the side of one of the Norfolk pines, her arm already raised.

In the next hundred yards Lizzie allowed him to gain on her. It was difficult not to follow his instinct to crouch forward, defying the absurd conditions she had placed on the race. Mason was close enough now that he might reach out to touch the black jacket of her upright back. And then the rapid swirling of the next few seconds. Lizzie threw herself forward until her upper body was level with the horse's back, her cheek touching the massive swell and working of its shoulder. She turned so her face was visible to him for the first time. He saw the nacreous glint of the eyes no more than a few feet from his own glance. On the hollowed mahogany cheek he saw the whorl of its ink-stained design. Her lip was raised to display white teeth in their discoloured gums. He had time to take in that what rode beside him was the head he had chosen in the fetid windowless hut on the world's far side. Yet it was Lizzie too, her bent form skimming beneath the invisible stretch of razor-sharp copper wire that passed through Mason's throat as neatly as a cheesecutter cleaves through cheese.

Lizzie wheeled Rosebud so the mare stood panting close to Bella. Mason's head had bounced on the short autumn grass twenty yards further on from where the women watched, and rolled into a clump of furze. While Candida, startled by the sudden release of the reins, galloped on, the figure on its back tilting with what seemed unnatural slowness, before falling from its saddle, one booted foot caught in its stirrup, the rider dragged until the mare stopped abruptly, and the riding boot fell loose.

*

Lizzie's calculations had been exact. Bella tightened the wire's brace as she saw the horses curve at the crest of the hill, raising her hand to turn the screw attached to the side of the pine. Hadn't Oliver warned not to ride in the park without informing him? The wires that he believed would bring him fame, rigged in unexpected places. Dr Osmond confirmed how the death, you might say, was extraordinary, but quite explicable. He also insisted that the ladies not see the head, with its purplish contusions and its oddly regular lines etched across the forehead from the fall, before Mason was buried, with a brief and secular ceremony, within view of Sir Jack's Tower.

Should a wire be run, the women liked to say, from the removed and replaced panel they had attended to in the Tower's rarely visited upper room, a wire run down to what they referred to as Mason's mound, it was not impossible, with a little imagination, to project a conversation of sorts. But that was not a matter for today. With her sardonic turn of mind, Lizzie said, as she and Bella lay embracing together, she supposed it all depended on how successful a scientist Oliver might be.

Bella's tongue was licking at Lizzie's upper arm. She lightly circled the younger woman's breast, small but upright as a thimble.

'What was that?' Bella asked.

Lizzie told her again.

'Maybe more than that,' Bella said. Kissing her friend's full lips. 'More than that.' Unsure now what it was she may have meant. Each intent on the moment's vigorous demands.

J WIREMU KANE

Ringawera

Ārani Creek

Sian's key was barely in the café door before the news reached her.

'*Terrible* thing,' the lady from the Salvation Army store said. 'That lovely old man. Dead in the creek.'

Sian crossed Ārani Creek several times a day. The path and bridge made for an easy shortcut, skirting around the back of the hospital on the walk from her house to her café in town.

'A dog-walker spotted him from the path,' she heard one of the council workers saying to another. 'Just below the boulder trap there. Must've slipped and fallen. Poor thing.'

Sian's hips throbbed and she paused. She didn't like to take her anti-inflammatories in the morning. Some days they fuzzed up her thoughts and other times they made her feel near manic.

In summer, the creek was a series of glassy riffles that moulded around any stones larger than a pebble, leaving their tops dry and dusty. The water gathered in a deep, silty-bottomed pool before gliding under the bridge and into a culvert that funnelled it away from the hospital. Sometimes on her walk home she saw swifts chase hovering insects over the pool, kissing the surface and sending out ripples like waveforms.

Sian had seen the orange and white of police tape and the yellow glow of hi-vis from Ārani Road on her way to work that morning. She had altered her route. Police had a way of eyeing her brown skin and curly black hair that she didn't have the energy for.

'Anyone know who he was?' she asked.

Her barista Brian shook his head. If Brian didn't know, no one in town could know yet. 'They've brought in cops from Hamilton,' he said over the shriek of the milk steamer. 'And they're not talking.'

'Terrible way to go,' her waitress said, leaning heavily on the counter.

'Order up,' Sian repeated.

'Imagine being alone out there in the cold.'

'It wasn't cold last night,' Sian said. She remembered her thighs sticking to each other in bed.

'Terrible,' Brian said, shaking his head.

Sian pictured the white of the moon and the orange of the streetlights glittering on water that barely altered its path around a crumpled body. It wouldn't have been quiet. The cicadas had been screeching at full volume and even in drought, the creek gurgled and chattered.

She tried not to compare it to a too-hot house with every window tightly shut, the only sounds the mechanical blast of the central heating and the beep of the syringe driver.

She shrugged. 'I can think of worse ways to go.'

Tokerau (north)

The retch originated deep in Rua's guts. It rolled upward as sweat pricked under his thick curls and emerged as a blast of warm air that tasted of McDonald's breakfast. His hand flew to his mouth too late.

Sian had walked several metres away from the car, fending off questions from her phone. She threw Rua a crooked half-smile of sympathy.

'Okay, but I really have to go now,' she tried for a fourth or fifth time. 'There's no reception in the valley so you'll just have to . . . you'll be fine. *She'll* be fine. I'm going now. No, I'm really going. Ka kite!' She hung up and looked over to Rua. 'You okay?'

He sat half out of the car, his bare feet on the gravel, his head on his knees. He tried to nod. His stomach clenched in protest. 'Yeah. Just a bit of carsickness. And you know, anxiety.'

'Yeah, I know.'

They had left Hamilton before dawn. It was barely light when they stopped outside Pukekohe, where one of Sian's mates filled every spare space in the car with cabbages and onions. They were now on the final stretch of the journey to their little tributary of Te Hokianga-nui-a-Kupe to farewell their Auntie Kuini.

The smell of cabbages didn't help Rua's stomach. He took in the gold-brown hills with dull splashes of bush in the gullies and bordering drains and creeks under a flat, grey sky. He searched for any feeling of familiarity, anything to say he'd entered his ancestral whenua, the one place he should feel at home.

'You'll ask if we have to . . .' Rua trailed off. Sian turned the car off State Highway 1 and onto a narrow side road. A reassuring yellow and black sign read *Marae.*

'We don't need a pōhiri,' Sian said. 'It's *our* marae.'

'I know. But it would help my anxiety if you'd ask.'

A Te Rūnanga-ā-Iwi o Ngāpuhi gazebo was set up at the

main gate. A large man in a hi-vis vest sat at a trestle table with a sign-in sheet and a walkie-talkie. From a tall bamboo pole, a Tino Rangatiratanga flag and a Confederation of United Tribes flag hung limply.

'Bernie,' the man said with a grin. He kissed Sian's cheek and solemnly pressed noses with Rua. 'Youse the ringawera?'

'That's us.' Sian scanned the Covid QR code and brandished her phone at Rua in delight. 'See? No reception! If Linney and Brian burn the café down, it'll have to wait a few days.'

'Drive round to the wharekai,' Bernie said, raising his walkie-talkie. 'I'll let them know you're heading up.'

'Um,' Rua murmured to Sian.

'My cousin here' – she jerked a mocking elbow towards Rua – 'would like to know if we need to be properly welcomed on first.'

'You're tangata whenua?' Bernie asked.

Rua felt his face grow warm. 'Yeah,' he said. 'I mean, sort of . . .'

'You got tūpuna on the wall in there?' Bernie jerked his thumb in the direction of the tiny whare where it sat across the paddock. It was a small, simple building of white weatherboard and red-ochre corrugated iron. Rua always thought it looked more like a classroom than a whare hui.

'Yeah, my granddad's picture is up there.'

'My great-uncle,' Sian chimed in. 'And my granddad, who's Rua's great-uncle.'

'Then you're tangata whenua.' Bernie's deep laugh leapt up an octave to a high-pitched giggle Rua couldn't help joining. 'Go on up.'

'They can wait,' Sian said as Rua hoisted a massive cabbage under each arm. 'Let's see Auntie first.'

They walked across the sun-bleached concrete and entered the little whare. It was cool and dark inside. The curtains were drawn against the glare and a huge air-conditioning unit was blasting frigid air towards the casket.

Two kuia with moko kauae sat vigil either side of the casket. One sang a waiata under her breath while the other ran wooden rosary beads through her bent fingers. They both nodded at Rua and Sian but didn't move from their posts to greet them.

Kuini's simple casket sat on the most beautiful mat of woven flax Rua had ever seen, the fibres tight as cotton, and was draped with a korowai trimmed with red, white and brown feathers.

'Doesn't she look lovely,' Sian whispered. She brushed a non-existent loose strand of hair from Kuini's forehead.

Rua murmured in agreement. He hadn't seen Kuini since the last tangi he'd made it up to five years earlier. Her skin was smoother than he remembered.

He looked up to the wall of portraits above. Christianity had declared elaborate carvings false idols, and the walls of the whare were instead hung with pictures of tūpuna: painted portraits, black-and-white photos from the late nineteenth century, all the way to crisp digital prints in modern frames. Rua smiled imagining his ancestors working their way around commandment number one with faux innocence.

His granddad was easy to find. His mother had the same framed picture in her room at home, a faded print from the eighties.

'Biggest tangihanga this marae has hosted in years,' voices behind him said.

'She marched alongside Dame Whina Cooper, you know.'

'And wrote her speeches for her!'

'That *can't* be true,' Sian said.

'Tonnes of VIPs . . . four or five MPs . . . the race relations minister, maybe even the Governor General . . .'

Rua stepped out of the whare and into the glare. The usually boggy paddock looked parched. The field beyond had been partially reclaimed by the creeping tidal mudflats and mangroves. Low cloud hung just above the Maungataniwha Range and the smaller, closer line of hills. Rua could just make out a glint of sunlight on the brown water of the Waihou.

'If we put one of those big gazebos here for some shade then we can keep the kitchen doors open all day,' Sian said as they walked to the wharekai. 'Get as much air moving as we can, it's gonna be a hot one.'

Rua found a bottle of liquid soap and counted to twenty while his hands turned red under the scalding water. Sian buzzed around behind him, making occasional clicking sounds with her tongue and consulting a clipboard.

'We can feed three hundred tonight,' she said as Rua searched for a towel to dry his hands. 'You and the other tāne can put the hāngī down first thing tomorrow morning. It'll be a late night of prep after we've fed everyone and then an early start.'

She gave Rua a look. *You sure you're up for this?*

'Āe,' Rua said. 'I'd better get those cabbages out of the car.'

'Then you can find the old bug zapper. I won't have flies in this kitchen, and the mozzies will be out later . . .'

Rua's hands were dry from overwashing. The wharekai had sat empty for months and he had spent over an hour scouring it clean of dead cockroaches and filmy spiderwebs. Tiny cracks around his nails stung when he switched to hand sanitiser. He picked at flakes of dead skin.

The walkie-talkie next to the sink crackled into life. Rua looked around the otherwise empty kitchen and raised it. 'Kia ora?'

'Kia ora, Rua,' Bernie's staticky voice said. 'The first group of manuhiri are here.'

'Already? There's no one here!'

'I'll come up and speak for us. One of the aunties can karanga at this end if Sian can do your end. Can you lead the singing? Unless you want to speak?'

'Fuck no.' Rua hoped Bernie wasn't from the Mormon side of the family. 'You speak. I'll do the singing. Does everyone know "E Hoki Mai Rā"?'

'Everyone is about four of us. We'll figure it out.'

'I need to put on a shirt . . .'

Rua half jogged to where he had pitched his small tent on the far side of the paddock, where it would catch a little shade from the mangroves in the afternoon. He kicked off the bright orange crocs that Sian insisted would 'save his feet' and struggled into a black shirt and trousers. He hoped his guitar was in tune.

He reached the whare hui just as the first note of Sian's karanga pierced the close air.

More tangata whenua had materialised out of nowhere and Rua joined the small cluster standing in front of the paepae. Someone handed him his guitar. Rua hadn't had time to feel anxious, but it stuck him in the throat as he plucked the guitar strings, checking their tune. He swallowed and whispered, 'E Hoki Mai Rā?'

There were murmurs of agreement. Rua ran over the chords in his head.

It was a small group of manuhiri that slowly approached the area of dry, spiky grass before the whare. Rua's eyes drifted to the tallest of the group. For a split second he was sure he wasn't seeing right. But with each step, his face grew sharper, and Rua knew it was him.

This country is way too fucking small, he thought.

He hoped nothing showed on his face, but Sian's had a knowing look as she joined them on the paepae.

'Can you believe it?' she hissed as she lowered herself onto the bench. Bernie stepped forward to begin his whaikōrero.

'Believe what?' he whispered back, aware of glares from the aunties.

'That's he's here!'

'How do you know him?'

'Cos he's that fucking cop from last week!'

A cop?

Bernie kept his speech short. Rua, Sian and the other tangata whenua stood again.

'Give me a chord and I'll do the opening line for you,' she said.

A fucking cop?

The line of manuhiri moved past him. Rua kissed cheeks and pressed noses. The cop was near the middle of the line. He showed no sign of recognition as he grasped Rua's hand and looked into his eyes. They pressed their noses and foreheads together.

A fucking cop, Rua thought.

'Tēnā koe,' he said.

Uiui (interrogate)

Sian shuffled up the hill towards home, imagining her view if she were taking her usual route along the creek. The convolvulus that crept along fence lines and up the California redwoods were in bloom, their flowers like old-time gramophone speakers in the shade between indigo and violet. Did the redwoods know they were on the wrong side of the Pacific? Could they feel it in the angle of the sun and texture of the rain and soil? *This isn't quite right,* she pictured them thinking as imported ivy climbed their branches and the moon's face was at the wrong angle.

The trees, birds and stones helped distract her from the shooting pain in her groin.

Try to keep as mobile as you can, everyone told her. So she did.

A kaumātua had come into the café that afternoon with more information. The body had been removed from the creek, but the tapu wouldn't be lifted for several more days. Sian remembered the soles of her feet feeling numb from stamping the last time she'd been part of such a ceremony.

There was an unfamiliar man outside her house. He was leaning against a car with no hubcaps and too many aerials, but stood as she drew nearer. Sian didn't quicken her pace. It seemed to take an age to reach him.

'Ms Mata . . . Mata . . .'

'Sian is fine,' she cut him off. 'You'll have to forgive me, I need to rest my feet.' She lowered herself onto the wooden steps up to the front door.

'We could go inside,' the cop suggested.

'On such a lovely day?' Sian squinted in the sun.

'I'm Detective Constable Nick Alexander,' he said. 'My colleagues and I have been doing some routine door-to-door due to the incident at Ārani Creek last night.'

He said the 'r' in Ārani the Pākehā way. His emphasis was on the wrong 'a'. Poor thing. She reminded herself that the A in ACAB stood for *all,* and that the traitorous brown ones were worse.

'You came all the way from Hamilton to do routine door-to-door?'

'We're being especially thorough on this case due to . . .' He looked as though he wanted to sit down too. There would be room if Sian shuffled along a little. 'How long have you known the deceased?'

'I don't know who it is.'

The detective riffled through a folder and produced a picture.

'Mr Dennis Hastings.' He handed her a photo of a nondescript white man. 'You know him?'

Sian studied the picture. 'I don't think so. He might come into the café, but hundreds of people do.'

'From what I understand, he and his um . . . *group,* are permanently banned from your café.' He handed her a crude photocopy of a second picture. In it, the same man held a sign reading PROTECT *EVERY* MEMBER OF THE FAMILY over the image of a foetus with an adult face and a simpering smile.

'Oh,' Sian said, her voice flat. 'He's one of . . .' She cut herself off from saying *those cunts*. '*Them*,' she finished instead.

'Speaking for the Voiceless.'

Sian snorted. 'They aren't *banned*,' she said. 'As I'm sure you know, my staff and I retain the right to refuse service to anyone we choose. And we choose not to serve members of *that* group.'

'You're pretty active in that local community Facebook group. And you've shared and liked many posts from an account called Niho Maunene.'

Sian stifled a laugh at the name. 'That account hasn't been active for months – and it was banned by the moderators pretty quickly.'

'Is it you?'

Sian's fingers dug into the wood of the steps. 'Do you think I'd tell you if it was?'

'It threatened members of Speaking for the Voiceless with violence.'

Sian looked down at the boards between her feet. They needed repainting. 'I don't remember that.'

The detective found another paper. 'This is from one of Niho Maunene's posts last year – which you shared,' he said. '*In Māui's final quest he aimed to defeat death by reversing the path of life. Crawling into the womb and out through the mouth of Hine-nui-te-pō, goddess of death and the underworld. He was immediately cut in half by the great lady's vagina dentata. Sharp teeth of black obsidian and waxy pounamu . . .*'

'And?'

'. . . *Our storytellers made it very clear what they thought of men messing around in uteruses that don't belong to them, and what the consequences should be.*' He paused. 'That sounds like a threat of violence to me.'

Sian felt her patience give way at last. 'You take things very literally, don't you?' she snapped. 'This Mr Hastings, was he cut in half by a vagina with teeth?'

She was pleased to see the detective blush. 'No,' he said. 'Head wound.'

'He fell in the creek and landed on his head?' Sian smiled. 'I see why you're involving me in this. Aren't you going to ask me where I was at the time of the murder or whatever?'

'No one is saying it's murder –'

'Then why are you here?'

'I –'

'Sian?' someone called from the back of the house.

'I'm out front, babe,' Sian called back.

'What are you doing out here in this heat?' Linney's voice grew louder and clearer as she rounded the house. 'Oh,' she said as she spotted the detective. 'Hi there. I'm Linney.'

'Linney is a work colleague who lives a few doors up from me,' Sian said. 'This is Mr –'

'*Detective* Constable Alexander.'

'Sure,' Sian said. She shifted along the step and Linney sat down next to her. 'He was about to start asking me some actual questions, or he was going to leave.'

'Sorry about her.' Linney smiled. 'She gets grouchy by the afternoons. Sore hips.'

'Thank you, Linney.' The muscles in Sian's thighs and lower back were cramping. She was overdue for her muscle relaxant.

'Linney?' the detective said, consulting his list. 'Is that short for Lindsey? Lindsey Warner?'

'Yes, that's me.'

'I need to talk to you too, please. And is there also a Ms Veronica Mata . . . Mata . . .'

Something must have shown on Sian's face.

'Is that your sister, Sian?'

'That was her *wife.*' Linney's voice sounded like static. 'Who is no longer with us. You need to update your records.'

'It's fine, Linney.'

'It is *not* fine.'

The detective looked mortified, his face red and crumpled. Sian felt a tear burn a path down her cheek and turned away from him to wipe it. 'I'm very sorry,' he said, his voice thick. He made a show of looking in vain for a tissue.

'Sorry,' he said again. 'Can I just ask, *both* of you, if you heard or saw anything unusual last night? Between 10pm and 2am?'

'No,' said Sian.

'No,' said Linney.

'Thank you. Have a pleasant afternoon.'

Sian and Linney sat in silence as the detective returned to his car.

When he had finally gone, Sian held out a hand and Linney pulled her to her feet.

'Handsome,' Linney said.

'Don't,' said Sian.

Āniwaniwa (moon halo)

'I'm just gonna . . .'

'The bathroom is next door,' Rua said.

'Cool.' The man rolled over and stood, picking up the towel from the bed and holding it to his crotch. 'Is it okay if I have a shower?'

'Yeah, man,' Rua said. 'The towels hanging up in there are clean.'

'Cheers.'

He still didn't leave. Rua felt a bead of sweat dripping down his back and another forming in its place.

'Oh, and can I grab another puff on your vape before I head off? I haven't had weed since before lockdown.'

'Yeah, of course.'

'Cheers.' He pulled the bedroom door shut behind him.

Rua wriggled out of bed, untangled his discarded underwear and climbed back into them. The flat was empty – his flatmates were scattered across Te Ika in their family bubbles – but he still felt exposed being naked there. He padded down to the other bathroom to clean himself up.

Rua flushed a stiffening wad of tissues. He could hear the clunk of the gas hot water and the hiss of the shower. His toothbrush was in there with . . . had they exchanged names? His profile name had been 'Looking'. He found an old tube of toothpaste, rinsed off the dried stuff from the tube and swished a chunk of toothpaste around his mouth with a swig of water from the tap. There was still a pleasant fuzz in his head from the sesh they'd had earlier, and the hum of relaxed muscles and worn-out nerves in his pelvis.

The pipes stopped gurgling as the shower was turned off. The flat was silent again. It still had a sulky, neglected air, mad that it had been left to sit empty during levels 3 and 4. Rua towelled the sweat off his chest and back and found some bodyspray to apply. He would have a shower after Looking had left.

Looking was sitting on the bench out on the deck. He wore just his K-mart brand black, trunk-style underwear and a damp towel draped over his shoulders. He took a deep inhale on Rua's dry herb vape. He patted the space next to him on the bench. Rua sat down, arms folded across his bare chest, oddly pleased that Looking hadn't got all the way dressed.

'Aren't you cold?' he asked.

'No. Are you?'

'No.' It was warm for June. He took the vape and inhaled. They'd probably look quite cool passing a joint or blunt back and forth. No one looks cool vaping.

Rua took in Looking's shaggy lockdown hair, not overgrown enough to hide his widow's peak. His brown eyes were big and a little too far apart. It somehow made him look more handsome.

'What are you thinking?' Looking asked.

'I'm thinking . . .' Rua looked up. The full moon was surrounded by a perfect halo of white light, though half of it was obscured by a rimu tree in the corner of the section. 'I'm thinking how considerate it is of ice crystals high in the atmosphere to refract light in such a way that . . .' He pointed up at the halo. He felt his mind soften and loosen at the edges. Some of the tension in his jaw and temples gave way.

Looking chuckled silently, his shaking shoulders brushing against Rua's.

'And that I wish weed were legal,' Rua added, blowing a cloud towards the moon.

'Soon,' Looking said. 'Hopefully.'

'Hopefully. Though then cops couldn't use the smell of weed as an excuse for warrantless searches of brown people –'

'A shame we can't see the whole thing.' Looking stood up and looked towards the back fence. I bet we could from your neighbour's place. Is anyone home there?'

'No, not for months.'

'Then let's do it.' Looking crossed the lawn to the fence and started feeling for foot and hand holds.

'Seriously?'

The silhouette of Looking vanished over the top of the fence.

Rua's feet left dark patches in the dew on the lawn. His hands were unsteady on the damp wood of the fence and his stomach scraped against the boards. He glimpsed the jagged shape of Mount Pirongia against the deep blue of the sky before half tumbling into his neighbour's garden.

Looking was lying on his back on the trampoline. Rua joined him, moving with exaggerated care to stop the springs creaking.

'There!' Looking pointed up.

The moon was directly above them, the entire halo visible, enclosing a circle of richer blue around the white disc. Only the brightest stars were visible: the three points of Orion's belt, Venus and Mars, the pointers and the bottom star of Te Punga. Takurua, the dog star.

'It looks like a lid on the dome of the sky,' Rua said. 'Like a giant would lift it off to look through to check in on us. They'd probably be mad. *Look at the fucking mess they've made!*'

'Can you let some carbon dioxide out while you have the lid off, please?' Looking asked the imaginary giants.

'No that's ozone,' Rua cried. 'We need that.' He felt Looking's shoulders shaking again.

Looking reached over and traced the pale scratches on Rua's stomach, his touch the slightest tickle. 'You okay?'

'Yeah,' Rua said. 'This is nice.' He could smell his own bodywash on Looking. He liked it. 'Āniwaniwa,' he said. 'A halo around a heavenly body. Āniwaniwa.'

Their hands found each other.

Ringawera (kitchenhand)

After the first group, the manuhiri started arriving in a steady stream. The kitchen sounds were punctuated by the wail of karanga, the crackle of the walkie-talkie and fragments of whaikōrero carried on welcome breezes. And waiata, new and old. Thighs, arms and chests were slapped, guitars thrummed, feet stamped.

The ringawera joined the singing as they worked.

'PIKI MAI KAKE MAI RĀ!' Sian heard Rua's voice from his place at the main sink. From there he directed mugs and glasses into the steriliser, plates to be scraped off – green bin for the pigs, keep the napkins separate for the compost. Any paper over there – it can be used to start the fire in the morning. Sian had never presided over a cleaner or more efficient kitchen.

Rua's parents arrived before dinner. Rua's mother, Maia, hugged him around his waist while his nieces and nephews clung to his legs and shoulders.

Sian greeted them too, hugging her favourite aunt and uncle and kissing the kids on the tops of their heads.

'You two are so good,' Maia said. 'How are the hips?'

'Holding up,' Sian said. 'And the doctors keep telling me thirty-nine is too young for a double joint replacement.'

Maia touched Sian's cheek and smiled before she was whipped away by two of the aunties.

Koha were delivered to the kitchen door almost too quickly for Sian to direct.

A chilly bin full of snapper. 'If someone could gut those,' she said. 'No need to fillet them, we'll roast them whole for tonight. Save some to marinate. Or we could slice it up thin for sashimi – do we have soy and wasabi?'

An even bigger chilly bin of live crayfish. 'The important manuhiri can have the tails,' she said. 'Make sure the cop gets one. A big one. We can make stock with the shells, heads and legs. Keep all the flesh that comes out. We can do a deluxe mac and cheese, that way everyone can have a little.'

She left the oysters for others to shuck. 'Half shell is much quicker. Then we can grill half and leave half raw for those that prefer them . . .'

She sliced the pāua herself, simmering the dark meat in a rich sauce of cream, onions and bacon. 'It's for the VIPs,' she said when it attracted longing looks, but she let anyone try a spoonful or two.

'Here.' Sian forced a small bowl into Rua's hands. He had tied a bandanna around his forehead to keep his curls out of his eyes. It was already soaked with sweat. 'Take this somewhere cool and eat it before you pass out.'

'Yes, Chef.'

Things ran more smoothly than Sian could have hoped. Everyone wanted the same thing. To impress the guests, to make Kuini's spirit proud, to avoid the shame of not providing every manuhiri welcomed onto the marae with more than they could eat.

And they had their own reasons too. Sian knew Rua never felt like he was Māori enough to belong on the marae. That his eyes dropped when his reo faltered. That he wished he could live closer to Te Tai Tokerau. Dishes were something he felt he could do.

And Rua knew Sian's reasons. The whole whānau did.

They know I didn't get to do this for you, Ronnie, she thought. To cook for you. To make your spirit proud.

Ronnie's mother, Debbie, had been scandalised at the idea of Sian doing the cooking. 'No of course not!' she'd said. 'It's too much for you to be dealing with on top of everything else. I've already spoken to a nice caterer, she did Paul's mother's funeral and I tell you, it was lovely . . .'

There was no 'everything else'. They had just wanted her to sit still and look sad.

'Can I do anything for you?' they'd asked.

You can let me cook! she had wanted to scream. Let her pretend it was onions making her eyes water and steam and heat flushing her face. Let her use her hands instead of forcing mugs of tea into them and patting them with dry skin.

'Oh wow,' Sian said as she was presented with six eels, already split and gutted. 'We can smoke those in the morning when the fire is going. Hang them in the walk-in.'

She instructed a group of younger cousins on how to prepare stuffing for the next day's hāngī.

'Everything for the hāngī goes back in the big walk-in fridge,' she said. 'I don't want it getting mixed up with tonight's dinner.'

She spotted the cop entering the kitchen. Trying to help. Drying a dish with a hand towel instead of a tea towel. Kotahi, Rua's older brother, showed him his mistake.

The cop looked lost. Sian felt an unexpected pang of sympathy.

'Kotahi,' she said as her cousin breezed past her. 'When the tāne put the hāngī down in the morning, ask Rua's cop if he wants to help.'

Hāngī (earth oven)

'Here.' The cop gave a hesitant smile. 'I'll help you with that.'

'Oh.' Rua hoped his cheeks weren't as pink as they felt. 'Thanks.'

They each took a handle of the heavy wire basket lined with the thick outer leaves of the cabbages. The predawn light was grey. Rain drizzled just enough to catch on glasses and in irritating hollows while stirring the dusty ground to mud.

The valley was blanketed in cloud that rolled up and down the steep-sided hills like enormous breaths.

'I don't think I caught your name,' Rua said.

'I'm Nick.'

They added their basket to the pile next to the pit and a stack of wood draped in scratchy blue tarpaulins.

The rain would probably find a way in, Rua thought. It always did. He wiped sweat and rain drops off his forehead. His ankles stung where mud clung to them.

They joined the group of men clustered under a makeshift shelter of canvas and bamboo poles.

'Once the fire catches it'll be tino pai,' Kotahi said.

'You still use river stones?' someone asked, inspecting the rocks stacked under the wood. 'I could've brought up some railway irons if you'd said.'

'Our koro probably laid those railway irons,' Rua said.

'Stones have done us for thousands of years,' Bernie said. 'We ready to light this thing?'

Rua watched the flames while seated on a round of a log. They'd been up until the small hours prepping the baskets. His eyes were itchy, the lids sore and swollen even before a gust of woodsmoke swirled into his face. He sipped black coffee with too much sugar from an Arcoroc mug.

'I've never put down a hāngī before.' Nick pulled up a log and sat next to Rua.

'Did someone make you coffee? Or tea?' Rua asked. 'Milo?'

'Yes they did. Everyone is taking especially good care of me. It's almost making me feel bad.'

'Sorry.'

'Don't be.'

Rua rubbed his eyes. The stinging only worsened. The smoke hung at head level and seemed annoyed that the rain was stopping it from drifting away.

Nick shuffled closer to Rua. 'I was gonna go for a bit of a drive after this,' he said, looking into the fire. 'Try and find some reception.'

'Okay.'

Nick kept his eyes fixed on the fire. 'You could come with me. If you want.'

'There are breakfast dishes . . .'

'The MPs are supposed to get here soon.' Kotahi pushed Rua aside to make room for himself on the log. 'And cameras from Māori TV and Te Karere. You know they want footage of MPs with their hands in the sink.' He clapped a hand on Rua's shoulder. 'Show the cop around our beautiful whenua.'

Rua felt the stirrings of a dry retch. 'I –'

A crack like a gunshot split the air. Rua froze, expecting to feel the white-hot pain of a bullet somewhere. Nick leapt to his feet, hand at his hip where a holster might be. Every dog in the valley started barking.

'What was *that?*' Rua heard Sian calling from the kitchen door.

Bernie moved as close to the fire as he could, holding a long-handled rake with steel teeth. He scraped at the side of the fire and out rolled two pieces of a stone that had cracked almost perfectly in half.

To Rua it looked like a hatched taniwha egg. He half expected a slippery, scaled creature to emerge and burrow a muddy channel down to the tidal mudflats and into the Waihou.

'You don't get that with railway irons,' someone muttered.

Rua was asleep before they left the valley. Fitful sleep that tasted of smoke and mud and felt stuffy despite the car's air conditioning. He woke dry-mouthed and confused, and the sun and water felt in the wrong direction. Through the fogged-up windscreen, he saw the sprawl of the fancy hotel and, beyond the massive yellow pyramid of the north head, a narrow wharf reaching out towards it.

'I didn't mean to wake you,' Nick said. 'I wasn't going to stop, but . . .' He gestured at the harbour mouth and the Tasman beyond. 'We ran out of road.' He looked at his phone. 'Give me a few minutes, I need to make a call.'

The rain had stopped. Rua got out of the car to let Nick make his call. Steam rose from the wooden planks of the wharf. The Tasman stretched forever, churned up grey with layer after layer of white foam under towering clouds.

Not the Tasman, Rua reminded himself. *Te Tai-o-Rēhua.* Tasman was some Dutch goon who so grossly underestimated the size of the Pacific he thought he'd hit the bottom of South America. Rēhua was Antares, the god star, the star of summer. Rēhua meant long days and humid nights full of the drone of cicadas and crickets. Rēhua meant January.

Nick finished his call and joined Rua.

'All good?' Rua asked, seeing Nick's drawn face.

'Yeah.' Nick's voice was distant. 'Just work stuff.'

'Work stuff,' Rua echoed. Cop stuff. His stomach gurgled again.

They walked past a small group of tourists in the hotel carpark, snapping photos of the clouds over the dunes. Rua tried to keep his breathing slow and even as they crossed the road and stepped onto the wharf.

'A taniwha lives here,' he said, pointing to the south head. 'Āraiteuru. She had eleven sons and each of them carved out an arm of the Hokianga. Waihou, her strongest son, he smashed his way inland through the cliffs and burrowed out the channel, throwing up the hills to each side. He made our valley and came to rest at Lake Omapere. His brothers carved out the shorter arms. Waimā, Orira, Mangamuka, Ohopa, Wairere . . .'

'I don't know any of my stories,' Nick said.

'Where are you from?'

'The East Coast.'

'Ngāti Porou territory? Then you have stories, you have the whale rider.' Rua took a deep breath and beat his chest with his palms. '*Uia mai koia*,' he sang, '*whakahuatia ake, ko wai te whare nei e? KO TE KANI! Ko wai te tekoteko kei runga? Ko Paikea! Ko Paikea! HEI!*'

The Pākehā tourists had joined them on the wharf. They looked over at Rua and applauded. He felt his cheeks grow warm.

'I like singing,' he said, hoping he didn't sound too defensive.

'It's beautiful,' Nick said. For a second Rua thought he was going to take his hand. He looked down at the swirling water through the gaps in the plank. When he raised his eyes again, Nick had turned back towards the shoreline.

'Tell me another story,' Nick said as he fished in his pocket for his car keys.

Don't, a part of Rua warned, but he was already speaking. 'Once there was a boy,' he began, 'who had the singularly useless magic power of hearing the words people wouldn't say out loud. At school he enjoyed the praise he received at first. Bright, articulate, a real credit to his family. Until he heard the rest of the words. Bright and articulate . . . *for a Māori*. What a credit . . . *to his working-class, Māori roots. This one's a smart one, he might finish high school or even go to uni*. He also heard other things people would never say to his face. Words he didn't understand and an identity that adults seemed intent on thrusting on him.

'When he was seventeen and still trying to figure himself out, he made the mistake of attending a party in the rural Waikato. There, some friends of friends took exception to the way the boy dressed or spoke or carried himself.

'Later, the boy, mostly physically unharmed due to luck rather than mercy, went to the police to report his own attempted murder. The officers were . . . bored? Unimpressed. Maybe a little amused. And as the downhearted boy left, he heard the words not said out loud.

'*What did the little faggot expect, showing up looking like that? Asking for it.*'

Rua didn't want to meet Nick's eyes. He focused on the lower part of his face instead.

'I don't . . . I don't know how you want me to respond to that,' Nick said, rubbing his chin. It was clean shaven. Rua had liked his post-lockdown scrubby beard.

'Honestly, I guess,' Rua said.

'Honestly?' Nick paused. He looked inland towards the low hills. The rain was rolling down the harbour in a wall of blurry grey and white. The sun would probably already be out again back in the valley. 'It was a little close to home,' he said at last. 'I remember the praise. The desire to please. Wanting to be the *good* Māori.'

Rua had been on the verge of apologising. Instead, he felt his irritation rising. 'That's all?'

'I don't know what you want me to say.' Nick looked down at the ground. 'You're angry with me.'

'A little.'

'For what? For being a detective?'

'For being . . . here.' Rua regretted the words instantly. Nick's face seemed designed to display hurt – his wide-set eyes, his naturally downturned mouth. 'Sorry, that was –'

'I get it. This is supposed to be your safe space.'

On the car ride back they drove through the shower and out the other side. Rua watched the clouds roll out to the coast, leaving the hills steaming. He wanted to say something to Nick. The way Nick's lips trembled and opened noiselessly, he thought Nick wanted to say something too. But they were both silent.

Takahi whare (tramp the house)

Sian's weariness hit all at once and her legs nearly gave out from under her. The hāngī was down, the last shovelful of soil patted flat.

'Have a rest,' Auntie Maia said. 'You've done Kuini proud, no one will go hungry.' She leaned in and kissed Sian's cheek. She smelled clean and somehow kind. 'You've done Ronnie proud, too.'

Sian didn't know how to respond to that. She smiled as her eyes pricked. 'Just one last thing to take care of.'

Her phone didn't start beeping until she was almost back on State Highway 1. She pulled over and called Linney.

'Sian! I wasn't expecting to hear from you until tomorrow. Is everything okay?'

'Yeah,' Sian said. 'I just needed a little drive. The hāngī is down.'

'Great, that must be a relief. How is everyone?'

'Good.' She paused. 'That cop is here.'

'The cop from last week?'

'Yeah.' She chose her words carefully. 'Don't worry, turns out we're only related by marriage.'

Linney gave a short laugh. 'I'm not the sort of person cops ever worry.'

Sian rubbed her eyes. They stung with tiredness. 'Everything fine at the café?'

'Perfectly so. Get some rest, babe.'

*

'Where are we going?' Sian had asked as she climbed into Linney's car. It had just struck midnight and level 3 lockdown had ended.

'To do something naughty.' Linney refused to say anything more.

The checkpoints on the way out of town were gone at last. The traffic was still sparse. Sian soon figured out where they were going.

'Linney!'

'It'll be fine,' Linney said. 'No one has been there since March and you know where Debbie hid the spare key, right?'

The car bumped along the pitted gravel driveway. Linney made Sian wait in the car while she climbed out and opened the heavy wooden gate. Sian half expected to see Debbie standing on the front porch, glaring at the intruders, but of course the house was empty. Debbie was trapped in Sydney with her sister and had been since March.

Debbie . . .

'She's much more comfortable here at home,' Debbie had said. What Debbie had really meant was *she* was comfortable in the stifling old homestead, too far out of town for casual visitors to drop by. Where heavy fabric draped everything in jewel tones, pigeon-blood red curtains, midnight blue quilts over dazzling white sheets and the pink crocheted hat pulled down to cover sparse hair.

Sian had never felt at home there, and Debbie loved to encourage that feeling. From the heavy-framed wedding photo with Sian's face turned away from the camera, to the low tables she enjoyed perching herself on, daring Sian to say anything.

It had got worse at the end. Debbie had been horrified at Sian's suggestion she stay with her wife. She had even put a wrinkled hand to her mouth in a show of disgust.

'No! I can't have you sleeping in here. It wouldn't be . . . comfortable.'

'I can sleep in a chair,' Sian said. 'Or even on the floor. Honestly, anywhere is fine.'

'The Airbnb is only fifteen minutes away.' Debbie reached out to pat Sian's hand. Sian was tempted to rip it away. 'She'll still be here in the morning.'

Sian had squeezed Ronnie's hand and felt the struggle of her pulse, slowed by morphine and midazolam. She *wouldn't* still be there in the morning. Sian wasn't sure how she'd known.

Debbie had barely spoken to Sian after the small, non-denominational funeral service. Sian knew she should resent the slight, but all she had felt was relief.

The house felt happy to be open again. Linney had brought a chisel and they pried open every window that had been painted shut. Sian oiled the hinges on the fanlight windows above the bed Ronnie had died in and wrenched them open for the first time in years. They drew back every heavy drape and the lace curtains underneath. They propped open every door and let the winter air swirl into every dusty corner.

They didn't have anyone else with them, so they tramped out the house together, just the two of them. They stamped their feet until Sian's hips throbbed, and the soles of her feet were numb. They shook loose every speck of dust with their stamping and drove out anything that needed to be set free.

Sian ripped layer after layer of bedclothes from the big old bed until just the fitted sheet remained. They sprawled across it and smoked a joint, watching the smoke rise and then get suddenly sucked out through the fanlights.

Sian cried into the pillows, her face, jaw and neck aching from the sobs while Linney pretended not to notice.

Before dawn, Linney closed all the windows and pulled the drapes back across. Sian remade the bed for the final time.

Any remaining weed smell had dissipated, and the close smell of potpourri was returning. Sian was sure she'd got the order of the bedclothes wrong.

'What'll we do if Debbie says something?'

Linney's car rumbled down the gravel driveway.

'She won't. And if she does, you'll deny all knowledge. Right?'

Sian nodded. 'Right.'

Pōhatu (stone)

Rua trudged down the paddock towards the mangroves, the two halves of the broken hāngī stone tucked under his arm. Despite the almost carnival atmosphere of the night before, there was a tired, heavy feeling over the marae on day three of the tangi. People were starting to feel how long they'd been away from their homes, their jobs. The little valley felt overstuffed with people and their feelings.

They were to bury Kuini that afternoon. Tents were already being dismantled, empty beer cans and wine bottles smuggled into recycling bins with sheepish looks at the Mormon contingent.

Below the ridge the whare was built on, the ground fell away suddenly down towards the creeping wetlands. A boardwalk snaked through the overgrown mangroves. Rua walked along it, feeling the rough boards under his cracked heels. He needed to raid his mother's tent for moisturiser.

Then the smell of cigarette smoke hit him, sharp against the salt, mud and evaporating water. 'Of course,' he muttered as he spotted Nick sitting on the edge of the boardwalk, exhaling smoke.

'You got weed?' Nick asked as Rua approached. 'I hear this is where people sneak off to smoke.'

'Is this entrapment?'

Nick shrugged. 'I'm not very good at it if it is.'

Rua sat down and handed Nick his vape. His feet dangled above the mangrove roots, which poked out of the mud like alien fingers.

'Cheers.'

'I guess I wanted you to appreciate,' Rua said, as if they were still mid-conversation, 'just how . . . vulnerable I feel around cops. How exposed. Being Māori. And queer. And having . . . multiple mental illnesses. And enjoying weed.'

'Yeah,' Nick said. 'I think I get it.'

Rua felt his stomach twisting. He forced himself to speak.

'Are you here because of Sian and that dead creep?'

Nick didn't answer right away. Rua's stomach clenched. He took the vape and inhaled.

'I'm here,' Nick said at last, 'to pay my respects to Kuini, just like everyone else. But, when I told my boss where I was going and who would be here, he asked . . . he asked if I would just . . . keep an eye out.'

Rua had been expecting the answer, but was surprised at how quickly he felt his heart speed up. Blood thundered in his ears and temples. He was glad he was sitting down already.

'And you told your boss,' he said, struggling to keep his voice even, 'that a marae is a sacred space. That tangihanga is one of the only rites we have left that colonisation hasn't forced its way into.' His voice was rising. 'And that anyone even remotely culturally competent should know that.'

'I mean, I know that *now* –'

'I'm trying *so* hard to not hate you.'

'I'm sorry,' Nick said. 'I really am. I . . . you're, what, thirty?'

'I'm thirty-three.'

'I'm going to be forty-one this year.' Nick seemed to sag as he spoke. 'It was different then. Being Māori was something I was always taught to be ashamed of. And all anyone would tell me was that being gay meant you would get AIDS and die, and I couldn't, so I couldn't be . . .' His breathing was ragged. 'I had no one to look up to, no one to confide in, I had . . . I had no one.'

'Nick, it's –'

'I had no one. I *have* no one, I have –'

'Breathe,' Rua said. 'Bring your knees up, head down and just breathe. Nice and even. Watch me and follow my breathing. In and out. Nice and even.'

Nick's breathing gradually slowed. All the colour had drained from his face.

Rua draped an arm around his shoulders. 'Better?'

Nick nodded. 'It gets worse,' he said. 'My boss . . . he wanted me to keep an eye on, on *you* too.'

'Me?' A humourless laugh escaped Rua's mouth. 'Why me? Because of that stupid fake Facebook account?'

Nick's eyes widened. '*You're* Niho Maunene?'

'Sian didn't tell you that?'

'No, she didn't. And before I got here I didn't know that *you* were Rua. I just thought of you as "CanHost".' He shook his head. '*You* really wrote all those things? You don't even live there!'

'I went over for the big counter-protest Sian helped organise,' Rua said. 'I put it together from a bunch of comments from the town hall meeting.'

'You compared anti-abortion protesters to the last bit of shit you can't squeeze out!'

Rua took a deep inhale on his vape. 'I was joking!'

'You said they deserved to be –'

'I was being dramatic. I thought that was obvious. I don't want to hurt anyone. Ever. I . . . If you didn't know I was Niho Maunene, then why me?'

'We had a list of people that attended the counter-protest.'

'Oh.' Rua's jaw clenched. 'And you saw the names Eruera and Matawhaorua and figured there are your murderers?'

'Not me,' Nick said. He turned away from Rua and let out a long sigh. Rua looked down at the mud. A crab crawled out of a hole, shuffled sideways and vanished into another.

'You can tell Sian it's all over anyway,' Nick said. 'The coroner has ruled it an accidental death.' He let out a long sigh. 'The only reason we investigated as thoroughly as we did was because those Speaking for the Voiceless arseholes were pressuring my boss. Their leader was sure that whoever was behind the Niho Maunene account had smashed his mate's head in.'

Nick seemed to notice the broken stones sitting on the boards next to them for the first time. 'Why are you carrying rocks around?'

'It's the hāngī stone that split yesterday,' Rua said. He picked up one of the halves and turned it over in his hand. 'I wanted to make sure it doesn't get used again by mistake.'

He stood up. With an exaggerated pivot, he hoisted the stone to his shoulder like a shot put and hurled it out into the mangroves. It crashed through some branches and landed with a splat. A white-faced heron rose from the trees in slow-motion and threw Rua a look of disgust before flapping away, its neck hunched into its chest.

'Sorry!' Rua called after the departing bird.

Nick looked down at the mud. 'I don't know what to do,' he said.

'You'll figure it out. If you could do something about the way your buddies target brown people, that might be a good start.'

'Yeah, that'll keep me busy, for sure.' He gave a shy smile. 'And what about us?'

'I dunno,' Rua said. 'Friends? Even though I'll get so much shit about it from my radical, cop-hating mates.'

'E hoa, that's friend, right?'

'Yeah. E hoa.'

'I'm learning.'

Nick stood and picked up the other half of the stone. He pitched it like a softball player. It flew out past the mangroves and landed in the creek with a satisfying plop.

Kāti i konei (end it here)

The car rattled at a frequency that made the bones in Sian's face ache. Rua was driving and on a whim had taken the narrow road of scuffed metal that wound up the valley rather than the sealed route.

'I haven't been this way in forever,' he said. 'And you know, it's the one part of the world where we're not . . . not on someone else's whenua. You know?'

'I know.'

Neither had wanted to stay for the poroporoaki. They had both reached their limit of speeches and interacting with whānau. Sian had long grown tired of the silent *aren't you doing well* nods and *sorry for your loss* cheek kisses.

Rua tapped his rough fingers on the steering wheel and sang to himself. '*Ki ngā ringawera, tino papai ngā kai* . . . is it *ngā* kai? Or *te* kai? I've heard it both ways.'

'So have I,' said Sian. Rua seemed happier since talking to Nick. She hadn't noticed him dry-retch in days. 'You really think your cop isn't beyond redemption?'

'He's not *my* cop,' Rua said. 'And I hope so. He seems to want to try.'

'Sure,' Sian said. 'Maybe he'll be the *one* person to successfully bring down the master's house with the master's tools.'

Rua shrugged. 'We all tried,' he said. 'He already called me out for judging people not as far along their journey as we are. I'm trying to be . . . nice.'

*

Sian usually allowed herself one joint at the end of the day. It helped her sleep after a day of paper-thin cartilage grinding on bone as her upper body balanced on her hips. She had just finished rolling it when she heard a frantic knock.

Linney burst through the back door before Sian could stand, her eyes wild, her cheeks flushed.

'Sian! I think . . . I think I did something. I *did* something bad.'

'How bad?'

Linney's face was answer enough. Sian stood and guided her to the couch.

'Are you hurt?'

Linney shook her head. Sian lit the joint and handed it to her. Linney inhaled deeply and remembered to aim her stream of smoke out the open window. Sian took a cautious puff herself, enough to dull her cramping muscles but not enough to cloud her mind.

'Tell me what happened,' she said. '*Exactly* what happened.'

Linney took several deep breaths before finally speaking.

'It was stuffy at home, and I was restless,' she said. 'I thought a walk would help. I got to the bridge and stopped to look at the ducks.'

Sian could picture it. Linney leaning on the curved metal rail of the bridge, watching the family of ducks that had taken up residence in the creek, bumping and bobbing in the water as they slept.

Linney wouldn't meet Sian's eyes. 'Someone else was there,

standing too still and quiet. I didn't see him until he moved. I asked if he was okay and he said . . . he said I'd kill my babies, that I'd told him I would kill as many of my babies as I wanted.'

'What?'

'It was one of the anti-abortion guys. One of the ones we had to stop coming into the café.'

Sian's fragmented thoughts were beginning to settle and arrange themselves. Linney's words were starting to make sense. Sian remembered something Rua had written on the community Facebook page as his wrathful alter ego.

I worry for the people in these men's lives. If they're willing to display such open misogyny in public, how do they treat women in private?

'Did he touch you?'

Linney nodded.

If they think outside a hospital is a good place to show how little they care for the bodily autonomy of others, what harm do they do when no one can see them?

'Oh, *honey* –'

'Just my arm,' she said. 'But . . . but it scared me. I shook him off easily enough, but he was blocking the path. I needed to push past him, or turn my back on him to go back and I . . . I didn't know what to do.'

Sian felt her chest tightening.

'I picked up a stone and . . . and I told him, *If you touch me again, I'll . . . I'll fucking kill you.*'

Linney reached out for Sian's hand and Sian let her take it.

'Did he touch you again?' she asked.

Linney wouldn't look at her.

'Yes,' she said.

Sian took another drag on the joint, trying to slow the racing of her thoughts. She was surprised by how calm she felt.

'The stone,' Sian said, squeezing Linney's hand. 'Think carefully. What did you do with the stone?'

Linney shut her eyes. 'I didn't drop it right away.' Her voice now had a dreamy quality. Sian moved the pāua shell ashtray holding the half-smoked joint to the far side of the coffee table. 'But I didn't have it at the corner by the Murphys' place, because I checked my hands under the streetlight there. For blood.' She opened her eyes and looked imploringly at Sian. 'There wasn't any. I barely touched him! He tripped . . .'

'Stay here. I'll be back in two minutes.'

Sian dragged herself to her feet. She slipped on the pair of jandals she kept at the back door and hobbled down to where the back gate opened onto Ārani Road. She shuffled along the footpath, her eyes straining for the glint of light on wet stone.

Sian found the river stone on the grass verge outside the Murphys' house. She felt almost light on her feet as she scooped it up, turned and jogged back to the house, her hip joints groaning in protest.

Linney hadn't moved from her spot on the couch. She looked up at Sian, her lip trembling.

Sian gave a short nod.

'Have a shower, go to bed. Nothing happened.'

'But what if . . .'

'Deny all knowledge, right?'

Linney rubbed her eyes and nodded. 'But what will you do with it? With the stone?'

Sian shook her head.

'Don't worry about it. I'll think of something.'

ANTHONY LAPWOOD

Around the Fire

> You never know what is enough unless you know what is more than enough.
>
> —William Blake, *The Marriage of Heaven and Hell*

'Daddy?'

Piper signals that she wants me to crouch, and so I crouch. She tilts her face downwards to avoid my eyes. Her breathing is slow and distinct, determined.

'What's up, sweetie?'

She hesitates, then cups her hands around her mouth. She moves beside me and her voice in my ear informs me she'd like to say goodnight to Misty, our family cat. She steps back and waits for my response.

'You still miss her?'

Piper bobs her head.

Misty.

'All right,' I say. I call over to Kate and Tyler, the eight-year-old girl teaching the five-year-old boy the names of things in the living room, using a made-up language. 'I know it's been a little while, but how do you feel about visiting Misty, to say night-night?'

'Misty!' Tyler shouts. 'Dead as a doornail!'

'True,' I say. 'That's true.'

Kate says, 'Will it be weird?'

Maybe it will.

'Why would it be weird?'

Kate shrugs, says, 'She was a good pussycat.'

'A lovely pussycat,' I say. 'Now, go polish your pearlies, all of you, then let's re-group.'

With something more intriguing than bedtime to anticipate, the kids move as one more or less dutiful organism towards the bathroom.

Misty was hit by a car one Saturday morning about eighteen months ago. I had eventually caught the sound of her strained, intermittent meows through the kitchen window, as I was sorting out a pile of sandwiches for everybody for lunch.

Approaching the road, a thick dread solidified in my stomach. There was a fleeting moment of relief as I lifted Misty from the gutter, anticipating a lot of blood and seeing none. But her weight shifted oddly as I tried to cradle her body, and it seemed clear her chances of survival were nil. Misty's back third hung crushed and limp, a bag of broken parts. Rushing her to the vet's would, surely, only raise the kids' hopes unfairly, and we'd never get the body back.

Michelle met me at the kitchen side door, claiming she'd sensed something was wrong. She seemed affronted by the wheezing creature in my arms. The kids were still occupied with their toys inside the house, out of sight. We quickly hatched a plan. Michelle would keep the kids distracted while I took care of things. I snuck Misty into the garage and wrapped her in an old towel, then lay her on the concrete slab floor. Its smooth surface was cold against the joints of my fingers. I emptied a small cardboard box of its pottles of vegetable seedlings and tucked Misty with her towel into that – anything to help keep the warmth in her ruined body. Then I roamed back and forth, feeling sicker and sicker as I considered the options. By the time I settled on a solution – a sharp-edged shovel and a covering for the box – Misty had, thankfully, died.

We held a small ceremony, after the lunch Michelle finished putting together, and Piper read the whole of her favourite Greedy Cat book – the one where Greedy Cat grows so fat his owners have to install a dog door to allow him to pass in and out of the house – as a form of prayer. Most evenings before bedtime, in the following couple of months, the kids and Michelle and I visited the grave in the back corner of the garden to wish Misty pleasant dreams. Now and then, one of the other two kids felt compelled to offer something. Tyler told fantastic, half-remembered mash-ups of tales he'd recently encountered. Cinderella hiding from her evil stepsisters inside a drainpipe until Incy Wincy chases her out screaming, only for Cinderella to return carrying a woodcutter's axe.

Not long after Misty's death, Michelle whispered furiously to me one night in bed, our backs already turned to each other.

'I saw you in there, mucking around.'

'What?'

'In the garage,' she said. 'You left that cat to suffer.'

'What do you mean?' I was suddenly cold all over.

There is, indeed, a clear line of sight between the kitchen window and the garage window through which the seedlings get their sunlight.

'You didn't do a damned thing,' she said. 'You did nothing at all to end her suffering. You're a gutless wonder.'

'Perhaps you're right,' I spat. 'I cowered before death, while you so bravely constructed sandwiches.'

For which I'd already done the prep work.

'I guess we're both shitty people,' I said, and sighed in the dark.

Michelle sighed in return, and the sheets twisted as we curled our bodies up, hugging our separate disappointments, that unbreachable strip of the bed growing larger between us.

Maybe the children have detected that gloomy linkage between their dead cat and their mother. If so, this recognition – more felt, surely, than reasoned – must be behind Piper's suggestion to say goodnight to Misty this evening, many months after we last did such a thing and now that their mother has been AWOL a fourth day.

'Will it be weird?' Kate had asked. Maybe she'd meant, 'Will it be weird, saying goodnight to Misty without Mummy?'

The three of them return from brushing their teeth and stretch their mouths wide open for inspection. I cover my eyes with my hands.

'Blinding. Close those mouths up and put your coats on.'

'Can I wear Swanny?' Kate asks when we're gathered in the laundry.

'Fine,' I say, and Kate slips her oversized tartan poncho over the top of her pyjamas.

'We shouldn't stay out long – it's chilly,' I say, as I wrangle the kids out onto the lawn. 'We don't want to catch colds.'

I tell Tyler to be still a minute and pay his respects, and we all stand there together, facing the lemon tree that marks the grave. The tree is surviving well – small but bushy, full of fruit – owing in no slight degree, no doubt, to Misty's help. Though, we located it in a bad spot. It's a good place for the grave, out of the way, but tucked too far back into the corner for its acidic treats to be collected easily.

'Why is ten afraid of seven?' Piper says to the dark ground, delivering, apparently, a recent joke for her prayer.

'I don't know,' Kate says, and giggles because she does know, she was there when I told it to them. 'Why is ten scared of seven?'

'Because seven *ate* nine.'

Piper and Kate laugh.

'That's a funny joke,' I say. 'I wonder where you got that from.'

'Not telling,' says Piper.

'Did you maybe hear it from someone like Daddy?' I say.

'No.'

'Did you maybe say Daddy was really funny, when he told it to you last week?' I grab hold of Tyler's shoulder. I tell him, 'Stop squirming around.'

'No!' Tyler says.

'No!' Piper says.

I told it to all three of you, when I made pancakes with bananas and syrup for breakfast last Sunday. All three of you laughed. Even your mother laughed, or smiled a bit.

Tyler shoves my hip and I let him go.

'I see. Did you come up with that joke yourself, sweetie?'

'No.'

'Where did you hear it?'

Piper shakes her head.

'All right, then. Another big mystery in this big, mysterious world.'

'It's from Misty!' Piper says.

'Oh, really. When did Misty tell it to you?'

'Misty was smashed by a car,' Tyler says, somewhere behind me.

'Just now,' Piper says, ignoring her brother, and she turns away from me to face the grave again. 'Sweet dreams.'

'Yes, sweet dreams, Misty,' I say. 'Now let's get back inside. You lot have school tomorrow.'

The sun's already gone down behind the stretch of hills and the evening feels later than it should.

Kate takes Piper by the hand, poncho sleeve engulfing both, then Tyler stomps through the tufted grasses, trampling on the grave. He snatches up a pair of fallen lemons, one in each hand.

Piper's mouth gapes.

'Vandal!' Kate screams.

'Jandal!' screams her younger sister.

Tyler stands in the grasses, clutching his lemons and staring in confusion at his older sisters, then at me, and probably about to start crying.

'He didn't mean any harm,' I say, but the girls stalk away, still holding hands. 'It's okay,' I tell Tyler. 'Watch your pyjama bottoms and pass me your treasure, for safe-keeping.'

He hands me the lemons and runs across the lawn, overtaking his sisters. He pulls the laundry door back from the rock keeping it ajar, and goes inside.

My daughters pause just inside the orbit of the porchlight, bright and warm in the early winter dark.

'I hope you wiped your feet,' I call to Tyler through the doorway. 'What's the hold up, girls?'

'You ask,' Piper says.

'You ask.'

'You're older. You ask.'

This seems to convince Kate, who turns and angles her head to look into my face. Her glowering expression is made more serious by the pockets of shadow deepening her features.

'When will Mum come back?' she says.

'Not long. Just a few days.'

'How many?'

Your mother would be the one to ask.

'I don't know exactly how many. It won't be long, I promise.'

'Why don't you know?'

Not from lack of trying. Perhaps you kids could charm your grandpop into passing your mother's phone to her, and then coax your mother into offering some sort of helpful comment – something as simple as, *Hello, how are you all? I miss you. I'll be home tomorrow.*

'Daddy?'

'Your mum just needs some quiet time and once she's had enough of that, she'll be back with us again.'

'Is that why you aren't working as much?' Kate says.

'Daddy's boss at the kitchen said Daddy had some time owing and so Daddy took it. It's a happy coincidence.'

'Are you going to lose your job?'

'No, sweetie. It's not like that at all. Daddy just took some time so Mummy could take some time.'

Though maybe it will get like that, if the new bozo keeps chef's-kissing the operator's arse and criticising Daddy's cooking – which is still pretty good cooking, considering they make Daddy reuse gross fucking leftover fish in the fishcakes, for example, while they pocket a premium dollar. It's undignified, treating product that way, but it helps put food in your two – your three – fussy mouths.

Tyler reappears and presses his hands against his face and blows a big raspberry, then runs back through the laundry and down the hallway.

'Rude!' Kate shouts.

Piper maintains her stare, boring right through me. 'Where did Mummy really go?'

'She said she's going somewhere that is secret and special,'

Kate says. And Tyler's rudeness, and Daddy's job security, are forgotten just like that.

'Do you know, Daddy?'

I would tell you where Mummy went, if it wouldn't hurt you to hear it because your grandpop is a sack of shit who knows that harbouring his daughter means I can't say a thing to you about what's happening. The minute I tell you kids where Mummy is, you'll say, *Can we see her! When can we see her!* And I'll be left having to explain no and why not.

'She's gone camping with some old friends, like I said.'

Kate and Piper look at each other. Kate raises one big sleeve of her poncho for privacy.

'He doesn't know anything about anything,' she says.

'I can hear you,' I say. 'I'm still right here, with my big ears.'

'Mummy needs a break,' Kate says, sleeve lowered again. 'From you.'

'Did she – did Mummy say that?'

Kate looks at Piper, who opens and shuts her mouth.

'Misty told us,' Piper says.

Yes, naturally, why not.

'It's a little bit true,' I say. 'Your mum and I agreed that a short holiday – a break – would be a good thing. Only a few days, we agreed.'

My daughters meet this statement with silence.

They don't raise the possibility of a phone call, which I was stupid enough to suggest could happen, on the first day, and which after four days has not yet transpired. 'She must be out of range, camping,' I'd eventually said. 'Yes, she said she was going camping and might be out of range. I'm not sure where exactly they've gone – somewhere peaceful, no doubt.'

'You dropped the lemons,' Kate says finally.

'It's because my hands are cold,' I say, and crouch to pick up the lemons. I'm suddenly overcome by visions of an unsupervised Tyler playing with knives, drinking floor cleaner, drowning himself in the toilet. There's a loud bang on the lounge window and I turn – expecting the panes to shatter and my bloodied boy to tumble out and convulse among the shards – only to see his face pressed against the glass making ghoulish goldfish faces. 'Go and check your brother hasn't tracked dirt all through the house,' I say.

'Dirty grave dirt!' Piper says.

'Dirty grave dirt,' I confirm.

They disappear inside. I stand there looking at the lemons – partially rotted from sitting in the damp earth too long. There's another bang on the window and all three of them are lined up, grinning at me, from inside the living room, cosy with all the lights on and the heat pump purring.

'You all right in there?' I say.

They say nothing, and keep grinning.

'What's happening, kids?' I say, raising my voice slightly.

They keep on grinning.

'What's the joke? I'm getting worried out here.'

More and more grinning, then Kate shouts, her voice slightly muffled through the glass, 'The door's shut!'

I glance at the laundry door, which is indeed closed. Standing under the porchlight there's nothing to see in the darkened laundry, only a tired, flabby reflection in the door's glass, two lemons in its fists.

'You have me locked outside, do you?' I say.

I place the lemons back down on the ground then make a show of working the doorknob, and of course it just rattles uselessly without turning, because I still haven't fixed the stupid thing.

'Very funny, you lot.'

'You'll have to go camping,' Piper shouts. 'You camp out there and we'll camp in here.'

Kate is pulling at the blanket that lines the back of one of the couches, draping it across the back of the other couch so that it makes a kind of tent.

'I'm not sure I'm in the mood for camping, you know?'

They can't hear me properly.

Kate is encouraging her siblings to gather in the sheltered space. They're comfy in there, the girls at the back, just fitting, with Tyler in the front, all dressed for bed in their pyjamas. They look happy.

I tuck my hands into my armpits, glad for the thick knit of my sweater. They're so damned chuffed in their tent, with Daddy stuck outside, but I have a trick up my sleeve, or rather, under a paving stone.

And it's good they're enjoying themselves.

'Can you open the window a crack?' I shout. 'So I can tell you a story?' I take a seat on the path close to the window, careful to stay within the porchlight's radiance so they can see me clear enough, just past their own reflections. 'I won't need to shout for you to hear me that way. But not too far, or else the heat will get out and the cold will get in.'

Kate prods Tyler, who gets up to try the window, but in the end he needs help from Piper.

'That's perfect. Now that we're all gathered around the fire, tell me –'

'There's no fire, *Daddy*,' says Piper, settled back into position.

'We must use our imaginations,' I say, and Tyler rubs his hands together as if near a flame. 'Okay, tell me, what story would you like to hear?'

'A *good* one,' Kate says.

'A good one,' the younger two agree.

I think for a minute. There's a story I haven't told them in a while, and it feels an odd one to bring up in these circumstances. But now that I've thought of it, it's like an itch. I don't want to be a prick about things, suggesting any judgements about their mother, but couldn't it help? Maybe it will remind the kids that we all come from somewhere? That even I come from somewhere. That where we come from and where we end up are different places in some ways, the same in other ways. Are these things that the kids will understand – that any kids would understand?

'How about an old favourite?' I say.

I suppose their fascination with this story comes from its sense of adventure. I wonder if its implications are also accessible to their young minds, and are part of the excitement. Maybe that's unlikely. But perhaps they do have an awareness of the danger at the story's heart. It's difficult to know at which point the apprehensions of children shade into the worries and fears of adults. Are such anxieties always there, buried like seeds, waiting to germinate, given the right amount of attention and encouragement? I don't want them to worry, only to understand. I've always told the kids a simpler version – holding back certain details and consequences, finishing somewhere neater and less true than where the story actually ends for me, if it has an ending at all.

I begin, this time, on a more honest note.

'Your granddaddy, that's my daddy, left your grandma, that's my mother – '

'We know about generators,' Kate says.

'Yes, of course,' I say, noting that the error isn't really much of one. 'He went away when I was young like you. He went to live by himself, because he was unhappy and he wanted to be happy again. Unfortunately, he was the kind of person who finds happiness in some bad places and by doing some bad things. He liked to feel the wind in his hair, is how he talked about it.' I've already gone racing past the signposts saying STOP, saying WRONG WAY. The connection to their mother must be apparent even to a person as oblivious as Tyler. I peer through the streaked glass. Their attentive little faces gaze back, blank as buns on a baker's rack. But the changelessness of their expressions means they're processing something. Is it the shift in the story's opening, to admit to Dad's leaving? Or the parallel with our present family situation? Or are they waiting for me to get on with it?

'My dad wasn't anything like your mother,' I say, trying to curb any wildly undesirable interpretations.

Creases form in the dough of Piper's features.

'*Nobody* is like Mummy.'

'That's right. Mummy is very much her own creature.'

I continue with the story.

One Friday evening, after many weeks of stalled pick-ups – where Dad would phone at the last moment to say he was out of town and couldn't have us for the weekend after all, and we'd dutifully unpack our bags, which, after a while, we only stuffed with useless things like old teddy bears and toilet rolls, as a joke that confounded then eventually amused our mother – on that Friday evening, not long after dinner, our dad sputtered up the driveway in a white panel van and came to a sudden halt like an asthmatic dragon making a crash-landing.

'Who the heck can that be?' Mum said, and tugged the net curtain back from the lounge window. She saw the squat figure climb out of the van and her face dropped. There was a loud knock at the front door and Dad hollered that he needed the help of two strong young lads to aid him in an adventure.

'I heard there's a pair around these parts that fit the

description,' he said, as Mum opened the door. She had a look of deep bitterness on her face.

'New vehicle,' she said.

'Traded in the old dunger and got myself a new dunger,' Dad said. 'Heya, boys! Got your stuff ready?'

'It's not your weekend,' Mum said.

'C'mon.'

'It's not your weekend.'

'Whaddaya mean? I haven't had a weekend with 'em in a long time. Aren't I due some time with 'em?'

'Your weekend was last weekend and every second weekend before then, and you either show up or you don't. This is my weekend.'

'You've had a lot of weekends. Now it's time for some time with their old man. Grab your stuff, boys.'

Our mother must have felt us standing right behind her, just as real as the force of our father in front of her. She must have known that she would have to put aside the technicalities of her argument. She'd made her point, and it was a fair one, but she'd also done the emotional maths. Who was more wrong – the parent who hardly showed up, or the parent who stood in the way? She was smart, our mum. She would have been thinking ahead – to what she could do between this weekend and the next time that Dad failed to show up, or showed up at the wrong time. She was already drafting a letter in her head, something a lawyer could help her formalise.

I was nine, my brother was ten. It would be easy to overstate some insight about our psychology, about the effect of our father's unreliable presence in our lives. Disappointed, perplexed – certainly. But any questions resting uneasily in our minds were displaced by the thrill of him simply being there. And by his teeth – yellowed by years of smoking rollies – showing in a grin on his bristly face, and by his new dunger, which seemed absolute proof of his promise of adventure.

'I'd better not step across the threshold here, boys,' he said. 'I'll go up in a puff of smoke if I do.'

Mum helped us pack while he waited in the van. He leapt out again when we stepped out of the house carrying our little duffel bags, opened the passenger-side door and pulled a lever to tip the seat forward. He took our bags and tucked them behind a pair of single seats mounted behind the two front seats.

'You two climb in there and take a seat each, and make sure you make it click, all right?'

Dad manoeuvred the front passenger seat back into position, then with a quick salute to Mum he got back in the driver's side. The small side windows were covered up with paper and paint, and I had to look through the gap between the front seats to see outside.

Mum was out of sight until Dad reversed down the drive, then she came into view through the front window, one hand poised in a frozen wave, a look on her face like she'd just done, or seen, something dreadful.

'I need to tell you boys something,' Dad said, when we were a few minutes down the road. None of us had said anything since we'd left the house. I think it was something in Mum's look, the image of her in the doorway like a phantom, that had kept us silent. 'I'm guessing you probably packed your bags for the weekend, just a few pairs of T-shirts and pants, and a few pairs of undies?' He looked at us in the rear-view mirror and we nodded. He tapped his temple. 'I figured as much. There's a bag in the back there with a few more clothes for ya. It's good, warm stuff. Might be a bit big for you, young fulla, but you'll be fine.'

I nodded back at his eyes in the mirror.

'What do you reckon of Dad's new ride? Pretty great, huh?'

We agreed, without much excitement, that it was pretty great.

'Lots of room back there. That's why I picked this one out. Go on and take a look around. Ah! Don't undo your blimmin' belts. Safety first, all right? Just loosen the strap a bit and take a quick look behind ya, in the space back there.'

The van was long and the area behind our seats was spacious and free of any fixtures, but it wasn't empty. It was full of plastic bins and canvas bags, backpacks, a couple of chilly bins, cardboard boxes. A real assortment of stuff, all stored neatly.

'You don't need much in this life, I tell ya. I know you've got a good thing going, with your mum in that nice house – but I don't miss that house. Any house is more than your old man needs to get by.'

Dad told us to lift up the flap of canvas resting in the gap between our seats. It covered something long that extended right back inside the van. Under the canvas was more canvas and a bundle of metal poles.

'It's a tent!' Dad said, and he laughed.

My brother and I stared at his smiling eyes. He frowned and his expression went dark for a moment, then he laughed again.

'We're goin' camping, boys!'

We'd been camping a few times as a family, but not since Mum and Dad had split a couple of years before. My memories of camping were blurry. I was sure I'd liked it, though. I looked at my brother and his glowing face confirmed things for me – camping was fun.

'That's not what I have to tell ya,' Dad said. 'Well, it is what I have to tell ya, but I also have to tell ya something else. Listen carefully, all right? I know your mum said back there that this was a weekend trip, but she must have got her dates wrong. I know she doesn't make many mistakes, your mum. But this time, she got her dates a bit upside down and wrong way round.'

We stared dumbly into the rear-view mirror, hanging on his words. Did Mum make mistakes? She sometimes did things that we didn't enjoy, like making us eat Brussels sprouts, which we hated, even though she always said that when we were toddlers we didn't hate them, we loved them. That felt like a kind of mistake, like Mum was confused about what we wanted.

Our stunned and pliable minds were easily shaped around the question Dad put in front of us: is Mum a liar? The other option never shimmered into being for even a moment: is Dad a liar?

'Everyone makes mistakes, all right,' Dad said, turning onto the highway. 'No soul on Earth is perfect, ya understand?'

We said we understood, and his eyes smiled again.

'No harm, no foul. Now, what I have to tell ya, apart from that we're going on a camping trip, is that we're going on a camping trip for longer than just the weekend. We could be gone around two weeks, maybe longer, depending on how things go, all right?'

My brother and I stared at the seatbacks in front of us, then at each other. I waited again for some clue from him about what to make of this declaration of Dad's, about what to feel. My brother's face carried a look of uncertainty, and a rumble of panic started in my stomach. Then his face broke into a smile and he screamed, 'A real adventure!'

'A real adventure!' I screamed back a moment later, the rumble subsiding.

'A real adventure,' Dad agreed.

*

We traversed almost the entire North Island coastline in a fortnight in that panel van, never camping any place for more than one evening. The only exceptions were Raglan and Tolaga Bay – a few days into the start of the trip, and a few days from the end, respectively – where we stayed two nights each and where Dad said we'd find a soulful peace like nowhere else on Earth. We arrived in these places as we did in all the others: with fifties rock music blasting from the van's tinny stereo – golden oldies from Dad's own father's childhood, on the one mix-tape Dad possessed. (Radio broadcasts were permitted for his ears only, while we played outside, or slept in the canvas tent.) As the van slowed to a coughing stop in the outskirts, Dad would declare, 'Perfect spot to pitch up, right around here someplace.'

Raglan left the deepest impression, setting us apart from the rest of the world through the awe we felt at the monstrous, unspoiled sight and sound of the surf. Dad cast a line out from the beach on the second day, the sea calmer by then, and filled a tin bucket with fish, which he cleaned and filleted at the water's edge, showing us the proper motions of the blade, its thin steel dancing through and beneath the silvery skins and the pale flesh. Of all the gear in the back of the van, Dad was proudest of his portable smoker – accompanied by a bag of thick brown sugar, another of mānuka sawdust, and a bottle of purple-tinted methylated spirits. The fish, served hot between folded slices of white bread, dripped over our fingers, warmed our stomachs, and overran our senses with its sweet-and-savoury effusions. We ate under the bright stars. In the morning, Dad threw another round of fillets on the smoker for breakfast, with enough left over to snack on as we hit the backroads again.

'Feels good, havin' that wind in ya hair, doesn't it?' Dad would shout over the noise of rushing air – his window cranked right down – and the crackling music from the cassette tape. His eyes shone in the rear-view mirror. But there were periods also of long silence, his words muted whenever he did speak, his eyes dull.

The police caught up with Dad – with the three of us – when he returned us home. A marked car was parked on the kerb outside Mum's place. Dad drove the panel van, chugging out black smoke, straight up the driveway. We didn't know it then, but the police were inside the house, delivering Mum another update on their lack of progress in tracking down 'the Stolen Sons', as we had been dubbed, it transpired, by an enthused media. Dad would have been following that public narrative closely, his ear to the van radio, and I'm sure he would have objected to the accusation embedded in the name 'the Stolen Sons'. After all, hadn't he knocked on the door before taking us away in plain sight? Hadn't we gone willingly? And hadn't he always intended to bring us back?

Dad told us to grab our bags and skedaddle, then he levered the passenger seat forward. We clambered out and stood on the driveway, and saw the two police officers emerge from the house, Mum behind them. We turned our eyes back to Dad, who smiled with his thumb to his nose and fingers wriggling in the air. Mum rushed up behind us, encased us in her arms. She took our bags and ushered us into the house as Dad started yelling out his window. 'You pigs coming, or what? We goin' to your place or mine? You're welcome to step inside, because I tell ya, this here is all I've got!'

We watched through the doorway as Dad got out of the van and presented his wrists behind his back for the police to handcuff him. Mum asked over and over if we'd been hurt.

'They're fine – probably better than ever,' Dad was shouting after us. 'Bye, boys! It's been a blast. Be good to your mum, all right?'

A few neighbours stood on their lawns gawping, while others peered around the shields of their front doors, everybody watching as Dad was pushed into the back of the police car and driven away. Our neighbours seemed both sickened and elated at witnessing the demise of a father depraved enough to kidnap his own children.

Dad was a runner, in essence. That big adventure was his way of trying to feel good about going away, having one last, rollicking time with his boys before leaving us forever in his past. He must have known a restraining order would be Mum's next move. Not that it would need to be enforced. Shortly after he finished his stint in prison, rumours reached Mum that he had made a break for distant shores – Australia, Morocco, Tunisia, Cambodia were all suggested – outrunning a long list of creditors claiming their various forms of debt.

We were snacking on tomato-sauced fish fingers ('Fish!' we had said. 'We want fish, fish, fish!') and a large glass of Kola each, when the police returned an hour later to photograph the panel van. They said they'd need to speak with us someday soon, once we'd had a chance to rest. (And they did, again and again, social workers too, checking that we hadn't been touched, beaten, hypnotised, until at last they were convinced that basically we'd had a fun time, for all the real pain our adventure caused others. Not least our poor mother, whose death, by stroke at age forty-eight in the same poky house we grew up in, close friends and family members attributed to the stress of that fortnight sixteen years prior – and I tend, unhappily, to agree.) Satisfied that we were not in any distress, one police officer got behind the wheel of their own car while the other got behind the wheel of the panel van, and off they went. Dad's new dunger vanished round the corner in a cloud of its own dark smoke like the end of an elaborate magic trick.

*

Perhaps they're dreaming of tin buckets full of fish, of crashing waves, of glinting stars. None of the kids have made it past Raglan. All three are curled around each other like sleeping kittens. My joints and muscles, stiff and sore with the cold, creak as I push up from the ground. I amble over to the third paver back from the laundry door, then crouch and prise the paver up with icy fingers, flick a worm away from the key hidden there in a shallow depression in the soil.

In the living room I stand in the enveloping warmth of the heat pump and feel my body defrost and loosen up. Then I peel away the slackened roof of their tent and rouse the girls, lifting them over the couches and setting them woozily on their feet. I lead them down the hall to their bedroom, where they fall asleep again as soon as the blankets are at their ears.

When I return, Tyler is sitting on the couch waiting for me.

'Dad,' he says, and rubs his eyes with tiny fists.

'That's my name, don't wear it out – or you'll owe me a new one.'

'They're not my treasure,' he says groggily. It takes me a moment to realise he's talking about the lemons. 'Cats don't like lemons, or oranges, or any stinging fruit.'

'Is that right?' I say, scooping him up. 'I had no idea.'

He's quiet as we plod down the hallway to his room. It's smaller than the girls' shared room, but they also spent their first year or two in this one.

'Teacher told us she puts the skins and rotting fruit around her garden to scare angry cats away. I thought Misty wouldn't like having lemons on her.'

'Good thinking. I guess she wouldn't like that.' Tyler crawls under his blankets and I pull them up to his chin. 'That's very good thinking.'

'Will you fix the lemon tree?'

The crux of the matter.

'I'm not sure I know how,' I say.

Getting a lemon tree was your mother's idea. I wasn't sure. It seemed overly suburban, a real badge in the sacred school of mediocrity. We already had the SUV, which, sure, is very practical. Next up, shop exclusively at overpriced supermarkets (not just for the premium cheeses and preserved meats and specialty food ingredients, but for everything, for ten-dollar cauliflowers – everything). Next up, orgies with the neighbours. It's a G&T tree, your mother said, which was an argument I found persuasive, though G&Ts are absolutely another badge. This is the life I am destined for, I realised. It's not just my profession, playing up to the middle classes – it's my whole fucking existence. Even a divorce would feel exquisitely, horrifically of the type.

Am I thinking, properly, of divorce?

'You really don't reckon the tree's any good?' I say.

Tyler, eyes closed, rolls his head slightly against the pillow.

'It was my suggestion to put it as a marker,' I say. 'I'm sorry I didn't ask you kids what you thought before I planted it on top of Misty.'

Tyler doesn't hear me – he's already asleep.

I break the neck on a bottle of bourbon and pour out three fingers into a coffee mug. It burns in my stomach like a small campfire.

The night before she left, Michelle asked if I remembered what I'd said after Misty died. I stared at her, across the dinner table still crowded with dishes, unsure what she meant. The kids were in bed and we'd been scrolling through crap on our phones for an hour, as usual, she nursing a cold cup of chocolate, me a bourbon, neither of us saying a thing – until she asked that question.

'It's been stuck in my head,' she said. 'It's been sitting there like a hot coal.'

'I don't know. I've got no idea,' I said, taking a drink but finding my cup empty. 'I remember you called me a gutless wonder.'

'Yes. I doubt I could have helped Misty either. I'm sorry, Jeff.'

'It's getting on. Let's clear these away.' I stood and collected the dirty plates, dropped them noisily into the sink, and ran the hot tap. 'Are you going to tell me what I said?'

She sat a moment longer, then gathered up the pudding bowls and added her dishes to mine as I dipped my hands in and out of the scalding water.

'You said that we're both shitty people – and I think you were right. We have become that way. I've asked myself why.'

'I was upset.'

'Let me say this, while I have the words. You seem dissatisfied, Jeff. Not just with me, but with everything. You've always had that tendency, like there's something bigger you want to chase, though I don't think you really know what it is. I've tried to be understanding and loving and forgiving. I've made some wrong steps too, I know. But I've realised I feel the same way, that something important is missing, and I don't know what to do.'

'It's not true, Shell. With Piper, Kate, Tyler – I could never be dissatisfied with them,' I said, sure of that one good thing.

'That's – bracingly honest of you.'

'I don't hate our life, if that's what you think.'

Michelle was quiet as she took dishes from the rack.

'Maybe the question isn't what's missing,' I said. 'Maybe it's what sort of life do we still want to make together?'

'We keep going in circles,' she said. 'You should take some

responsibility. I need to do the same.'

The next morning, Michelle said she was going to her Dad's place to take a break, that I'd need to look after the kids, that she'd be back soon but couldn't say exactly when.

'Keep their routines up,' she said, and started the engine of the old runaround. She left the SUV for me, rightly, so I could shuttle the kids about routinely.

'Chef's kiss,' I said, putting my fingers to my lips.

She turned her head to check behind her, then reversed out of the carport, down the drive and onto the road, all in one smooth motion, ignoring the engine's complaints.

Even if you have to think hard, which if I'm honest I don't, you can always find room for improvement. Not a single fucking soul on this earth is perfect. We just want to find our happiness, usually with as few wrong turns as we can possibly manage, so long as we know what the wrong turns look like.

Mum had never wanted us, her two boys, to think we were at fault for that fortnight with Dad, so she kept the deeper facts of the situation to herself. But she gave up some of them, reluctantly, as we grew older, becoming stronger in our hearts and minds, and as we began to uncover and infer more details on our own. At first, it seemed that the biggest mistake – and perhaps it was the only real mistake, the mistake linking up all the rest – was that we had never made a phone call back home to Mum, to say hello, to say we were okay. Dad told us that the phone box was dead, or that we had to race the sunset, or that Mum didn't answer when he dialled – lies that came easily to him. It was a dishonesty bred by duplicity. Me, Piper, Kate, Tyler, if we went someplace, we would do it right and keep on calling. Michelle would pick up, surely, and talk with us. And we would tell her about all the fun we're having. How we've cooked and eaten whitebait netted in rivers by ourselves – Tyler will have those in a fritter, perhaps, given a nice batter. We can tell her about the amazing coastal cafés we've stopped at – everything served absolutely fresh – as we hunt out fantastic sights by day, packed into the SUV. And how by night we stretch out on the beaches, sand still warm from the sun, and gaze at the stars, more stars than the kids have ever seen, since they've been stuck, as they always have, looking up from within polluted suburbia.

Just for the kids, I wish Michelle would answer, would talk.

The suggestion of an adventure – that would compel her fucking father to pass the phone, would compel her to say a few words.

I tip another few fingers of bourbon into the coffee mug, then head to the laundry, stick the rock between the door and its frame, and go out into the biting cold to the lemon tree.

Tyler's footprints are clear in the soft earth.

The girls aren't fond of citrus, though they'll eat it in a cupcake, in a tart, in anything loaded with sugar. Tyler eats almost nothing we put in front of him, and if it wasn't for our shared brow line, wide and flat and curled at the ends like single quote marks, I might think he was another man's child.

We can keep the tree, but not there. It can't remain over Misty. We'll need a new grave marker, but I will fix that too, in time.

I put the empty mug down on the ground and replace Tyler's footprints with my own, then reach through the branches and grip the narrow trunk with both hands. The astringently scented leaves scratch my face and twigs catch in my sweater. I tug and feel a movement in the earth, the roots releasing. I expected this to be more difficult. I tug again and the roots give way a little more. I steady my stance, then wrench upwards and the lemon tree comes ripping out of the soil. I stumble backwards and in a quick, dumb instant, I'm on my arse in the dirt, my head bashing onto the hard lawn, the tree on my chest. The bush claws my skin, lemons knock against my ribs and face, a citrus perfume blankets my head – while the stars circling far above begin to blur.

The lemon tree is slumped across my body like a lover. My brain aches. The air is cold on my skin, and my face and hands are numb.

I shut my eyes and concentrate on breathing.

I should have used the fucking shovel.

There's a fizzing in my head, the slow suck and spill of surf. I concentrate on drawing air in – holding it, letting it go. Soon, beneath the surf's noise, another sound arrives, building in volume, resolving into something familiar. The rattle and whine of an engine, like that of our struggling runaround.

I open my eyes.

The wide beams of a pair of headlights divide and fill the night as the vehicle tentatively enters the carport behind me. I squint in the sharp light, and the sound of the fizzing sea spills from my mouth.

Then the headlights shift as the vehicle reverses and turns, the stranger behind the wheel realising that, at some point, a mistake has been made and a correction is required.

SAM KEENAN

Afterimages

The morning I disappeared, I walked out with an air of knowing. I passed the concrete wall with its faded 'Men Wanted' posters next to the newly pasted advertisements for Lifebuoy deodorising soap. I walked by the ding in the iron railing that the ambulance made when Mrs Nunes fainted because the voice on the radio said 'We are at war'. I passed the entrance to the pathway that led back towards my previous life at the university, of which I was once so embarrassingly proud. Claire would get back and find the cups in the kitchen clean and well placed. The surfaces would be all white and sparkling. 'Jeepers,' she'd say, and wonder what strange happenings must have occurred to result in such a vastly improved roommate. She'd make a mental note to shout me a drink at the milk bar on her night out with Tom. The inkling that something wasn't quite right would settle upon her slowly, the way fog quietly comes to rest in the dark, then startles at dawn with its whiteness. Her worry would keep her company all evening, haunting the hours I did not come home. Later that night, she would be alarmed enough to call Tom, ask him to come over, then say, 'Nah, don't,' because she worried about Mrs

Rothbury seeing him and calling her a floozy. Instead, she'd sleep, and only call the police when the sun rose.

I had become fainter, hazier, with a soft glow to my edges. I knew it before I disappeared, and I knew it was my doing. That's what you get for meddling with the universe. That's what you get for finding the hidden parts resting beyond the surface of things.

Shadows thicken in the trees. I hear cars passing the eastern entrance of the Reserve, a dog barking two streets over. Frost paints everything silver.

I didn't always want to disappear, of course. It wasn't like it was my lifelong ambition. At first, it was a passing interest, like collecting stamps or old postcards, only I became more and more proficient, and then I was pretty much done for. All it took was a small turn inwards, a kind of delicate attentiveness, the world revealing its secret things as if it were giving up the last missing piece from a jigsaw puzzle.

I almost wish I hadn't noticed, but Dad sparked my fascination early in life. From our house in Ōhura, we'd watch the wind whip across green paddocks that spilled into an infinite nowhere. Dad could feel the nowhere. He'd sit on the deck in the evenings after I returned home from school. He'd rub the bayonet scar on his calf and after a long silence he'd say, 'There's nothing anymore.' The way he said it was sort of casual, as if he'd looked in the biscuit tin in the pantry and found only crumbs.

My interest was piqued well before the fathead postgrad suggested, the day before I disappeared, that my overbite was a safety hazard.

The dark dissolves, and I am there again, standing in front of him.

'I mean, can you even see the floor?' he guffaws, nudging his pal. He'd been greatly peeved the previous summer when he missed out on the lab assistant job we both applied for. Now he'd beaten me to graduate studies, he was intolerable. I could tell he looked down on me as I struggled to balance working in the lab with finishing off my degree. Still, I had two majors to his one.

I summon all my farm-girl roughness to tell him what's what. 'Mate, my overbite isn't nearly as obscuring as your stupidity.'

What is the chemistry of good self-esteem? Possibly a sudden surge of energy to your temples. Probably about 70 to 120 volts. I look at my watch as the fathead's pal laughs, and I can almost see the fluorescent lab lights through my flesh. I hide both wrists behind my back and hope neither of them notice.

The day I disappeared I stood behind the professor at the beginning of Stage I Chem. I am there, rolling my eyes beneath my good-girl hairdo as all the undergrads in front of us laugh. That's what you get for pinging my bra, Sir. Earlier, I lied about the lab mice: 'Sir, there was a spontaneous outbreak of Sendai, and I had to euthanise them all and incinerate them.' (I let them go because I could no longer stomach seeing them in their little glass prisons.) At morning tea, about the sugar in Sir's coffee: '"None" does sound an awful lot like "nine", Sir.' (I surely can't have been listening all those times Sir told me he was diabetic.)

Sir's eyes are very blue and pale and unattractive. I watch the spit pool in the corners of his mouth, and I think of how much his face has in common with an overflowing bottle of soda. What is the chemistry of attraction? Probably regularity.

I used to watch a looker of a man every Wednesday at the French Maid Coffee House. I found it interesting to measure my reactions to him, like it had something to do with relativity or particle physics. His features were remarkably regular. I sipped my tea and observed the Typing girls fawning over him, giggling, whispering, elbowing one another.

What is it about symmetry that makes us so pathetic? Why is it we can't rid ourselves of illogical thinking? I am terribly unsymmetrical, yet my mind is metronome-regular. I am all sorts of perplexing, my parents' blond hair an unexpected contrast to my dark curls and heavy brows and lashes. Everyone thinks I'm from somewhere exotic, that I'm Italian, Greek, Spanish. Even my mother thinks I was mixed up with some other baby at the hospital. You should see the sympathetic looks I get from the old ladies on Lambton Quay – like I have just arrived from some war-torn European country and am not some ordinary New Zealand girl living with her ordinariness.

Consider eyes, noses and mouths, and their mathematical proportions. Is it not possible to calculate the angles that are pleasing? Only, the universe tends to disorder. Like me, it is inclined towards useless experiments. Perfect symmetry is the accident, something we would rightly perceive as a freakish mishap instead of an accomplishment.

I find none of this consoling the morning Sir froths in front of me, attempting to explain the atomic qualities of helium. The faces of the new undergrads are likewise disappointing: young men and their ill-placed admiration. I barely remember that feeling of looking up to my professors, that belief that they knew some deep secret. Miraculously, there is a gap in Sir's rambling. It's now I find my most peevish tone. 'Yeah, yeah, yeah,' I say, meaning, 'Trust me boys, this knowledge is going to be pretty useless when you're on an aeroplane to Europe to obliterate the Führer.'

Sir glares at me. 'Get out,' he says with the last shreds of his composure.

I play dumb. I stick out my lower lip, and I say, 'Surely you don't mean it, Sir? However will you demonstrate the next experiment without me?'

'Get out!' yells Sir, and I curtsy. I hold Sir's gaze unflinchingly, and I back slowly out of the room as if I am a retiring prima ballerina in the historic moment of her departure before the final curtain comes down.

I stare through the glass door in the vacant hallway. I smile at Sir rambling on, trying to recover, actively avoiding my gaze. I inhale with an almost divine satisfaction, because after today there'll be no Sir walking up quietly behind me in his office, no feeling his fingers between my shoulder blades as he plucks at the clasp of my bra. There'll be no hearing that God-awful 'heh' noise, the sound he makes when he thinks he's delivered the world's best punch line – 'heh' – like a fat sparrow that's snagged a particularly delicious bug. And there'll be no accidentally dropping and smashing a glass on Sir's desk having felt his hands on me, no smarty-pants line from him like 'Still working on not breaking things?' at my performance appraisal. And there'll be no subsequent recollection by me of the boy at my college who would fall into me and grab my pubescent breasts then say, 'You should be flattered, a girl like you,' and no thinking that boy had probably been correct and that Sir's attentions were something I should be grateful for.

It's easier to be yourself when you're about to disappear. There's no vested interest left. It's a peculiar kind of indifference. Like when you're fired from your first office job at Faber's

Furnishings because your manager thinks you took the apple he'd saved for his morning tea, so you stuff your handbag full of apples from his fruit bowl on the day you leave as you hum 'Any time is apple time' and smile broadly as you pass your co-workers' many disapproving faces.

You have to make the best of lousy situations. Take the war. Surely it's best to slip out early before the whole world goes belly up. Mystery is subatomic. It's sitting there right now, waiting patiently to be discovered.

I started discovering it a week before I disappeared. It was the afternoon Tom, Claire and I were sprawled in the back garden, moving our towels with the sun, feeling the earth's soft turning in the sad square yardage of suburbia. There is something mightily wretched about trying to get a tan in Kelburn: the towels in their tragic arrangements, the looming grasses, the neighbours who at the sight of any skin above ankle level set themselves to gasping. The earth, the hills, the damp, the very sky conspire to keep us pale.

Claire and I lie down, and all is quiet for three seconds before Claire shrieks – Can't Tom bloody watch where he's going? And Jesus! Christ! Now her towel is covered with dirt!

Tom fumbles backwards. His short leg has always been inconvenient. Of course he'd wanted to fulfil his duty like all the other boys, but would it not have been off-putting to have a lad like him hobbling around Berlin when there are many other preferable specimens who would reflect favourably on our country's military prowess? It is of course very sad and humiliating and shameful to be turned down for service, but – as he explained to the recruitment officers – if he tries extremely hard over the months and years left to him, he may be able to live with this mortification. It's harder now, now he sees the lads sent back, the half deaf, the de-fingered and de-armed, the horribly imbalanced because of inner-ear perforations, the boys who always wear socks owing to a lack of toes. We see them walking in the Gardens with their crutches and eyepatches and empty pinned-up sleeves. When I disinfect the lab, I think of the boys whose names I recognise when the announcer reads the daily dispatches. I fancy, owing to my imperfect cleaning, their handprints are still with us, like ghostly afterimages, on railings, on door handles, like traces of a lost world.

'Coming to Veronica's?' Claire asks after she's rearranged herself and Tom has gone to fetch lemonade as penance.

'Can't. Got after-labs,' I say, my mouth half full of macaroon.

'Are you ever not at the lab?'

'I'm never not always at the lab.'

'Is it not très boring?' says Claire, using the one word she remembers from third-form French.

'Très boring, très awful, très all the bad things.'

'Life is très overrated.'

I nod in agreement. I didn't know then that I was on the verge of a way out – escaping the ridiculousness of getting the sun to alter my colouration into a more pleasing pallor, of days spent liberating plates and cups from the traces of their previous inhabitants, of being unaccepting of the dirt that invariably gets under fingernails and being seen as socially questionable should it remain there.

The sun turns my forearms an angry pink, and I try to extricate myself. 'I'm burning,' I say.

'Aw no, Ruth! Stay the afternoon. Tom is boring me to death!'

'Be a responsible nurse, Claire,' I say. 'You really should be discouraging third-degree burns.'

'Aww jeez.' Claire flops back down on her towel.

I go inside and change, then set off towards the Reserve.

Mrs Nunes waves as I pass her kitchen window. Dishcloth in hand, she mouths something as she smiles and nods. I wave back and imagine she's said something wildly out of character like 'Curse everything' or 'Pays not to give a damn'. I am aware I have an odd gait and that my walking intently gives me the look of a mad woman. I hold my self-consciousness like an angry flame inside me as I march below the viaduct, past the silent grey monuments of the cemetery, to the newly planted entrance of the Reserve.

Like most everything I do, my frantic walking is an attempt to not think of my brother. Problem is he comes back in unexpected things. There he is in the silence of the bush, its drawn out, unpunctuated no-sound like the non-arrival of his letters home. He's there in the air, all lucid from sunlight, in the waterfall swollen from yesterday's rain when the hill was drawn over with a gauzy mist, making a haze of the ferns, the pongas, the starburst leaves in the cabbage trees. I breathe in, trying to will away the hurt of his absence. I lengthen my stride. I move faster.

I walk until I am all soreness and ache, too tired to be startled by the suddenly descending kererū or the thin *pip pip*s of fantails below the wet green canopy. It's then I see the tree and its iridescent darkness, its leaves swathed in a black shimmer, as if night has been caught and atomised and strung across it.

Once before in my life, I was so tired that I saw things. My brother was still here, and I was still at high school. My mother would get up in the early hours and pace the lounge, talking to my absent father: 'Now Jeremy, I'm going to tell you what's gone on with your girl.' 'Now Jeremy, you stupid bugger, now's about the time you should come back.' I'd sit in the slice of light that fell from the lounge through the open door of my bedroom. I'd watch Mum in her nightdress, her hands gesticulating, her midnight hair a jagged halo. I'd quietly shut the door and try to sleep, but her muffled voice would carry through the walls, then her sobbing, and by the time she went back to bed, I'd have to get up to catch the bus. I sat tiredly at school, trying to pay attention to the teacher, but when it was last-period Physics, the diagrams took off from the blackboard in front of me and I had to swat away every equation as my classmates stared and laughed.

This is what I think is going on deep in the Reserve when I see those million pinpricks of dark in the late afternoon sun, tiny and pulsing, as if light and shadow had been reversed in that tree's thousand leaves.

I don't stand there in awe or alarm. Instead I feel the delayed regret of discontinuing Botany. Poor previous self – assigned such an inept field trip partner in Lewis, whose catastrophic misidentifications earned us that C. I had calculated that even if I aced the rest of my assessments, I could have only just entered the uninspired country that is a B+, so there was nothing for it but to withdraw.

Logic surfaces and tells me the dark pulsing points in the tree have nothing to do with botany and everything to do with physiology. Logic says that such visual disturbances are more likely than not the result of exhaustion, even if the exhaustion was self-inflicted for the purposes of both forgetting brother and doing something other than sunbathing. To assume the existence of a new unknown entity is to fail to apply Occam's razor.

But then I get to thinking about that paper I keep finding on Sir's desk, the one about the Coma Cluster that he's been translating from German for what seems like fifty years. Now there's a heretic, I thought of the author when I read Sir's spidery scrawl. You wouldn't think science would permit entry to someone who thinks the universe can only be held together by some vast cloud of heavy darkness – some as yet unseen, untested, phantasmal cement. According to that paper, the universe would fly apart without that invisible heaviness to stop it. Of course, heaviness can be seen all around us – in objects, solidity, particles. Only there is not enough of it in these tangible things to prevent everything from flying apart, so there has to be some imperceptible heaviness. And what might that invisible heaviness comprise? Consider souls, the ones the various religions are harping on at you to save, lest you find yourself embroiled in eternal damnation or assigned a lab partner called Lewis. Contemplate the peculiar experiments of the last century: all those spiritualists weighing people as they depart for wherever they go to when the machine that is their body gives over.

The tree pulses in front of me, its little points of dark hovering in the air as if those places had been sucked inwards into shadow. The atmosphere is ghostly around it, like fabric, torn and limp, softly seeping. My breath quickens. I retrieve the scissors from my nail kit and I take a cutting. From my pocket I pull an envelope marked in my mother's handwriting with my loathed nickname, 'Ruthy'. I remove the £1 note and place the sprig of leaves and darkness inside it.

As I walk up from the lower valley, a kind of weight strikes me, and I drag it behind me like the skirt of a long dress, catching on ferns and mosses, trailing the detritus of leaves and their damp decay. I keep walking. I look into the glowing worlds of other people's interiors. I gaze into a lounge on Glenmore Street where a boy stands staring at the floor as a man yells. A woman comes to the window. From beneath the rollers in her hair, she flashes me a look of vengeance then draws the heavy curtains around their heavy secret lives.

My life is a series of avoidances. I'm in the lounge figuring out how I can get into the lab without encountering Sir.

I'll happily take a three-block detour to dodge unwanted encounters. I know Sir's schedule off by heart: the hallways he's likely to traverse, the percentage of possibility that he might drop by a particular after-lab to see how I'm getting along. You've got to watch girls like me, right? We need special attention. Sir has a particular interest in improving my ability to clean the blackboard. How do I always manage to get chalk on my chest? Sir is, of course, doing me a favour in brushing it off.

It's late, and Justin and I are in the lab. I gasp at the sickly stench of sulphur lingering from Stage II Chem. I feel a waft of it following me like a spectre and I drop a beaker. The sound is a sonic boom ricocheting off the windows and the floor.

'Another statistical casualty,' Justin observes, as if it were a pilot shot down over Italy.

The empty lab has a particular sound to it. It is the sound of flat surfaces, of symmetry, of linoleum, of all the no-voices of the no-people that should be here but are now in some no-place overseas. Justin throws the glass shards into a metal can and the clang rings through the building. We tick everything off the status checklist, and he offers to walk me home, but I tell him not to bother. When he leaves I look out over the street lights and the vast blackness that is the harbour. In the lab at night, every sound is amplified: the mice skittering behind their glass sliders, the irregular fizz of the fluorescents, the security guard two floors down making his rounds. The only sounds in the room are me and the clock, its tick as regular as machine-gun fire.

I take out a tray from my locker. I open the small white envelope, slip out the dark sprig I collected hours earlier, and weigh it on the triple-beam balance. I slide each line carefully and discover an impossible weight. I remove the sprig and weigh it again, given my capacity for error, and once more, it is absurdly heavy. I go to Sir's bench and take out his prized analytical balance. Again, a ridiculous weight. I wonder if I am seeing things. Perhaps my vision is shot and I have managed to drag a large branch home without knowing it. I grab a beaker and fill it with water. I attach a small piece of wire to the stem of the sprig and hold the sprig under: 2 fl. oz. I take it out and dunk it under again. 2 fl. oz. I look at the dark pinpricks through the water, their wispy blackness like Indian ink.

What do people do with knowledge like this? Is it worth sharing when you'll likely not be believed? Even if you are believed, someone with more scientific and academic respectability will no doubt take it over (read: Sir), and all you've found will be polluted and his and it'll all be for nought. That Coma Cluster guy, how was he given space to advance his theory, despite it breaking every philosophical maxim? I put the sprig back in my locker. I walk home indirectly – down the dark paths through the Botanic Gardens, hoping that I'll be swallowed by the blackness before I reach home.

My fading is not something I observe immediately. I'm not one to examine my hands, or my legs, or my face in the mirror.

'You look kind of pale,' says Claire when I walk in, and I figure that yes, I am kind of pale, kind of a weird pallor, maybe owing to working with Sir, maybe owing to general malaise, maybe because of how my mother is and how my father isn't and what may or may not have become of my brother. Or maybe it's the war in general, the many absences of all the people I once knew.

'Yeah,' I say, like my paleness is unremarkable. If I am paler than normal, it's probably because I have spent the last three hours cleaning surfaces and trying very hard to avoid breaking things.

I only gradually notice a change in my translucency, a ghostly sheen to my skin, an increase in the people I walk past who don't acknowledge my existence. I've always had a gift for absence in presence. I could have been a spy, you know. I could have ended the war by being invited to one of Hitler's meetings then clunking him smack on the head with a cricket bat in full view of his guards. And while everyone exclaimed 'What in the Hell?!' I'd just calmly walk away, strutting past the armed soldiers and down the long stretch of roadblocks and sirens like some invisible catwalk girl. Only, I am not symmetrical. That is the art, see. If you want to be stealthy and silent as the mildew growing on your bedroom curtains, just uneven your face a bit. It will let you see things others don't notice.

I probably could have changed my life's destiny. It's all cause and effect, and just a tiny push off course would have led me to some other outcome. Perhaps I could have held up my two-year-old-toddler hand and said, 'Hey, troubled parents – umm, no thanks,' and set off with my toddler knapsack, kissing goodbye to their various problematic personality traits rather than inheriting them. Perhaps it is always too late to change the course of history, and the mathematical equation of our destiny is something we have no say in. It's some consolation that disappearing is life's greatest magic trick. I mean, here I am, confounding the laws of physics and thoroughly messing with Einstein's theory of relativity. I am truly spectacular with my no atoms, no bones, no letters home, no lungs for breathing in. But boy is there some tedious housekeeping upfront. You get out a library book. You have to put it back before you disappear because it'll be well overdue, and fines tend to mount up when you have no body with which to return things. And it would be very rude and inconsiderate to lumber your roommate with every aspect of house-related maintenance. And you can't be leaving dirty clothes, right? I mean, how embarrassing for the world to know that your human body is capable of making your undergarments unclean. I am struck by the ridiculousness of it all, but I think of my mother and decide to prioritise the reputation she has for wholesomeness – albeit among those who have never entered our home. There are other things to think of too, like how to settle the things that need to be settled when past you was disinclined to settle them, and was permissive to those who deserved humiliation.

I lose track of my situation easily. Disappearing sure messes with clock-time and calendar-time and any kind of linearity. I wake up and the sounds of the world are drowned in radio static. The cold sits heavily upon me. I don't remember myself. Birds shudder in the trees and the wind lifts things from the earth. Gradually, I remember my mother's voice, and my father's absence, but nothing of who I am. Shapes gather like ink blots until they dissolve into atoms, electrons, glittering valency. *What is the chemistry of loss?* I hear the words in what was my voice, then a long frisson of silence.

I wake again later, and the trees seem taller. Bits of my life are returned to me: the arctic white of my lab coat, American soldiers dancing in the soda bar, machine-gun fire on the wireless, the sudden gasp of a lit match. I remember days being delivered to my doorstep and how I lived in them, and I am awakened into parts of my life as if they are unfolding.

I am walking in the hall inside my house, looking into Claire's room, where the bed is piled with cans and suitcases and newspapers: all the things we'll need if we lose the war. And there we are, playing the 'how would you rather die?' game: me with my knowledge of chemistry and biology, Claire with her first-hand experience of injuries in the ward. Claire says pneumonia. I say bomb. Claire says arsenic. I say cyanide. Tom says 'For Christ's sake!' We say, no harm in exploring options.

I am at home with Mum in Ōhura the Christmas before I disappeared. The neighbour has changed the hinges so the front door opens outwards, and when Mum lets me in, she bangs me in the face. The altered hinges have given Mum an extra yard of floor space to start a new stack of things, and this she finds most exciting. I shuffle against the wall so her enormous hall stacks don't go tipping over. I walk past them to the kitchen stacks and the lounge stacks. I creep into the small sleeping space between the stacks in the spare room and put down my bag. The music stack is as it ever was: the cardboard box at the base with the word 'study' in my father's scrawl, the loose music books with their pages in various states of disrepair, the fabric binding on the spine of *Beginners' Mozart* like a patched-up injury.

My brother and I moved one of Mum's stacks once. The curtain stack appeared to be a monument to the many houses my parents had lived in before coming to Ōhura. There were the curtains the colour of threatening clouds from 13 Hamilton Street, the thick velvet from Cedar Way and the gauzy nets from God-knows-where, all with the strange musty smell of bygone places. When we moved the curtains, my brother and I were hypnotised by the floor beneath. There was the carpet of our childhood – its bright floral bouquets on a sea of pale green, the roses in their hues of pink and yellow, the brown and apple-green clusters of leaves. Everything around the stack was the colour of dust, of time, of slow accumulation. In that moment, I almost understood my mother's compulsion – how things like old curtains might allow you a door back into your previous life in the same way as a glimpse of old carpet, or a scent from your childhood. All these links to what was – as if everyday life were like those montages soldiers report seeing as death nears: a perfect swan dive the summer before the war, a family argument at the dinner table, a quiet moment with your mother when she seems entirely present.

'Bernie says I'm *fully* prepared,' says Mum as she stands in the new yard of hall space.

I nod. 'Yeah.' When the world ends, we will surely have enough mildewed reading material and broken appliances to pass the afternoons.

'Here,' says Mum. 'I found this for you, Ruthy.'

She hands me a hair brush with all the bristles missing. 'Thanks,' I say with an intonation suggesting that, yes, yes, this broken hair brush is a most thoughtful gift.

'We can melt down the plastic and make something.'

'Good plan,' I respond, laughing inwardly at the thought of us suffocating from all the noxious gases, or setting the whole house alight.

My mother seems to register something for the briefest of moments, as if she's found something below my words. 'Maybe it's the war,' she says. 'Maybe it's the fact a bomb could crash down upon us at any moment.'

I do a double take, but she's already back to showing me her most recent acquisitions: a broken gramophone, an aerial, a stained pink jersey knitted in 100 per cent wool.

My mother sets her white hair in perfect curls every morning. Turns out my brother's unrelenting absence is a most effective whitening agent. I laugh every time Mum places the money she would have spent getting her hair dyed at the hairdressers in a box labelled 'die savings'. I think of my brother as still somewhere in the sky over Italy. People aren't dead until you give them permission, see. Only my father broke the rules. He did it before the war. It happened inside the hay barn, below the roof and its gentle curvature, above the soft echo of the floor, in the in-between place bordered by support beams and rafters. After the cows left, my mother burned it down, said goodbye to its lofty ceiling and the sweet smell of hay. I was thirteen. My mother set my father's place at the table for years afterwards. I remember his plate sitting there, empty, like a little pool of grief while my brother and I stared at the gap he had left in the world. I didn't know about the spaces we leave then. I didn't have the consolation that no energy is destroyed and the missing silhouette that marked my father's leaving was his presence in reverse. A photograph has its negative, an inverse, an opposite that exists in balance within it. Matter gathers itself into the semblance of no matter.

Claire says my extracurricular research will surely win the war. Her job has her tending to all sorts of injuries. 'Do you think,' she asks, 'they will be consoled by the fact their legs are there in reverse?' I sort of roll my eyes and she sort of rolls hers back. Everyone knows about phantom limbs, but something solid to stand on is so much more practical.

I'm twenty, and my brother and I are at home arguing.

'Can't we just shoot you in the foot?' I suggest. He's sitting on a ramshackle chair Mum recently procured from the Wilsons' skip.

'How about laying off the grim ideas, Ruth, okay?'

'Mum is going to go spare, actually go spare, like more so.'

He shifts in the chair and it makes a screech as if it's also uncomfortable, and couldn't he just get off it and give it a rest.

'Nothing doing, unless you want me banged up in Shannon,' he says.

'Yes. That would be perfect,' I say. 'Deal.'

'You got to be kidding, Ruthy. I'll never be employed again.'

'Well, Dad never was.'

My brother gives me one of his looks.

Mum arrives, and my brother says nothing to her about having to leave, and she's all chipper because he's home, and how does he like the new dining table, and she's found him a second-hand copy of *How Green Was My Valley*, and he can start reading it tonight. I say nothing and look into my bowl of soup. My brother asks if I would like the salt and pepper. Somehow my anger makes it impossible for me to answer. It feels like when we were little and we played hide-and-seek in the hay barn, and I hid too well and my brother was all 'I give up! I give up!' but my voice kept hiding inside me, so I couldn't yell back 'Here I am!'

It's the weekend of the camping trip, and Tom is talking in his sleep about being set upon for desertion. He mumbles about his shortened leg being not all that shortened. He's twitching and wriggling and defensive at his dream sergeant's accusation that his hobbling at the recruitment outfit must have been on account of him hamming it up.

Claire and I can't stop laughing, and we take turns being the dream sergeant, yelling things and asking questions. Finally, Claire says in her deepest voice, 'Private, choose your form of execution!' and Tom wakes up all wide-eyed, and any vague sympathy we have is tempered by the fact that it is now 2am and we've had absolutely no sleep.

*

We're at the house on a Friday night, and I'm half ignoring Tom with his slicked back hair and his lounge jacket, begging for a compliment.

'You guys going out?' I ask.

'Right on! The hall dance. I thought you were coming?' says Tom.

'That doesn't sound like me at all.'

'Aw, come on. Where's your stompers?'

'Hey, look, I'm saving you and Claire the embarrassment.'

'Suit yourself.'

When they leave, I sit in the lounge with the lights off. I listen to the sound of the cars. I hear a morepork far up the hill beyond me. In the dark of the back garden, I see the jagged outline of the grass. I walk into the bathroom and catch a glimpse of my face in the mirror, my thick brows, my deep dark hair, the angle of my front teeth. I smile, marvelling at my face's wrongness. Here is a universe. Here is an unremarkable girl and her unremarkable face on some unremarkable Friday night in the almost early morning.

I turn on the radio and listen to the glum sounds of late-night jazz, only I'm all tin ear, born into the wrong era with its jarring supposedly swell sounds, which I find impossible to like.

An exchange.

'Ruth, is this what I asked for?'

'Yes, Justin. It is what you asked for.'

'I asked for the size 3 dish.'

'A size 1 and a size 2 equal a size 3.'

'Agreed, but I have to mix in the same dish.'

'Oh dear. Whatever shall be done?'

Justin kind of smiles, and I kind of relax my grimace.

'I reckon you could flip your wig less often,' he offers.

'Agreed,' I say, brushing it off. 'Perhaps our judgement is skewed. Perhaps you are the most demanding man in the universe and my flipping my wig is completely proportional.'

'Very likely,' Justin says with his lop-sided smile, and I feel a kind of heartsickness at all the things life probably won't offer a girl like me, like a normal world not saturated in loss, like a life that isn't awash with emptiness.

I am eighteen and spending the mid-term break back home. My mother is regaling me with stories of local girls made good: 'Did you know that Greta Hume made the paper for her one-woman painting show? How does she do that *and* run the bake sale? And what about Kylie Fenton, she just kept on believing in herself despite her circumstances. That's what you should do, Ruthy. You should just believe in yourself.'

Well here I am doing it. I mean, has anyone else mastered the art of disappearing so thoroughly, gone from being pale and unthreaded like a tapestry to being completely undone? We are all residue of some long-ago cataclysm. I am a result of a billion trillion collisions, an infinitesimal probability – it's why my mother doesn't think I am hers. I am the space where the child she imagined is.

I yell as if from an adjacent room, as if I am back in Ōhura with my mother and father, but it's only me and the cold and the trees.

I'm in my college uniform, and my mother is chastising me for crying at school.

'You have every advantage, Ruthy,' she yells, enraged by my tears and general lack of sunniness. She is bewildered when the tears keep on coming. I nod, and I nod. I agree I have had every advantage. I agree I have a loving family. I agree that life is not meant to be easy. I agree with every word she utters. I know my mother would have preferred it had I been born Greta Hume with her all-around excellence and fortitude. I imagine she has secret fantasies that Greta is her real daughter, with her blonde hair and her manners and her perpetual smile.

I'm eleven. Mum is at Aunt Carol's and Dad goes to bed early. My brother and I wake to a bird-call we don't recognise, and we walk outside into the morning hours. We don't see the door shut behind us as our feet crunch on the grass. We follow the sound through the blue-black air until it fades into nothing. We go back home, and we knock and yell at the front door, only Dad doesn't hear.

'He could sleep through World War Two,' Mum used to say before there was a second world war.

He keeps sleeping as we shiver in the barn trying to coax Bailey, his horse, to lie next to us. In the morning, Dad is beside himself for sleeping through our cries and leaving us out in the cold. He says he could have killed us, and he cannot be trusted and what has he done.

'Don't tell Mum,' we say, but it's the first thing he says when she comes through the door. We see her trying to look sympathetic but we can also see the worried anger flushing under her skin.

Dad gives us that look, the one that upsets Mum because she's sure he's somewhere else hearing mud falling from the sky and men calling out in the dark.

I'm ten, and Dad is wearing his hole-ridden jumper, the frayed remains of the rope knit twisting up his chest.

'Ruthy,' he calls. 'Ruthy where's your mother?' and I point at Mum fretting and pacing at the washing line.

The curtains lift and I lift with them.

I am six, and Dad is outside building a new gate. I'm watching him from the settee in the lounge, and I can see how his tremble upsets the nail he's holding. I shout to my mother that I'm going outside to help, and she says 'No' and I get upset and say he needs me to hold the nails. She yells 'Get to your room', all thunder-faced and stern, and I continue to watch Dad from my bedroom, as he holds each nail and it falls over, and I count the first nail fall twenty-three times before he manages to keep it still enough to whack it in.

I'm very small, and I want to sit on my father's shoulders instead of taking five steps for every one of his. He reaches down and lifts me over his head. The sky is full of blue, and two swallows are circling and dipping above us. I can hear the deep, low moos of the cows in the next field. I try to answer them by making my deepest, lowest 'moo', and Dad laughs. I feel his laughing as I sit on his shoulders. It is like the up-and-down of the roundabout at the A&P show, and I giggle and say 'roundabout' and Dad laughs again.

I am the shadow below the storage shed at home, the dark in the delicate stems of roses, the mottled shape cast by a maidenhair fern. The rain pours and I am inside it, filling it with ghostly matter, willing it to fall. Trees lengthen above me, and a warmness pulses inside the bitter cold.

*

It is the day before I disappeared, and I walk along Lambton Quay. I try to enter the lives of others: this man with his mouth etched in a downturn, this woman who rushes with a look of distress, this child who cries as if he has discovered an abysmal truth. The sun is painfully bright above us. There is nothing like the despair of mid-afternoon, and I think of how very tired I am living in the room of myself, this perpetual company of my body, my face. I have wanted to be spread over things, to disperse and experience some kind of oneness, but humans were never meant to experience what it is to be interlaced with things. Consciousness is hardly compatible with scattered atoms.

I'm dropping a plate of biscuits. I'm feeling Sir's fingers grasping at my back.

I'm walking with Justin to the Reserve, having only slightly mentioned the tree with the darkness sucked into shadow. I talk about how it's more interesting in life to do something that leads to new knowledge or discovery, even if it means giving up on everything else.

'You're talking kind of disturbingly,' says Justin.

'Really?'

'Yeah. I mean, what is "giving up everything else"?'

'An interesting experiment.'

He sighs in exasperation and we walk in silence for what feels like forever.

I can feel the slowness of my breath even though we are walking fast.

The light makes a thin leap above us.

'I can stay and keep walking if you like,' Justin says.

'What? Why?'

'I'm not sure you are okay.'

'I assure you I am perfectly okay.'

'Really?'

'Yes! Now be gone.'

'I'm trying to be helpful, and I've been polite enough not to mention your . . . your fadingness,' he says, which I take in a metaphorical sense, which I take to mean that a person's mannerisms grate against you when you're in their company so many waking hours, and they become boring and predictable, which is very like a kind of fadingness. So I inform him that I embrace the general beigeness of my personality, thank you very much.

'Your flesh, Ruth. I'm talking about how I can see the sunlight through you right now.'

'So you mean I'm like one of your girlfriends, and you think I'm all sunlight and moonbeams.'

'Don't play stupid, Ruth. You're like anaemia times a thousand.'

'I've been pale since the beginning of time.'

'Well it's become rather alarming.'

It's then I politely thank him for his concern and generosity. I say I'll see him tomorrow at the lab, and I hope he has a good time at the movies, and despite my prickliness and sickly appearance, I have very much enjoyed the walk and being his lab partner. He looks a bit startled, but he departs anyway.

I watch him weave his way through the trees. I notice the light falling in blurred shapes around him. I listen. I strain to hear his feet crunching the leaf-littered path, but there is just the slow sifting sound of the wind.

SAMANTHA LANE MURPHY

Like and Pray

When her daughter died in the small hours of a Saturday morning, Kelly knew she had a lot of work ahead of her.

But at 3am, there wasn't a lot that she could actually do. She sat silently by the oversized hospital bed, her hand compressed in the grip of her husband's, listening to him speak to the social worker in a voice that made him sound like an old man. He was not old at all. They were both twenty-eight. Anna-Kate had been four.

Kelly had been drinking weak tea all night, because they kept giving it to her while Anna-Kate tried to breathe, and now that it was all over, Kelly desperately needed to wee, so she excused herself and went to the bathroom.

The funeral would have to be organised. That would cost money. She should cater it herself, then, make little sandwiches out of bulk-buy bread, tomato and ham. Maybe Desiree would supply them with flowers from her garden, because Kelly (remembering her wedding) knew how expensive that would be. Desiree had always liked Anna-Kate, always squeezing Anna-Kate's chubby little arms and saying something like how she might grow up into a little fatty if she wasn't careful.

Maybe Desiree would cut up all her flowers for the service, if Kelly asked. Maybe Kelly could talk Darren into stopping by on their way home, and she could just go out there and do it herself, while it was still dark. Walk around the garden with her nail clippers and behead every single loving daisy.

Heavenly Father, she was crying now. It was an unpretty braying sound. *Hee-haw, hee-haw*, echoing back at her in the bathroom. This made her laugh, laughing and crying and sitting with her jeans and knickers around her ankles and her bum on a warming toilet seat, the water beneath a weak tea yellow.

And no one knew. Everyone in the world thought that Kelly and Darren were asleep in their bed, and Anna-Kate was too. Well, no, not everyone in the world was thinking that. A lot of people were asleep, and even more didn't know them at all. But there were still a lot of people who would need to be informed. At the church, at Darren's work, at the store. Her mother, Darren's parents. And, realising she'd have to speak to Nadia, too, she took her phone from her handbag and thumbed it un-idle.

She found a nice picture of Anna-Kate, one of her favourites. Her flyaway curls, halo-like, her tiny hand squeezing an orange wedge, her pink dress with the white polka dots and the little plastic belt that went with it. You couldn't see the damp sticky smears where orange-juice hands had gripped at her skirt, the wrap of fresh Band-Aid on a knee where she'd ground it into the play-yard dirt. No one would see that, just this sweet girl, smiling in the sun.

Kelly uploaded this image to Facebook and captioned it:

> Anna-Kate Lundell declared deceased at 2 30 am
>
> :(

And she posted it to her public timeline. Hitting Post felt like screaming and silence pressed in on her ears and her nose was thick-feeling and she could sense her own heartbeat in the swollen flesh around her eyeballs. But she had stopped crying, and her phone idled to blackness in her hands.

She wiped herself dry and pulled her pants back up and went to rejoin her husband.

It made her uncomfortable to see her husband cry. It was something he tended towards, more than most men. When they were younger and argued more, his eyes would start to glisten and shine. His face reddened. Kelly sometimes wondered if it was an upbringing thing, if his mother had spoiled him, if his father hadn't involved himself enough. She thought about it not because she wanted to be cruel but because if she were going to have a boy, they'd have to figure out how to ensure he didn't wind up quite so sensitive.

But they'd had a girl.

Darren pulled over without saying anything and sat in the driver's seat with his hands parcelled together like prayer. He wasn't crying in clear rivers, but a kind of film of briny grease oozing from around his eyes, slowly spreading down his face.

'God, oh God,' he whispered.

Kelly watched him and then watched the early morning trickle of cars on the road. Her face felt numb and she realised she was clasping her hands too, tight and stiff and sweating in her lap. She counted three, four cars, before she said, 'I'll drive.'

'I'm sorry.'

'No.' The version of herself that had not also lost a daughter reached across the car and cupped the side of his neck and said something, something, nothing she could think of. This would do: 'Let me drive awhile. It would make me feel better.'

They swapped. They passed each other at the front of the car without making eye contact. In the passenger seat, Darren slumped and shivered in place. Kelly started the car. She had the thought about having the thought about speeding and colliding with one of the sets of headlights streaming down the opposite way, and instead drove at a normal speed, on the correct side of the road, and felt a little better for doing so.

Darren said, 'I need to call my parents.'

'Not now. It's four in the morning.'

'They get up at six.'

Kelly didn't say anything.

'For hot yoga.'

'It can wait,' Kelly said. 'For after hot yoga.'

'Crikey, Kelly. I can't let my parents do hot yoga while their granddaughter –' And something inside him seemed to crumple again.

'We go home,' Kelly said. She drove straight and true down the road, even though she felt like she was driving through fog, through a storm, through an earthquake. 'And we get some sleep.'

But she didn't sleep. Darren did, almost instantly, his back to her. Kelly curled into a ball and held her phone inches from her face. There were two messages in reply to her update. One of them was Viv in London, saying her deepest condolences, and Jos in Sweden, spamming question marks.

Kelly looked again at the lovely sun-filled photograph. Maybe they'd use it for the funeral too. No, too informal. One of their family photographs, the one with the little lacy collar on the dress. That would be appropriate. Not like a beach photograph, dynamic and full of possibility just out of frame, but something as static and immortal as a little doll, something that would be like a picture of her freshly dead body, the blue around her mouth, the crusted mucus, the glassy swollen eyes, but nicer, nicer.

The sun began to shine through the closed curtains. Maybe Kelly had dozed off too, but she roused again to see that notifications were starting to come in. How strange, that upon seeing over twenty waiting for her to read, her heart leapt in excitement. She normally raked in an average of ten or so, sometimes something more impressive if it was in the interests of the church, and the thrill came unbidden, unasked for, and she braced against it like a cramp until it passed.

The familiar names, the expected messages. The offers of friendship and commiseration, the shock and the confusion. The prayers, the many prayers.

Tomorrow would be Sunday. She and Darren would go to church. They'd be received like royalty.

On the other bedside table, next to a framed picture of a soft-focus Jesus Christ, Darren's phone was buzzing, and she felt him stir and sigh beside her. Kelly slid out of the bed. She passed by a mirror, and the woman in the reflection who looked a little like she'd been hit by a car after all gave her a bleak and hungry glance before disappearing into the frame.

As she went, she said, 'Alexa, please make some coffee.' She heard a beep from the kitchen.

From the bedroom, she could hear Darren's voice. He was talking on the phone. The rumble of the coffee machine threw a blanket over the distinct words, but Kelly could imagine what they'd be. He was always apologising to those people. They'd come over, probably this morning, not asking if they should. They'd embrace him.

They'd embrace him and Kelly realised two things. Those things were that her husband had not put his arms around her yet, and that their marriage wasn't going to survive this. She wanted the third thing to be that she didn't give a shit.

It took longer for Darren to emerge than she thought. By the time she heard his footsteps, she had drunk half her coffee while his went cold. He came in and he was dressed, with his shirt tucked in. She was still wearing her knickers and her camisole. He wasn't looking at her and instead went to the tray on the counter where they put things like their keys, which is what he took. He'd shaved his face. He looked well rested. Kelly hated him, an impulse that hit her from the back of the skull.

'Alexa made us some coffee,' she said.

'I'm heading out.'

'Where?'

'My parents.'

'You can't,' she said, and believed it was true. He couldn't, not because it was wrong, but because it was impossible. 'You can't go.'

Darren stopped and he turned back to her, but he wasn't looking at her. Now she saw the haggard shadows under his eyes. Her hate left her. She wasn't in control. It could come back at any time, the hate. Darren was saying, 'I can't believe you did that, Kelly.'

'I had to.'

He didn't hear her. 'They deserved to know, to be told personally. We're family. I told you I wanted to tell them. Your sister, have you talked to her?'

'You know I haven't.'

Darren seemed to sag, like a marionette with some vital string cut free. The one that was propping up his anger, maybe. Then he said, 'Come with me. Will you come with me?'

It was easy to imagine. The little living room, the dream catcher in the window, the uncomfortably small couch where she would sit with Darren and they'd be hugged together in it, and their hips and outer thighs sandwiched there would get warm, and Maddie and Paul would ask them so many questions. When did you get to the hospital? What was her temperature? Didn't she seem sick that day? And they would say nothing unkind. They would just keep asking, persistent as detectives. Maybe they'd still be in their yoga pants throughout the interrogation.

'You go,' Kelly said. 'I just can't, Darren. If it's what you need, then you go.'

He stood there for a few more moments before he rounded the table, a hand going out, which she took, and she drew him nearer. His arm went around her shoulders and she stayed sitting as she leaned into him, and he held her.

She slept on the couch that morning, exhaustion taking her, and she dreamed of Cottesloe Beach rendered in yellow and blue. In this dream, she lay on a beach towel in her one-piece and a tie-dye sarong, a floppy hat that she saw as a shadowy wing over her eyes, her skin shiny with a fresh coat of coconut-scented sunscreen. She felt the bristle of shaved hair under her palms, felt sand roll between layers of slick flesh. There was a dull roar of noise from behind her but she refused to turn, would only lounge there on her elbows with her crossed ankles. As long as she didn't turn, this beach day would continue forever.

There was Darren, nearer to the ocean. He wasn't in his boardshorts but a white cloth smock that tied at the neck and extended to his ankles, covered his arms in loose sleeves. It flapped against his legs like a sail on a mast. She didn't ask why he was wearing a temple garment, or why she wasn't. She waited for him to turn and see her and smile, but he was just looking up.

Between them was Anna-Kate, crouched like a bullfrog on the sand, the curls in her blonde hair pulled at by the wind, the tensile strength of them insisting on ringlets. She'd been early to walk, but now she was crawling to Kelly like she hadn't since she was thirteen months old. Come to me, darling. Good girl.

Darren was moving. He was walking to Anna-Kate, and Kelly saw him reach down and help her to her feet, help her wobble her way back to Mummy, except that's not what he was doing. He cradled her to his chest instead, her face no longer visible to Kelly, and he turned away, walking for the ocean. Kelly realised with a hysterical urgency that the roaring was not coming from behind her but from those crashing, frothing waves.

Darren walked and the water lapped up his legs, sticking his robe to his skin, and Kelly felt the memory of walking out into the lake, guided by a pastor. Her feet were slipping in mud, her teeth beginning to chatter, but his hands were warm and firm around hers, and he pulled her out and out into the lake.

But she wasn't in the lake. She was lying on the beach in her bathers and her husband was walking into the surf with their baby. She could barely see her anymore but knew she was there like she knew the sun was in the sky. She lay on the beach as the ocean crept up for his hips, where it would start biting at Anna-Kate's hanging little feet. As it swallowed his legs and his waist and then his torso, she felt the way the pastor's hand had conformed to the shape of her forehead, pushing her back into the icy lake water, which rushed up and flooded her nose. They would have to insert a tube to encourage airflow. They would have to put her on oxygen, or she would never wake up again.

But she did wake up, to the shrill sound of her phone going off.

In a fugue state, she half-fell off the couch and reached for where it was vibrating across the table. The sun was coming in at a harsh angle through the windows, the gauzy curtains doing nothing to blunt the bite of heat. She was still dressed in sweat-damp sleep things and the dream that was also memory and something else was leaving her brain, shredded to nothing. She thought she remembered Darren in his robes on the beach. That must have been funny.

'Alexa, what time is it?'

'It is 10:42am.'

Then Kelly saw her phone was bright green with an incoming call, and a name glowed white from the centre: NADIA.

Kelly stopped herself from reflexively answering and instead stared at that name. The ringing just wouldn't stop. Nadia would be on the other end, her phone pressed determinedly to her ear, her jaw set haughty and her eyes cold. It would be an angry call, Kelly knew this as a matter of instinct and fact, and she didn't want to deal with it half-asleep, or half-anything. Kelly made herself decline it, only realising as she did so that her daughter had died last night and maybe that was why Nadia was calling. Because Nadia's niece had died.

Her eyes gravitated to the bright red bubble of Facebook notifications, and saw 99+.

And there were more, on investigation, and as soon as that 99+ disappeared, a 1 appeared in its place. Then a 2, a 5, a 24, a 67, until the ceiling of 99+ was struck once again. Names scrolled by, names she didn't know, complete strangers, and even then, she expected to see condolences, offers of sympathy, sad reacts.

Hannah Churley

Glorious day! King Jesus, please BLESS this family,

BLESS Anna Kate! Please BESTOW upon them your MERCY! Hallelujah!

Michelle Sawyer
In the darkest nights, you light it up, o Lord, o Lord

Jenny Caroline DeGracey
God of revival ! God of Renewal ! Bless Anna-Kate ! We invite His holy intercession ! Awake ! Awake !

Carl Gay
'Now all glory to God, who is able, through His mighty power at work within us, to accomplish infinitely more than we might ask or think.' - Ephesians 3:20

Beverley Gordon
Breathe, breathe Your divine breath into the body of AnnaKate and may she rise NOW!

Keightlyn McMillon
We agree! We agree! We agree for our powers to flow through to Anna-Kate! Bless the Lundell family with the presence of the Holy Spririt in Jesus's name!

And on, and on.

And the screen went bright green, with Nadia's name in its centre, and Kelly denied her call again, with more irritation than dread this time. The sweaty rectangle in her hand felt about as illuminating as the world seen through a letter slot, so she abandoned it on the couch and went for the study she shared with Darren.

On her way, she blindly reached out for the door in the hallway that had been knocked open in a panic last night, refusing to look inside as she clicked it firmly shut.

Equipped with keyboard, mouse, and a bigger screen, finding the centre of the cyclone came easier. She reasoned someone had to have shared her post, for whatever reason, and when she found that early chain, she sat still with her hand to her mouth, her heart racing.

His name in bold, sharing her post, his own words affixed on top of them:

> **Pastor Paul Blanston**
> It has been made known to me that an innocent soul has departed this earth most unexpectedly and I believe unjustly. Anna-Kate Lundell was pronounced deceased by doctors in the early hours of this day. On learning of this tragedy I have prayed upon it to know God's will and He has spoken to me of that will. He has spoken to me and said that it is my solemn duty to Him that I gather every mighty believer on this Earth and that our prayers together will restore the soul of Anna-Kate to her earthly form so she may walk among us again.
>
> Our God is a God of great miracle. We believe in Him as we believe in King Jesus, who bested his grave and the land knew the weight of his Holy feet once more, and it became blessed. I ask our family of the Church of the Called Ones to lift up our hearts in unified prayer. Stand in the belief that God will raise Anna-Kate once again as he once raised his son Jesus Christ. Believe and believe well!

Pastor Paul Blanston was a handsome man, all the girls at the store could agree on that. Glossy blond hair swept from a side-part, a square jaw, broad shoulders, all those qualities that women might desire and men might wish they had for themselves. Kelly had always thought that it wasn't those things alone, but also his eyes. Pastor Paul's eyes were unusually pretty, maybe even womanly. It wasn't just the colour, though – it was something else. Easier to see in photographs and videos, of which there were many. Kelly had only been to a few of his live sermons, and she'd found herself watching the screens mounted above the stage rather than the man below them, all the better to see his lovely eyes.

And he'd called for unified prayer. In the time it took for her to read his post through, her notifications had hit the 99+ ceiling again.

She felt like her brain was floating in a pool of warm milk, leaking through the floor of her skull into her nervous system. She felt like she'd taken the Tramadol she used to take in the days after Anna-Kate was rescued from her small body with a scalpel and gloved hands. Like a millionaire was praying for her. She also felt exactly like she'd fallen asleep in the late morning, sick with the heat streaming through the curtains, the itch of unwashed knickers, stale coffee staining her saliva. She left the computer to wash herself, and when she dressed, she put on her good jeans, her nice blouse. She blow-dried her hair with quick curling motions to bring out her natural waves.

Her daughter was to be resurrected, and Kelly knew she had a lot of work ahead of her.

They lived in a quiet cul-de-sac, an inverse grin of houses. Darren felt as though he was being watched as he drove home, and found himself going slower than normal, like he was sneaking in. It was a radiant day, but maybe someone up there was looking out for him because he saw no life stirring on his neighbours' front lawns.

Now, on *his* lawn, there was someone.

A woman he did not recognise was sitting on the red brick steps leading up to the front door. Not a woman, really – a girl, in shorts, with long centre-parted hair and a top with fluttery sleeves, and in one hand she was holding a pear, he thought, and in her other hand was her phone, fingers laced around the PopSocket as her thumb skimmed the screen.

When Darren parked and got out, the girl looked up in a dozy way, and grinned a blissful grin. Beside her was a basket of more pears, and bananas and grapes and a rock melon, and a bed of flowers, and a big fluffy bow.

'Blessings upon you,' said the girl. She had an American accent. 'You're Mr Lundell, right?'

'Um,' said Darren. 'Who are you?'

She stood, slipping her phone into her back pocket, holding the pear out from herself. 'Dani,' she said. 'I'm a revivalist. Do you hug?'

Darren stood helplessly as she flowed down the steps to wrap her long arms around his shoulders. He felt concern for the drip of her fruit on his shirt, such an instinctual thought drilled into him by the numerous times he had lifted Anna-Kate only to find she had some morsel of food in her hand, the inevitable connect of sticky fingers, and grief once again slammed into him like the swing of a mallet for his guts. Tears freed themselves from the corners of his eyes, stinging raw, but he resisted the easy collapse into this embrace.

Still, maybe Dani sensed it, for she pulled back to look up into his face. Her smile didn't go away. 'No sadness today,' she said. 'Only ecstatic joy, my dude. Everything's going to be fine.'

He thought, what the fuck is happening right now.

'Can I help you? Or something? I need to get inside. Is this your fruit?' It rattled out of him in quick succession as disentangled himself from her hands, hefted the fruit basket, palmed away the tears. 'I don't mean to be rude,' he said, which most times meant that he wished whoever he was talking to would stop being rude.

'The lady with the nice garden over there dropped that off,' Dani said, pointing, and then dropping her hand. 'I came out and she said it was because she heard about your daughter dying. I said, it's all good, you can keep all your fruit, no one's dead today, but she left it anyway.'

Darren's arm already hurt from holding up the basket, staring down now at this creature who kept grinning at him. He asked, 'Where is Kelly?' and it came out much louder than he intended.

Dani didn't flinch, still smiling. 'Inside, with my mom.'

Darren left her there. Inside, he found Kelly dressed like she was about to go to Belmont shopping forum with her friends, in nice tight jeans and her hair clipped up high, her face freshly made up. Not the haggard woman he left on the couch hours ago, not at all. She was sitting with a woman he did not recognise. Was she a social worker? A funeral director? They were consulting a sleek-looking tablet, which the stranger held in skinny, veiny hands, and then they looked up simultaneously.

'You must be Darren,' said the woman, with an accent and a smile that confirmed she was the mother of the girl outside. The same horsey brown hair, only worn in two long skinny braids.

'You're back,' Kelly said. 'I thought you'd stay the night.'

'Of course not,' said Darren. He set the fruit basket down. 'What's happening? Is this for the service?'

'Yes,' said the woman. 'We're just selecting some images of your lovely daughter. You're both quite the photographers. You should get into that fruit, Mr Lundell. You look like you could use the hydration.'

Kelly was on her feet, eyes shining. 'Darren,' she said. 'This is Rosemary Love. She's the lead social media consultant with the Church of the Called Ones.'

'For WA,' Rosemary added, with a humble hand on her chest.

Behind him, Darren felt Dani trail in, roaming through the house like it was familiar territory, coming to perch on the arm of the couch.

'And she's going to help us,' Kelly said.

Darren had talked with his mother and his father about help. His mum wanted to do a lot of helping, which seemed like a series of specific tasks to do with handling paperwork, how her friend Terri had a catering company that would give them a fair rate, how she was only a phone call away if he needed to talk. All delivered between short and sharp blows of her nose into an infinite supply of tissue paper, as if impatient with her own physiological reaction to grief. His father had also offered something like help, but it was of an abstract kind, mumbled and noncommittal, and neither of them could really bring themselves to bridge that conversational gap.

None of it felt like help. It felt like busywork. Eventually there would be a funeral. Eventually they'd lower Anna-Kate into the ground in a baby-sized coffin, polished bright Barbie white, and as far as Darren figured, no one had to do anything, really. It would all come together on its own. Or it wouldn't. And who cared?

And now someone else wanted to help with busywork, by giving them more of it. If Dani held out her half-eaten pear for him to bite from, he'd consider it of more immediate use right now than anything anyone else could offer.

But he asked the question anyway. 'Help with what?'

Kelly placed her hands on his shoulders, like they were teammates about to go out on the field. She said, 'Help bring Anna-Kate back.'

*

It had been a bright day like this one when he'd fallen in love with Kelly. He'd seen her before they'd switched to their robes. She'd been a string bean with a heavy fringe and bright clips, in a denim skirt that went down to her knees, white sneakers, and a T-shirt that had *Cheer For Christ* printed across the chest. It hadn't been love, then, but he'd felt for the first time the urge to actually walk over to a girl and talk to her for no reason other than he thought she was pretty. But she'd looked over at him and smiled in a way that didn't seem very friendly.

And that had made him think about Kelly Davidson even more.

When they'd lined up for their baptism, rows of pale bare feet on the uncomfortable rocky shore of the lake, she'd been two people ahead of him. All he had to do was lean a little to the left to see past Margot Townview. Kelly had removed the clips from her hair, which now fell in sun-streaked chestnut around her shoulders. There was a hole in one ear where she'd removed an earring too. He could imagine these motions, like the way his mother would sit at her vanity, take down her hair and methodically remove her jewellery. A deeply female and mature ritual, fine-fingered and elegant. He wondered if Kelly had a mirror like that in her room.

And then she was walking to the side of the lake, meeting the pastor already standing waist-deep in the steel-blue water. Darren wasn't sure what happened next, exactly, only that when Kelly came back up from being dipped into the water, she was coughing and heaving, and clutching onto the pastor. They walked together to the edge of the lake, but as they moved for the shallower edges, Kelly's knees bowed beneath her own weight, legs slow, like she was powering through syrup instead of water, and the pastor was dragging her, now.

Kelly's face pale, frightened and sleepy at the same time.

Darren had moved first, splashing out into the water, looping an arm around her and helping the pastor pull her towards the lake edge. She was limp in his arms and heavier because of it, and it felt for one frightening moment like the lake itself was trying to draw her back. That if he let it, she'd slip out of his arms and disappear into the water.

Later, they said that the Holy Spirit had entered her so powerfully that her mortal body had gone into shock, made her vulnerable to the cold water. It was a day that Darren thought about when, several years later, her doctor prescribed iron pills for anaemia, and it was a day that Darren thought about now as he watched the audience.

The audience. That was how he viewed them, these church goers. He and Kelly were seated at a place of privilege off to the side of the stage. The stage, not the sanctuary.

Darren's childhood church had been a modest service conducted in a high school, where the wives put collapsible picnic tables out front and balanced jugs of watery orange cordial with towers of disposable cups. You walked through the big front doors and into the auditorium, air conditioning blasting away the dry heat. Even though the kids used it for theatre, it had felt as much a church as any cathedral, to Darren. Maybe it was just the familiarity of the thing.

And then Pastor Paul came to town.

These people, the Called Ones, built up their church a year faster than the megastore development a block away, even though it seemed like it was just as tall, just as wide, just as decorated in glossy steel and smooth floors and tall ceilings hanging with spotlights. The stage was massive, the auditorium itself gigantic. There was a band, fully electric, with speakers hidden in the shadowing heights dispersing noise into the empty space.

This was not a place that echoed, the way cathedrals seemed like instruments themselves, carrying prayer and choir into new harmonies. This was a space that amplified.

And then that screen. That screen Darren tried not to look at but was forced to, because it was too big and too bright to ignore. It was currently filled with a picture of Anna-Kate's face, her delicate toddler features, her big eyes that seemed like they were laughing at all the ridiculous things in the world. He remembered the first time they'd had a day in the city, when she was just past twelve months old. He'd been anxious about how rough and rude downtown could get, and the first time a car blasted by, horn wailing, he'd whipped around, expecting that face to crumple into tears. Anna-Kate had laughed instead, the way she laughed when he made elephant noises, or fart sounds, or his Wookiee cry whenever he dropped something. He'd thought, there's something to that instinct, to finding everything a little ridiculous.

There was an absurdity to everything now, and it sat uneasy in him, the same way blasphemy made him uneasy. Uncertain exactly if this blasphemy was his own horrible compulsion to laugh, or just this: the picture of his dead daughter blown up on a ten-foot-tall screen, his own nearness to it, the way he could see the black lines between individual pixels, if that's what he was seeing. He'd wanted her to grow bigger, but not this big.

'Look upon this sweet, innocent girl,' Pastor Paul was saying. 'This girl whose time has not yet come. You all know by now that this is a very special service, that you've been called here for a reason. We're going to use our great power on this day, and do wonders.'

Kelly stood, and Darren didn't. She turned to him, and he saw her hand lift like she was preparing to reach out and grab his. His own rested on his knees, unmoving, cold, and he looked at her and just shook his head. That look crossed her face, that profound discontent. The kind she wore when he left his car keys inside the house, noting this infraction down for later reckoning. He sensed her attributing it to something defective inside him. Irresponsibility, carelessness, some hidden subconscious compulsion within him that wanted to sabotage their morning, their day, their marriage entire, when really the keys were just hidden beneath a folded newspaper and he'd assumed they were in his coat pocket.

And now he wasn't going to go with her up onto that stage, and he wondered what reason she would give. Cowardice, hatred, the malicious impulse to keep their daughter dead.

She walked away from him, climbing the steps. Pastor Paul was looking at her with his arms out, and embraced her in a careful way so as not to disrupt any microphones. Darren wondered where *were* the microphones? Pastor Paul wasn't holding any, and he couldn't see a visible headset, and yet his voice boomed over their heads, in surround sound. Voice of God stuff. Powerful enough to hang the earth from the sky, all its billions of trillions of tonnes.

He felt a hand close around one of his. Rosemary Love, sitting beside him. Her nails were painted a bright pink and her hands had a starved aspect, with blue veins visible beneath thin, lotioned skin. He looked at her to convey gratitude even if that was not what he was feeling, but he could press his mouth into a shape that would signal it. She wasn't looking at him, instead gazing adoringly up at the stage, but he did it anyway. In case someone was watching.

It was hot up there. That was Kelly's first thought. It was hot and Pastor Paul himself was holding on to her hand, which was also hot, or it was his hand that was hot, and it was getting hotter and making her palm sweat, but he held on so tightly that she would have to struggle to free herself, which she did not want to do. The lights were brighter than she had expected, dazzling her eyes so much she could not see the crowd. She looked down and saw the clusters of cameras filming the service, sightless black lenses, people in headphones with their heads bent as if in contemplation.

She didn't have a microphone. Up close, she saw now that a wire had been laid through Pastor Paul's hair, which must have been shaped and sculpted to hide it. The tiny flesh-coloured microphone was taped almost invisibly to his forehead, just peeking past his hairline. She'd never seen anything like it, had never noticed it before, and it was hard to stop looking once she spotted it. Spotting it felt lewd to her in a way she couldn't define. Her hand was getting clammier and clammier. Soon it would start dripping, she was sure, just dripping onto the stage.

'And I was awoken that night,' Pastor Paul was saying, echoing around the gigantic arena. 'To nothing. Silence, and stillness. My room was a coffin. It was as though the whole world just up and died on me it was so quiet. Because when God speaks to you, He doesn't shout. He doesn't raise his voice. He just quiets it all down so you have no choice but to heed Him. And that night, He woke me to that silence, and He spoke to me.

'God said, Paul, it is time for you to make use of the considerable power and influence that I in my wisdom have granted you. There is a woman out there who is praying so hard to me right now. There is a woman whose prayer deserves to be heard, to be uplifted.'

From the void (although Kelly's eyes were slowly adjusting, and she started to see them, shadow pebbled with faces, tufts of hair catching errant light, the occasional starlight gleam of an activated cellphone) came murmurs. A slowly building rise of assent. It reminded her of the screed of comments, the disembodied Hallelujahs, the Amens, the In Jesus' Names. Beneath it, the sound of creaking, of motion. Kelly squeezed Pastor Paul's hand, or tried to, but her fingers felt trapped.

'And so I summon you all on His holy day,' Pastor Paul said, his other hand now raised in half Sieg Heil. A stage magician's gesture, as though lightning might spring out from his fingertips and ignite the darkness. Kelly was not entirely convinced that this was a strict impossibility. 'His chosen, His called. Within you lies the power. Within you lies His will.'

Bless you Anna-Kate, God is mighty, God is just. The swell of noise was climbing louder. Kelly was used to being submerged in it, but standing before it she felt like she was awaiting a great wave. A drowning.

Pastor Paul was now praying. He had opened his arms outstretched, still keeping clutched her hand, and so she was forced to participate.

She was meant to be praying, Kelly realised. This struck her as obvious and not new information. They'd run through the service beforehand, reassuring her she wouldn't be mic'd, but that God would hear her just fine. But it occurred to her then, standing on a stage and sweating beneath spotlights, that Kelly had not offered a single prayer since Anna-Kate had died.

But before, not long before. Sitting in the back seat, holding her little body in her arms as Darren drove them to the hospital. Not going fast enough, if there even was a fast enough. Her hand clasped over Anna-Kate's forehead as if to keep her consciousness firmly compressed within her skull. Her wheezy breath tickling Kelly's chin, struggling in and out. Kelly had said, *Please, please, God, please.*

'Please God,' she said, then. She felt like the edges of her words were being picked up by Paul's forehead microphone, an echo of her words thrumming through the auditorium.

'Wake up, Anna-Kate,' said Paul, and this was echoed back to them in other voices, fractured. 'Anna-Kate Lundell, come back to the light. Your time is not over.'

The thought occurred to her that she wished it was some other woman who had lost her child and was praying her back to life. Kelly was confident she could pray for that woman. She could hold that woman's hand and say with absolute certainty that God would look after her, would do right by her. She could sway in the crowd and in the darkness and speak the name of some other little girl and believe wholeheartedly that they together could perform a miracle. She could also tell that woman that she would feel whole again, that grief isn't forever, that of course she is loved and that she did nothing wrong. That none of this was her fault. When inevitably they failed to restore this woman's daughter to her earthly body, she would tell this woman that even though her little girl was barely four years old, it was her time to go, and that's that about that.

But she was that woman, and it felt like being asked to pull herself out of the cold lake. That she had to open her mouth to pray now, despite the lack of air in her lungs. She *was* speaking, half-repeating the boomified utterances of the man beside her, half something else, but she couldn't hear herself to say what.

She could hear her own heartbeat throbbing in her ears. Her own breath winnowing high from her chest. God, it was fucking hot up here.

Her vision vanished to a pinhole, and she was floating.

Darren watched his wife buckle. He watched Pastor Paul hold on to her before she could hit the stage completely. The moans and groans of the audience continued as ceaseless waves while his daughter smiled gap-toothed from the screen.

People wearing black T-shirts with the Called Ones logo stamped on their chests all leapt into motion, collecting the swooned Kelly out of Pastor Paul's arms, helping her to sit. One of them was opening a bottle of water, another supporting her head, and they were all smiling. This kind of thing happened all the time. Kelly was not the first and would not be the last person to collapse on that stage, overwhelmed, face white. Some of them convulsing. Some of them faking it. Hell, maybe all of them. Maybe Kelly too.

And Darren left.

Oh, he knew the husband thing to do. The husband thing to do would be to surge forward. It would be to yank his arm from Rosemary's reassuring clutch, *that's my wife and she needs me*, and to vault up onto the stage. To take Kelly's face in his hands and say her name a bunch, maybe even scoop her up in his arms, shrug off the pleading hands of the worship assistants. There's a hysterical piece on the cutting-room floor where he judo chops Pastor Paul in the neck, probably before the scooping. What happens after that, he couldn't quite imagine that far, but he could feel the instinct towards this first sequence as sure as he'd known all the steps of their wedding dance. Synchronicity.

Instead, he stepped out into an empty foyer, and then out into the parking lot, where his imagination ran out once again, vis-à-vis what happens next. But at least there was air. Air filled with nothing but wind in sun-parched trees, a distant ambulance wail, the electrical hum from overhead powerlines.

'Did you feel it, in there?'

And a voice, someone following. Darren looked back to see Dani. She stopped at a distance. Maybe it was something in his face. She didn't stop smiling, but he was beginning to think that was just how her face worked, like a dolphin's fixed grin.

'You and Kelly were amazing.'

'I didn't do anything,' Darren said. 'I left. And she just – is she okay?'

'She's wonderful,' Dani said, now making an approach. Her fine hair picked up in her own personal wind and floated behind her. She moved like she was stepping from cloud to cloud. 'God's power is awesome, and it'll wham you like that, when you're up there. I really felt like we generated a lot of it today. You felt it, right?'

Darren wanted to yell at her. To tell her he felt nothing. Not God and not anything, certainly not whammed. He didn't even feel sad anymore. Instead, he said, 'I just needed to get some air.'

'I could use some too,' said Dani, stopping beside him instead of going back inside like he'd hoped. 'Miracles are hard work, huh?'

'What happens next?'

'Well, the pastor's done talking now, and they're gonna play some –'

'I meant Anna-Kate. What happens? We get a call from the hospital, saying there's been a disturbance at the morgue? Or can we bury her first? Should we have someone on standby with a shovel? I mean, you're the revivalist.' Darren felt the words rattle out of him and go rolling on ahead, out of reach. He'd resolved not to yell at a child but this didn't feel much better. Her smile had faded. He could feel his own, spreading against his will. Primates sometimes show teeth as a sign of aggression. Or was it submission? He said, 'You must have seen this go down all the time.'

'No, sir,' Dani said. 'I have not.'

'So we're gonna be a world first, huh? I mean, after Christ.'

'Mr Lundell.' Dani reached out, a hand on his arm, a hand on his chest. 'You're upset. And scared. You don't have to be either of those things. When God returns your daughter, He will deliver her with excellent love and care. It'll be like waking up to Christmas, you know? Just a brand-new day, with joy in your life, like it never went bad to begin with. That's what I believe. That's what we're praying for.'

'So it's like Santa,' said Darren. 'Bring her down a chimney, set her under a tree.'

Dani didn't let go. She clutched tighter. 'Oh Lord,' she said. 'Please help Mr Lundell in his moment of doubt and fear. Give him the strength and power to return him to his perfect faith so that he can lift his voice in prayer.'

As she spoke, Darren peeled Dani's hand off his shirt sleeve as gently as he could, even as her other hand gripped his collar. Shaking her off was like escaping a tentacle that kept replacing its grip somewhere new.

'Do you know why miracles don't ever happen?' Dani said, once he'd broken free. Her eyes were bright. 'Mr Lundell? It is not that His power is deficient. God has already decided to bring back Anna-Kate, just as He has decided to cure hunger and cancer, to bring peace on Earth, to reward the good. He has placed this power within us. All we have to do is believe, and we don't. It's us, Mr Lundell – we're why. We're why He hasn't. It is *our* lack. *Our* absence. Please, sir, Anna-Kate needs you right now, more than she ever will in her life.'

Darren stood silent, staring, at this willowy creature who had begun to cry, and God, he envied her that. He envied her free tears and her certainty, the shrill fear that had entered her voice, because she believed something he did not: that his absence would kill his child and ergo, logically, his presence would restore her life.

If only.

'No,' Darren said. 'Lucky Anna-Kate, she doesn't need anything, anymore.'

And then he went to his car.

Kelly was trying to remember something. She was trying to remember why it was that water formed on the outside of a cold glass also filled with water. All she could bring to mind was her belief as a child, which was that the water inside the glass slowly seeped through somehow, that it was always leaking through. That the rounded curve of the glass itself was not as solid as it seemed. As a result, she liked to drink quickly so the water wouldn't escape.

She was drinking it slowly, now, and trying to remember the truth of the matter. Strange how so much you learned in high school just seemed to evaporate.

It was the opposite of evaporation. Condensation?

She drank another sip of her water.

'. . . and I told her. So, she's going to upload the video to Twitter,' someone was saying. It was Rosemary, and Kelly was partially aware she was talking to her. 'With the hashtag we talked about. And Beckers said she'd retweet it when it comes up. Oh, you know Beckers, that little thing that was on Idol a few years back . . .'

Kelly put down her glass of water and picked up her phone. Her screen was plagued with more notifications. She felt nothing. Just irritation, clearing them with jabs and swipes of her fingers so she could get to the information she was looking for.

She opened a browser and input *why does water condensation outside of glass* into the search field.

'. . . after we upload the stream to the main channel, and Dani's been Instagramming the whole thing . . .'

The air is cooled to its dew point on contact with the cold surface, and the water vapour in the air forms into liquid. Right, of course. Instead of the opposite thing, where heat turns liquid water into vapour, steam rising out of a boiling pot, scorching her fingertips when she lifts the lid to check on her asparagus.

'. . . setting up a GoFundMe for you and your husband, with a modest percentage directed towards the church, just as compensation for everyone's time and effort . . .'

But why? Why does the cold turn gas into liquid, and liquid into solid? Why not the other way round? That had always been Kelly's problem with facts. You could ask *why why why* all day and eventually you'd run out of answers and run out of facts. The observable universe, floating on top of a depthless void of ineffable unknowableness, where God lived. Kelly could not fathom the idea of treading the world with the belief that He did not.

'. . . what *you* need to do is rest up. How are you feeling now?'

The world seemed to swim back into focus at Rosemary's question. Her hands had gone out to touch Kelly's wrists, and Kelly looked up into kind eyes and a waiting smile.

'Much better,' Kelly said. 'Good, I think.'

'Wonderful,' said Rosemary. 'Would you let me drive you home?'

'I should really find Darren.'

'Oh, honey. I'm afraid to say that he took off a little while ago. Dani let me know he wasn't feeling quite right.'

Kelly nodded. She was fairly sure she should be angry at him. But the feeling didn't rise.

'And for your sake,' Rosemary went on, holding on to Kelly's hands, 'I hope you can forgive him for that. From what I can tell, he's living in a world right now where he'll never see his daughter again, and that's a truly sad and lonely world to be in. We have to keep the door open.' She squeezed Kelly's fingers. 'At least for now. And when she's returned to you both, I'm sure everything will start making sense again.'

'When?'

'Pardon?'

Kelly pulled her hands out of Rosemary's. 'I mean, we just had the service. When does she get here?'

Rosemary frowned, pulling away. 'Mrs Lundell,' she said, keeping her voice quiet, and, Kelly thought, a little admonishing. 'That's not for us to say. But we're going to keep lifting our voices. Right now, international Called communities everywhere are praying for the waking of your daughter. For now, we have to be patient.'

'Why?' Kelly could feel her voice shake, and also get louder. Both of these things felt entirely beyond her control. 'God is God. He made the whole universe in six days and then got the Sunday off to make the first man.'

'And the resurrection of King Jesus took three days,' Rosemary said. Some of the lines around her eyes had smoothed away. 'And can you imagine, having loved Christ, having known him? Having been held in his arms? And then witnessing the disgusting death he was put to, with all of that hope and joy sealed up in a tomb, and spending three days not only mourning his passing, but wondering what it meant for him to die? Wondering what purpose they had, what their lives were meant to be after this tragic occurrence? And maybe in those three days, the non-believers had let their hearts turn cold and spiteful, while the others saw the work ahead of them, the work of faith, and were justly rewarded with great joy, and not shame, when he returned.'

'I thought it was the fish thing,' Kelly said. 'Jonah spent three days in a fish belly before God told the fish to throw him up, and Jesus was like . . . yeah, I want it like that.'

'Well,' said Rosemary. Kelly could see she was trying not to be irritated. Irritated, like that was the strongest emotion either of them could summon right now. 'Regardless of *when*, there's a lot to do, and you need to find rest where you can get it. Let's get you home.'

Kelly followed Rosemary out of the little room she'd been escorted to, out into bright white hallways. She'd never been backstage before. She'd never thought of her church as having a *backstage* before. Up ahead, the broad-shouldered shape of Pastor Paul Blanston strode in the opposite direction, casting Kelly a wide smile. His hand brushed her shoulder as they crossed paths. 'You were great up there,' he said.

'Thanks,' she said.

Outside, churchgoers milled around, chatting, smiling, having a nice Sunday. Some of them looked at her, smiled wider, waved, said some things, seemed to know better than to approach her. The same way a celebrity might navigate a pool of more timid bystanders, she thought. Or a victim, still wearing blood on her face.

She trailed after Rosemary to her blue hatchback, but automatically looked for the white Honda she shared with Darren, and then saw Darren, opening the car door, popping up like a meerkat. 'Kelly!' he said, and Kelly stopped.

As did Rosemary, a flash of surprise on her face. 'Mr Lundell,' she said. 'You're still here.'

'Yeah,' Darren said. 'Figured I'd get the air con started.'

'Very thoughtful,' said Rosemary. She pivoted back to Kelly, her expression inscrutable, before it broke with a smile. 'That's great, then. I'll give you a call later tonight, let you know how everything's going.'

'Okay,' said Kelly. 'Maybe we'll have news for you, too.'

Rosemary's smile pressed into a thin line, and she gave

them both a wave, continuing on to her car. Kelly readjusted her bag under her arm and started towards her own, sneaking a look at Darren as she circled round to the passenger seat.

They both got in. The air inside was blessedly refrigerated. They closed the doors and stared out the windscreen, and sat in such silence that when Kelly's phone rang out, they both jumped.

She looked at the screen, to find NADIA's name glaring up at her.

'I can step out,' Darren said.

'It's fine,' Kelly said, and dismissed the call. Immediately, it rang again, and Darren covered it over with his hand when she went to hang up a second time. 'You want to talk to her, then? Go ahead.'

'Crikey, Kelly,' Darren said, but took the phone from her, bringing it to his ear. 'Hi, Nadia, it's Darren.'

Kelly could hear NADIA's voice on the other end, shrill and spiky. She pressed her fingers against her ears to block out the specifics, listened to the muffled version of Darren talk to the indistinct tiny-voiced cartoon version of her sister. *She can't talk right now, it's been — no, it's true. She'd — we think she had a bad flu, she'd been sick and it just, almost overnight. Yeah. Well, I'd rather not — we can't know that, can we? Yeah, it's all a bit crazy right now. I'm sorry for that, all this, just, I reckon it will die down a bit after today. I'll see if she can call you back later. Okay, thanks, Nadia. Thank you. I'm, yeah, I'm all right, thanks. Okay. Bye.* Kelly dropped her hands, took back her phone, switched it off.

She waited for Darren to tell her to call NADIA back later today, like he promised, and instead he said, 'I can't do all of this, Kelly.'

'I know.'

'I want to mourn our kid. I just want to do that, now, with

you, and not without you.'

She looked at him. He'd been crying, hadn't he? In this car, alone, with eyes that were red and were begging her to rescue him, to dive in after him, to drown alongside. How could he want to do that to her? She couldn't forgive him.

'Well, Darren, I *don't* want to mourn our kid,' she said. 'Who *wants* to do that? You know, that's the sick thing, what you want. That's the crazy thing.'

She stopped looking at him, stared out instead at the parking lot. People were still out there, milling around, trickling out from the gaping doors of the church, dispersing into the rows of cars. Lots of sunglasses and hats to combat the bright sky, lots of squinting and smiling. Small children, too, running in circles, or clasped to their mothers' hips, or bundled into prams with shades. There would be people who had a nice day today, all of these people, maybe everyone in the world.

She felt Darren hold on to her, and for a moment, she did not know why. He pulled her across the space between them, and she waited for some kind of instinct, an urge to push him away. Instead, he wrapped her up in his arms, and she realised she'd already started crying. In gasping breaths, Kelly filled her lungs with cold air, sharp and clear.

'Let's make a deal,' said Darren, above her head, after what felt like hours. 'We go home. We check every room, and we check hers last.'

She pulled back. Her eyes felt like they were full of sand, and she used her thumbs to wipe them clean. She looked at her thumbs, at the mascara smears, and rubbed them away with her fingers. 'And then what happens? When she's not there.'

'I don't know,' Darren said. 'But I will be.'

'And then we do things your way?'

He held out his hand to her, and she took it. She tangled her fingers with his and trapped them in between.

Kelly said, 'I'll think about it.'

Darren nodded, and held her hand, tight.

KATHRYN VAN BEEK

Sea Legend

It was the end of the second day when Hemi saw the octopus. He rubbed his eyes. He'd almost gone mad from sleep deprivation on past trips, but he'd never hallucinated before. It had been two long days on the trawler, and they'd been knocked around by continuous swells since they'd hit the Southern Ocean, but surely he wasn't delusional – yet. He peered back over the gunwales. An enormous, bronze-coloured octopus looked up at him. It clung to the side of the boat with its long tentacles, the spotted patterns on its skin shimmering through the mist.

'Luke – Tai! We've got a passenger.'

Tai looked up from repairing the net, his wraparound sunglasses dark beneath the shaggy fringe of his mullet. He lifted his chin and returned to his work. Luke, who'd been stacking the last tubs of black oreo dory in the hold, climbed out of the hatch. He stood beside Hemi, admiring the stowaway.

'Good eating.' Luke's voice carried over the din of the engine. 'Stick it on the barbie, add some chilli sauce.'

Hemi appraised Luke's slight frame. 'You reckon you could take it?'

'I've got the best spear gun you've ever seen.'

The octopus eased its white suckers from the steel and slipped back into the ocean. Hemi raised his eyebrows. 'Didn't like the sound of that.'

'The things you see out here,' Luke said. 'You could tell people, but they wouldn't believe you.'

'I took an angler to show my ex once. She didn't even believe it was a fish.' Hemi bared his teeth and rolled his eyes in an impression of an angler fish.

'That's nothing compared to some of the weird shit I've seen on the *Sea Legend*.'

'What kind of weird?'

'Oh, like . . .' Luke's sunburnt face flushed even redder. He glanced up at the wheelhouse. 'Well, you'd have to ask Dad. There's that non-disclosure thing, remember? You would've signed it when you got the job.'

As though he'd heard them, Pat strode from the wheelhouse and stood at the top of the steps leading down to the deck. The masthead floodlight picked him out in the haze like a spotlight on a mainstage, illuminating his wide stance and muscular shoulders. His scowl. 'Forgotten something?'

Hemi felt his stomach hollow out. Surely he hadn't fucked up already.

'Oh, shit.' Luke grimaced. 'I'm on dinner, aren't I?'

'Damn straight.'

Luke groaned, and Hemi exhaled.

'No canned chicken,' Tai called. 'Cook some real kai!'

'Or what?'

Tai looked up at Pat, who nodded. 'Or Hemi will chuck you overboard,' Tai said.

Hemi grinned and made as though to grab Luke.

'Oh come on, the chicken wasn't that bad,' Luke protested.

Pat walked down the steps, his weathered face creasing

into a smile. He pulled his phone from his pocket. 'Get him in a headlock, Hemi. I'll get a photo for the wall of shame.'

Hemi complied, looping an arm around Luke's neck. 'Is that why your last deckie left? The canned chicken?'

'Andy didn't like the direction we were going in,' Pat said as he took a photo. 'And we didn't like the direction he was going in, either.'

Pat stepped nearer to take another photo, giving Hemi a close-up of the long, silver scar that snaked along his jaw from ear to chin.

'Are we done yet?' Luke asked. 'I can't actually breathe.'

Hemi let go, and Luke boxed him on the shoulder before heading down below.

'We'll need some good tucker tonight,' Pat said. 'Tomorrow's going to be a big day – I can feel it in my bones.'

Hemi looked out over the water, wondering what Pat could sense that he couldn't. There was no land, no other ships – just darkening skies, viridian waves and a few circling mollymawks. Pat came and leant on the rail beside him. He was a few inches shorter than Hemi, but had the bearing of a bar-room brawl champion.

'How are you finding the *Sea Legend*?'

'Great, yeah.'

'Got your sea legs?'

'Yep.' Fuck. He thought he'd hidden yesterday's excruciating seasickness. 'I've never seen swells this size, though.'

'You're not worried about being so far south?'

'Why would I be?'

Pat turned to Hemi, his grey eyes squinting against the salt breeze. 'I knew your dad, you know.'

A large roll took Hemi off guard, and he stumbled. He braced his legs against the gunwales. 'Okay.'

'We were deckies together once or twice.'

Mollymawks cried behind them, squabbling over the offal Tai threw into the water.

'I wasn't exactly planning on sailing down here,' Hemi said. 'But a chance to crew the *Sea Legend* was too good to pass up.'

She was an older boat, but pretty with her gleaming white and teal paintwork. Everything from the red tasselled chafing gear on the net to the lifeboat canister under the steps was pristine, top quality, and stowed in its proper place. With her top-of-the-line technology and Pat's fabled knack for finding fish, the *Sea Legend* promised shorter trips and higher pay than most of the rust buckets he'd crewed.

'You said you're going for your mate ticket.' Pat said. 'Are you serious about that?'

'Yeah, I am.'

Pat nodded. 'I'll get you some time in the wheelhouse so you can sign off some sea service.'

'Ace.' At the rate he was recording sea service in his workbook, he'd be able to get a job like Tai's within a couple of years. He looked over to where the mate, all biceps and tattoos, leant over to close the transom doors. The knife sticking from his jeans pocket sliced the air, the blade perilously close to the net.

'Watch it,' Pat yelled. 'That's a hundred and fifty grand worth of net!'

Tai glanced over at them. His thumbs-up said he'd received the message, but behind those glasses his eyes could be saying anything at all.

Hemi turned to go below. He looked up at the security camera above the door. The red recording light blinked and he smiled and waved. He wasn't planning on getting lost at sea, but he liked to leave these visual mementos stored electronically for Sam – just in case. He stepped through the door into the middle deck and hung his windbreaker next to the life jackets and foul weather gear, then washed his filleting blade in the basin and opened the knife drawer. Stainless steel filleting, butcher and boning knives swam inside, shifting back and forth with the movement of the boat, like sprats. He blinked hard to clear his tired eyes, replaced the blade and turned towards the bow and the two ladders. One led down to the cabin, the other up to the wheelhouse and galley. Hemi forced himself to climb up towards whatever Luke was cooking. Not long now and he'd be able to sleep.

After a feed of singed sausages and eggs, Hemi and Luke retreated to the cabin, which was already rank with wet clothes and stale sweat. Hemi pulled off his boots and jeans and stuffed them into his drawer beneath the bunk he shared with Tai. He clambered up to the top, still wearing his socks and the old merino tee Kayleigh had bought him when they were together. He wriggled beneath the covers and waited for Luke to turn off the light. Pat's and Tai's boots tapped on the wheelhouse floor above them. Soon they'd be tag-teaming for the lower bunks, each catching a few hours' sleep before sunrise.

Luke climbed into the opposite bunk and studied Hemi. 'Why are you going for your mate ticket?

'Why aren't you?'

'I'm just going to make some money, have some fun.'

'Yeah, that's how I started.' Hemi tried to drown the memory that floated into his mind. The look in Kayleigh's eyes when she'd arrived home early to find him stoned and playing video games when he should have been building wooden block towers with Sam.

'Character's what you do when no one's watching,' she'd snapped, snatching the joint from his fingers and feeding it down the garbage disposal. Since getting that 'women returning to education' scholarship at the grand old age of twenty-three, she'd been full of big ideas. 'You don't want to be a stoner deckie all your life, do you?'

'Do you?' Luke said.

Hemi rubbed his eyes. 'Sorry?'

'Do you really want to spend your whole life at sea?'

Hemi shrugged. 'It's in my blood.'

He glanced up at the photo of Sam he'd blu-tacked over the surfing collage Andy had left on the wall. In the original photo Hemi, Sam and Kayleigh had been together on the beach, but when he printed it out he just printed Sam – white teeth flashing in a smile, red spade digging into sand. 'Turn the light off, would you?'

Luke clicked off the light, and Hemi closed his eyes. He saw the enormous octopus clinging to the side of the boat, its bulbous mantle and glistening arms. He saw the scar that ripped along Pat's jaw like a tear in a page, the angler fish he'd taken home to show Kayleigh. She'd screamed when he pulled the sneering monster from the chilly bin and chased her with it. It had just been a laugh. But in the sludge of his brain, slippery as fish guts, one thought was firm: he'd let her down.

'Hard to believe they're so old,' Luke said.

'Eh?'

'Oreo dory.'

'What are you on about?'

'Some of the ones we catch are three times older than Dad is.'

Hemi scrunched his face. 'Were we talking?'

'Nah, I'm just thinking.'

'Shut up, man, I'm trying to sleep.'

But Luke was already snoring. Hemi listened to the rhythm of the waves smashing against the hull, and drew the covers up tightly around his shoulders.

*

Pat had been right. The water was alive with fish, and the day had been set to the tempo of shooting the net, hauling it in, and processing the catch. This shot the net had only been out for an hour and it floated behind them, the length of the boat again and already bloated with dory. Mollymawks bobbed in the water around them, and the air vibrated with the twanging of the warps as Pat winched up their haul. He paused for Luke to take the orange buoys from the net's greedy mouth, and for Hemi to remove the heavy iron chains. They heaved the bulging cod-end up the stern ramp, through the open transom doors, and fixed it into position. Luke ceremoniously unlaced the net and fish flew out onto the deck. Hemi dragged away anything that would slow the processing down: first a rig shark, then a large bouquet of red bubble-gum coral. The coral was as big as Sam, but maybe four hundred years to Sam's four.

'The kauri of the sea,' he said to Luke.

'Fucking thing's sliced up the net.'

Luke grabbed one end of the coral and helped hoist it back into the water, where it was folded in by a wave. Meanwhile, Pat was working the net, struggling to free something that looked like a drowned sea lion.

'What have you got there?' Hemi asked.

The tip of the creature's tail slid from the net, and he shivered. Pat whirled to face him, eyes flashing.

'Into the hold, Hemi – what the fuck are you doing?' Pat roared.

Hemi froze, unsure if this was some kind of joke.

'We've got to get this fish iced, stop fucking around!'

Confused, Hemi opened the hatch. As he stepped onto the ladder he gave the security camera a curt nod. The red light was no longer blinking.

Hemi climbed into the refrigerated hold and waited for tubs of fish to be lowered. Previous catches were packed in ice and stacked either side of a locked utility cupboard. It would be faster to have him on deck to help with the bleeding, knifing and sorting rather than banished down here, where he was freezing his nuts off and feeling every pitch and roll of the boat. He shook his arms to keep warm, remembering every horror story he'd heard about fishermen being frozen to death, welded into cupboards or chucked overboard by unscrupulous skippers. Pat had asked for Hemi's references, but what did Hemi know about Pat? He'd jumped in his car and gunned it from Dunedin to Riverton the moment he'd got this job. He'd texted Kayleigh to tell her he was going to sea, but hadn't given any details. If he never came home, no one would even know where to look for him.

Finally there was a yell from Tai, and the first blue plastic tub of iced dory was lowered into the hold. Hemi unhooked it from the line and stacked it against the bulkhead. He returned for the next tub and soon they were in a rhythm: lowering, unhooking and stacking tub after tub of the diamond-shaped fish, until Hemi was as much a machine as the growling monster in the engine room. Unnecessary senses peeled away and all he saw was a long blur of blue plastic against the white hold as tub after tub was lowered and stacked. He heard a shout, and the fuzzy stretch of blue was interrupted by a face appearing in the hatch. Tai came into focus.

'Last one,' the mate yelled.

'Thank Christ.'

Hemi hung on to a grab rail and allowed his body to relax into the rhythm of the waves as he waited for the final tub to be lowered. Even with his eyes closed he could see fish after fish, lips downturned, fins sharp, peridot eyes glaring.

*

Hemi sat next to Luke at the galley table. Tai was opposite, still wearing his sunglasses, and behind him Pat presided over the diesel oven. Tai popped the cap off a bottle of beer and foam spewed over the table.

'Shit.' Tai mopped at the mess with a tea towel and opened the rest of the bottles over the sink, passing one to Hemi. As he reached for it, Hemi glanced over at the wall of shame. The photo montage below the condiments shelf featured Tai doing the fingers, Luke brandishing a crayfish, Andy pretending to swallow a filleting knife and Pat holding a curvaceous blue cod. Added to these was the photo of Hemi with his arm wrapped around Luke's neck.

'How'd you print that out?' Hemi asked.

'Portable Bluetooth printer,' Pat said without turning around.

Luke smirked. 'Dad's got all the mod cons.'

Hemi peered at the photo. He must have been speaking, and his mouth looked twisted and mean. Luke's face was mottled red and his eyes bulged in mock terror. If you didn't know better, you'd think he really was being assaulted.

'I hope Maritime New Zealand don't see this,' Hemi said. 'They'll never sign off my Fit and Proper Person form.'

'A fit and proper fisherman.' Tai took a swig of beer. 'Does that exist?'

Pat opened the oven and a heady fragrance filled the air. A seafood steak gleamed in the roasting dish, golden-skinned, surrounded by diced kūmara, potatoes and capsicum.

'You'll enjoy this, lads,' Pat said. 'A step up from fried eggs.'

'And several steps up from canned chicken,' Tai added.

Pat handed them each a heaped plate, then joined them at the table.

'Doesn't look like dory,' Hemi said. 'Is it the shark?'

'It's something a bit different,' Pat said.

Hemi picked up his knife, lowering it again when Tai shot him a sharp look.

'*Nau mai e ngā hua o te wao, o te ngakinga, o te wai tai, o te wai Māori*,' Tai began.

Hemi bowed his head, confused. Since when did anyone on this boat bother to bless food? But Pat and Luke had also lowered their heads with unusual reverence.

'*Nā Tane, nā Rongo, nā Tangaroa, nā Maru. Ko Ranginui e tū iho nei. Ko Papatūānuku e takoto ake nei. Tūturu whakamaua kia tina*!'

Hemi added his voice to the incantation. '*Tina*! *Hāumi e*! *Hui e*!'

Channelling their inner All Blacks, Pat and Luke chanted the last line. '*Tāiki e*!'

They raised their heads, and Pat lifted a forkful of meat to his lips. As Hemi watched, Pat's eyes moistened with the steam rising from the meal. He finished his mouthful and blinked, droplets clinging to his eyelashes. He blinked again and the tears slid down his face. Hemi looked at Tai to see if he'd noticed. As he ate, Tai's face was expressionless. But a bead of liquid escaped the rim of his sunglasses, hung for a moment on his cheekbone, and slipped down his jaw. Hemi turned to Luke, who speared forkfuls of kai with one hand and wiped tears away with the other, shoulders shuddering with each breath. There was none of the usual galley chatter, just the growling engine and pounding waves.

Hemi picked up his cutlery and cut into the meat. The knife broke through the caramelised crust and slid into a shocking pink centre. Flesh spread either side of the blade. He brought a forkful to his mouth and closed his lips around it. It fizzed on his tongue for a moment, then burst into full flavour.

The meat had a sweet, tart taste that reminded him of blackberries, of his late nan and the times they'd gone berry picking together, staining fingers and mouths with dark juice beneath wide summer skies. It had a light, salty taste that stirred a memory of collecting pipi with his dad, twisting feet into wet sand, scrunching toes around cream-coloured shells. He hadn't known he had that memory, but there it was, the two of them knee-deep in salt water, laughing as they filled their bucket with kaimoana. The meat had an umami, spring onion taste that conjured summer nights with Kayleigh, her soft, secret places and her sun-dried cotton sheets. And it had a gentle, milky taste that recalled Sam as a baby, giggling and gurgling as Hemi and Kayleigh took turns kissing his belly and inhaling his innocent scent. Hemi blinked. The tears that had gathered in his eyes fell down his cheeks and over his jaw. He brushed them away, embarrassed.

'It's always intense, the first time,' Tai said.

Hemi looked at the mate. His own face, reflected in Tai's sunglasses, looked back at him. He smiled, and his reflection smiled, and he was on the verge of laughing. He felt drunk, or high.

'What is this stuff?'

Tai shrugged. 'Some kind of deep sea thing.'

'Does it give you . . . dreams?'

'Yeah, man. It's giving all of us dreams.'

Hemi looked at Pat and Luke, still lost in their own minds. Memories swirled and ebbed as Hemi finished his meal. One by one the men lay down their cutlery and leant back in their chairs.

Finally, Pat pushed his plate away and stood up. 'Hope you enjoyed that, lads.' He put a hand on Hemi's shoulder. 'Luke and Tai can tidy up. You'd better get some sleep before your shift in the wheelhouse.'

Hemi beamed. 'Really?'

'We'll soon see what you're made of.'

They were still submerged in darkness when Hemi felt Pat's firm hand shaking him awake. With the boat pitching as though each wave was a cliff, Hemi struggled to get out of his bunk, pull on his jeans and boots and grab his workbook without falling. He climbed up to the wheelhouse, where Pat was already back in the helm chair, drinking coffee from a lidded cup. The skipper peered out at the night sky, cross-checking whatever he saw out there with the eight computer monitors arranged in a horseshoe around him. Like every other inch of the *Sea Legend*, the wheelhouse had been meticulously refurbished. Rows of knobs and buttons, dials and gauges were set into polished hardwood, and shone beneath the lights.

Hemi reached for a grab rail. He looked at the monitors, trying to focus on the colourful screens showing navigation, seabed mapping and scenes from the sea floor.

'This one's not working?' He pointed at a blank screen.

'CCTV's on the blink.' Pat winked and pointed to another screen displaying video feeds of the propeller, nozzle, rudder and engine room. 'We're capturing the important stuff.'

'I thought we had to have video?'

'We've got our Automatic Location Communicator on. That's all MPI really needs to know.'

'Makes sense,' Hemi said, swaying from the grab rail.

'Bycatch is a fact of life. No sense being hauled over the coals for it.'

'Makes sense,' Hemi repeated.

Pat glanced at him. 'There's some coffee in the plunger. You'd better wake up before we get started.'

Hemi lurched aft to the galley. It had been cleaned, the beer bottles tidied away, the dishes scrubbed and stowed. But the memory of the previous night still hit him like a thunderclap. He opened the oven. There was the roasting dish that had held their strange meal. There on the wall was the photo of him assaulting Luke. And there was the table where they'd all sat and wept. Hadn't they? How many beers had he drunk? He took the stainless-steel plunger from its wooden frame, poured the coffee and took a deep swig. Then he returned to the wheelhouse, where Pat looked him up and down.

'There's one thing they don't tell you about moving up through the ranks,' Pat said. 'Once you become a mate, that's bait for the ladies.'

'It is?'

'The adventure, the romance, the money – it drives them crazy. It's even better once you're a skipper.'

Hemi grinned at the thought of a fisherman having groupies like a rock star. He saw himself stepping off a trawler and into a crowd of women forming a guard of honour from the wharf down to the pub. He walked along the aisle they'd created, and all the women smiled and murmured, and as they smiled they morphed into rows of Kayleighs, and the Kayleighs flicked their hair and held their arms out to him, and as they did so they morphed into rows of Sams, and the Sams looked at him with their big brown eyes and cried 'Daddy!'

Hemi plonked down on the bench seat. 'I just want to provide for my kid,' he said, opening his workbook. He flicked past his sea service log to the question-and-answer section, and cleared his throat. 'Health and safety is of paramount importance on a fishing vessel. Write down the locations of the following: radio beacon.' He looked up. 'That'd be in the lifeboat, right?'

Pat flicked a dismissive hand. 'Today we'll cover some of the stuff that's not written down.'

Hemi closed his workbook and stashed it between the bench seat's leather cushions. 'The main thing to know is that we're family out here, and we stick together. What MPI doesn't know won't hurt them. Loose lips sink ships, financially speaking.'

'Right.'

'Right. So let's say you haul up your net, and you've got a dolphin. The ALC's on and the cameras are on. What do you do?'

'Note it on the trawl catch form.'

'Good. And what do you do if you've got a dolphin and a nice chunk of coral, and the ALC's on but the cameras are off?'

Hemi paused, trying to gauge what Pat wanted him to say. 'You just write the dolphin on the form?'

'You don't write anything on the form, and you take the coral home for your missus.' Pat gave him a wink.

Hemi nodded, wondering if he could win Kayleigh back with anything found beneath the sea.

'Okay, so the ALC's on, cameras are off, and you haul up an albatross. What do you do?'

'You . . . chuck it back over the side?'

'Good lad.'

Hemi tilted his head. 'Have you? Pulled up an albatross?'

'We've pulled up all sorts of things.' Pat turned to Hemi, his eyes bright. 'People say fishing out here's dangerous, it's foolhardy – but they don't talk about the thrill. A trip can be like a drug hit. But if you do get a hit, you've got to remember one thing.' He smacked a hand on the dashboard for emphasis as he spoke. 'Stay on the fucking boat.' He drained his cup and held it out to Hemi. 'Must be time for a top-up.'

Back in the galley, Hemi refilled both cups with the last of the coffee. When he returned to the wheelhouse, Pat was crouched before a cabinet beneath the radar screen. The open cabinet door revealed a black foam interior. And nuzzled in the foam, barrel gleaming, was a Glock handgun.

Hemi took a step back. 'Holy.'

Pat looked over his shoulder. 'All that talk of bycatch. Thought I'd better check my ammo.' He closed and locked the cabinet. 'You never know when you might have to put something out of its misery.'

Hemi ran a hand over the polished wood. 'Is all this custom-made?'

'I could've bought a new boat for what it cost me.' Pat wiped imaginary dust from the controls. 'But she's lucky, the *Sea Legend*.'

Pat took his coffee and returned to the helm chair. Hemi stared at the screens, trying to make out what each was telling him. As he watched, the lights seemed to flicker beyond the monitors, through the windows and out across the black water. Hemi rubbed his eyes. The sea was filled with neon-blue fairy lights. The boat rose over a wave, and the lights rose and shifted too. This was it. He'd actually lost it. He was hallucinating.

Pat whistled. 'The squid are putting on quite a show.'

Hemi exhaled. 'Squid. Yeah.'

The baritone of the engine and the drumming of waves against steel accompanied the ballet of light. The constellation of sapphires rose and fell to the rhythm of the waves, the rhythm of his breath. So it was here that it had happened. He too floated over the abyss, miles above the sea floor where bones of lost sailors had become grains of sand. The words dropped from Hemi's mouth before he could think.

'What was Dad like?'

Pat stared out at the squid, each outlined with pin pricks of light. 'Tall. Strong.' He turned and met Hemi's eyes. 'A fit and proper person, you might say.'

Hemi nodded. 'Nan said he drowned trying to save someone.'

'You could say that.'

Pat's fingers went to his chin and traced the length of his scar. He withdrew his hand and looked back out at the dissipating squid lightshow. Gleaming beings floated away until there were just a few glowing tendrils in the water, and then none at all.

'That's enough for now,' Pat said. 'You grab some breakfast.'

Hemi fished between the bench seat cushions, but his hand came back empty.

'I've lost my workbook.'

Pat looked around and shrugged. 'It'll turn up.'

As he made his way to the galley, Hemi heard Pat shout behind him. 'Jesus wept!'

He turned to see Pat working the controls. After some frenzied manoeuvring the skipper leant back in the chair and ran a hand across his brow.

'Fucking whale.' He shook his head. 'We almost sailed into a fucking whale.'

Hemi staggered out to the galley. A whale? At this point he wouldn't be surprised if they came bow to nose with a taniwha, or Tangaroa himself.

They shot the first net early, brought up a good catch and then shot the net again, calculating that they'd have time to haul it up before the darkening sky brought too much trouble.

Working on the slime line, Hemi could feel the tough, oily heads of the dory through his gloves. He ran his sharp blade along and through each fish, his hands like blurs as he raced himself and the weather to get the catch on ice.

'Watch it,' Tai yelled.

Hemi looked up. Tai lifted his gloved hands and manipulated his ring finger, flattening it against his palm and then against the back of his hand, as though it was triple-jointed.

Hemi stared. 'How are you doing that?'

'I don't have a finger there anymore, do I?' Tai twisted the empty glove finger. 'And neither will you if you don't watch what you're doing.'

Hemi forced himself to slow down and concentrate on what was fish, what was glove and where the knife should slice: fish, gloves, knife. To the rising howl of the wind they packed the dory into tubs, stacked them in the hold, and then trudged up to the galley for smoko.

Once they each had a coffee in their hands, Luke beckoned Hemi and Tai in for a selfie. 'Fisherman life!' he said.

'What are you, a fucking influencer?' Tai leant in for a photo.

Luke draped an arm over Hemi's shoulder.

'Say "boat bros".' Luke fumbled for a good shot.

'Boat bros,' they said, and Luke took the photo.

Pat blew in through the door. 'Net's looking full,' he said. 'But we're heading for some weather. Let's work fast and knock off early.'

Hemi drained his coffee and followed Pat outside. Back on deck, Pat winched up the swollen net and Luke unlaced it. Fish poured forth in a torrent that soon slowed to a trickle.

Pat stopped yelling commands, and the mollymawks ceased their squawking.

Hemi looked to see what the hold-up was. Pat was working the net more gently than usual. Black dory slithered from the cod-end as the skipper struggled to release something bigger, a shark or a barracouta. Tai gripped the net and helped widen the opening, but the creature still wouldn't come free.

'Hold steady,' Pat said. He reached into his pocket, pulled out a knife, and sliced a large square of nylon from the $150,000 net. Through the opening, the creature's tail slid out: long, opalescent, lunate. The creature was the size of a dolphin, and coloured like the inside of shells.

Hemi looked at Luke, astonished.

Luke's eyes, fixed on the creature's tail, were blazing.

Pat reached in through the hole in the net, under the creature's arms, and eased her out. She slid onto the deck like quicksilver. Her eyes were huge and black. The dark-finned dory gasped their last breaths around her, tails flickering and then quieting. But the creature was alive.

A call emanated from her, sweet and eerie. The notes shivered up Hemi's spine and leapt in his chest. He wanted to fall to his knees before her, but he couldn't move – and nor could the other men. Pat's neck muscles strained beneath the collar of his jacket as he struggled to resist her lure. At last he tore his eyes from her and pulled from his jacket pocket a tiny plastic package. He broke it open, removed the contents and stuffed them into his ears. He rummaged in his pocket again and threw earplugs to the crew.

Hemi squeezed the tips and inserted them. The sounds around him dampened and dulled, until all he could hear was his pulse throbbing in his ears. Pat looked around at the men, his eyes fixing on Hemi.

'Pick her up and follow me,' he yelled, motioning with his arms to ensure he was understood. 'Tai, check the net for more. And get the dory processed.'

Hemi took a step towards the net.

'Shouldn't we throw her back in?' he yelled. He mimed throwing her over the gunwales.

'For fuck's sake, Hemi, do what you're fucking told!' Pat screamed.

Hemi moved towards the creature. He reached for her and she drew back with an ululating call like a frightened gull's. He bent closer and she thrashed violently, the whip of her tail sending dory hurtling across the deck. But encircled by the winch, the net and the men, she had no way of escape. At last Hemi was able to get a grip on her body and gather her in his arms. He bent beneath her weight and flipped her onto his back, draping her around his neck in a fireman's carry. The feel of her soft skin filled him with fire. Her fierce heart beat against his shoulder.

Hemi followed Pat down into the hold, one hand grasping the cool rungs of the ladder, the other clasped around the creature. Heavy clouds loomed overhead. The creature continued to make her haunting call as they descended into the belly of the trawler.

Pat unlocked what Hemi had assumed to be a supply cupboard. The door opened to reveal a small room filled entirely with a large tank. A handful of shells was scattered on the tank's base, seaweed drifting above them. Without Pat needing to instruct him, Hemi climbed the step up to the tank, leant over the edge and released the creature. She slipped from his arms and sank, her hair unfurling in the water. Hemi felt his heart sinking with her. He stepped down and followed Pat out the doorway. They both turned back to look at the creature. She lifted her head and gazed at Hemi.

Pat banged the door shut, locked it and climbed back on deck. Hemi trailed him, emerging from the hold into the other world, where Tai and Luke, excited as children, competed to gut dory. At the sight of Pat they looked up. Pat removed his earplugs and stashed them in his pocket. Hemi followed suit.

'Did you find any more?' Pat asked.

'Nah.' Tai prodded a rogue barracouta with his foot. 'She's all good?'

'All good.'

Luke flung his knife down and let out a whoop. 'I'm getting a Ducati!'

A grin broke out beneath Tai's sunglasses. 'I'm getting my Ford Mustang!'

The pair pranced around the deck, driving their imaginary vehicles, the rolling waves underfoot making them look drunk.

'All right lads, I've got some calls to make,' Pat said. 'Back to work. This fish isn't going to knife itself.'

Pat returned to the wheelhouse. Hemi pulled his knife from his pocket and joined the slime line. Tai stopped his play-acting and picked up a fish, running his knife expertly from head to tail.

'She looked like a good one? No damage?'

'Damage?' Hemi asked.

'They can get banged up in the nets, break their arms, snap their tails.' Tai didn't stop his rhythm of knifing, washing and packing. 'And there's no fixing them, because we don't have the expertise. Because technically, they don't exist.'

Luke skidded to a stop on his invisible Ducati. 'We did try to patch one up. Remember?'

'Yeah, we fucked that up,' Tai said.

Luke shrugged. 'There's no market for the munted ones. But they make a good meal.'

Hemi thought back to the previous night, to his knife slicing through that vivid pink flesh. He looked at Luke, aghast.

'What, did you really think last night's dinner was shark?'

Hemi felt bile rise in his throat. To the sound of laughter, he turned and leant over the gunwales. The sea spumed below.

'You're supposed to be fishing, not sight-seeing,' Luke said.

Hemi felt the boat heave against the waves. 'Are we turning?'

'No sense staying out any longer,' Luke said. 'Not with our money-maker in the hold.'

The last fragments of clear sky disappeared behind dark clouds.

'Sea's turning purple,' said Tai. 'Let's get this fish on ice before the storm comes.'

By afternoon it was too rough to continue working. Hemi lay on his bunk, head churning, guts roiling. He closed his eyes and saw Kayleigh's smile, smelt the sea salt in her hair. She stirred beside him and he opened his eyes, and she opened hers, and they were black, deep onyx black. Blood surged through his body. His mouth opened, and he ran a hand along her silvery skin. She shone like the moon.

'Kayleigh?'

'Hemi,' she replied.

She drew him in for a kiss, hungry lips bruising his. He gripped her long hair and held it in a knot at the base of her neck. His other hand wove around her waist. They fell together through warm, dappled waves.

Tai woke him, shaking him back into the world above the sea.

'What time is it?'

'Time to feed our passenger.'

'Why me?'

'Us. They're best fed in pairs.'

Hemi stepped down from the bunk and found himself sailing through the air as a massive roll dropped him to the floor. He tugged on his boots and followed Tai up the ladder, each step a struggle as the boat bucked beneath him.

In the galley, Tai threw a handful of fresh seaweed on a chopping board.

'How do you know what they eat?' Hemi asked.

'We don't, really.'

Hemi watched as Tai cut the seaweed into thin slices,

holding the chopping board fast to prevent it from flying off the bench.

'What will happen to her?'

'Pat's got a buyer. His people will meet us behind Pig Island, before we reach shore.'

'But then what? Then what happens?'

Tai shrugged. 'Whatever the buyer wants.'

He tipped the seaweed into a container, snapped a lid over it, and stepped out onto the deck.

Hemi followed, closing the door behind him. A shadow fell over the deck, and he looked up to see a giant swell rearing above them, blocking the sky. Hemi instinctively fell to his knees, clutching a rail. The lifeboat canister, in its cradle beneath the steps, was almost within reach, but it was too late to deploy it. Hemi braced for the icy deluge. Instead, the boat surged beneath him as it rode up the wave. The wind tugged around him, playing discordant harp on the lines. Then Hemi's stomach dropped as the boat plummeted into the trough.

'How many years' experience did you say you have?' Tai yelled, mocking.

'What are these, freak waves?' Another tsunami was rising before the bow.

'We're in the Southern Ocean. They're just waves. Come on!'

Hemi got to his feet and followed Tai through the hatch, securing it behind them. For all Tai's bravado, if one of these monster waves broke on deck and entered the hold they'd be buggered. They descended the ladder and made their way through sliding crates of dory to the cupboard. Tai put his earplugs in, motioned for Hemi to do the same, and then pulled the keys from his jeans pocket.

The door opened. For a moment the tank was dark, and Hemi wondered how much of the creature he'd imagined. But when the lights shuddered on, she was as he remembered. She floated listlessly in the tank, eyes closed, hair drifting over her face and shoulders. Her skin, which had shimmered so brilliantly when they'd first hauled her from the water, was dull and grey. The boat heaved and Hemi and Tai clung on to the grab rails. The limp creature smashed into the sides of the tank. Water sloshed over the top and pooled around Hemi's boots.

'Is she okay?' Hemi yelled to be heard through Tai's earplugs.

'We just need to keep her alive overnight. Pat's steaming as fast as he can.'

Tai tipped the seaweed into the tank. The creature ignored it.

'I don't think she wants it.'

'What?' Tai removed his earplugs. 'What did you say? It's okay, she's gone quiet.'

Hemi pulled his earplugs out too. The creature was silent. 'I don't think she wants the seaweed.'

'She'll eat it when she gets hungry.'

Neither of them took their eyes from their languid, lithesome captive.

'Shouldn't she go to some kind of conservationist?' Hemi asked.

'You know some billionaire conservationists, do you?'

The creature opened her black eyes and stared at Hemi. She raised a hand to her lips and traced it down her body, leaving a glowing trail in the wake of her fingers. Her skin shining with its former lustre, she started her call. At first a murmur, it rose like a wave until he was bathing in it. He stepped closer and the pitch of her call rose. He took another step.

Tai wrenched his gaze from the creature. 'Move it,' he yelled.

He grabbed Hemi by the shoulders and pulled him out, slamming the door behind them. With shaking hands he locked it and stuffed the keys back in his pocket.

Hemi stared at Tai, his mouth open.

'Catching flies? Come on.'

They lurched back through the hold, through towers of dory.

Tai indicated a tub of bycatch as it slid past. 'Aren't you on dinner tonight?'

The tub slid past again, and Hemi saw the beheaded and gutted rig shark shimmering beneath the ice.

'How will I carry a bloody shark in this weather?'

Tai's eyebrows rose in a challenge. Hemi hesitated, then grabbed the shark and stuffed it down his top. Fuck it. He stank like fish anyway.

They crawled back out onto the deck, where the sky was sea and water rushed underfoot. Hemi glanced up at the security camera. The red light blinked back at him. He froze, then gave a fixed smile.

Within an hour the wind had screamed itself to a whimper, the waves had worn themselves down, and the worst of the weather was behind them.

Potatoes browned in the oven as Hemi prepared the shark. He whisked beer into a bowl of seasoned flour, dipped the fillets in batter and dropped them into a pan bubbling with oil. Nan would be proud. The tempting aromas lured Luke, and then Tai, into the galley.

'Does Pat want some?' asked Hemi.

'I'll drag him away from the wheel later,' said Tai.

Hemi dished up and sat at the table. As he ate, he glanced at the wall of shame. There was a new photo – of someone passed out on a bunk, a bottle of liquor in one hand and a filleting knife in the other. It looked as though it had been taken after a bender, but it must have been taken during his afternoon nap, because it was a photo of him.

'What the heck?'

Luke snorted a suppressed giggle.

'Who did this?' Hemi asked. 'Why the fuck would anyone do this?'

'Kayleeeeigh,' Luke sing-songed. 'Who's Kayleeeeigh?'

'What?'

'That's what you were saying. Kayleeeeigh.'

Something gripped Hemi's gut with one hand, his heart with the other, and squeezed. 'Fuck you.'

'Lighten up, mate,' said Tai. 'It's just a joke.'

'Yeah, look at this one of me.' Luke pointed to a picture of his sleeping self, sporting a pair of bushy eyebrows drawn on with black marker. 'And this one of Tai,' he added, indicating a sleeping Tai with a pair of lace knickers on his face. 'It's a *Sea Legend* tradition.'

'But my one's got a knife!' said Hemi. 'It makes me look like a maniac!'

'It's funny!' Luke reiterated. 'It's just funny, okay?'

Hemi clenched his teeth and sawed a chunk of potato in half, his knife squealing across the plate.

Tai pushed his sunglasses to the top of his head. Beneath them, his eyes were surprisingly warm. 'Good kai.' He gave Hemi an approving nod. 'Great batter.'

Hemi felt the tension within him subside.

'Don't you guys ever get sick of fish?' asked Luke.

'You know where the canned chicken is,' said Tai.

Luke rolled his eyes. 'So anyway, on to the important stuff,' he said. 'Superleggera or Streetfighter? The Streetfighter looks mean but the Superleggera is top of the line.'

'Guess it depends how fast you want to die,' said Tai.

Luke made a face. 'At least I'm getting something cool.'

'Are you, though?'

'Cooler than some lame Ford.'

'Well, I'm not getting the Mustang, anyway.'

'Decided you're a Holden man?'

'Gunna pay off my mortgage.'

Luke groaned. 'Boring. What are you going to get, Hemi?'

'With what?'

'With your share.' Luke pointed his fork at the hold.

Hemi frowned. 'I dunno, yeah, a vehicle would be handy. Some kind of ute.' Some kind of ute he could drive up to Kayleigh's in, tooting proudly. Something with room for her in the front, Sam in the back, hunting gear in the tray. He pushed his plate away. 'It's not right though, is it?'

Luke and Tai looked at him, grins dissolving.

'Do the mahi, get the treats,' Luke said. 'It's no different from selling any other kind of fish.'

'Yeah, but it's not a fish.'

'What is it, then?' Luke asked, daring him to say it, to name the impossible.

Hemi shrugged. 'They didn't believe in giant squid either, until there was scientific proof.'

'So?'

'So I wouldn't have believed it if I hadn't seen it myself. But we all know it's not a fish.'

Luke narrowed his eyes. 'There is no proof, though, so it doesn't exist. And if it doesn't exist, then we're not doing anything wrong. Anyway, didn't you say you want a ute?'

Tai stood up. 'I'll give Pat a break,' he said, disappearing into the wheelhouse.

'And I've been wanting my Ducati forever,' Luke continued. 'We hardly ever get one alive. This is a big deal, Hemi.'

Pat staggered in, his eyes red and glassy. 'What's a big deal?

Our big catch?' He heaped his plate and sat at the table. 'We should be in behind Pig at around 4am, and I'll need you lads looking sharp to help with the transfer. No dramas and we'll be back on shore tomorrow morning. And we'll all be a bit richer.'

Luke looked at his father, an eyebrow cocked. 'Hemi seems to think it might be a little bit wrong.'

'Ha,' said Pat, with a cadence more scornful than merry. 'It's only wrong if money's not right.' He fixed Hemi with a beady look. 'Remember what I told you in the wheelhouse?'

Hemi frowned.

'We're family, and we stick together,' Pat said. 'Say it. Or whānau, if you prefer that.'

'We're family, and we stick together,' Hemi said.

'And what MPI doesn't know won't hurt them.'

'What MPI doesn't know won't hurt them.'

Pat nodded. 'And fit and proper people don't nark.'

'And they don't fool around with knives,' said Luke, indicating the photos. 'And they don't try to strangle me.'

'That reminds me,' said Pat. 'Did you ever find that workbook?' Hemi shook his head. 'I'm sure it'll turn up. You're a bright lad. You could have a big future at sea.'

Hemi looked up and met Pat's flinty eyes. 'I'd like that. Yeah. And I'd really like a ute.'

Pat steamed towards Pig Island, the *Sea Legend*'s engine growling as he put her through her paces. Hemi followed Luke and Tai down to the cabin, where they stripped off their outer layers and flung them into their bunk drawers, Tai's jeans landing with the satisfying clunk of denim and metal against wood. They got into their bunks and Luke turned off the light. Some kind of electricity rose through the darkness from the hold and into the cabin, and sparked in Hemi's veins.

'I can't make up my mind,' said Luke.

'About what?' asked Tai.

'Red? Black? Red and black? Black and yellow?'

'What?'

'My Ducati. Is yellow too showy?'

'Luke!' Tai's voice was a warning shot. 'I'm too tired for the dippy la-las. Count sheep or something, would you?'

There was a loud sigh and some rustling as Luke rearranged himself in his bunk. Then there was more rustling, and his indignant voice piped up. 'But yellow? What do you think about yellow?'

Tai groaned. 'Jesus! All right, I'll start you off. Picture a nice fluffy little lamb. It walks along a lovely green hill and then it jumps over a fence and skips away. Okay, that's one. Now picture another lamb doing the same thing. Two. Now three. Four . . .'

The line of sheep jumped through Hemi's mind. With each jump tension drained from the cabin, until Tai's snuffling and Luke's snores wafted through the night, forming an off-key duet. But Hemi's sheep continued to jump, until they were no longer lambs leaping over a fence but fish flying over a net, and then the fish were bigger, one bigger still, and it was the creature, trapped in the net and thrashing, looking up at him with her black eyes, lips parted in a plea for help.

Hemi pulled off his covers, slipped from the bunk and lowered himself to the floor. He paused for a moment, straining to hear Tai's and Luke's snoring over the engine. He eased open his drawer and pulled out his boots. He inched his fingers along the bunk, under the sleeping Tai's torso, and opened Tai's drawer. He felt for the jeans, sweeping with his arm, creeping close until his face was surely level with Tai's. His fingertips grazed fabric. He scrunched the denim with one hand, grabbed his boots with the other, and rose to his feet, hoping the keys in Tai's pocket wouldn't fall to the floor with a clang.

Outside the cabin Hemi stepped into the jeans. He was taller than Tai, with a narrower waist, but they fit well enough. The keys sat against his hipbone. He pulled on his boots, gripped the rungs of the ladder and climbed. The light from the wheelhouse streamed down from the open hatch above. Pat was just overhead, but from his helm chair would be unlikely to notice movement below.

Hemi crept through the foul weather gear towards the door and tried the handle. Locked. Clearly, Pat wasn't taking any chances. Hemi pulled out Tai's keyring and tried one key, then another, until he felt the lock slide beneath his fingers. He grabbed a lifejacket, opened the knife drawer, felt for a blade and stashed it in his back pocket. He opened the door, squeezed onto the deck and turned the key in the lock behind him.

He stood with his back pressed up against the door. The sky was black, the waves were black, but the masthead's floodlight illuminated much of the deck. The security camera would be on, and Hemi tried to imagine what it – and Pat – could see. For now, he was behind it, but as soon as he stepped out onto the deck he risked being spotted. His best bet was to creep around the machinery, hiding in the long shadows. The hatch itself was veiled by the shadow of the winch.

Hemi reached in under the steps and pulled the pin to release the fibreglass lifeboat canister from its cradle. He dragged the canister out and placed it on top of the life jacket, concealing the jacket's reflective strips.

He knelt and crawled across the deck, pushing the canister with him, hurrying between shadows. He could only hope that Pat was as sleep-deprived as he was and wouldn't notice Hemi's shape flickering across his screen. At last Hemi reached the pool of darkness that surrounded the hatch. Leaving the emergency equipment wedged beside it, he opened it and crawled inside, half expecting to be stopped by a bullet. If Pat hadn't seen him already, he might notice the open hatch cover on his camera feed.

Hemi scrambled down into the dark hold. A thin strip of light glimmered then blazed beneath the utility cupboard door, guiding his path. He reached the door and twisted the key in the lock.

The creature shone, luminescent, her colour restored. She gazed at Hemi, and a current jolted through him. He stepped up to the tank and she rose from the water. She wrapped her soft arms around his neck. Hemi hauled her out and stood with her in his arms, beating heart against beating heart, before flipping her over his shoulders.

Hemi hurried through the hold and made his way back up the ladder. He struggled from the hatch with the creature on his back, sure he'd come face-to-face with Pat's Glock, but found no one on deck. He reached the stern, opened the transom doors and crouched down. The weight of the creature shifted over his shoulders and he bent to draw her into his arms. But there was a flash of light and she flew from him and into the ocean. He watched as she swam beneath the waves, a glimmer in the dark sea.

An alarm screamed. Hemi threw his lifejacket on and buckled it tightly. He lashed the lifeboat's line to a railing, tossed the canister into the sea and yanked the rope. The canister opened and the lifeboat inflated. Behind him, the other men shouted as they ran on deck. Hemi pulled the lifeboat closer to the stern. Eyes fixed on the canopy opening as it rose and fell, he dived in.

Hemi righted himself and looked up at the steep hull of the *Sea Legend*. Pat was on the other end of the line, body taut with resolve, pulling him back in. Hemi whipped the knife from his pocket and cut the rope. A wave caught the lifeboat, and in a second he was metres away from the *Sea Legend*. Pat groped in his pocket and pulled out the gun. Another wave caught the lifeboat and bore it away.

Hemi could no longer hear the shouting. The *Sea Legend*'s lights dipped in and out of view, and he knew the crests of the waves were higher than the canopy of his craft. A powerful torch beam shone across the ocean, back and forth over the waves that rose like bulwarks around him. A volley of shots sounded overhead like a howl of frustration. Hemi felt around in the lifeboat and located the beacon. A simple flick of the switch, and it would transmit a signal to the coastguard.

The *Sea Legend* and her lights were no longer visible. There was no clanging engine, no cargo scraping in the hold. All Hemi could see was the light shining through the fabric and water beneath him, the luminescent body of the creature as she danced and dove. All he could hear was the sound of the waves, and the call of her song.

DAVID GEARY

The Black Betty Tapes

Transcripts of V, AV & AO
Sec. Level: Ivory [P-WoRd Pro-EX] #IRIS
R – INTERVIEW CAT-CH#22 [UNSIGNED]: DOUBLE DUMMY BRIDGE

TR: We played a lot of cards together. She's good. We started out playing two-handed bridge with a double dummy. Then she said she'd prefer two-handed 500 but was often quite tired so we cut back to short hands of euchre.

Then one day she just couldn't figure out the left and right bowers. You can't keep correcting someone like . . . I tried to teach her poker and pontoon. Those are simpler games, but the counting and what beats what: pairs, straight, flush, full house . . . it wasn't sticking. I stacked the deck and dealt her a royal flush. That pleased her, but after she was like, 'No more American games.'

I skipped Go Fish. We stopped playing altogether, and then she called me into her chamber one night to show me how she was trying to play patience, but it'd turned into something else, samba crossed with crib crossed with snap?

It was either brilliant or nonsense. That kind of sums up the whole affair really: sublime or ridiculous, or somehow both at the same time.

TR & Q – SURVEILLANCE J$TNT4 [AO = AUDIO ONLY]

Q: Yes, let's play snap. Snap! How does it work?
TR: Just try to find two that are the same, ma'am.
Q: What about the colours?
TR: Don't worry about the colours.
Q: Snap! I won! . . . snap! Stop letting me win!
TR: You're just really fast.
Q: Don't play me for a fool, Bond.
TR: Oh, are we playing that again?
Q: What's wrong with James Bond?
TR: Nothing.
Q: And you were MI5 before –
TR: My name is –
Q: Don't tell me. Parker? Peter Parker!
TR: Close. Peter Parker is –
Q: Baron Parker!
TR: Closer. He was the one before me.
Q: What happened to him?
TR: Retired.
Q: Forgive me. You all look a bit samey. Snap! Queen of hearts, queen of spades – she knows where all the bodies are buried. Why don't you play properly?
TR: I don't want to hurt you.
Q: Hurt me! I have my family for that. Take my hand.
TR: Ma'am.
Q: Squeeze.

TR: Owh!
Q: Well, if you're not going to squeeze me, I'm going to –
TR: That wasn't –
Q: I know, I had my brooch clip in my palm and I stabbed you. Sorry, but never underestimate me.
TR: I never –
Q: Even when I'm going stark raving – never doubt me?
TR: I won't.
Q: When I'm gone, I would like them to add another card to the deck for me, another queen. Promise me that.
TR: I'm not –
Q: But you were once a famous spy, like James Bond?
TR: Ma'am, if you're a famous spy, you're not doing it right.
Q: Touché. Do you consult the tarot?
TR: . . . No.
Q: I'm in love with the Hanged Man. He keeps coming up when I consider you in my plans.
TR: What plans?
Q: Originally, in Italy, it was a punishment. To be hung by the foot until death. Commoners could feed the criminal to prolong the agony. Me, I'd just prefer the chop. Like Anne number 1 – a clean sideswipe with a French broadsword, as opposed to sloppy two-chops Queen of Scots. You know, I chopped the noggin off a chicken once. It ran around headless, hopped up on a shrub and laid an egg. And so in the end is our beginning. The Hanged Man isn't all bad. It's the card of ultimate surrender, sacrifice to the greater good. So, are you ready to surrender to me?
TR: Ma'am?
Q: I've been waving my hand, slapping on a smile and behaving myself for far too long. All the while my family have been getting up to all sorts. It's frustrating.

TR: I can imagine.
Q: No, you can't. Thanks for the game. Find me an artist so I can pose for the card, will you?
TR: Yes, Ma'am.
Q: And I shall get them to make one for you, too: Hairy Legs! The Joker!

[AV] TR INTERVIEW #3-9-8-^ STATIC – SPOOKS #1

TR: Our responsibility is to protect her first, the family second, and her from the family is third. People ask me, all the time, 'What is it really like?' I don't tell them, but it's more like *Game of Thrones* than you could ever imagine. Great show. Right on about how tribal, venal, low-down and dirty we can all become when it comes to the crunch. Anyway, the Furries –
IN: Furries?
TR: Bearskin guards. Bent as. One of them said they saw something, a ghost, on the battlements. We have cameras everywhere. Checked. Just the usual fog. But she's grown more . . . superstitious. One of the Furries mentioned it to her in passing and next thing she's snuck up there. On the roof. Anything could have happened. Checked the CCTV. It's foggy. Hard to see anything. Then maybe you can see some shapes in it, maybe you can't. Then there she is, her majesty, stumbling around, and the fog seems to divide into three . . . shapes. Then all the cameras cut out and there's just static for fifteen minutes. Next time they come back on, she's gone. Filthy fog again.

TR & Q SURVEILLANCE [AO] 777-+ 7 – SPOOKS #2

TR: Sorry to ask, ma'am, but what were you doing on the roof?
Q: Getting some fresh air. Sometimes, I just can't breathe down here.
TR: We have the guard who –
Q: Don't . . . he's a good lad.
TR: Ma'am, I'm responsible for . . . everything. You won't see him again. What happened up there?
Q: There were . . . there are more things in – what happened to Shakespeare?
TR: Sorry?
Q: I hear someone desecrated his tomb?
TR: Who told you that?
Q: I forget. A whisper. I need you to organise all the heads of Europe to come here, for a special dinner. Soonish. I have an announcement to make.
TR: But –
Q: Come on, one of the Gs is happening, G7, G20, gee-whizz. Make it happen. Now I'm walking the dorgis, then we'll work on the menu.

TR-INTERVIEW # 668 – The Neighbour of the Beast 😁 Shakespearean Serial Killer [SURVEILLANCE]

IN: Where were you when Shakespeare's remains were being stolen in Stratford?
TR: London. With her.
IN: Will she verify that?
TR: Well, you know, she has her good days. Check the videos. Hold on, you must have already done that. You know –

IN: You studied Shakespeare at uni?
TR: I studied a lot of things: military history mostly, some geography –
IN: Is that where you learnt about Sykes and Picot? And Winston's Hiccup?
TR: That's not true. Churchill just boasted drunk about dividing up the Middle East in an afternoon, but it was really a French and a British bureaucrat who –
IN: Sykes and Picot, yes, she keeps mentioning those names, names you gave her, so it's true to her. You put it in her head – this idea of carving up countries.
TR: Every superpower carves up countries. That's the history of –
IN: Are you aware of the Royal College of AIR?
TR: AIR meaning Artificial Intelligence and Robotics? No.
IN: No one likes a smartarse.
TR: Officially, I don't know about them.
IN: Well, unofficially, they can do some amazing things with DNA and algorithms and –
TR: Sorry, where is this going?
IN: Shakespeare's skull has been missing for many years.
TR: And you think someone has somehow extracted his DNA and programmed a Shakespearean serial killer?
IN: They're killing in the manner of his plays, following his scripts, leaving notes.
TR: Creative. I did once write an undergrad essay about how I thought the Bard was overrated. Still do. Got a C minus. Don't get me wrong, great poet. Awesome at a catchy phrase or couplet, but hampered by exposition dumps, in-jokes and plot holes. So what do the killer's notes say?
IN: That's restricted.

TR & WIFE WIFI #111 – [SURVEILLANCE AUDIO] SH*T DAY – MARRIAGE ON THE . . .

WI: How was your day?
TR: Shitty.
WI: Shitty how?
TR: Some shit happened and it's my job to clean up the shit so that's what I did, and then more shit happened, and so tonight I'll be dealing with all that shit, and when I wake up there will be another huge pile of steaming shit. You?
WI: Good. So, this shit –
TR: You know I can't tell you or –
WI: You'll have to kill me? Do you want to hear about my day?
TR: . . . Sure. How –
WI: Can we at least pretend we're interested in each other's days?
TR: Are we? I had a shit day, it was shitty to live it, and now you want a highlights package?
WI: You haven't even asked about your daughter.
TR: Haven't had a chance. I've walked in the door, and you –
WI: Ambushed you? I'm the improvised explosive device you never –
TR: Yes, I spend all my time defusing shit, and some real bombs, and some real shits of people, and some shits wearing bombs, and then when my guard is down my wife blows up in my face. How is Zoe?
WI: Well, I changed her and then she shat herself, so I changed her again and she shat herself again. And guess what?
TR: What?
WI: She's got the shits, and now I've caught the shits off her. I think we both got it off the shitty effing cat.

TR Grim! Hate that shitty effing turdy toady cat!

WI And when she wasn't shitting, she wouldn't eat, and she threw a fork at my head and it stuck in. See!

TR: Oh, yeah, little dents . . . no, I don't see anything. I gather it bounced off. Oh, there it is on the floor still. I'll just pick it up and –

WI: Stab me?

TR: What? No, no, what are –

WI: So I yelled at her. Swore at her. I grabbed her arm and squeezed really hard. I didn't slap her, 'cause that would leave a mark, and she started crying and said she was going to tell you that I was mean, and I hurt her.

TR: Right. So you're trying to get ahead of the story before some –

Z: DAD! DAD! DAD! DAD! DAD! DAD! Mum hit me.

TR: Did you throw a fork at her?

Z: You can't hit children. It was on the TV.

TR: Sod this, I'm off to the bistro.

WI: We won't be here when you get back.

TR: . . . Going to your mum's?

WI: No, I've met someone.

TR: You've –

WI: At the daycare. A solo dad, Michael. Wife died of breast cancer. He does the Ride, raises money, Pink Ribbons, all that. His nickname is Quadzilla. Turns up in Lycra like he's just done the Tour de France. Bulges in all the right places. And he's really interested in me and my day. How I'm feeling. And he's got a little daughter, too. The kids get on like a house on fire. So, I want a divorce. Can you kill someone with a fork?

TR: Come on. We met in the service. You know exactly where you can put a fork. Do you want to see a counsellor?

WI: No.

TR: Great, me neither.

WI: Jesus, that's a relief.

Z: Mum, what's happened? Are you in trouble for hitting me?

WI: No. And I didn't hit you. I just squeezed you too hard . . . mostly because I love you so so much.

Z: What's wrong with Dad?

WI: Allergies. Mostly to spending time with people he should love. And being present when he is with them. Not ghosting and –

TR: She's seeing ghosts.

WI: Sorry?

TR: She . . . my boss, she's seeing ghosts. That's what I'm dealing with.

WI: Okay, not a great segue, but weird.

TR: Weird sisters, actually. And that's just the tip of the ice pick in the back of my head. The Firm . . . the family, there's so many of them to keep tabs on. Every day, all the time, you're dealing with affairs, abortions, burying bodies, blackmail, hush money. A plain old STD dose of the clap is welcome relief. Not to mention the paedophilia, necrophilia, incest, bestiality, drug addiction, fraud, sexual assault, manslaughter, murder, car accidents, suicidal tendencies, and that's just the dorgis.

WI: You're making jokes just as I'm about to –

TR: You want to know about my day? That's my day. Triaging all that. And, on top of everything else, I'm dealing with Double Trouble. The top dogs, the A-listers, they all have doubles, lookalikes who sit in the cars, and leave the buildings, cover the seams, and wave hands from a distance, and generally allow the real deal to have some kind of private life. But, and this happens more than you can imagine, they like to spend time with their doubles. Because, you know – Narcissus loves a mirror, and they rationalise it as needing to spend time together so that they can get the voice and the mannerisms and the walk right. But really they're falling for each other. And, God help me, today we were dealing with someone who ended up shagging themselves. I'm sorry you had a forking shit day.

WI: Ha. I didn't really meet someone.

TR: But you know I'm going to check.

WI: See, you do care, darling, but please don't. Can't we have our . . . our little secrets? [BUZZING] That's your phone, your secret phone.

TR: I know.

WI: You can check it. Is it her?

TR: It'll just be more shit. How's your tummy now?

WI: Why, you want to have sex?

TR: No! I was genuinely –

WI: We can have sex. I dosed us all up with witch-hazel – me, Zoe and the effing mad moggie. See that scratch.

TR: Ouch. Let me kiss it better.

WI: So she's seeing ghosts?

TR: Yeah, and I haven't even told you about the – I'm going to take this, then Zoe is having an early bedtime, and then so are we.

WI: Promise?

TR: Promise.

TR & Q TRANSCRIPT – CHOP CAM – CODE ZZ(STRIKE 99:{fR} – KITCHEN NIGHTMARES

Q: Where are we going? I don't like helicopters. I get dizzy.

What happened at the dinner?

TR: Someone poisoned all the heads of Europe and our prime minister.

Q: Oh dear. Who? The Russians? Chinese? Americans? ISIS? IRA? Haven't heard much from them lately. Where are we flying to?

TR: A safehouse.

Q: Remember that time you picked me up and we flew over London and parachuted down to open the Olympics? I was watching it today. You were hunky-spunky back then.

TR: That . . . that wasn't me.

Q: But it was me?

TR: It was you, but –

Q: Why are we going to a safehouse?

TR: Because your life could also be in danger.

Q: I don't think so.

TR: Ma'am.

Q: I did it. The ghosts on the roof. There were three of them. So much smoke. I thought one was Margaret. You know, she chain-smoked three packets a day, and, yes, had reasons to be sad, but, oh dear, I should never have called her poor Margaret Misery Guts. She's come back to haunt me. Because she thinks I got to be happy and live the high life while she –

TR: Ma'am, you're not . . . yourself.

Q: Another one of the spectres I thought might have been Diana. Very thin. Threw up behind one of the chimneys. Then, the one that was most clear to me was Victoria. She commanded me to reclaim England and the Empire, or chaos would reign. More chaos. I mean, it's been awful, hasn't it? Hasn't it? Hasn't it all been going to hell in a handcart? And our beloved country weeps, it bleeds, and each new day a gash is added to her wounds. It smacks of every sin that has a name.

TR: Ma'am, you couldn't –

Q: Our chef, he's connected to . . . I said it was going to be a big surprise.

TR: True. And everyone assumed that at your age you were going to –

Q: Step down? Never. And – you'll like this – if the food didn't get them, then we had the same thing on the serviettes that the FSB use on Russian underwear.

TR: Ma'am, I have to make calls. Here's a sleeping pill. Please take it.

TR INTERVIEW/INTERROGATION #1–1 – CHINA GIRL? [God has given you one face and you make yourself another]

TR: I honestly don't know anything about the transplants or the cosmetic surgery. We flew to a safehouse in the Scottish Highlands. I flew back to London immediately to do damage control. Next I knew, someone above my security level had moved her again . . . or it seems, some other party she'd been dealing with had taken her. And I wasn't in contact for three months.

IN: Is that usual?

TR: No.

IN: Where do you think she went?

TR: Well, the Chinese are way ahead when it comes to transplant tech. They've been able to do all the R&D on the Falun Gong and Uighurs without any pesky ethical reviews. And that's what she told me when she reappeared on the heath.

IN: What did she say exactly?

TR & Q [AUDIO] 923^^ THE QUEEN IS DEAD!

TR: How did they establish contact?
Q: A fortune cookie.
TR: What did it say?
Q: *Who wants to live forever?* . . . So what do you think?
TR: About?
Q: How I look?
TR: Oh. You look . . . fabulous.
Q: I know, don't I? So pleased. I gave them a pic of me at twenty-five at my coronation, *et voilà!* Goodbye frumpy baggage. I like the Chinese. How they turned things around. They have a fly problem, so they just get everyone to catch flies. That takes some gumption. And they adopt a one-child policy, then if anyone breaks that rule they just make them leave the baby by the river. Too bad if you're female. They're not wasting time and energy on the illusion of democracy and election cycles, and pug-ugly unions. They just declare themselves 'Leader for Life'. And that's what I've done. I am having a new coronation as Elizabeth III.
TR: The Americans want to talk to you.
Q: Has-beens. China has leapfrogged right over the Yanks in everything. They don't try and invade countries with armies. The Chinese state backs their banks to take over the local businesses, then they force the local politicians to adopt policies that are friendly to them. Perfect example, that port in Ceylon . . . no, Sri Lanka. See! They've also helped me with my memory. New wonder drugs. It's all coming back to me now. They probably

put a chip in me. I don't care. And they showed me how to control everyone with the social medium. They have an app that tells you how much power people are using, tracks them every time they leave the house, and facial recognition software to see if they're having dangerous emotions – it's just brill.

TR: Oprah wants to talk to you.

Q: Oh, Doprah can go –

TR: She'll pay.

Q: How much?

TR & WIFE #2 [AV] – A BETTER DAY?

TR: We divide the royals into four categories. If you go back through their family tree, or hedge with so much intermarriage, they all fit in there somewhere. Some are a spicy combo of all four: Sad, Bad, Mad and Glad.

WI: Glad? Gay?

TR: Gay.

WI: So what's she?

TR: Sad.

WI: How come?

TR: I'm sorry.

WI: What for?

TR: Being a dud of a husband . . . friend . . . not being present. I've got a lot on –

WI: Hey, you're you. I knew exactly what I was signing up –

TR: I'm thinking of leaving the service.

WI: But you love her – it. You love your job.

TR: No, you just said, you love her. I don't –

WI: It's just the way you talk sometimes. I mean how can a girl compete with –

TR: You're not competing. You're – I'm going to resign. Family reasons. I want to see Zoe grow up.
WI: And what will you do?
TR: Don't know. Teach something. Maybe learn to cook. Open a bistro.
WI: You! Cooking!
TR: I'm pretty good with a knife. I might like gardening, too. We could move somewhere quiet, with real grass. Get a dog. You like dogs.
WI: So who is the baddest, gladdest, maddest?
TR: I shouldn't have told you that. I shouldn't –
WI: No, it's been fun. It's not like –
TR: Your bit of fluff, he's got a dog, right? A schnoodle. Zoe likes playing with it? Quadzilla has a dog, right?
WI: So you did spy on –
TR: If you take Zoe to your parents on Sunday, me and my stuff will be gone when you come home.
WI: . . . That's it?
TR: That's it.
WI: Shit.

TR INTERVIEW/INTERROGATION/CONFESSION @R-9 [AV] – *The Falcon and the Snowman* #playwithinplay

IN: Tell us about *The Falcon and the Snowman*.
TR: We talked a lot about the Americans. She wanted to know what they were really like. So I got her that movie. That's it.
IN: Did you discuss it afterwards?
TR: Sure.
IN: So, imagine I've never seen the movie. Why would it tell me everything I need to know about Americans?

TR: Well, it was a book, on our reading list at Sandhurst, understanding FBI-CIA ops, or somesuch. I mean she knows about Chile, Allende being toppled. You know, Pinochet wanted to meet her when he was hanging out in London. Thatcher was never going to toss him out to face his war crimes. And the Americans definitely didn't want their connection made more explicit. I mean, everyone knows that story.

IN: Do they?

TR: Well, they should. But there's a tipping point, whereby it reaches the general public, and suddenly they're all experts. And it usually takes a movie, and an Oscar or two, or –

IN: You're getting off-track. I asked –

TR: *The Falcon and the Snowman* didn't win anything big, but it had great actors, Sean Penn and Timothy Hutton. Bowie wrote the theme song, 'This Is Not America'. I mean I told her that the Americans feel like the old kings and queens, that they have a divine right to rule. That all the oil under all the soil is theirs, and you just happen to be in the way, living on top of it. So that's not news, but take Australia, a friend – an ally. In 1966 the Americans established this 'weather station' in the middle of nowhere, place called Pine Gap. But it's, surprise, actually a spy station, and helps detect and guide missiles. In 1972, Gough Whitlam, a liberal-leaning PM, gets in, declares he's going to open up Pine Gap, so every Australian knows what's going on in their lucky country. Unlucky for him, the CIA goes into overdrive to depose the PM, sets up a dodgy loan for Whitlam to buy back some Aussie assets. Then the CIA expose it as dodgy. Whitlam gets dismissed in parliament. Governor-general fires him. A Yank-friendly PM gets put in his place. Remember that New Zealand prime minister, Lange, the one who brought in their No Nukes policy, well, he said after leaving office that the Americans had had a plan to kill him. And everyone was like, 'Oh, yeah, paranoid overreaction.' But that's probably true. If they can't kill your career, then it's always Plan B.

IN: What's your Plan B?

TR: I don't –

IN: Where is this going?

TR: The only reason we know any of this is because an American, Christopher Boyce, ends up working as a desk jockey for the CIA in the US, doing surveillance on Whitlam, and thinks this stinks. He tells his drug-dealing buddy Andrew Daulton Lee, who tries to cash in and sell the info to the Soviets in Cuba. But they both get caught and sent back to the US, and are charged and convicted of treason, when really they were Edward Snowden before their time.

IN: You admire Snowden?

TR: . . . After she'd seen the film, she's like, 'I loved it! So a governor-general can fire a prime minister!' That was her takeaway! And, yes, that's where she got the idea to issue a royal decree to get the GG to fire all the prime ministers in the Commonwealth, and re-install herself as Queen Elizabeth III, Ruler of the Empire . . . for life.

IN: And you didn't try to stop her?

TR: I didn't know! After her three months in hiding, she had these other advisors. I mean she always had those, but I was not in the loop.

IN: What loop were you in?

TR: I tried to stay close to her.

IN: By sleeping with her.

TR: . . . Nothing happened.
IN: You were in the same bed.
TR: She was afraid . . . of . . .
IN: So you just spooned the Queen . . . after you manipulated the videos in her bedroom to show old footage of her sleeping alone, so we couldn't see –
TR: She saw daggers . . . coming for her. She saw . . .
IN: Ghosts?
TR: Ghosts.
IN: Are you aware of the RC AIR's work on horrorgrams?
TR: No.
IN: Whose idea was it to declare war on France and redraw the maps of Europe?
TR: Hers. Old habits die hard. Listen, any sign of Charles?
IN: Just reports he's holed up down an abandoned coal mine in Wales. Waiting till things calm down.
TR: Don't hold your breath.
IN: That's our analysis, too. Twenty years of instability, at least. Also, your wife –
TR: We're separated.
IN: She's missing. And your daughter, too.
TR: Well, she was in the service, and I told her if anything ever happened to me, that she should take –
IN: We think the Israelis may have her.
TR: Shin Bet or Mossad?
IN: Unclear.
TR: Why –
IN: Because you were blabbing to her about your work! Because everyone always wants dirt on everyone else! And because she'd be useful in a trade.
TR: With whom?
IN: With us!
TR: I didn't tell her –

IN: It's either them or IRIS.
TR: IRIS! We made up IRIS.
IN: You, you made up a terrorist group?
TR: Yes. After the poisoning, there were the usual suspects, but we thought it would be useful to promote some new kid on the block. There was no IRIS, no Irish Islamic State –
IN: Well, there is now.
TR: It was a joke.
IN: They just claimed bombings in Belfast and Tel Aviv. And you do have Irish ancestry, yes? With a name like Terry Rowe?
TR: Yes, but I also have English, Scottish –
IN: And your grandmother was Palestinian.
TR: Lebanese Jew. My grandfather was in the British army in Palestine, but she –
IN: Was a prostitute.
TR: A waitress.
IN: A terrorist, in part responsible for the 1947 bombing of the British Officers Club in Haifa, in which seventeen people were killed.
TR: No. You're making shit up.
IN: Would you consider yourself a person of colour . . . ish, with your olive . . . ish complexion? A diversity hire?
TR: I was top of my class at –
IN: Your nickname at Sandhurst was 'Death'? Death Rowe?
TR: My middle name is De'Ath but –
IN: Why are you laughing?
TR: This is all a frikkin' joke! What has this got to do with –
IN: Well, firstly, HR have big questions about what will happen with your pension and benefits if you're . . . let go.
TR: Let go?
IN: You don't realise what you've done, do you? Your

background and everything will come out in any official investigation. And, believe me, they will dig up everything, make shit up, make out you're some deep mole. Say your family has been in the spy biz for years. That you were radicalised by –

TR: If I was radicalised by anyone, it was her.

IN: Okay, my advice, in the future, don't say that. Well, you have now, but, but I'm trying to help you here.

TR: Oh, this is your 'good cop'?

IN: Good as it gets. So was she some kind of . . . kind of witch, too? Put a spell on you? Charmed you? That's your defence?

TR: Never underestimate her.

IN: Listen, if you want to see your wife and daughter again, you'd better tell us everything.

TR: I'm telling you everything.

IN: Who was she working for –

TR: The Queen?

IN: Your wife!

TR: No one.

IN: Your apartment was bugged by us, but we also found signs of some other strange intelligence. Your wife had secret bank accounts. She downloaded numbers and messages off your phone while you slept. She passed this information on to a man at a daycare.

TR: Quadzilla!

IN: Who was he?

TR: I don't know. I mean, I knew he was interested in my wife, but –

IN: There could be a trial.

TR: Of me? . . . Charged with what?

IN: You'll be able to plead to something lesser, might save your skin. On that, they're bringing back flaying. Public executions, old-school stuff. Proving very popular. Welcome to the revolution that you started, soldier. Do you want some water?

TR: What's in it?

IN: Nothing. Here's a jar. You can drink your own piss till you decide to tell us something useful.

BLACK BOX *YCHOP-TERM9 – TRAGI-COMEDY AT AN AIR SHOW – Transcript #6 – NOW, GODS, STAND UP FOR BASTARDS!

W: It's not a race, Hazza. We fly the choppers in formation. Side by side, showing our unity.

H: Dare you to thread through the London Eye.

W: No. Don't be a maggot. Not today.

H: Come on, we've got to at least fly under one bridge.

W: Not a chance. We –

H: Nervous nosebleed! Pecksniff! Hey, I can't . . .

W: Watch out! You're too close!

H: Wills, I've lost –

W: We've tipped rotors!

H: ****

W: ****

H: Holy ****

TR INTERROGATION / CONFESSION #7 [AV]

IN: That's from one of the black boxes. The princes' last words. What do you –

TR: It's tragic. What else can I say? Essentially top lads dealt bummer hands.

IN: You've examined the footage?

TR: Of course.
IN: What's your take on the drone?
TR: It's a bird.
IN: You can pilot a helicopter, yes?
TR: I'm not –
IN: You would be able to instruct someone on how to interfere with –
TR: I didn't –
IN: You know how someone with malignant intent could take over the controls of a helicopter?
TR: It's not rocket science.
IN: Although, that is something you also studied? . . . Note, the accused has nodded, reluctantly. The paparazzi had drones in the air this day trying to capture footage of the Royal Air Show. What security measures did you take to prevent them interfering with aircraft?
TR: The usual.
IN: You didn't step it up for what was –
TR: Of course. We jammed all transmissions. Surveillance of persons of interest. But any nutjob with thirty quid can buy a decent drone, so –
IN: What would it take to make a drone that looks like a bird? Specifically, an owl?
TR: I don't know. Ask Harry Potter?
IN: Who's Harry Potter? Is that code? . . . What would it take to make an owl drone?
TR: It's next level, but not much.
IN: Did you have access to one of these?
TR: No.
IN: Why not?
TR: I could get clearance, but I've never asked to use our –
IN: But someone else could supply you with one? Or you could instruct them on how to use it?

TR: There's nothing to be gained by killing –
IN: The women are in charge now.
TR: What, you think –
IN: We'd be stupid to ignore any option.
TR: Listen, the boys tipped rotors, but they both recovered. Tipping a rotor doesn't necessarily mean a crash. In fact, they both stabilised their crafts. Then they decided to turn it into a dogfight.
IN: So you don't believe some other parties could control the choppers to do that, like some big X2BOX game?
TR: No! It's . . . okay, it's possible, but why –
IN: Ratings. It's going to be the most-watched video of all time. It's surpassed the planes hitting the Twin Towers. People will always ask: Where were you when the princes fought a dogfight to the death at the crowning of Queen Elizabeth III? So where were you?
TR: With the Queen. In the stands. Protecting her.
IN: And afterwards?
TR: Taking her away to a safehouse as quickly as –
IN: Like you did so well to that other safehouse? What is your job?
TR: To protect the Queen.
IN: What about serve?
TR: My first priority is to protect.
IN: Was she feeling threatened by her grandsons? By Harry, in particular?
TR: I . . . ask her.
IN: I'm asking you. Who do you serve? Who are you?
TR: Look, I'm not some criminal mastermind!
IN: What about terrorist mastermind? Did you ever play the X2BOX X10 computer game *Snoop Dogg's Chopper Doggfight!*, where helicopter gunships in the shapes of various dogs dogfight?

TR: . . . Is this the bit where I ask to see a lawyer?
IN: Yes. It's that bit.

TR & Q_8888#^ [AO] The Uncanny Valley – It's Not You, It's . . .

TR: It's not you.
Q: Then who is it?
TR: Actors.
Q: Actors! I've had it up to here with actors. I forbid it.
TR: It's too late.
Q: . . . None of it is me?
TR: No, they're all actors playing your family, and you.
Q: Well, I mean that's some relief, because some of it is not how I remember it, or how it happened. It's mostly lies.
TR: I'm sure.
Q: I want all copies destroyed, and no more –
TR: You started this, remember, ma'am?
Q: Never.
TR: In the 1970s, you allowed cameras to film the family, growing up. It helped humanise you all. And it created a hunger for more. It's seen as a good thing.
Q: How can it be?
TR: It enhances the brand. It makes you personable, but also adds to the . . . the mystique. And it means you're still culturally relevant.
Q: So who do you think is best at playing me?
TR: They're all just actors, ma'am. Glamorous, can deliver a line, cry on cue, but they don't do the hard yards. End of the day, they go home and it's just a job. For you, it's, it's your life.
Q: True. True. But I'm an actor too, you know. I should

get a BAFTA, and an Oscar. God knows who the real Elizabeth is. I've been performing like some parrot puppet for so long, I've forgotten who . . . I'm me when I'm in the stables, just me and the ponies, or with the dogs. I've lost a lot of people, you know. And now those stupid boys. I don't have friends. It's very lonely. I have . . . you. I look forward to our chats. Thank you for being a friend, and –

TR: It's an honour to be regarded as such, but now I must check the perimeter. IRIS have been busy, and we've upped the level to Orange.

Q: I didn't think IRIS were real? I thought we made them up? Can I come? With the dorgis?

TR: No.

Q: But what shall I do?

TR: My advice, ma'am, is don't watch, don't watch any more of these shows.

Q: But . . . but I want to find out what happens next.

TR: I will block some channels.

Q: I forbid it.

TR: I'll put on the show-jumping and dressage.

Q: Oh, oh . . . Unsex me here . . . and fill me . . . from the crown to the toe . . . full of . . . make thick my . . . What's that from?

TR: Ma'am, you need to sleep.

Q: I can't. Someone murdered it.

#4 [AV] TRY-TIME! INTERCEPTED ZOOM 3.0 DARK WEB TRANSCRIPT – Q & TR with DHO
[RIP = Dame Rawinia 'Winnie' Ikanuihārotoiti-Powers, prominent Māori politician and businesswoman]

RIP: We've considered your proposal and I'm sorry, but we can't accept it.
Q: Why not?
RIP: Well, we can't trust –
Q: Me? I've offered to tear up that treaty, give you the land back.
RIP: There would be significant backlash from some white folks. There always is, even with the smallest parcel. And if we scrap the treaty then we've got nothing to base our claims on. We'd be back to square one, opening ourselves up to extractive colonialism all over again. Sorry, but we'd rather just go with the devil we know.
Q: I'm not the devil.
RIP: Arohamai, sorry, of course, but you're also . . . not quite yourself.
Q: I'm the most me I've ever been!
RIP: Are your family taking care of you?
Q: My family!
RIP: If you need a holiday, we love to host manuhiri. We run some five-star resorts down here. Come down, chill out, and kōrero . . . let's talk. We like to do things kanohi ki te kanohi, face to face.
Q: Damnation, I thought you'd jump at the chance to claim your sovereignty back.
RIP: We've been trying. If your treaty was honoured, well, yes, it would be lovely to have an independent state, but right now we need to concentrate on education, educating our people, and the Pākehā, so we can at least have independent states of mind.
Q: Well, that's disappointing. And so you won't be sending any of your warriors as reinforcements, to do your dance on the front lines, in our war with France?

RIP: Kāo! No, we won't be doing that.

Q: I'm sorry about World War One.

RIP: Really? What aspect?

Q: All of it. They were right. We could have stopped it. The royals of Europe were all related and so we could have pulled strings, put our collective six-toed feet down, but the bottom line is each royal family was itching for bragging rights and wanted to see whose toy soldiers would win. World War Two – not so much on us. The politicians who punished Germany with the World War One reparations created the filthy soil for Hitler to grow from. And, my uncle Edward, apart from being a terminal womaniser, was indeed a Nazi, and M15 wanted to assassinate him, but his brother, my poor father, wouldn't have it. So Edward meeting that American divorcee and abdicating, well, it saved his wretched life . . . and set up mine. Oh, and I'm sorry about what Philip said, that 'Do you still throw spears at each other' remark. He was a man of his time.

RIP: That wasn't us. He said that about an Australian Aboriginal group.

Q: Oh. Who am I talking to?

RIP: Auē!

Q: It's just, look at it from our perspective, wherever we go you insist on dressing up and doing your traditional song and dance and hoo-ha. And sometimes that involves spears, so, to be honest, I thought it was blown out of all proportion. And it's not like Philip didn't say some dicey things to the Scots, like about struggling to find one who was sober to take a driving test, and those haggis-eaters are pasty white, so it wasn't about race. Anyway, apart from encouraging everyone to honour the treaty, what else could we do?

RIP: Pay your fair share of tax. And encourage your corporate mates to do the same. I mean, these Cayman Islands tax havens, they – Hello? . . . She hung up! Way to end on a stink buzz. So much for #kuinitanga.

[NB: It was assumed that after QEIII's Annus Horribilus #2, whereby her representatives the Governors General fired the elected governments of all Commonwealth countries, and QEIII took power and ordered them to supply armies for a doomed campaign against France, these countries would immediately declare themselves republics. It hasn't happened yet. To the contrary, they all released special 'Black Betty' Christmas stamps with her new visage.]

TR &^763^ – [AV] TRIAL TRANSCRIPT – YOUR HIGHNESS 😁

[PRO = Prosecutor; J = Judge]

PRO: Let me get this straight. Her Majesty was 'hearing voices', 'seeing things', 'talking to herself incessantly', 'conversing with what she called at various times spooks, spectres, spirits, ghosts, goblins, gremlins and gargoyles', 'was unable to distinguish between herself and actors portraying fictionalised versions of herself and her family's lives', and yet you took it upon yourself, not being a doctor of any sort, to diagnose our beloved Queen, whom you have vowed to serve and protect, and supply her with illegal street drugs?

TR: She was –

PRO: In a distressed mental state, and you gave her drugs so you could manipulate her further to your own ends, until we were all witness to her tragic psychotic break live on the BBC, while attending a Royal Gala performance, when she set fire to the Globe Theatre then tried to set fire to herself?

TR: That was . . .

PRO: What?

TR: An accident.

PRO: Or a witch trial?

TR: What? No, this is a witch trial.

PRO: The prosecution rests, Your Honour.

TR: Your Honour –

PRO: No further questions.

TR: You haven't allowed me to answer the ones you posed.

J: I'll allow it . . . well, go on.

TR: She'd had multiple surgeries –

PRO: Thanks to you!

TR: That left her in a lot of pain.

PRO: Not to mention allowing our Queen to become addicted to painkillers!

TR: The royal physician would not allow her to try medical marijuana.

PRO: Your Honour, our Royal Highness –

[AN UPROAR]

J: Order! Order! Or I will have the court cleared.

TR: She requested edibles for the pain, and it seemed to work wonders. I didn't know she was also sneaking the odd smoke, hence perhaps the regrettable fire at the Globe. She was also getting these terrible headaches and so micro-dosing –

PRO: Magic mushrooms for migraines! What about ayahuasca?

TR: No.

PRO: What restraint! You did however use this lethal hallucinogenic drug in your previous work with M15 when interviewing 'persons of interest'?

TR: Sometimes it proves more effective than waterboarding –

PRO: Oh, so you admit to breaking the Geneva Convention and torturing –

TR: There are medicines beyond our . . . I had witnessed her decline, now I saw a radical improvement. On a good day she was back to her brilliant self, and more, she found . . . another gear. She was transcendent.

PRO: So you fell in love with her?

TR: It was no . . . ordinary love.

PRO: Oh, what sort of love was it? The sort where you drug your boss and get her to try and take over the world for your own terrorist gains?

TR: The fire at the Globe was perhaps also Shakespeare . . . himself . . . or some malevolent form of him. You know they stole his skull a long time ago and –

PRO: Who? The grave-robbing evil aliens who clone –

TR: There are more things –

PRO: Your Honour, he's referring to this homicidal maniac, still at large, killing hack journalists in the manner of Shakespeare's plays, who is obviously some deranged method actor/director/writer, whose poisoned quill has inspired copycat killers. And the Bard's archaic language is now desirous, so Shakespeare has become a . . . virulent virus. A Peter-Pandemic, where they all wish to never grow old, and organs are bought and sold. But everyone should also know, you can't escape the blue shadow. And those infected will be detected. They'll get their fifteen minutes of shame, like the accused here, whose name we've heard enough, and should be snuffed out – I request an immediate judgement of guilty, and the mandatory sentence for treason, as per Elizabethan times. The prosecution rests.

J: You already rested!

PRO: I re-rest . . . again. Thank you.

J: Defendant, you still have the chance to obtain counsel.

TR: Thank you, no.

J: A man who defends himself has a fool for a client.

TR: This charade is nothing but foolery.

J: You could also change your plea to one of insane –

PRO: Yet there is method in his –

J: No!

TR: I'm not insane.

PRO: Beg your forgiveness, your honorable, and I don't know why I'm doing this exactly, to step out to act as both prosecution and defence, when I'm not entitled to double-dip, but I, too, would advise the defendant to invoke the insanity clause, by reason that his wife is now believed to be an agent of the dark web – a spider capable of brewing poisonous potions sourced from the original medicine women of these lands. That she took control of her hapless husband and forced him to commit these unnatural acts. And that her dark forces have now taken control of heir to the throne, Charles, until she can rally an army and storm the capital to install him as a puppet prince, who –

J: Enough! Silence with your claptrap conspiracy theories.

PRO: Conspiracy faeries, to be more –

J: Muzzle him! . . . Defendant, your turn!

TR: I'm not insane.

J: Very well, begin!

TR: Firstly, can I ask why I wasn't allowed a jury trial?

J: Because we're not having that kind of circle-jerkus circus. The general public, twelve goodish men and women and the gender-fluid, well, they're fickle strumpets and can be got to. People have a gut feeling about something or someone. The headshrinks tell us they get this within the first five to ten seconds of the original encounter, and after that no matter what truths are presented, no matter what logic and reasoning, the jury members are trying desperately for a way to confirm and rationalise their original instinctive reaction. Once you give them that morsel, some scrap of doubt or proof – no matter how unreasonable – then it's enough to make it reasonable to them. And so we get false negatives. Whereas I, although not without my own privileged prejudices, am 'woke' enough to include these biases in my deliberations. That said, the arguments here seem quite cut and dried.

PRO: Which is what you'll be!

J: Muzzle him! Defence, your move.

TR: Our Queen – Elizabeth III – now embodies all the qualities of a higher being. The spirits have come to her and she is having visions of our futures. We need to kneel before her, listen hard, and follow. She is the Queen of Heaven. Our God who was only cruel to be kind.

PRO: The Devil can cite scripture for his purpose!

TR: The empty vessels make the loudest sound!

PRO: Burn the witch! Burn, Hollywood, burn!

[AN UPROAR]

J: Take them both down! Hell is empty and all the devils are here.

DWEB 7P [AV] INTERVIEW – S.TAPE 😁 [Level – PentH. – EXXX] [DELETED] [REDACTED]

TR: They examined her before she got married. To ensure she was a virgin. When she gave birth, a bunch of goons stood around and watched, took notes, filmed it. Her whole life has been recorded. Yes, she's rich beyond . . . but nothing belongs to her. She wanted . . . she wanted to take back control, of her story, so when we . . .

[REMAINDER REDACTED]

Q & THE SUCCESSOR = TS [AV] – BODYCAM #34-L

TS: Here's the tapes for you, your Majesty . . . Excellence.

Q: Just call me Black Betty. Everyone else does. They've even remixed that godawful song. It's number 1.

TS: I . . . I couldn't call you – you – you are – are –

Q: Stop stuttering! What's on the tapes?

TS: Conversations between you and . . . and the traitor, interviews, interrogations, some of his family chats with his wife and daughter. Also, they've gone missing.

Q: Down a sinkhole in Caledonia? Or Hibernia?

TS: Unclear. We're investigating the usual suspects, but there's strong evidence that IRIS played –

Q: IRIS aren't real! We made them up.

TS: Well, be that as it may, build it and they will come, and now IRIS has manifested in various forms.

Q: You know, he told me it takes a special person to kill a child. That you can find a man who'll kill a woman easy enough. But a child, well, we've all been one, haven't we? I think I was one, once . . . I mean look at this photo . . . full of life and hope, unaware of the horror, horrors to come. That is me, isn't it?

TS: Yes . . . yes.

Q: What card games can you play?
TS: I don't play cards.
Q: I'll teach you.
TS: Forgive me, but I'm under strict instructions not to play cards with you.
Q: From whom?
TS: Will there be anything else?
Q: *I wasted time and now doth time waste me.* Who said that?
TS: I'm not sure. I'm not much of a reader.
Q: You're not much of anything, are you? Shakespeare. *Richard II.* Has the Bard Butcher struck again? You know some think Jack the Ripper was a royal and –
TS: Ma'am, I'm under instructions to protect you from –
Q: Protect! You're my jailor! Imprisoning me in my own home! I want the latest news!
TS: This is for the tapes, as you asked for, a *Walkman*. It's fairly self-explanatory. The cassettes go –
Q: I know. Leave me! Imbecile! I shall confer with my muses, my spirits. They're much better company. Where are my tarot?
TS: Your Excellence –
Q: Have you hidden them again? Also, I've been working on my Christmas message. I expect they'll want to vet it, but it will explain –
TS: That's not my department, but –
Q: Have they got stand-ins standing by? Actresses?
TS: Actresses?
Q: Yes! Whoever will whore themselves next to play me? Mirren? Dench? Colman? Blanchett? Streep? Or are they all dead? Have I outlasted them?
TS: I really can't –
Q: Any news of Charles?

TS: Oh, yes, muddled and fanciful reports that he was hiding out with neo-druids when the Queen of the Faeries turned him into a blind pit pony down a mine in Wales.
Q: Don't diss the faeries! Stranger –
TS: I must go.
Q: Then go! . . . He's gone. We're safe. Can you hear me? Ghosties? Bugs in the wall? In the teapot? Sewn into my clothes? I know you're there. Or did you really insert a chip inside me when . . . I watch a lot of movies. I'm not stupid. Where's my dorgis? Their collars! I bet you put bugs in them, too. Sisters? Where are you?

BROADCAST FOR TV, 88*UTUBE, SOCIAL MEDIA INDUSTRIAL COMPLEX. Take #1: XMAS MESSAGE – ANNUS HORRIBILIS Part II – 'Madness in great ones must not unwatched go . . . but is great for ratings!'

They say there is no fool like an old fool and that couldn't be truer after this last year. I'd like to say how sorry I am you had to witness . . . for want of a better phrase, my madness. I mean look at me. Mutton dressed as lamb. Old, cold mutton at that, but it's at times like these that I'm particularly grateful for my family, what's left of them, and how they've rallied around in these tragic times. The terrible crash, where we lost our precious boys, will forever be a dark stain on our history. But the paparazzi continue to hound us with their drones. And they will continue to pay.

It's times like these we realise how brittle our existence is, and how quickly all we understood to be good and true can be lost. Many of you have lost loved ones in the riots, battles, wars, uprisings and crackdowns. Thankfully, we now have a system of re-education to ensure our future stability and have put the heaths and moors to good use for building the camps.

So I want to wish you all a very peaceful, and maybe quite a boring Christmas, for a change. At home, alone . . . like me, in front of the telly, watching your Queen – the real one – smiling and wishing you well, wherever you are . . . Where are you? Who are you? Have long have we got? What does it all mean? Don't bother with any of those big questions, just crack open another one . . . and . . . and a Happy New Year to you all!

Before I go, thank you all for all the lovely-jubbly messages, and postcards, wishing me to GET WELL SOON. I'm not really sick, just disappointed . . . and personally, I find that the best medicine is still my daily ration of Kellogg's cornflakes for brekkies, and a cocktail of gin and Dubonnet ahead of my midday meal. And every night before bed, I enjoy some bubbly. For me, heaven is likely to be a bit of a comedown. So, bottoms up! God Save the Queen, and God Save All of You! Where's the music? Cue the music . . . Put some music in now.

One more thing. You know, I've been looking back at old photos, of me in the army as a young slip of a thing, driving trucks and working on engines. You know I'm the only royal who knows how to change a spark plug. The only one with any real spark really. And I've got to say I was a bit of a spunkrat back in the day. And perhaps Philip was lucky to snag me. You know I met him when I was fourteen, and he was a dashing young soldier, and we wrote to each other in secret for years. Nothing naughty, but it's all about the subtext. Philip called me his Cabbage, from the French *ma petit chou*, my little cabbage or pastry . . . and he was no sour kraut. Ha. *Je parle français* . . . fluently. Though I don't like to show off, and as a general rule don't like the French and their dreadful diseases.

But I do regret declaring war on them this year. It was a rookie mistake, like marching to Moscow in the winter. To all of you who lost loved ones in this war . . . it's on me . . . and the spirits. They're all here. Behind every palace portrait. They give me advice, wake me up, tease and torment me. *What have you done? How could you let our realm sink so low, go to rack and ruin?*

And that is why I tried to take it back from these two-bit charlatans and their moronic megaphones. Tried to put some dignity and backbone in the Crown, and in England. I'm just sorry that we fell short . . . however, perhaps this next gen, these young women whippersnappers, perhaps you will take up the reins . . . I have stables. I breed thoroughbreds, they race, they occasionally win races, and plates . . . whereas I am a loser, soggy dog biscuits . . . cut. CUT!

I lost my . . . you can cut there . . . truth is, you probably weren't even filming, right? Just amusing the old bat. Well, we are not amused. I don't see a light on. Is the camera even on? It is? I'd like to see the playback and then we can do take two. I just need a moment . . . oh, God, the implants again . . . There's leakage.

9-8+GT – [AV] TRANSCRIPT – Q & TR MIKED. UPSIDE DOWN WORLD #1: MISERY LOVES COMPANY [ILLUSTRATION: THE HANGING MAN TAROT CARD]

Q: Psst. It's me . . . I'm in disguise, like that duke of . . . whatever. Are you awake?
TR: Ma'am?
Q: Yes. You know, you should thank me.
TR: For?
Q: For having you hung upside-down outside the palace, for the public to toss rotten things at. The Vote on the

telly and social medium was for old-school – hung till almost dead, disembowelled, innards winched out and then twirled around your neck like a scarf of sausages to hang you like at the end of that Scottish film, then quartered and –

TR: Did you want something?

Q: The Hanged Man – it's not always a bad tarot. It can be seen as time suspended, and you get a unique perspective on the world. Have you had any unique perspectives?

TR: Well, the sun was out today, and some women wore short skirts, so I saw up a few.

Q: I get that you're low but there's no need to give in to our baser instincts.

TR: The thing is, there's very little variance in that department, and yet we keep looking up.

Q: Aha! See, you've found some wisdom. You know, funny story, I ended up with dorgis because Margaret had a dachshund and I had corgis and . . . oh God, I've slipped into my anecdotage again. Shoot me now. Let's just say everyone spends far too much time sniffing each other's bums. But don't you want it all to mean something? I mean, one dark day I shall breathe my last, and I'm interested to know from someone so close to the end, if there's any . . . any moment of clarity.

TR: No. In my case there's only intense pain, and . . .

Q: Go on . . . I'm listening . . .

TR: Sorry, no epiphanies. But, yes, I guess I'd like one final moment, when I can truly let go, like when you thought you were relaxed but your shoulders were up two inches. And you take that breath that allows you to let the struts go. Truth be told, this has done wonders for my spinal compression. But, yes, if I could find one of those moments of –

Q: Were you ever charged to kill me? I won't be offended. I may have gone over the line. Boundaries were never my . . . who are you?
TR: Me . . . I'm a ghostie . . . woooo. OWH!
Q: Shush, or I'll kick you in the face again.
TR: Woooo, ghosties coming to get ya! OWH!
Q: Stop teasing. You know, I was chatting with old Henry. How he and the first Anne, when they got married, had a royal barge. And he had the first letters of their names entwined on it. And at first the commoners cheered when they floated down the Thames, but then there was a ripple of laughter. And pretty soon everyone was laughing like drains at them, because –
TR: It spelt HA, HA, HA. OWH!
Q: Only I finish my stories. And we royals, we can make jokes about ourselves, but not you lot. You know I came here, in disguise, at great personal risk, to see how I would feel about helping you escape. Maybe do an old switcheroo with an unlucky double. But not now. Now I'm feeling like I might like to crush your larynx. I'm getting much more in touch with my feelings these days. And Elizabeth I, she's been a great help. You know she was Shakespeare's ghostwriter and never got the credit.
TR: Poppycock! OWH!
Q: Ugh, see, now you've dragged me down to your level. I'm withdrawing from public life and starting a religion, just like Henry. And like you talked about at your trial, calling me God, Queen of the Heavens. That was genius. Do you want to join? . . . Why not?
TR: What part would I play?
Q: I'm not sure. You know, I've been watching all Shakespeare's plays again, and so much of it is utter claptrap, in-jokes, like you said, and saying things five

ways when one would do, and not following his own 'brevity is the soul of wit' aphorism. But the thing that really struck me in the DVD extras was how he never gave the actors a whole script. He only gave them their parts to learn. I think that's like life. And some of us don't even get a script. So perhaps you could write your own. I mean, personally, I'm making it up as I go. I mean I have 'a script' but I've never written it down. Sometimes we just close our eyes and improvise, right. You're asleep . . . or you're dead. Adieu, my sweet prince, may the worms, the maggots. . . something something . . . something that rhymes, but not faggots, which were just big bonfires really. Toss on a guy. Actually – epiphany! You're the new Guy Fawkes! . . . I'll go . . . I'll stay . . . I'll pray.

AUDIO: ANON. ANSWERPHONE MESSAGE, LEFT FOR THE PALACE

QEI, II, III – it's me. I'm following your hit list. Taking out the tabloid hacks who attacked you. Taking down the *drone of paparazzi*. All I ask is that you stop them butchering my plays. Stop them trying to update my plays by putting them in outer space, or doing Indo-Afro-Futurism, or gender-free, or what tf . . . and definitely stop them trying to do them trad. old-school styles. As if. You don't have a time machine. I have the only time machine! Dissolve the RSC ffs . . . four hundred years have gone by now, can't you put on something new?

Regards,

ANON.

PS: Tom Waits (who I do rate) said: *The world is a hellish place, and bad writing is destroying the quality of our suffering.*

And so, adieu – we hawks have handsaws and will continue to publish these hacks' pieces.

[NB: Pounds of flesh, with similar bloody notes as above skewered to them, have since been tossed over the palace walls. Some were impaled on the battlements where they rot and attract flies, and vultures, which Black Betty has introduced.]

AV TRANSCRIPT – Q MIKED – TR MIKED. UPSIDE-DOWN WORLD #2

TR: The dorgis!
Q: Oi, stop licking his face. You'll get traitor germs. And I'll have to put you down.
TR: Mmm, fancy dog food breath, I can live off that for another day or two. Pedigree thoroughbred horsemeat nibbles, dorgi din-dins, is it? The slow nag from the seventh at Ascot? Are you still taking it upon yourself to deliver the fatal bolt?
Q: How do you know about that?
TR: It was in the dossier. It's one of the ways you could . . . harm . . .
Q: Others? Myself? How are you?
TR: I've seen better days.
Q: Me too. Update: I talked to Oprah. It didn't go well. I mean, haven't we all wanted to top ourselves at some point, especially when we're up the duff? But we buckle up. I mean I was hoping we could form some sort of alliance. Two of the most powerful women in the world, but all she was interested in was me spilling my guts, and I ended up railing and ranting about . . . Americans and their me, me, me exceptionalism. I brought up your

Falcon and the Snowman, but she'd never heard of it. She was just wanting to talk about Diana and how she almost destroyed me. You know, I'd scrap the virgin clause if I could have my own way. We need women who've lived, and . . . and I wanted to set the record straight with her, that neither I, nor my dear mother, when asked about Diana having an official royal funeral, said, 'No way, toss the bitch in a skip.' We're not those kinds of people. We maintain decorum. But Americans, they're all heart-on-your-sleeve, spill-your-guts-all-over-the-floor, but there's nothing behind it? They perform grief and apologies, flagellate for the masses, indulge in trauma drama, thinking it's true catharsis. It's not. It's as shallow as a bird bath. They're plastic people.

TR: What's up with your feet? I saw the shuffle.

Q: Oh, I'm booked for feet transplants, but I don't know. Anyway, enough of my suffering, any new perspectives today, my . . . my oracle?

TR: No. The blood in my head, it's pounding . . . and the dead weight of my guts on my lungs and heart, it's . . . how many days is it now? Four?

Q: It's been a week. You know, you have your own channel – a GoPro trained on your face. It's like the Yule log, or a goldfish in a bowl. And Ladbrokes is taking bets on when you'll finally expire. Oh, your eyes. Yikes! It's even worse close up.

TR: What's happened to them?

Q: Blood vessels have burst. They're completely red. IRIS took a screenshot, turned it into a meme, and they're appearing on walls all around the city. They blamed Banksy, but we still can't find him, so they just rounded up the top fifty graphic artist-slash-satirists, bundled them up like they were all pens and pencils, and burnt them in Trafalgar Square.

TR: No!

Q: Yes, if the wind's blowing the wrong way you can catch a whiff. So, no wisdom for me today?

TR: There is a saying in Hebrew: *The cloth always tears at the seam.*

Q: What does that seem to mean? So there are bugs in my seams!

TR: Probably, but it's what those of us in security focus on: the seams. The places in between events. The soft spots. That's what Rabin was doing, walking from his speech to his car. Reagan – walking from the Hilton to his car. Kennedy, in a car –

Q: And Julius Caesar!

TR: No, he was just in a meeting of the Senate.

Q: Oh, meetings, meetings, meetings, shoot me now. So who is going to shoot me?

TR: I don't know. Just . . . watch your seams.

Q: And I really am so sad about Harry, poor little bastard. But he wanted to give it all away. Convert royal residences into refugee hubs centring wellness, but –

TR: So you –

Q: That's not us. That's not our job. They want me to appear at the coronation of Kate and that American actress. They've agreed to power-share. There's going to be a concert on the roof of the palace.

TR: Madness, again?

Q: No. Kate wants another Spice Girls reunion. The actress wants Beyoncé's 'Run The World (Girls)'. Then there's going to be some all-in motley-medley led by Paul McCartney and Stevie Wonder doing 'Ebony and Ivory'. You know, Oprah and I would have slayed, but . . .

TR: But –

Q: If you were still with me. You would have put a stop to all that, backed me up. Slayed them. Instead, I've got some new . . . thing, non-binary persona non-entity robot.
TR: Really, a robot?
Q: Yes, I think so. I call it the Terminator. I'm not sure it even has genitals.
TR: Where are they now?
Q: The genitals?
TR: No, the robot?
Q: Oh I did a bait and switch with one of the doubles . . . sorry, I'm going to step back a bit. You're a bit iffy-whiffy.
TR: Listen, cut me down. I'll go to the loo, clean myself up, and then you can hang me up by the other leg. I could last another week.
Q: Um . . . no. I brought you a slice of pie from the kitchen.
TR: Where's my daughter?
Q: Relax, it's not steak and kid . . . sorry, that was –
TR: Titus.
Q: You what?
TR: It's you! In disguise! The original actor/writer! Shakespeare himself! Titus Andronicus baked the children of the prisoners who raped his daughter and killed his sons into a pie, and fed it to their mother, then killed her. The Roman emperor then kills Titus, and Titus's last son kills the emperor and takes his place.
Q: What a gory story. Listen, you stink and I have perfume. A little spray to keep the pong away and –

[REVIEW #1 from BBC SPORTURE-CAM #dG77 – GAME ON! Described Video Captions]

[She takes a perfume spritzer from her sleeve. He swings

away. Suddenly, he has a hand free. He grabs her spritzer hand. Pulls her to him. Swings his free leg up around her throat. A canny wrestling move – the Neckbreaker! Sayonara C-4! Lots of likes on the livestream. Comments: '*DO IT!*' 'Just another random who got too close to the traitor.' 'Who cares!' 'Yesterday he lashed out with his free foot and kicked a homeless guy pissing on him in the groin. Made the midnight highlights package.' 'Help tip the vote to keep him alive, hydrated and fed.' #HangingMan is trending.]

TR: What's in the bottle?
Q: Perfume!
TR: Who gave it you?
Q: I got it myself.
TR: What's it called?
Q: Guerlain L'Heure Bleue.
TR: Describe it.
Q: Spicy-sweet citrus with aniseed and bergamot, a powdery dry-down.
TR: What year was –
Q: Created in 1912, designed to represent the evening hour when the sun has set, but night has not yet fallen, 'the hour when one finally finds oneself in renewed harmony with the world and the light'.
TR: You're not her! The real queen has lost her sense of smell with all the nose jobs, and she'd never remember all that. I'm going to break your –
Q: Okay, okay, I'm not her. But she's poison in my ear. A bug. If you let me go –
TR: Who am I talking to? I've got your double here. I'm going to break –
Q: No! She's not a double. She's a clone. A gift from . . . *Who wants to live forever*? A China doll.

TR: You didn't have the heart to do it yourself?
Q: I'm watching from the roof. Can you see me?
TR: My eyes are –
Q: I can see. They're on the telly. Bloodshot. You've fulfilled the #IRIS prophecy. Believe me, I'd be there in person, but there's been some side-effects. They have to wheel me around now. It hasn't been the perfect end . . . Romeo. How does that end? A knife? Poison? A kiss?
TR: A kiss.
Q: (SINGS) Who wants to live forever?
TR: Around your little finger I was twirled. But now I am sick of your little world. Goodnight, sweet . . .

[REVIEW #2 from BBC SPORTURE-CAM #dG77 – GAME ON! Described Video Captions]

Whoa! He kisses her down below! Lets her go. She staggers back. Collapses. The crowd boos. She takes out the perfume bottle. She stops. Holds her ear. Freezes. Listens. Grabs the dog. Retreats. He wriggles, wails, writhes. The rope breaks! Perhaps he took a sharp brooch from her while in the clinch? He lies on the ground. Tries to get up, but one leg won't work. A mob gathers around him, streaming, posting, liking. He gets up on one leg. He hops away. The mob follows. Surrounds him. He disappears beneath them. Sirens. Police. Security. Whistles. Big dogs. Teargas. Mob disperses. A hunt. Vultures. Drones. He is gone. Vanished. The gallows remain. Credits.

[STATUTE #333: STATE OF EMERGENCY – MARTIAL LAW – DOUBLE TROUBLE #2 SINISTER SISTERS [ILLUSTRATION: BLOOD RED EYE –

SYMBOL OF IRIS TERRORIST GROUP]

The #IRIS symbol has appeared in London, the UK, Ireland, Europe, and now internationally with posters, graffiti, and in social media. Anyone believed to have created or promoted its distribution forfeits their life with no recourse to due judicial process. By decree of the newly crowned Sisters – Duchesses of Cambridge & Sussex, Queens-4-Life ֍ ∞ ҉

<u>'The Black Betty Tapes': Your Highness 😁 * Footnotes</u>

I. The agent who inserted 😁 emojis etc. and created the glib titles for these transcripts has since been removed.

II. The agent who was removed subsequently filed a WDC (Wrongful Dismissal Complaint).

III. The WDC was originally upheld and the agent reinstated, but this decision was appealed by the Crown and eventually went to the Privy Council, where Lord Denning (RoyBot) gave the deciding argument that the 😁 emoji did indeed indicate bias towards the transcripts, which threw into doubt the legitimacy of not just this transcript but all the other transcripts.

In LDR's words: 'These should be neutral documents. We find the original dismissal a rightful one and deem that the tongue and hands of the agent should be taken and nailed above the entrance of the other agents' cubicles. This to serve as a lesson to the other agents that such work is to be undertaken with utmost seriousness. We further instruct that the original recordings be found and checked against the transcripts, and any errors be amended.'

In their defence, the agent testified that the above collection of transcriptions, etc., was only a first draft, and for *THEIR EYES ONLY*. The draft titles were thus created to aid the agent in recalling what each transcript was about before final editing and encryption, whereby the offending emojis and titling would be removed. This 'draft' copy only came into circulation due to an urgency for it to be read by all concerned parties and stakeholders, and the agent's superior lifted it from the said agent's Cloud folder and distributed it before final tweaks could be made.

LDR considered this and was sympathetic. However, he deemed that matters of such national importance should never be approached in such a glib fashion, even at the draft stage. He did, however, demand that the superior of the agent also be charged for not checking the contents more thoroughly before distributing them. LDR determined that this superior should lose one hand and one ear for having a hand in this travesty and not listening to our better agents, who would have cautioned against rushing to put such tripe and blasphemy into the arena.

NB: 'RoyBot' is an abbreviation of Royal Robot. The real Lord Denning shuffled off this mortal coil on 5 March 1999, but his extensive judgements were downloaded into an AI and an algorithm was created so that new evidence and arguments could be inputted and his new self – LDR – make future judgements (and thus save the judiciary and taxpayers much expense in not having to hire humans). This R&D was undertaken by the RC AIR (Royal College of Artificial Intelligence & Robotics) and thus 'RoyBots' went into the *Oxford English Dictionary*.

[END TRANSCRIPTS 99-fr.om]

EPILOGUE: STATUTE #334: STATE OF EMERGENCY – MARTIAL LAW – SHOOT TO KILL

[ILLUSTRATION: A PLAYING CARD OF QEIII – BLACK BETTY, SURROUNDED BY REGALIA, WITH A HANGED MAN INTERWOVEN. DORGIS, HORSES, KELLOGG'S CORNFLAKES, GIN AND BUBBLY, GHOSTS OF FORMER KINGS AND QUEENS, AND SHAKESPEARE'S STOLEN SKULL ALSO FEATURE]

The portrait above of QEIII – BLACK BETTY has appeared as an ID card among underground rebel cells loyal to her deposed majesty, who currently resides at 'The Tower'. Anyone found in possession of this card forfeits their life with no access to judicial process. By decree of the newly minted Sisters – Duchesses of Cambridge & Sussex, Queens-4-Life ֍ ∞ ҉ The Queen is Dead! Love live the Queens!

[ILLUSTRATION: Kate and Meghan facing each other on a newly minted 'Limited Edition' collector's card with royal seal. Cost: £50. They stare into each other's eyes. There's some deep connection between them, but both hold something unseen behind their backs. They appear to have risen phoenix-like from the ashes of a chopper crash. The Tower of London appears in the background. The silhouette of Queen Elizabeth III can be seen at a barred window. She tenderly kisses a skull. In the dark underworld beneath the tower, the silhouette of a mighty woman performs rites with dismembered animal, bird, and human parts. A cat, an owl and a toad stand guard, singing 'Who Wants To Live Forever?']

CONTRIBUTORS

Jack Barrowman was born in 1992 in Wellington, New Zealand, and has been regretting it ever since. In 2014 he won the David Carson-Parker prize for his MA screenplay, 'The Sun at Night', and his work has been featured in the New Zealand International Film Festival, the Miami International Science Fiction Film Festival, VUP's *Monsters in the Garden*, and the walls of his own tomb. He likes soup.

Octavia Cade is a speculative fiction writer with a PhD in science communication. Her cli-fi novel *The Stone Wētā* was published in 2020, and close to sixty of her short stories appear in publications including *Clarkesworld*, *Strange Horizons* and *Asimov's*. A short story collection, two poetry collections, a book of essays and several novellas have been published by various small presses. Octavia was the visiting writer in residence at Massey University in 2020.

David Geary (Taranaki iwi and Ngāti Pākehā) created a playlist for his story. You can find it on Spotify: 'The Black Betty Tapes'. It starts with 'God Save The Queen' by the Sex Pistols and finishes with 'Your Queen Is a Reptile' by Sons of Kemet. David's recent fiction appears in *Pūrākau: Māori Myths Retold by Māori Writers* (edited by Witi Ihimaera and Whiti Hereaka), and he's rapt to work with VUP again, and its fabulous editors, after VUP published his play *Lovelock's Dream Run* (1993) and short story collection *Man of the People* (2004). He tweets at @gearsgeary.

Joy Holley lives in Wellington and completed her MA in creative writing at the International Institute of Modern Letters in 2020. Her writing has been published in *Starling*, *Sport*, *Stasis* and other journals.

J. Wiremu Kane (Ngāpuhi) lives and writes on the ancestral lands of Ngāti Hei and Ngāti Maru. He graduated with a Master of Professional Writing (First Class Honours) in 2020 from the University of Waikato. His novels, short stories, and essays seek to expose the gaping, unhealed wound that colonisation has wrought on this whenua and its people.

Sam Keenan was the winner of the inaugural Sargeson Prize in 2019 for her story 'Better Graces'. In 2017, she was runner-up in the Sunday Star-Times Short Story Competition for her story 'Interim'. Her short fiction has appeared in *Landfall* and the *Sunday Star-Times*. She lives in Te Whanganui-a-Tara with her family.

Samantha Lane Murphy was the recipient of the Modern Letters Fiction Prize in 2020 for her short story collection 'Hard Wear and other stories', completed during her MA year at the International Institute of Modern Letters. Based in Wellington, she persists in writing things of small to reasonable length, and not all of them on social media.

Anthony Lapwood's fiction has appeared in a variety of publications in Aotearoa and abroad and been broadcast on Radio New Zealand. He has an MA in Creative Writing through the International Institute of Modern Letters. His first book, *Home Theatre*, a collection of realist and non-realist stories, is forthcoming from VUP. He lives in Te Whanganui-a-Tara and can be found on Twitter and Instagram @antzlapwood.

Vincent O'Sullivan, who lives in Dunedin, has published poetry, short stories and novels with VUP. His latest poetry collection, *Things OK with you?*, came out in March 2021 and *The Dark Is Light Enough*, a biography of Ralph Hotere, won the General Non-Fiction Award at the 2021 Ockham New Zealand Book Awards.

Nicole Phillipson's short fiction has previously appeared in *Sport, Starling* and on Radio New Zealand's *The Reading*. She holds graduate degrees from the International Institute of Modern Letters (2016) and the Iowa Writers' Workshop (2020).

Maria Samuela has had stories published in *Turbine*, *Sport*, *Takahē* and *adda*, and on Radio New Zealand. In 2019 her story 'Bluey' was shortlisted for the Commonwealth Writers Short Story Prize. She's held residencies at the University Bookshop (in association with the Robert Lord Cottage) and the Michael King Writers Centre. In 2022, her collection of stories, *Beats of the Pa'u*, will be published by VUP. Maria's parents came to Aotearoa from the Cook Islands in the 1950s, and she grew up in Porirua. An early version of 'The Promotion' has been read on Radio New Zealand.

Emma Sidnam is currently completing her double degree in law, English literature, and creative writing at Victoria University of Wellington. She regularly performs slam poetry in the community and her work has appeared in *Asterism*, *Capital Magazine*, and the AUP anthology *A Clear Dawn: New Asian Voices from Aotearoa New Zealand* (edited by Paula Morris and Alison Wong).

Kathryn van Beek has an MA from the International Institute of Modern Letters at Victoria University of Wellington, and has won several awards for her plays and stories, including the Mindfood Short Story Competition and the Headland Prize. In 2020 she released a collection of short stories, *Pet*, which is also available as a podcast.

Rem Wigmore is a speculative fiction writer based in Aotearoa. Their solarpunk novel *Foxhunt* was published by Queen of Swords Press in 2021. Their other works include *Riverwitch* and *The Wind City*, both shortlisted for Sir Julius Vogel Awards. Rem's short fiction appears in several places including the *Capricious Gender*

Diverse Pronouns Issue, *Baffling Magazine*, and the second *Year's Best Aotearoa New Zealand Science Fiction & Fantasy* anthology. Rem's probably a changeling, but you're stuck with them now. The coffee here is just too good. Rem can be found online at remwigmore.com and on twitter at @faewriter.